The Island

To Anna

Have a Blessed Christmas
and a Happy New Year

Love C P Gunter

Author
signature

Enjoy!
N Lee

this is a true story!

The Island

By

Nancy Lee

NORTH STAR PRESS OF ST. CLOUD, INC.
St. Cloud, Minnesota

Prologue

MR. WILLIAM DUNLAP HAD A VISION—a dream that floated under his closed eyelids twice before it registered on his brain—and he sat bolt upright in bed, his eyes wide, an amazed look on his face. With both hands, he smoothed back the long wisps of hair usually strategically placed to cover the balding top of his head. As his wife snored softly at his side, he threw aside the covers and slipped from the warmth of his bed.

Pacing back and forth across the width of the bedroom, his bare feet getting cold on the wooden floor, he repeated under his breath, "Yes, of course! That would work! Why didn't I think of it before?! Of course!" On spindly legs extending below the hem of his nightgown, he did a jig that would have made his sleeping wife very proud—if only she had seen him. "Of course!" he repeated with fervor.

He pulled back the curtain of the northeast window and intently stared out. The town of Cloquet rested quietly on the shore of the St. Louis River, silver moonlight sparkling on the water. And there was the island, the centerpiece of Mr. Dunlap's plan, gently cradled in the river's encompassing arms. He smiled and slipped back into bed. With his covers tucked around him, his feet warmed quickly once put near the feet of his wife. Smiling broadly, he fell back to sleep.

The island in Mr. Dunlap's vision was a small piece of earth dropped like a glob of clay from the creator's hawk and trowel, fallen into the river as it coursed south. There it remained from the beginning of time—unnoticed, unappreciated, and undeveloped—until the 1880s. The island existed untouched. The river flowed by, yet the distance to either shore was minimal. Trees grew, flowered, died, and grew again. The only inhabitants with any claim to the island were animals, birds, fur traders coming and going, and of course the local Ojibwa, who rightly claimed ownership.

On the south side of the St. Louis River, a lumber town, Cloquet, had sprouted up. Lumber barons from the East gazed longingly at the majestic stands of northern Minnesota pine and set about gaining logging rights. Within the blink of an eye, Cloquet was born.

People settled, sawmills were built, railroads ran in all directions, lumber companies hired men, and logging camps sprouted up in the midst of the tall white pine forests. Civilization had arrived, and with it came standards of proper behavior that were soon established for the residents dwelling in Cloquet. A city ordinance stated, "There will be no establishments that serve liquor built within the city's borders." A vigorous discussion, one might even call it a battle, arose between the " imbibers" and the "non-imbibers."

The ruling made many people very unhappy—especially the lumberjacks, who always seemed to work up a tremendous desire for various deadly sins while confined to the lumber camps for the months of deep winter. When the logging drive ended and they moved back into town in the spring, they expected to work hard, drink hard, and some would then wreak havoc on the surrounding area. The city leaders were aware of the mayhem taking place in other lumber towns and wanted no part of that behavior in their fine city.

Then Mr. Dunlap had his nocturnal vision. On the island there would be no restrictions on what businesses could be developed, none whatsoever. The city itself would remain pure. The island, not in the platted boundaries of the city, would be something else. Mr. Dunlap envisioned purchasing the island for nominal cost, then collecting bounteous fees from the enterprising business people, to whom he'd sell lots where they would build the businesses so desperately needed by the thirsty loggers—and townspeople who would frequent the saloons on the sly. This idea was gold plated. But first he had to buy the island. He had done his homework; he knew the island was in the possession of the Ojibwa tribe living on the nearby reservation.

In the most enterprising business transaction of his life, Mr. Dunlap secured the deed to "island number 4" from the Indian Council for, legend has it, a one hundred pound bag of flour. In 1882, the island was surveyed and platted as the town of Dunlap. From that moment on it was known as Dunlap Island, where the narrow lots sold like hot cakes.

Following the business transaction of his life, Mr. Dunlap took his wife, children, and profits with him and moved to St. Paul, Minnesota, where they lived happily ever after in relative luxury from his newly found affluence gained by his island sales.

The one hundred pound bag of flour had little or no consequence in the lives of the Indians on the reservation, however.

Now, dear reader, I invite you to return with me to the Island as it existed in the year 1917. Both the town of Cloquet and the Island unknowingly stood on the brink of disaster, but no one could foresee what the future held. Day by day, month by month, life passed by until the characters you're about to meet were plunged into the horrors that would occur on the twelfth of October, 1918. Dunlap Island itself was a major player in the tragic events of that day, prompting one mystified newspaper reporter to close his article with these words:

THE DEVIL CERTAINLY TAKES CARE OF HIS OWN!

❧ 1 ❧
Spring 1917

BY LATE AFTERNOON ON FRIDAY, the only piece of furniture remaining in the narrow room was an old brass bed structured with four large corner posts, each topped by an ornate brass ball for decoration. Other pieces of furniture—a dresser, a bedside table, a lamp, a braided rug, a small oak chair—had been hoisted, carried, and packed in the wagon outside the front door of the small house. The room appeared to be nearly empty. Yet, with a more careful glance into the shadows of the fading afternoon sun, an observer might make out the figure of a man.

Lying on the bed, his broad shoulders covered by a quilt, Hank Larson faced the far wall. Silently cursing his injury and feigning sleep, he was conscious of the activity as his lumberjack friends and his wife, Daisy, carried the Larsons' few belongings out the front door of the small house on the alley. The men moved quietly, packing boxes with the modest possessions Hank and Daisy had accumulated over the years. In and out and back again they came. Hank could picture his friends, his wife, and the confusion of this unfortunate—but necessary—move. Time passed. Soon the wagon outside the front door was filled to capacity.

Pausing at the front door, Daisy turned to the men as they came for the last load. She glanced at the half-dozen hefty young lumberjacks and millworkers, smiled, and spoke softly, fervently willing herself not to cry. "I can't tell you how much Hank and I appreciate all you've done since Hank's accident."

Being men of few words, the lumberjacks and millworkers instantly waved aside her praise. One by one, they offered comments:

"Hank was always one of us, one of the finest river pigs ever!"

"I've known Hank since I was a kid. He made me want to run the logs."

"Whatever you need, Daisy! Just let us know."

"When you get settled on the Island, we'll be at your door more often than you expect!"

"You'll get tired of us coming by so often and eating up all your donuts!" All the men laughed, knowing of their large appetites.

Then a young logger, Frank Shaw, removed his hat and said, "Hank saved my life, Daisy!" His voice was choked, his eyes diverted as he took time to collect himself. "I'll never forget that moment. Hank saw I was in trouble." Swallowing with difficulty, he continued.

"Hank saw me go under, ran across the logs, threw me a rope, and pulled me from the river." He took a deep breath, then whispered, "From my grave. All those logs were coming right at me, covering me over, pushing me deeper into the river!" Frank turned away, not wanting anyone to see his tears. "Without Hank, I'd be dead!"

Daisy put her arms around the young man and held him close. "Hank said many times he'd do it all again, Frank," she whispered, "especially for you!"

Frank took a deep breath and stepped back. "I know, I know!" he said softly, then turned and headed out the door.

The meager possessions of the Larson family, all carefully wrapped and covered, were tied down securely for the trip across the river. With the help of Hank Larson's husky friends, everything would be delivered and set up in the refurbished shack on the north shore of the Island, where it was bordered by the northern arm of the St. Louis River. Linens, clothing, two chests of drawers, a small bed, lamps, benches, end tables, an old trunk, an oak rocking chair, a small round table with four small chairs, books—all the items once making their modest house a home—were now ready to find a new residence.

The main item for the second trip on Saturday was the large brass bed. It had been in Daisy's family for years. The spring, mattress, quilts and bedding and anything else that hadn't fit on the first load would fill out the second. For now, the items stayed in the house. Old Syd, Mrs. Brush's hired man, checked the ropes holding down the contents of the wagon, took a final chaw of tobacco, then climbed up to sit next to Frank. The lumberjacks climbed on wherever they found space. Some jogged along behind.

"Let's get this over with, men!" Old Syd shouted, slapping the reins. Letting go a well-placed splat of tobacco juice, he set off for the bridge and Dunlap Island.

Daisy Larson watched the wagon make its way down the street. How she loved those kind young men. Taking a deep breath, she blinked back tears and entered the little house that had been her family's home for the past eleven years.

I won't cry! she thought as she stood in the middle of the empty room that had served as their kitchen and parlor. *Poor Hank, lying there in bed, knowing all this was taking place. He never said a single word!* Tears formed in spite of her determination not to cry. She brushed them away.

Quickly she put on her apron and set about sweeping the floor. *No sense in standing around feeling sorry for myself.* She'd repeated this mantra a hundred times that afternoon. Taking one more look around the little house that stood between the alley and the woodshed, behind the large ornate home of Mrs. Brush, she reached for a cloth to wipe the dusty windowsills a final time.

At last, nothing left to clean, she hung her apron on the peg by the door, and quietly entered the small room that had served as their bedroom. For a moment she stood silently beside the bed. Her beloved husband lay there, still and pale, his eyes closed, his face to the wall. Yet Daisy could tell he wasn't asleep. She reached out and brushed back the thick blond hair from his forehead. He turned toward her.

She knelt by the bed and took his face in her hands, bringing it close to hers. He opened his eyes slowly, as though hesitating to return to the events of the real world.

With her lips next to his ear, she whispered, "Hank, all this trouble will come to an end soon. We'll begin a grand new life on the Island." She took his hand and raised it to her lips. She had always loved his hands—so large and calloused, yet strong and gentle.

Reluctantly he opened his eyes, looked at her, and shook his head. "How can you say that?" Despair filled his voice. "I'm a cripple. I can't work. I can't support you and Henry. Since the accident, I feel I have no purpose anymore!" He clutched her hand in both of his so tightly it hurt. "And now, thanks to the bank, we're being turned out of our home because we can't pay the rent!"

He let go of her hand, turning his face to the wall once again. "I'm grateful we have a place to go to. I'm thankful Mrs. Brush could work that out for us." He paused and took a deep breath. "But it's certainly not anything I would've planned—for any of us!"

Crying didn't come easily for Hank Larson, but lately, with all that had taken place in the past few weeks, he found tears erupted no matter how he fought against them.

What kind of a man am I? he'd often ask himself. *Crying all the time!*

The springs creaked as Daisy lay down beside him, her arm across his chest, her head on his shoulder. Wiping away his tears, she kissed his cheek and whispered in his ear, "We're still together, Hank. Remember that! You and I will come through this—together." Pulling his face gently toward her once again, she kissed him full on the lips.

"I thought you were dead, Hank!" She swallowed the lump that immediately filled her throat. "Just think of how I felt when I heard what had happened! I was so afraid!" She paused, then spoke softly, her breath and words on his cheek. "I felt like I had died as well. Can you truly understand that?" Her tears mixed with his. "Now I know we can come through this together—the three of us!"

"Are you sure this'll work for you and Henry?" He covered his eyes with his left hand. "Eleven is too young to be the man of the family!" A deep sigh escaped his lips.

"He's your son, Hank. He's strong and fearless. He feels like I do—that it's a miracle you're here with both of us—a family, that's what we are!"

With a final kiss on his lips, Daisy rose from the bed, tucked the quilt around her husband, smoothed her dress and put back a lock of hair that had come loose from her braid.

"I'm going up to Mrs. Brush's house to get us a bit of supper." She wrapped a shawl across her shoulders. "I'll check on Henry. The last time I saw him he was deep into a game of chess with Mrs. Brush."

As she opened the front door of their little house, the fragrance of spring flooded the room. "This can be an adventure, Hank." She turned and called to him. "I'm looking forward to living on the infamous Island. Maybe I'll learn to enjoy an occasional shot of whiskey!" And with a deep laugh, she was gone.

Hank smiled in spite of himself, turned on his side, once again facing the wall. *A shot of whiskey, huh? She has courage, that wife of mine!* After a moment, another thought filtered through his mind before he fell asleep once again. *What if she's right? What if there really could be better times ahead?*

BEFORE THE SUN DESCENDED behind the western trees, Old Syd returned with the empty wagon. The men remained on the Island, ready for their supper at the Riverside Boarding House. Syd parked the wagon in the alley where, early in the morning, it would be filled with its final load.

When the new day dawned, the Larsons and the wagon would make their last trip across the red bridge to the Island to begin their new lives as "Island Folk"—or as some of the unkind people of the town liked to say, "Island Trash."

By mid-morning, the men and wagon had long since left. Yet Mrs. Brush remained seated by her kitchen window. She had watched the Larson family set out for their new home. Well into her eighties, she looked frail—slender, unruly white hair, a bit of a tremor in her veined hands. Yet on the inside there lurked a strong, intelligent, determined woman, her eyes alert and eager.

I did the best I could for them, she thought. *They were the family I never had. I kept them under my wing as long as I could.*

Her memory drifted back almost a dozen years to when the young couple moved into the small house behind hers. The house had been a temporary shelter for Mrs. Brush and her husband many years ago as they awaited the completion of their beautiful new home. Once they moved into their elegant Victorian home, the bank accepted the narrow lot containing the modest house on the edge of the alley as collateral. Thus, over the years renters had come and gone when able to afford a more permanent home. Then, in 1906, Hank and Daisy Larson arrived with their meager belongings.

A handsome young man and a lovely young woman—soon to be parents by the looks of it—eventually walked up the path to her back door where they knocked and introduced themselves. She invited them in for coffee. Ever since that initial contact, she knew she loved them both. When baby Henry arrived, named after his father, her cup overflowed.

Her life expanded, offering her a chance to be a surrogate parent and grandparent, a friend and mentor, a confidant and adviser. Her life, lonely since the loss of her husband some years before, blossomed with the Larson family coming and going through the back door, always leading to her warm and welcoming kitchen.

Then—tragedy. Hank's accident and the bank's sale of the little rental house on the alley turned all their lives upside down. "Live with me!" she implored them. "Look at all the room in this big old house. There's more than enough space for all four of us."

But Hank was a proud, stubborn man and would not hear of such an arrangement. "No way will I impose on you or anyone else!" he said with conviction, whenever Mrs. Brush broached the subject. "Just because I'm a cripple, I won't become a charity case!"

But she did work behind the scenes by way of her hired man, Syd.

Old Syd had come to her with a fine idea. "There's an old cabin sitting empty down on the Island. I think you could make a quick deal with the family of the logger that used to live there until a few months ago." He smiled his crooked smile. "They'd be more than happy to be rid of it, and," he went on, "I don't think it'd take much to make the cabin snug and secure. And, since it's such humble place, I don't think Hank'd take offense."

Syd went on to explain that a few months ago the logger who owned the cabin had been found dead, floating in the river, his body caught by an overhanging branch a mile or so downstream. "He was quite the drinker. No one's surprised he disappeared one night," Syd explained, shrugging. "At first no one even knew where to look for him—so they just waited. Sure enough, his body eventually floated up on the river bank, got caught on a branch, and was found by another logger angling for his supper." Syd wasn't one to get upset with the ups and downs of other people's lives.

"The fisherman was really disappointed when he found a dead body on the end of his line," he chuckled, "instead of the big northern he thought he was about to land!"

So Mrs. Brush made the deal. She bought the old cabin for a song, put Old Syd in charge of its rebirth as a home for the Larsons, and made a deal to exchange rent money for a weekly supply of Daisy's baked goods, for Daisy and Henry's help with household chores, and Hank's manly advice about maintenance and financial issues. Hank was totally outvoted, yet somehow seemed to find peace with the treaty—such as it was— even if it meant a move to the infamous Island.

Now they were gone, out of her sight and headed for Cloquet Avenue. *Life will never be quite the same again*, she thought. She smiled to herself as she rose from her chair and placed her cup of cold coffee in the sink. *I did all I could for now, but*, her smile widened, *I still have a couple of surprises up my sleeve for the Larson family.*

Later that afternoon, the back door opened and Old Syd, humming to himself as he always did, stepped into the hall, where he removed his jacket. "Have a quick cup of coffee—it's waiting for you on the stove. Then put your coat back on," she ordered. "We're going outside to freshen up the rose bushes today."

Mrs. Brush was back in charge.

ও২ର
On the Island

THE RIVERSIDE BOARDING HOUSE was the most popular, best-run boarding house on Dunlap Island. Big Jack Swanson, a former lumberjack and camp cook, ran a tight ship. The men who ate and slept under his roof were only too happy to abide by his rules, as the food was great and the rooms were clean. They were:

1. No fighting in the dining room.
2. No chewing or spitting in the dining room.
3. No cursing or swearing in the dining room. (This was to protect Maggie's tender ears. Big Jack's young daughter often worked beside him in the kitchen.)

Since Big Jack purchased the boarding house five years earlier, shortly after the sudden death of his young wife, the Riverside had fewer fights and mishaps than any other establishment on the Island. The rules were a factor, but the main reason was Big Jack himself. Having been a lumberjack, he understood the needs of the men who paid to live under his roof.

Also, Big Jack was just that—BIG! He could wrestle any adversary to the ground. Few men challenged him anymore. Being tall, broad of shoulder, strong of arm, and wily as a fox, Big Jack let it be known it would be a very foolish man to dare confront him in his boarding house. That man would soon find himself flung over Big Jack's shoulder, tossed out the front door, and left sprawled in the dusty road.

Big Jack was an extraordinary cook. Maggie loved to watch her father's huge hands butcher meat, knead the mammoth mounds of bread dough, peel multitudes of potatoes, and fry eggs by the dozen, tenderly turning them "over easy"—with never a yolk breaking.

The two of them were a finely tuned team. Maggie's responsibility at breakfast was the oatmeal and coffee. She filled a large Imperial enamel cast iron pot half with water, half with milk, then brought it to a rolling boil that awaited the proper measure of oatmeal. She added a healthy fistful of brown sugar to sweeten the pot.

"Keep stirring, Maggie Girl!" Big Jack would call as he flipped pancakes on the large griddle. "We don't want lumps in the oatmeal!"

Maggie's other job was to ring the old brass bell on the wall close to the stairway leading to the upstairs sleeping rooms. Once everything was ready to be served, Big Jack gave her the signal to hit the bell—just three times—with the mallet hanging nearby. The upstairs seemed to explode with stomping feet, cursing, pushing and shoving as the men stumbled down the steep stairs to the dining room, eager for their breakfast—freshly made, warm, and tasty.

The coffee pot always sat to the rear of the stove, where it percolated patiently until time to fill—and refill—the cups of the hungry boarders. "Keep that coffee boiling away, Maggie! The boys like it real strong!" Thus, the coffee boiled away while the men ate, and was black as pitch by the time the final cup was poured.

Soon the men were off to work at the mills, and Jack and Maggie took a moment to enjoy their breakfast and plan their day. This was Maggie's favorite time of the day, especially on a Saturday. Then she had her father all to herself, and she always relished these moments, brief as they were.

"Well, Maggie Girl! We did it again!" Jack laughed as he buttered a huge slab of bread. "You keep an eye on that young guy at the back table. I think he has his eye on you!" Maggie was now eleven, almost twelve, and Big Jack teased her constantly about the young boys who worked in the mills and sat at their tables. All the men, young and not so young, knew that if they so much as looked sideways at Maggie, Big Jack would have them out the door before they knew what hit them. He teased, but she knew it was just for fun.

Maggie blushed and stirred sugar into her coffee. "Nope!" she said with conviction. "If I were old enough, I think I'd like Samuel Berg. He looks like a nice young man— but he's way to old for me!" She paused, then said, "I'm not really too fond of boys yet. Boys my age need to grow up!" She smiled.

Big Jack threw back his head and laughed. "You're right about that, Maggie Girl! Yep! I really like that Berg boy, too. He's got potential on the two-man saw!"

Rising from the table, he stoked the stove to heat water to wash the enamel-ware dishes in the sink. No china here. Too fragile for rough-and-tumble loggers.

"Now Maggie, I have a couple more chores for you—if you don't mind."

The chores clearly defined, Maggie set about obeying her father's directions. "Scrub and oil the dining room tables—the oil brings out the grain in the wood. Take a clean cloth and wipe off the salt and pepper shakers. After that, fold the napkins and put a pile on each table. Finally, sweep under the tables to clean up the mud, the chunks of manure, food droppings, and cigarette butts."

Big Jack scowled. "I keep telling 'em to smoke outside, but some of the guys sneak one in now and then. I can smell it!"

Maggie's final chore was to polish the front windows of the boarding house, plus the large glass panel in the front door that was usually covered with dirty handprints from the hard-working men coming and going.

Maggie never complained at her work. "I'll get started right away," she said. She went to her small bedroom off the kitchen for a jacket for the outside job. The inside work would be done in the blink of an eye. No one worked faster than Maggie Swanson! Then she'd tackle the front windows and the door onto the front porch.

A short time later, inside chores completed, Maggie struggled through the front door, both hands full of cleaning supplies—towels, soap, a bucket of warm water, vinegar for the shine, and a large sponge—all set to spiff up the façade of the Riverside Boarding House.

Once she had everything in place, Maggie took a moment to sit on the porch steps and enjoy the spring morning. Breathing deeply, she smelled the perfume of the damp earth, ready to bring forth green grass and fresh flowers. The early morning sun cast shadows of the buildings on the Island, with a strip of sunshine outlining each shadowy patch on the ground.

All seventeen of the saloons on the Island were closed at this time of the day. There wasn't a sound, except for the breeze blowing through the nearby pines. Most people who worked on the Island—and the few who lived there—started their day sometime in the afternoon. They worked late into every night. So far Maggie had the day—and the Island—all to herself. Taking a moment to relax, she leaned back against the porch railing, shut her eyes, and took another deep breath.

That was when she heard the faint unfamiliar sound—like the creaking of wagon wheels—far down Main Street to her left. She held her breath and listened carefully, trying to make out exactly what she heard, then heard it again. She stood and walked to the middle of the street, looked south. There it was—a large wagon, fully loaded, with one driver. Slowly the wagon turned off St. Louis Avenue, heading in her direction. Looking more closely she could see two figures walking beside the loaded wagon—a boy pulling a smaller wagon and a woman with her arms full of bundles.

Who in the world could that be? What in the world are they doing on the Island at this hour? Where in the world do they plan to park that wagon? Maggie was mystified.

"Dad!" she shouted. "Come see what's coming up the street!"

Big Jack, his apron covered with flour, burst through the door, stepped into the middle of the street and gazed down at the procession slowly making its way toward them.

"I can't believe my eyes," he said, as he ran a hand through his thick dark hair, leaving a streak of white flour. "I'm not sure, but the woman looks like it could be Daisy Larson, Hank's wife!"

A puzzled look covered his face. "What in the world are they doing, coming here—to the Island?"

ഔ3ଓ
Their Island Home

IN THE YEARS since Mr. Dunlap had his inspired vision, the Island—Dunlap Island as it came to be known—had flourished. In the blink of an eye it had been transformed. What had once been a gentle, green oasis became a location for the flow of alcoholic beverages, tobacco products, and "sins of the flesh." The townspeople watched from shore in dismay and disbelief as one saloon after another was built, furnished, and opened for business.

"Nice" people supposedly did not venture over the unsteady bridge leading from the orderly town to the depravity of the Island. Respectable people drew the curtains of their carriages if they had to drive over the rickety bridge in broad daylight. If a person crossed over under the cloak of darkness—well, that might be another experience all together.

By 1917, every available lot on the Island was filled. Not built with the best materials or the finest architectural designs, seventeen saloons were functioning at top capacity, greeting customers with open arms and a never-ending supply of liquor. On still evenings, Cloquet townspeople could hear the echoing of raucous events on the Island. They were convinced mayhem happened across the newly constructed red bridge—but never in the hallowed streets of their genteel little town. Curious townspeople often cast a suspicious glance across the river, but no one was turned into a pillar of salt for just looking.

JACK AND MAGGIE WATCHED the creaking wagon make its way up Main Street. Taking a closer look at the young boy loaded down with bundles and pulling a wagon as well, Maggie was sure she recognized him from her class at school.

"I know him," she whispered to her father. "That's Henry Larson. He's nice. He always picks me to be on his kickball team. Sometimes he sits beside me at lunch."

She saw the grin creep across her father's face and said firmly, "He's *not* my boyfriend!"

Big Jack laughed and pulled her heavy braid. "Yep. I know the family, too. Hank and I worked at the same camp one winter. They're good people."

Jack's smile faded. "I heard reports from some of the men that Hank had a bad accident on the river this spring. I wonder where he is—and how he's doing."

Maggie watched the heavy wagon move closer toward them, bundles stacked one on top of the other, threatening to fall into the street.

Big Jack stepped out to meet the wagon. He knew old Syd, and raised his hand in greeting. Maggie followed close behind and called to Henry.

9

"Hey, Henry. What in the world are you doing here on the Island?"

She reached out to help retrieve two burlap bundles that had just now fallen into the road. To Maggie's surprise, the bundles were squirming about. *Good grief!* she thought. *Could there be chickens in there?*

"This is quite a surprise!" she said. "We don't get much early morning company." She saw surprise on Henry's face when he recognized her.

"Hey, Maggie. Do you live here—on the Island?" he questioned, looking up as she indicated the boarding house to their right. "Have you always lived here? Is that why some kids call you . . ." He hesitated to say the words and picked up one of the squirming bundles to hide his embarrassment.

"Yup!" She smiled. "They call me "Island Trash." So if you're planning on moving here, you'll get used to it!" She laughed at the surprise on his face. "But just wait. I love living here, so I don't pay attention to those words." She picked up the second squirming burlap bag from the road. "Is there a chicken in here?"

As they visited, Maggie set about helping Henry reorganize the wagon and his chickens before they continued on their way.

Big Jack went to the large wagon, noting the slight woman with the energetic attitude who seemed to be in charge. Because of early morning coolness, she had a scarf about her head. A few escaping dark curls were tossed about by the spring breeze. Not large, she still gave off an aura of strength and determination. Standing there with a wiggling bundle under her arm, she reached out with her one empty hand to greet Big Jack as he approached her .

"I'm Daisy Larson, Hank's wife. We might have met before, but I'm not sure." She smiled up at him, and he returned her greeting.

"Everyone calls me Big Jack—I'm sure you can figure out why!" They both laughed. "I worked with your husband at the logging camp some time back. I really enjoyed his company. Haven't seen him much since I took over the boarding house a few years ago." He gestured toward his building. "Just where is Hank?" he asked. "I was sorry to hear about his accident on the river. How is he doing?"

Daisy looked away.

Syd took time to let loose a splat of tobacco juice before he interrupted their conversation. "He's in the wagon, Jack. Maybe you can help us get him situated in their home." He gestured to the old cabin near the end of Main Street and the northern arm of the river.

Jack was shocked. In two giant steps, he moved to the rear of the wagon, and, sure enough, Hank, wrapped in a quilt, lay on a mattress balanced on top of other contents.

Big Jack leaned over the edge of the wagon and reached for the limp hand lying on the quilt. Jack's hand was broad and strong and full of bread dough. It gently surrounded the injured man's hand, large as it was, and Hank slowly turned to face the concerned man hovering above him. The bright sun at Big Jack's back cast a soft shadow over the makeshift bed where Hank lay cushioned and comfortable.

Opening his eyes, friendly recognition washed over Hank's face. "Big Jack! I never thought I'd see you here."

"My God, Hank! I heard reports of what happened on the log drive this spring." Jack's eyes scanned Hank's pale face. "I can't tell you how sorry I am."

Jack continued speaking, as if brute force could will strength and health into Hank.

"I've got such great memories of our years in the woods. You were the best, the wildest river pig ever seen on the whole river!" Jack laughed aloud at the image of Hank Larson dancing his way across the rampaging river on unpredictable logs.

Hank looked up, caught Jack's eyes and held them a long moment. A smile slowly covered his face, and he shook the hand that held his. Hank said softly, with mock irony, "I could've run circles around you any day, you who always worked as a cook's helper!"

Then everyone laughed, and suddenly the moment took on a less somber air.

Big Jack untied his apron and tossed it over the porch railing. "Please, Mrs. Larson, let Maggie and me give you a hand. Just tell us what to do!" After he and Maggie retrieved the rest of the bundles that had fallen into the dusty road, the procession once again started out for the cabin at the far end of Main Street—the Larsons' new home.

Henry observed the scene with amazement and thankfulness. The sadness in his eyes lightened a bit as Big Jack's strength and good humor infused the cloud of sorrow and pain he, his mother, and his father had been under since the accident. Maggie walked at his side, telling him of all the benefits she had discovered while living on the Island.

"I'll take you fishing, if you want." She was just warming to her subject. "I also go hunting and swimming. Then there's people-watching—when people come and go from the saloons. That is really interesting," she said with a giggle.

Soon they stood in front of the cabin. "I'll come by and get you whenever you can come out. I'll show you everything I know!" She smiled at him. "You'll love it here!"

He tried to smile. She was a girl, after all. He'd never had a friend who was a girl.

Jack could see the cabin had been spruced up a bit, and vaguely remembered workers there a few days ago. The place looked sturdy, clean, and comfortable. Old Syd pulled the horse to a halt, spit out his old chaw into the dust at his feet, bit off a new one, and slowly stepped to the road below.

Taking the key from Daisy, Jack opened the front door and stood aside to allow Daisy and Henry be the first to enter. Daisy smiled up at Jack and said with great determination, "I rather look forward to living here. What a lovely place!"

At that moment, it was. The cabin faced south. Bright sunlight streamed through the open door. At the rear of the cabin, the river flowed by gently, so close they could hear the water brush the shore. The cabin had been through a rebirth—thanks to Mrs. Brush. No longer reeking of mold and stale air, no longer unkempt and unheated, white-washed siding glowed in the morning sun, and newly caulked windows were shiny and clean. Shingles, some blown away by the winter winds, had been replaced. The grass had been cut.

The path to the door was soon a busy thoroughfare as everyone worked to turn an empty cabin into a warm and cheerful home.

Daisy quickly took charge. "Mr. Big Jack, I'd surely appreciate it if you'd help me get Hank comfortably seated in his favorite rocker. He can watch over us—be the boss! He likes to be the boss, you know," she said, with a sly smile.

Big Jack moved quickly to the back of the wagon. After placing Hank's arm across his shoulders for leverage and tucking the quilt snugly around Hank, Jack reached strong arms under Hank's prone figure and easily lifted him from the wagon.

"Sorry about this, Jack. Never thought I'd ever have you carry me anywhere!" Hank said as he tried to smile.

Big Jack began to laugh. "I'm keeping track of all this, Hank, so you just get yourself well. You wait—I'll have lots of jobs for you when you get better. You're my neighbor now, and neighbors help each other!"

Jack cradled Hank's weakened body through the front door into the parlor. The rocker awaited him next to the sun-filled window, strategically placed there by the movers. With great tenderness Big Jack placed Hank just as Daisy directed.

Daisy adjusted the quilt, placed a pillow at Hank's back, making him comfortable, and, with a loving kiss on his cheek, she was satisfied. Hank could sit in the middle of all the activity and be the boss, watching what it took for his family to begin their new life on the Island.

Jack, with Syd and Henry, returned to the wagon. They maneuvered the parts of the old brass bed through the door into the bedroom, where it was assembled next to the window. Daisy made the bed, carefully tucking muslin sheets under the corners of the worn mattress. Tossing a quilt on top, she stuffed two goose-down pillows into lace-trimmed cases she'd embroidered for her hope chest many years ago.

Big Jack's final assignment was to lift Hank out of the rocker and bring him to his freshly made bed. There he placed him, tucking him in as one would cover a child.

Hank closed his eyes in weariness. "Thank you again, Jack. What else can I say?"

"That's more than enough for me," Jack replied. "I'm glad I was able to help."

He motioned to Maggie. They headed for the door. "I'll be back with some supper for you later, but I have to go now. My bread dough will be raising all over the table."

Maggie said her goodbyes. "I'm so glad you'll be our neighbors," she said with a shy smile at Henry. Henry blushed—that "girl" thing again. With a quick wave, she followed her father back to the waiting windows of the boarding house that still needed washing.

She took her father's hand as they walked toward the boarding house. *Now I won't be so alone on the Island*, she thought, knowing great adventures awaited her and Henry.

Back at the cabin, Daisy worked her magic. The round oak table was situated so it could be useful in the kitchen or for serving a dinner on a special occasion. The four matching chairs fit perfectly. After placing a doily in the center of the table, she put a kerosene lamp on top. When lit, she was sure it would give a peaceful ambiance to the parlor. Hank's rocker waited for him by the window, where he could look out and see the activity along the street. He'd even be able to see the lights of the town across the river.

Everything was finally in position. Dressers, lamps, mirrors, family photos, the large Bible Daisy's grandparents had carried over from Norway many years ago, the trunk that contained family treasures—photos, clothing, important papers, family history, special keepsakes. By late afternoon, only one task remained—making up Henry's bed in the spare room. However, when Maggie arrived at their door with a pot of rich beef stew, a pan of warm buns, and a large plate of cookies, they knew Henry's room would have to wait. The Larson family could not resist the delicious food.

Later that evening, they watched the sun go down behind the pine trees to the west and felt the damp spring darkness seep into the house. Henry and Daisy carried in firewood Syd had packed in the depths of the wagon and stacked near the door of the cabin. Within minutes a fire glowed in the old stove, and the chill all but disappeared.

Daisy and Henry sat on the bed next to Hank. All three of them were weary. "It's been a very long day," Daisy said, smiling at Hank as she reached for his hand. "Only one more chore—Henry's room needs to be set up." Rising, she motioned Henry to follow her.

Before Henry stood, he leaned over his father and kissed his forehead. "Good night, Dad. I had a great time today," he said, pulling the quilt up to cover his father. Hank reached up and touched Henry's cheek. Hank's hand was cool, yet Henry could feel the warmth of the blessing his father had silently bestowed upon him.

Henry's room had been created out of a rustic storeroom. The door had barely hung on its hinges, so Syd had removed the door and taken it to the back yard to be used as a partial wall for the makeshift chicken coop. After making the small cot into a warm, comfortable bed, Daisy filled Henry's small chest of drawers with his few items of clothing, The final touch to the small room took Daisy only a second. Before Henry crawled into bed Daisy pounded two large nails into the wall, one on each side of the door. Then she attached a heavy rope between the nails and carefully hung a large, worn quilt, the squares of fabric faded with age, for a makeshift door.

Over time Henry came to realize the private space was not so much for him as he lay in bed, reading or dreaming of things to do the next day. The gift of privacy was for his mother and father as they ended each day, together in the old brass bed. Henry understood. His parents needed their privacy. Thus, on many nights to come, before drifting off to sleep, Henry would hear the muffled sound of his father speaking and his mother's soft, consoling voice replying.

SLEEP DID NOT COME easily to Hank that first night as he lay beside his slumbering wife, her breathing quiet and even. His mind was full of thoughts and fears and sorrow about what the future held for him and his family. Often, as the hours passed, his mind would thrust him back into time and he'd relive the moments leading to his accident, the split second when his life was changed forever.

He had always loved the feel of rolling logs beneath his feet and the sounds of the giant tree trunks bumping and scraping against each other, endlessly driven by the current of the river. Over the years he'd come to love his work, challenged by the danger, proud of his skill, confident in the experience he needed to direct the huge, unruly logs as they plunged down the river to the mill. His reputation and skill grew as the years passed.

Grimacing, he relived the moment when the first section of the spring log drive reached the curve in the river where the current swung the logs to the left. River pigs, with pole and spike, directed them toward their destination. Hank and Frank Shaw, his young protégé, had the final resting area in view. They were as good as home. Then Frank Shaw suddenly cried out and disappeared beneath the river of moving logs.

Bystanders often gathered along the shore to watch the logs approach the town. They'd cheer and clap as the log riders leaped from log to log and, with brute strength, kept the huge logs from catching on the shore or piling up in the narrow areas of the river. Crowds watched the river pigs maneuvering logs through mile after mile of treacherous water. People on shore often cheered for Hank, and he loved it. He'd respond by taking a risky leap from log to log or take off his cap and do a little jig—right there on the bark of the log, making the log spin beneath his boots. Like magic.

Then, because of one renegade log cascading wildly through the churning river, one misstep by Frank Shaw, working the river alongside Hank, and one second of lapsed concentration, the lives of Hank Larson and his family changed forever.

Some witnesses claimed there must have been a piece of ice remaining on one side of the log where Frank Shaw was doing his fancy footwork. That could have thrown him off balance. Some said a protruding branch from another log caught Frank's leg, causing him to stumble. Others claimed the young river pig turned quickly to wave at a lovely girl calling to him from the shore. No one seemed to know exactly what took place. They could only agree on one thing—that when they saw him fall into the freezing water with logs crowding him on all sides, pushing him down, causing him to disappear from view, they all felt with certainty that Frank Shaw was a dead man. No doubt about it.

Then, over the sounds of the river and logs, Hank Larson heard Frank's desperate cry for help as he plunged into the river. Turning quickly and seeing Frank disappear beneath the logs, Hank knew what had to be done. One unsteady log at a time, Hank made his way closer to where he had last seen the young man. Within seconds Frank had totally disappeared. Then, momentarily, his head would reappear above the logs, and he struggled to find something secure to clutch—anything to grab and hang on for dear life.

Balancing carefully on the logs, Hank readied the rope always attached to his leather belt. Wrapping it firmly around his own arm and body, he cast it to the drowning man, still struggling to keep his head above the water and his body out of the way of the crushing logs. After three frantic tries, Frank was finally able to grasp the rope. In desperation, hand over hand, Frank pulled himself to the surface of the water where he fought against being crushed. Straining mightily, Hank worked to direct Frank toward a large log coming up beside the struggling young man. As the log floated close, Frank reached out, wrapped his arms about the log, and prayed.

Hank Larson breathed a sigh of relief as soon as he saw Frank attached to the log and rescuers hurrying to his side. He had saved his friend but, as he balanced there on the tumbling logs, his attention focused on Frank, Hank had broken the loggers' number one commandment: "Thou shalt never take your eyes off the log-filled river!"

A renegade log approached him from behind, coming to the middle of the river. The current slammed it into a hidden boulder that had allowed smaller logs to pass smoothly over its surface. As soon as the large log collided with the submerged rock, it ricocheted up, bucking like an untamed stallion. People on shore watched in horror as the log reared up, then smashed down on the log where Hank Larson stood. In a moment it was all over.

People would talk of this tragedy for years to come. Like a giant, malicious fist, the log claimed its victim. Hank lay motionless across several smaller logs still bobbing in the river current, arms spread wide, with the larger log straddling several logs, plus Hank's legs and lower back.

For a moment there was total silence. All anyone could hear was the bumping together of the now-contained logs and the rushing current of the river. Then all hell broke loose.

People on shore were galvanized into action. Loggers and river pigs maneuvered carefully over the logs finally coming to rest by the Island. Several men hurried to Frank's side, removing him from peril. The more experienced loggers concentrated on Hank. And the situation looked bleak indeed.

River pigs, working together, used their hooks and poles to slide the huge log back into the water. Four brave men constructed a makeshift stretcher out of an old ladder and some blankets. Carefully they slid the ladder with Hank's inert body across the logs to shore.

By this time the great pine logs rested peacefully in the calm waters near the Island. When Hank regained consciousness, he was in the Cloquet Hospital. Since then, he had relived that moment when his strength and mobility were stripped from him just about every waking moment of every day. This night was no different. Daisy remained asleep, yet Hank's eyes still stared into the darkness.

MAGGIE SWANSON ALSO lay awake, looking up at the shadows of tree branches moving on her bedroom ceiling. She held a small framed photo of her mother she carefully studied every morning and evening. Maggie had memorized her mother's face. She could visualize the woman who had been her mother for such a short time.

"I wish you were still here, Mama. I still miss you," she whispered. Maggie's thoughts wandered back to the busy morning with the Larsons. *I'll bet you and Mrs. Larson could've been best friends,* she thought. *She's such a nice person.* She placed the photo on her chest and covered it with both hands, pressing it to her heart.

In the photo, Agnes Swanson looked directly at Maggie. Agnes sat erect, hands crossed in her lap. She had a soft, gentle look about her that belied the energetic spark in her wide hazel eyes. Her dress was tailored, except for the lace collar. A thick braid of dark hair circled her head, decorative combs keeping it in place.

I remember the collar, Mama, Maggie thought. *You told me you made it yourself to wear on your wedding day. It was so beautiful.*

Her thoughts flew ahead to the final time Agnes wore the lace collar. *I was only a little girl, but I remember how beautiful you looked on that day.*

The final time anyone noted the beautiful collar was as it lay on that still bosom of Agnes Swanson the day of her burial.

Maggie shook her head to chase away the memory of the sound of heavy clods of dirt being shoveled into the grave, falling upon the polished pine lid of the coffin, the beautiful coffin so carefully fashioned by Big Jack's strong hands.

During the service, Big Jack never let go of Maggie's small hand. She still loved to hold his large calloused hand. She treasured the moments he walked by her, ran his hand over her long dark hair and said, "Beautiful hair, just like your mother's."

"I miss you, Mama," she whispered. "Much as I love Dad, I do miss having a mother." Placing the photo back on her night stand, Maggie fluffed her pillow, pulled up the quilt, and closed her eyes.

Strangely enough, her final thoughts before sleep came centered on Daisy Larson. All the time she had been helping at the Larsons, she watched how Daisy reached out to encourage everyone, how she made everyone feel appreciated.

She thought, *I really love my dad, but maybe I could adopt Daisy Larson as a part-time mother. She looks like she'd be a really nice mother—if a person finds it necessary to borrow one. I'll have to think about that,* and then she drifted off to sleep.

🙠4🙡
A New Beginning

THE LARSONS QUICKLY ADJUSTED to life on the Island. Each day took on a rhythm of its own. Daisy and Henry were able to prepare Hank for the day comfortably seating him in the rocker by the window. Daisy would make breakfast for her two men before Henry set out for school. A thick slice of her homemade bread in a bowl, covered with hot milk, then sprinkled generously with brown sugar and cinnamon—that was Henry's favorite breakfast.

Henry took an old white enamel mug from the shelf over the kitchen sink and filled it to the brim with hot coffee, topped off with a large splash of cream—just the way his father liked it. The blue enamel coffee pot on the small wood stove percolated away most of the day. The aroma of the coffee and the warmth of the cup in his hands brought contentment to Hank's eyes.

Each day, Maggie waited for Henry in front of the boarding house. Daisy always smiled as she watched them walk together down Main Street to the bridge.

"Have a great day, you two," she would call as she watched from the door.

Then she turned to Hank. "It's your turn, Hank Larson. You always look like your hair's standing straight up." She brought the brush, comb, razor, towel, soap, and a bowl of warm water to the round oak table, situated next to Hank's rocker.

"Not today, Daisy," he protested. "I'll just run my fingers through my hair and wash my face—" He never finished. Daisy was never deterred from her task.

"Hank Larson! I love to do this for you, and," she laughed softly, "I know you like me fussing over you. So—just be quiet and let me work my magic."

And she did. After lathering his face, she drew the straight-edged razor carefully over his cheeks with a steady hand. All the while she spoke softly to him. "I love you, Hank Larson. Always have, always will." She wiped away a clump of soap and continued. With each stroke, she said how grateful she was they were still together.

"I've loved you since I first saw you, way back when you two boys and your dad came to work on our farm in North Dakota. Do you remember how shy you were back then?" She laughed as she trimmed his modest moustache. "You were such a skinny boy, all blond hair and long legs. You wouldn't ever look at me, and I really wanted to be your friend." Taking a comb, she parted his thick hair and, after wetting it down a bit, combed it to the side—where it stayed, at least for a while.

Hank never took his eyes from her face. "Ah, Daisy—you know the farmer's daughter never becomes friends with the hired help. My dad put the fear of God in me if I so much as cast a sidelong glance in your direction." He smiled teasingly. "Of course, he never knew all the thoughts and plans I made in my mind if I ever got my hands on you!" They laughed together. He reached for her, pulling her down into his arms—razor, soap, towel, and all.

They kissed tenderly. For a moment she rested her head on his broad chest, conscious of the beating of his heart. "Hank, do you ever regret how we came to be married? How upsetting it was for everyone?" She raised her head and looked into his eyes. "Well?"

Hank's face broke into a broad grin. "Daisy, my dearest girl, no one ever enjoyed breaking my father's rules and your father's rules more than I did." He kissed her again, suddenly feeling more like his old self than he had for some time.

She laughed as well, then stood before him and surveyed her handiwork. "You're looking very handsome, Hank Larson. I've decided I'll keep you!" Picking up her shaving equipment, she turned to go into the bedroom.

Without any warning there was a commotion right outside their door. Being early in the day, they weren't sure what to expect. Daisy set aside the shaving equipment and opened the door. There stood Syd, Big Jack, Mr. Jackson from the train depot—and most surprising of all, Mrs. Brush, all bundled up against the cool spring morning, looking very much in charge as she leaned on Syd's arm.

"Come in! Come in!" Daisy and Hank welcomed them. Mrs. Brush stepped inside as Big Jack and Mr. Jackson began to wrestle several large shipping crates in through the door. The outside of the crates displayed dark printing stating the contents held within— WEHRLE, MODEL NO. 22, FULL NICKLE BLUE STEEL RANGE $32.92. THIS STOVE HAS NO COMPARISONS, NO SUPERIORS, FEW EQUALS IN THE LINE OF STEEL RANGES!

Daisy and Hank were speechless. Once again the Larson family found it hard to believe the constant kindness showered on them from Mrs. Brush.

Mrs. Brush removed her gloves and coat, then seated herself at the table. Her favorite hat with the tall feather remained upon her head. "This is purely a selfish gift," she began. "How can you bake for me, Daisy, if you don't have an appropriate stove?" She stood and walked slowly over to Daisy, put her hands on Daisy's shoulders and said, "This is my gift to you, only you." Her smile created lace-like creases in her cheeks.

Daisy tried to speak, but Mrs. Brush gently touched her lips. "No words. Just do your baking and the entire city will be a happier place because of the aroma of your marvelous bread."

She paused for a moment, then added as though she just remembered, "And, by the way, not only will you bake for me, but four of my dear friends would also like to take part in the bread delivery program. How do you feel about that?" Before Daisy could answer, she added, "Of course, they'll pay you handsomely for your delicious baking."

Daisy enveloped Mrs. Brush in her arms, while Hank reached out his hand to his dear old friend. Taking his broad hand in her arthritic hand, she held it, gently bending her delicate frame to touch his hand to her lips. Then she walked back to her chair where she once again took charge of the situation. "Let's get this unpacking over with," she said with great authority. "I want this stove in working order before the mill's noon whistle sounds!" Under Mrs. Brush's watchful eye, with much straining and maneuvering of the heavy containers, the crates were emptied, and various parts brought into the small house.

Then assembling the new stove began. As the work progressed, everyone could see this was no ordinary stove. As all the boxes stated, everything about it was "superior."

Later that morning the men who strained and groaned to unpack the stove and place it in its new home were only too willing to stay for a cup of coffee from the pot that still warmed on the surface of the old wood stove. Daisy had some cookies from a previous day, and everyone ate their fill. Hank enjoyed the company and joined the conversation any time he could slip in a comment or two.

After the crates had been removed, the company left. The beautiful new stove radiated heat throughout the cabin. Daisy and Hank sat side by side, holding hands—still basking in the warmth of the generosity from their dear friend, Mrs. Brush.

ఱ5ౝ
Feeling at Home

B Y THE END OF THEIR FIRST TWO WEEKS on the Island, the Larson family was feeling quite at home. A number of lumberjacks who had previously worked with Hank stopped by to say hello. They also chopped and split wood, providing fuel that would last for some time. Even the chickens, who protested their move to the Island, settled down and—sure enough—started laying for the family.

Daisy's favorite time of day was when the first faint light began to filter through the windows. Slowly, silently she'd rise, dress and head for the kitchen. The sooner she set her batch of bread, the sooner it would emerge from the oven and be ready for delivery. If all went well, her patrons would receive their bread while still warm.

Milk, sugar, yeast, flour, lard, salt—she stirred the dough in her large crockery bowl. Making bread—six loaves a day plus two pans of buns or cinnamon rolls—gave purpose to her life and joy to those who ordered her bread. She loved the texture of dough, its pliant movement as she kneaded it, its aroma as it baked in the beautiful new oven, the sight of brown loaves cooling on the counter, the smoothness of butter gently applied to the crust to keep it soft.

The compliments she received from the families who enjoyed her baking didn't hurt, either. Thus, she began each day with this process—one she enjoyed and understood. Most of all, in her new kitchen, she felt in control of her life and her family. Lately there had been so many things over which she had no control.

Once the large bowl of dough was set on the warm surface of the stove to rise, she poured herself a cup of coffee and sat in Hank's rocker by the window, holding her warm mug close to her chest and shutting her eyes.

After a rest, Daisy would set aside her coffee and walk quietly to the bedroom door. She'd look in on her husband, seeing if he still slept, if he was comfortable and covered. Reassured, Daisy returned to her kitchen, thanksgiving filling her heart. She knew each day with Hank was a gift.

The dough having risen, Daisy could knead it before letting it rise for the last time. Another hour and a half would pass before she could form the final loaves. She punched and poked the soft dough, covered it, and set it to rise.

Three years earlier, Mrs. Brush had given Henry a wagon, and the boy had hardly been separated from it in most of that time. With his father's accident, the move to the

Island, and his mother's baking schedule, this beloved wagon took on an entirely new meaning for Henry and his family.

Henry and his wagon were now part of Daisy's growing baking business. As soon as the baked goods were pulled piping hot from the oven, they were set on the table to cool. Waiting until the loaves were just the proper warmth, Daisy would wrap each in a fresh towel and load them gently in the wagon. Henry would then grab the handle and take off down Main Street for the red bridge.

Reaching the streets of the town, he'd deliver the fragrant baked goods to the customers awaiting the golden loaves of bread—as well as cookies, buns, and even donuts on special occasions. The demand for Daisy's baked goods increased as word reached the ears of the wealthy women on Chestnut Avenue who would never allow their delicate hands to knead—or even touch—bread dough.

On his days off, Henry and his wagon coasted down the many hills in Cloquet. No matter how fast he and the wagon flew, he always felt in total control. *I can always apply the brake,* he knew. Somehow he never found it necessary to slow the wagon down. The neighbors shook their heads and clucked their tongues as he flew past their houses, his hair flying, grinning, and his foot nowhere near the brake.

When he had extra time, Henry would visit the fence at the horse barns owned by the lumber companies. At certain seasons over one hundred horses lived there. Henry watched them canter about, run together as though playing, and often watch him where he clung to the fence. The horses stayed a safe distance from him, looked him right in his eye, and tossed their thick, beautiful manes.

"Don't be afraid of me. Come closer," he would softly invite. He would hold out his hand and beckon to them. For a while, none responded to his call. Then one special spring day, a large brown horse walked slowly over to the fence where Henry waited and placed his muzzle in the outstretched palm of his hand. Henry could hardly breathe for the joy he felt in his heart.

The bonding of boy and horse continued day by day. As the weeks passed, a mutual trust grew between the boy and the large workhorse. Often Henry would produce a sugar lump from his pocket—thanks to Mrs. Brush—and the eager horse quickly lapped it up. Soon one sugar lump was not enough, and Mrs. Brush's supply of sugar lumps decreased mysteriously. Henry sensed something strong and secure about this horse, something that reached in and touched his soul.

Henry called the horse Samson. Strength and determination to survive—that was the picture he had of the Biblical strongman. The name was perfect for the horse. Henry longed for Samson's strength. So many parts of Henry's world had crumbled and changed in the recent past. Samson's strength reaffirmed Henry's desire for a life that would survive, that would endure, no matter what happened.

‰6‱
Hank's Healing Begins

BIG JACK SWANSON BECAME Hank's constant morning visitor. Once his boarders were out the door with lunch buckets in hand, Jack hurriedly packed up breakfast leftovers, stacked the metal plates in the sink to soak, and put the roaster full of meat destined for supper in a slow oven. Tossing his apron over a chair, he immediately set out for the Larsons.

Jack just happened to arrive once at the same time as Hank's doctor pulled up in front of the cabin. Henry was already off to school, and Daisy had headed to town to visit Mrs. Brush. Doctor Thompson had stopped by several times since Hank returned home, but on this particular morning, he came to discuss Hank's therapy. Jack was very interested.

"In my opinion, Hank, you're ready to get those damaged muscles back in working order." The doctor said, "That is, if you're ready for some painful and difficult movements."

If he had been able, Hank would have leaped from his chair in his eagerness to begin his rehabilitation. And Big Jack, who did leap to his feet, grabbed the doctor's hand, almost shook it off the doctor's arm, and declared, "I'm your man, Doctor. Just tell me what to do—show me—and I swear, I'll get this guy on his feet before you can whistle 'Dixie'!" And so the process of healing began.

Once Jack had designated himself chief caregiver and leg restorer, he was relentless. With his great strength mixed with uncharacteristic gentleness, the two men worked—and prayed—for a miracle. Kneeling at Hank's feet as he sat in his chair, Big Jack meticulously followed Dr. Thompson's program. Big Jack would straighten Hank's legs, one at a time, and carefully raise them up and down—never higher than comfort would allow. He reached behind Hank's knee to provide leverage while he slowly bent the lower limb up and then down—up and down—one leg at a time.

Over and over the two men would face each other as one tenderly, yet firmly, assisted in the rotation of the leg, while the other man gritted his teeth, resisted the pain, and prayed that movement and strength would somehow return. Hank would, at those painful times, close his eyes and visualize himself again riding the logs as they coursed down the river. In his memory, he could even sense the damp pine fragrance of the logs beneath his feet.

Then it was time for coffee and visiting.

"Whatever possessed you to became a river pig, Hank? I think that's most dangerous of all the jobs connected to the logging industry." Jack chuckled as he added, "You can tell how brave I was as a lumberjack. I became a cook!"

They both laughed.

"Well," Hank sipped his coffee before he responded. "The river pigs were always paid more because their work was more dangerous. Daisy and I really needed the money after moving here from North Dakota and Henry was born. So I took the job when it was offered."

"Did you happen to be involved in that huge log jam up the river six or seven winters ago? I think it was the last season I worked in the camp." Big Jack leaned forward, his elbows on his knees, cup in his hands, his mind searching his memory for an image he had carried there for all these years. "It was you, Hank, wasn't it, that blew up that giant sucker and started the whole log drive in one huge blast!" Big Jack set down his cup of coffee and slapped his large hands on his knees. "I knew there was something about you I just couldn't recall—and there it is! You wild man, you! I always thought river pigs had a death wish—and by God! You proved it that day!"

Hank started to laugh as his friend went on about a memory Hank had almost forgotten, one that belonged way back in his more youthful, more hazardous days.

"Hank, you gotta tell me what happened! I think I was there—in fact, I was on the other end of a rope attached to one of you crazy river pigs." Jack paused with disbelief flooding his face. "What if it had been you?"

Hank indicated that he needed another shot of hot coffee. Jack took care of both cups. "Well, Jack, you asked for this—so here's the story of the biggest log jam I ever worked." He laughed. "Pay attention!"

"As you know, during the time at the lumber camp, the teamsters hauled the cut logs to the edge of the river bank where they dumped them, and the logs piled up there until spring. Over the winter, load after load had been dumped on the steep edge of the river bank. The logs intertwined, one load on top of the other. Snow covered them, then melted and froze and more snow and ice covered them." Hank shook his head as he remembered.

"By the time the river ice broke up and the river started to flow, there was a gigantic pile of logs, seemed like a hundred feet high, from the edge of the river to the top of the bank, totally frozen layer upon layer."

"Wasn't someone in charge who could see a problem coming?" Jack asked.

"Evidently not," Hank replied. "Reports started coming to the camp that the pile contained over one and a half million board feet of pine. And guess who they called in to do their dirty work? The river pigs!"

Hank continued. "We grabbed our poles and spikes, hooks, and ropes, and—a little scared—we spread out over the giant puzzle of frozen, intertwined logs. 'Where was the key log?' we wondered. If one log was loosened, would the rest crash down on top of us? If the worst scenario came to be—where all the logs fell at once—would there be a safe place for those of us working on the logs?"

Big Jack shook his head. "I remember that log jam. You men looked like ants working your way across that monster pile. All of us cowardly guys stood at the top of the bank, holding ropes tied around the waists of all of you crawling over the logs."

He grinned and shook his head as he commented, "All of us tough guys at the top of the river bank used to joke about you river pigs down below, that the ropes weren't a safety precaution." Shaking his head as he remembered, he said, "We thought the ropes were the only way we'd ever find your bodies later in the freezing water below." After a thoughtful pause, Jack apologized. "I'm sorry, Hank. I guess it's not a joke."

"You're right. It was really life and death." Hank went on to recall how the river pigs worked to free all the logs. Finally, using brute strength, they came down to the main frozen mass that had snarled together earlier in the season.

"Some of the river pigs weren't fond of using dynamite, and signaled their friends to pull them up." Hank paused, took a breath, and continued. "Soon it was just me and crazy old Wilbur Schmidt. Wilbur was never scared of anything. So, we carefully placed the dynamite under several huge pines that seemed to pin the rest of the logs to the side of the bank, lit the fuse, and signaled like crazy for you guys on top to pull us up!"

Big Jack started to laugh, his big hearty laugh. "Oh, yeah! It's all coming back. Just as we got you two guys up the bank, the dynamite exploded. Logs flew in all directions, then crashed back into the river and, one by one, just kept floating gently downstream. The log drive was on! Wow! Nobody was hurt, and we were all cheering for you crazy river pigs!"

Rising from his chair, Big Jack placed his empty cup in the sink. "Hank, my friend, I can't tell you how glad I am to have you for a neighbor." He reached out his large hand and encased Hank's hand in his. "From now on I'm going to remember that story and, if I tell it to someone, I'm saying you were on the end of my rope, you crazy river pig! And I was the one who saved your life!"

Hank laughed, then turned serious. "And now you're saving me again, Jack. Thanks for everything."

With a wide grin on his face, Jack headed out the door and back to the boarding house, where a tub of potatoes needing to be peeled awaited him.

ᔥ7ᔧ
The Farmer's Daughter

I N THE EARLY SPRING OF 1904, Hank Larson, along with his father and older brother, sailed from Norway to begin a new life in America. Arriving on the shores of the New World, they traveled across the country to a large farm located north of Fargo, North Dakota, where they had been hired to work as farm laborers.

A wealthy landowner in the fertile Red River Valley, Mr. Torsten Fjestad, had over the years accumulated farm acreage as far as his eye could see, as much as his bank account would allow. Always on the search for hard-working farmhands, Torsten quickly responded to a correspondence and suggestion made by a relative still residing in the old country. His cousin posted a letter confidently recommending three men of his acquaintance who were highly thought of as farm laborers in Norway, and all three of them were looking for the opportunity to come to America.

Arrangements were soon made for the three men, Ole Larson and his two sons, Hank and Helmer, to journey to the United States from Norway, leaving Ole's wife and two daughters in the old country. Their plan was to work hard, earn good wages, send most of their money back to Norway, and eventually have the family reunite in North Dakota. At first, everything seemed to fall into place.

Without warning, tragedy struck, first in Norway, with the sudden death of Hank's mother from pneumonia. A year later in North Dakota, an accident occurred during the threshing season, taking the life of Hank's father.

In the fall of 1905, the threshing crew arrived at the Fjestad farm as the sun began to lighten the eastern sky. Before long, the operation was in full swing. Ole Larson, experienced farm worker that he was, should have paid better attention to what he was instructed to do. In Norway, where farms were much smaller, not many farmers saw the need for the large threshing machines like those working their way across the sprawling farms on the prairies of North Dakota. On this, his first morning on a threshing crew, Ole was eager to see the big machine in operation with the crew directing its every move. His job was simple—keep the belts and cylinders running smoothly, distributing a shot of oil wherever and whenever lubrication was needed.

All the workers had been warned against reaching in between the belts of the whirling machine. That could easily damage an arm—or take a life. The hours of the day wore on. Repeatedly Ole checked on the whirling belts, giving a shot of oil here, then moving to another belt for a shot of oil there. Tired and hot as the hours passed, and not remembering the numerous warnings he'd received, Ole carelessly leaned in to oil a boxing on the spinning cylinder of the thresher. Suddenly, his shirt sleeve caught in the cylinder shaft, wrenching Ole off his feet and drawing him into the deadly machine. The crew watched helplessly as Ole Larson was spun around time after time, crushing his head and shoulders on the front wheel.

One of the men sounded five long blasts on the steam whistle, announcing to the rest of the crew that a serious injury had occurred. Work halted. The men rushed to the site of the accident, gathering silently around Ole's body. No one could believe the damage done to the man. Ole's devastated sons fell to their knees in shock at the side of the mutilated body that had been their strong and loving father. Their world had fallen apart.

The tragedy shocked the entire farming community. For years the memory of Ole's gruesome death served as a warning for laborers working near the deadly whirling belts of the threshing machine.

After a funeral service at the nearby country church, Ole's remains were buried in the rich black soil of North Dakota instead of the rocky hillside of his beloved Norway. The plans for a future family reunion in the United States were gone forever.

Wanting a new beginning somewhere else, Helmer soon departed for the far west, hoping to make his fortune there. Hank, however, remained on the farm for two reasons. First, Torston Fjestad made him an offer.

"Hank, you're the best worker I've ever had working here on my land. I'd like you to stay on working for me." Torston clapped a hand on Hank's shoulder and leaned toward him in a confidential manner. "There might even be a substantial raise if you let your brother go west by himself and you stay on as my chief farmhand." A vigorous handshake sealed the deal. However, Torston had no idea of the second reason, even more important than the money, causing Hank to stay on the farm. Hank's reasoning focused totally on Daisy, Torston's lovely young daughter.

From the beginning Hank was attracted to Daisy, not because she was the boss's daughter, but because she made everyone feel more than special, more than accepted, more than welcomed. He couldn't help himself. He fell in love with her.

Being twenty years old when his father died, Hank had now grown from a boyish young immigrant to a solid, strapping mature young man. Typical of his Norwegian heritage, he was tall and sturdily built, with thick blond hair and clear blue eyes.

He realized it was now up to him to keep the farm running in the best condition possible for Mr. Fjestad. And it was also up to him to keep his feelings for Daisy to himself. This would prove more difficult than he thought, as he observed the many young farmers of the area riding their horses through the front gate with the sole purpose of courting Daisy.

Daisy didn't help his situation at all. "Hello, Hank," she'd call as she and her mother brought lunch out to the field workers. "I brought you an extra piece of chocolate cake—I know how much you like my cake."

Then she'd smile, and Hank would stammer his thanks as he took a big bite of the delicious cake. Once, after she served him, she smiled and said, "You have some frosting on your cheek." Reaching out to touch his cheek with her finger, she removed the frosting and placed it gently on his lips. She smiled. Hank blushed and was flustered.

Even when he mucked out the stalls, Daisy would often come by, settle herself on a bale of hay and visit while he shoveled manure into the wheelbarrow. *How strange*, Hank would think. *I don't know of any other girl who wants to be around this shit.* But there she sat, smiling at him while he shoveled and visiting the time away. He was always surprised how much they found to talk about—and laugh about.

"Tell me about your home in Norway," she would often say. "I've been told it's such a beautiful country." And he'd describe to her the fjords, the mountains and the rocky hillsides of his former home.

"I'd love to visit there some day." Then she'd smile, listening to his remembrances of the home and family he would never see again.

She sought him out when he was repairing equipment in the shed. Standing close to him, she watched his strong hands work the tools, often placing her hand upon his shoulder—or on his arm—or on his hand. Hesitantly looking at her, Hank was always surprised by how confident Daisy appeared while being so forward.

Then, one warm evening in early summer, while standing by the pump washing up before going to supper, Hank dried his face on the rough towel. Glancing toward the house, he saw Daisy walking defiantly toward him, a troubled look on her face. Petite as she was, Daisy gave off an aura of strength and determination. Hank could tell, even from a distance, she was upset. Placing the towel back on the hook near the pump, he turned to her. As she came closer, he saw the tears on her cheeks and the frustration in her eyes.

Daisy marched right up to him, looked him straight in the eye, and told him in no uncertain terms, "Hank Larson, I will *never* marry any of those farmers my father wants me to marry! Never!"

Hank blinked in surprise and took a step back.

Stamping her foot, she exclaimed, "I'll marry only the man I love—and that man is you, Hank Larson, whether you like it or not! I won't be auctioned off to the farmer with the most land!"

Her cheeks were flushed, her eyes wide. As a grand finale, standing on her tiptoes, she threw her arms around his neck and placed a kiss directly upon his lips. Then, looking defiantly into his wide, unbelieving eyes, she turned around and marched determinedly back toward the house.

Shock covered Hank's face, still slightly damp from washing. He placed his hand upon his lips where her kiss still lingered. He couldn't believe what he'd just heard. Slowly the meaning of the impassioned words became clear to him.

She loves me—the hired hand. How can that be? It dawned on him the true meaning of what had just transpired. "She loves me!" he murmured to himself. *Dear God! I wish I had grabbed her and kissed her and told her how I feel, how much I love her.*

I'm such a jerk! And a coward! That's what I am! He stalked off to the bunkhouse where he threw himself on his bed and stared morosely at the ceiling. *What a jerk*, he repeated to himself. *How in the world will I ever have a chance to tell Daisy I love her?*

Later that evening, while pitching hay in the barn, Hank noticed a buggy pulling into the yard. The neighboring farmer, a sought-after bachelor by all reports, stepped down from the buggy, threw the reins over the hitching rail, and headed for the front door of the house, where he was warmly greeted by Daisy's father. A stocky farmer in his early thirties, Mr. Orville Pearson was said to be an astute manager and have the best acreage for miles around. And, conveniently, his land nestled up to the northwestern boundary of Torsten Fjestad's land. After shaking hands, the two men disappeared inside.

Hank felt sick. Was this the farmer Daisy was supposed to marry? His mind went blank as the idea of losing her flooded over him. Pitching hay as though the devil himself commanded him, Hank attempted to work off his anguish and dismay at what might be happening to Daisy in the shelter of the parlor. Was there nothing he could do?

Within the span of an hour or so, the two men once again emerged from the house and stood visiting on the porch. Listening carefully while standing in the doorway of the bunkhouse, Hank thought he could hear an angry edge to the conversation. No handshake occurred, as far as he could see. No pats on the back; no warm farewell. The bachelor farmer leaped into his buggy, slapped the reins over the back of his horse, and trotted through the gate and out of sight.

What in God's name is happening? he wondered. Hank's mind went in all directions, coming to no conclusion. *Will I ever have a chance to tell Daisy I love her?*

Two days later, his opportunity arrived. The day dawned hot and humid, intensifying as the hours passed. After a hard day's work, Hank ate supper, finished his evening chores, and washed up at the pump before heading to the bunkhouse.

The heat made it impossible to sleep. Rising from his sweat-soaked bunk, Hank pulled on his trousers and stepped outside for a breath of fresh air. The evening breeze, warm as it was, cooled the skin of his bare chest and ruffled his hair. Above him the stars shone clear and bright in the night sky. As he ambled through the moonlit shadows falling across the yard, his thoughts were of Daisy.

He had not spoken to her since she shocked him by confessing her love for him. Deep in thought, he didn't hear a voice softly call his name. The second time his name floated through the summer night he paused, then looked across the yard toward the big house. And there she was, barely visible, silhouetted in the dim lamplight of her bedroom window. Daisy gestured for him to come closer.

Silently crossing the yard, keeping to the shadows cast by the wide border of lilac bushes, he at last stood beneath her window, looking up at her. Without making a sound, she motioned to him, signaling him to climb the porch railing, then up to the roof, and finally into her room. For a brief moment, Hank felt the entire process very daunting. Looking furtively about him, he pondered where her parents' bedroom might be.

For a brief moment he hesitated, then threw caution to the winds. *I'm not missing another chance to tell her I love her!* he thought. Thus, with one very agile—and quiet— leap he was on the railing, then silently pulled himself onto the porch roof. A second later he slipped through the lace curtains into Daisy's room. There she stood—dark hair freed from her braids flowing down her back, her white nightgown falling softly over the curves of her young body.

When she reached out to embrace him, he almost hesitated. Then his desire for her clouded any good judgment that remained, and he wrapped his arms around her, brought her close, and buried his face in her hair. Taking a moment to blow out the dimly lit lamp, Daisy once again returned to his embrace. Hank was not about to let this moment pass. His lips found hers. There was no turning back. Neither one spoke a word, but they both knew the outcome of this encounter. Darkness surrounded them. It was almost as though they were the only two human beings in the universe.

Daisy took a step back and loosened the ribbon at the neck of her gown, letting it fall to the floor. Though the room was filled with shadows, Hank could see her as she stood there—waiting. He could not believe how beautiful she was. Moving closer, she placed her head gently on his chest.

"Please, Hank," she whispered pulling him closer. He could feel her warm breath on his skin. "Stay with me awhile." She took his hand and placed it gently on her breast.

Hank pulled back. "I can't do that, Daisy. Your father'll kill me. What are you thinking? Don't you know what could happen if we," he hesitated, "do this?"

Daisy grabbed his ear and pulled his head down to hers. "Of course I know what can happen," she whispered. "I'm not a dummy. I'm a farm girl! I know how this works!"

Hank felt an urge to laugh at her confidence.

"I want you to love me, to give me a baby, to make me unacceptable to marry anyone else but you." He could feel her tears on his skin as he held her. "I need to be a soiled woman, can't you understand that?" He felt her body stiffen. "Then no one else will ever want me, only you, and I won't have to fight with my father!"

"Oh, Daisy," he could barely speak. "You'll never know how much I love you, I always have, but are you sure you want this? What about your fam—"

"Please, if you love me, then let me be only yours!" she whispered and, taking his hand, she led him silently through the dark to her bed. Throwing back the quilt, Daisy lay down on the soft muslin sheet, then reached for him.

Letting his trousers fall to the floor, he cautiously slipped onto the bed beside her.

"My bed's a bit squeaky," she whispered in his ear as they lay together on the cool sheets. "We don't want to wake my parents." Then, kissing and laughing quietly together about the squeaky bed, they attempted to make her desperate plan a reality.

However, the antique bed and springs had other ideas. Horrified by the first squeak, they stifled their laughter and silently slipped to the braided rug beside the bed. Tenderly, not allowing even one more sound to escape and awaken her parents, they held each other while discovering the delight of their first venture into sexual satisfaction.

Thus, what briefly began in the old brass bed—the same bed that later moved across the entire state of Minnesota—Hank answered Daisy's pleas to give her a baby. "Then they can never pull us apart! Never!" she whispered, to herself as well as to Hank. "Never!"

And, even on the wooden floor covered by the roughly textured rug, Hank did his very best to fulfill her desire—and his own as well.

Before the horizon showed the glow of approaching day, the lovers again stood at the window. "Come back, Hank," she whispered. "Please come back and love me again."

He kissed her one last time, and—not knowing how to answer her invitation—slipped from her room and dropped silently to the grass. Once again keeping to the deep shadows of the lilacs, he made his way across the yard and back into the stuffy bunkhouse.

Stretched out on his bunk bed, sleep eluded him. Hank was in a state of disbelief, gazing up as the shadows moved across the ceiling. He had always loved her. He knew he always would. Strangely enough, he felt no shame, not even one tiny sliver of shame.

Later that summer in mid-July, when once more he found the courage to make his way through the shadows, he took her in his arms and she returned his love totally, without restraint. The noisy bed once again remained unused and, just as the moon slipped behind a silver cloud, Hank returned to the safety of the bunkhouse where he breathed a sigh of relief.

I'm sure Mr. Fjelstad would shoot me dead if he knew what was going on. Oh well, I'd die a happy man! Turning over and punching his pillow, he fell asleep just as the sky began to lighten.

The summer days passed quickly. By the end of the fall harvest, when the crops were in and all the bins filled, Mr. Fjelstad, after estimating his profits, was pleased with his hardworking hired man and his better-than-expected financial gains.

Suddenly, all hell broke loose.

Daisy missed her monthly bloody show. She smiled wistfully as she pressed her hand to her belly, hoping against hope a baby grew within her. Soon she found herself retching into the one-hole outhouse behind the kitchen just about every morning, and her smile grew even wider.

Daisy's mother grew suspicious as she observed Daisy's frequent trips to the outhouse. She watched Daisy closely, suspecting something amiss. Then one day, after following her daughter on one of her hasty trips to the outhouse, Daisy's mother threw open the door and found her daughter vomiting into the open hole.

Her mother was shocked, but Daisy was relieved and confessed everything. She told her mother of her love for Hank and their nights together in her bedroom.

Her mother told her father, and both parents were horrified, aghast, appalled to discover their beautiful daughter was—who could believe it?—a fallen woman, and pregnant on top of it all. If that weren't shameful enough, the father of the bastard child— God forbid—was Hank Larson, the lowly hired hand!

Mr. Fjestad was not a forgiving man and had no forgiveness for his daughter or the young man he had so often praised as the best employee he had ever had.

"In my very own house!" he ranted and raved, his face flushed with disgust. "I can't believe it! In my very own house!!"

In the autumn of 1906, the ultimatum was issued: "Leave the farm, both of you, and never darken our door again!" Treating the two young lovers like a pair of lepers, Daisy's parents cast them out of their sight and away from the farm—forever.

HANK OFTEN TOOK TIME to contemplate the path he and Daisy had taken. He knew how difficult it had been for her when the two of them drove away from her home and all that had been precious to her. Her mother wept; they could hear her sobbing over the sound of the horses' hooves on the gravel driveway. Her father, on the other hand, turned his back on them with not so much as a "good luck" or "keep in touch."

At first Daisy wrote them often, telling them of their beautiful grandchild and the new life they'd made for their family. No response ever came. They did hear, however, that Daisy's younger sister, Ragna, became Mrs. Orville Pearson, fulfilling Daisy's father's desire for the coveted fertile acreage to the northwest.

After the accident, guilt haunted Hank while he contemplated what life had to offer him and his family at this awkward juncture of pain and inactivity. He had no idea what the future would hold for them, filling his mind with options and possibilities, solutions and alternatives. So far nothing had materialized.

Each morning Daisy returned to the bedroom after setting her bread. Hank looked forward to her coming to the side of the bed. He loved the feel of her hands on his skin as she helped him dress and prepare for the day and any company that might stop by.

"I thought you were so handsome way back then." She paused to manipulate his arm into the sleeve of his flannel shirt. "And I think you're even more handsome now."

Hank would try to protest, but she took pleasure in laying her love for him out in the open. "Just be quiet, and let me tell you how much you mean to me." And on she would go, recalling memories of their "shotgun wedding" at her rural church and the early days of marriage and, finally, the birth of their son.

"Poor Pastor Sorlie," she smiled, remembering. "He was so surprised when we came to him. He'd baptized me and known me since I was little, and there I was—a fallen woman. Do you remember his parting words we left the church after the marriage?"

She pretended to look stern as she repeated the words of her pastor. "He said, 'Go, and sin no more.' Well, I was grateful he even married us, after realizing we had brazenly broken the sixth commandment and made my parents so upset." A slight smile slipped over her face . "I'm sure he thought we'd just keep on 'sinning,' whether he married us or not! And he would've been right about that!"

Even Hank had to laugh when she cupped his face in her hands and looked him right in his eyes. "Yep, I have to admit the night you first came to my room," she paused dramatically, "and we 'sinned'—that will always be my favorite night of my entire life." She grew serious a moment. "You were—and are even today—such a gift and a blessing to me and to Henry."

They laughed together at the memories, at the way they had survived together, at the many twists and turns of their life as the years passed. Her voice filled the room with hope and gave Hank a desire to live each day to the fullest. "We're still together, Hank—the three of us. We can look ahead and plan for the future. Who in the world knows what surprises might come around the corner?" She lightly dabbed his cheeks and neck, clearing away the final remnants of shaving cream. "I know it's going to be something good." She put her arms around his shoulders and kissed him deeply on his freshly smoothed cheeks and lips.

He gathered her close in the shelter of his arms. Daisy seemed to carry with her the aroma of yeast and sugar, of flour and milk and freshly baked bread. He buried his face in her hair and inhaled the sweet fragrance that always surrounded her. Holding her close, for as long as he was able, feeling her lips warm on his, Hank prayed that, one day soon, they would again have the opportunity of "sinning" together, as they had those many years ago in their same old brass bed. Squeaky springs didn't matter anymore.

At last Hank found himself washed, shaved, dressed, fed, and sitting in the old rocker by the window in the parlor. Most days were filled with visitors who came to say hello and always stayed for coffee and a taste of Daisy's baked goods. Hank's friends stopped by after work or on their way to the nearby saloons. Masculine laughter filled the small rooms, constantly warming Daisy's heart toward these hardworking men who cared so much for her Hank. Everyone commented on how well Hank seemed to be doing, how ruddy his color looked, how strong his handshake was when he greeted his guests man to man.

Frank Shaw continued to stop by nearly every day. Hank was aware of the burden Frank carried because of the accident. "I'm here to do any chores that need to be done," he would say, twirling his hat in his hand, " or I can run any errands for Daisy or chop some wood or fetch some groceries."

Most of the time the Larson family invited the young man to stay for supper before allowing him to help in some physical way. Frank spent so much time with the Larsons that Hank found a new name for him—"the other Larson boy."

"You know what, Frank? I think I'll just adopt you and call you my son." Hank turned to Henry, who loved sitting in the middle of all the men. "What do you think, Henry? Would you like an older brother?" The men laughed and Henry nodded emphatically.

Then—at rare moments—when everyone was gone and the cabin was empty, Hank would lay his head back on his chair, close his eyes, a pray fervently. "Please, God, help me to heal. Help me to walk again so I can take the load from Daisy's shoulders and be a true father to my son." Reaching down to massage his damaged legs, he entreated God to bring feeling and function to those slack, impaired muscles. "Please, please, God, give me back my life!"

∞8∞
The Pastor

THE YOUNG SEMINARIAN'S footsteps echoed through the dimly lit hall as he made his way to the library. Seventeen graduates had already been interviewed throughout the course of the day and now, at last, it was his turn. Growing excitement churned in his belly as he paused before the massive wooden door at the end of the corridor. Late afternoon sun warmed his shoulders as it shone through the large window at the end of the hall and shimmered across the polished wood floors. He knocked.

The man seated at the head librarian's desk was the district president of the Norwegian Lutheran Churches for northern Minnesota. All who knew him and worked with him held him in high esteem, for he had a passionate concern for and interest in all the pastors who came under his direction. For the past two days he temporarily occupied the office of the director of the Seminary Library. During the time of these interviews, the director of the library took his briefcase and papers and found another place to work.

C.E., as he was affectionately called, sat at the desk with his chair facing the window, one foot resting on the heavy oak window ledge, the other draped casually over the ankle of the first. A lean and lanky sort, with a balding head, the hair growing in short spurts on the crown, his eyes were large and alert behind metal-rimmed glasses. Hearing the knock, he turned his chair around, ready to greet the next graduate. Rising from his chair as the young man entered, C.E. stood, extended a large hand in welcome, and smiled with his whole being. A large, unlit cigar churned round in his mouth as he spoke.

"Michael G. Jenson, I believe. Sit down. Sit down. You're the final graduate to be interviewed today, and I've been looking forward to meeting you." C.E. gestured toward a leather chair near the front of the desk. He took the chair opposite, thus sitting knee to knee with the young man. After a few minutes of small talk, C.E. came right to the point.

"Tell me, Jenson, why do you feel called to go into the ministry?" The cigar stopped churning. C.E. removed it from his mouth and put in the ash tray, while his cool blue eyes looked into the guileless eyes across from him. A moment passed.

The young man leaned forward, elbows on his knees, and looked with confidence into in blue eyes that studied him. Then the younger man spoke with confidence. "I was born to elderly parents. My mother was forty and my father sixty-two when I came on the scene." He suppressed a laugh. "All our family thought my father and mother were too old to have a child. They had lost several children over the years and had given up hope."

Leaning back in the leather chair, gesturing with his large hands, he grinned. "Finally, like a total miracle, there I was—big, healthy, and—as my parents told me hundreds of times—an answer to prayer." He paused.

"All my life I heard I was a gift from God, that I needed to be ready to answer His call. So, I stayed home to help my parents with the farm until they both passed away about a dozen years ago." He looked down to his large hands in his lap. "And then I heard 'the call,' telling me it was time for me to leave home and get an education."

Michael paused, looked directly into C.E.'s eyes and smiled. "There was never any doubt in my mind about it. I knew I'd become a minister. And here I am."

C.E. leaned back in his chair and contemplated the young man. Average height, thick through the body from all the farm labor, big hands, gentle eyes, and an aura of determined strength. *Yes, this would be the one to send to Cloquet. He could deal with the needs there—I'm sure of it!* he thought. He jabbed the cigar back into his mouth and once again the cigar began its rotation.

They visited over a list of items on the sheet detailing the requirements for ordination. The requirements were met, all recommendations were excellent, and, with the district president's signature, everything would be ready for the assignment to take place.

To close the interview, C.E. suggested the two of them should read scripture together. "Certainly," replied Michael G. Jenson. He reached into his pocket and drew out his well-worn testament. He thumbed through it and came to a passage. He was about to read when a hand reached for the book.

"Here," C.E. said, "let me share one of my favorite passages with you first." He opened the book, glanced at the page before him, then, with great disbelief, looked into the face of Michael Jenson. "Good heavens! You read in the Greek?!"

"Yes, I do. Every day. It keeps my brain disciplined and my skills sharp." Michael smiled at the surprise registered on the face opposite him.

"Well, you read, then. My skills at reading Greek are pretty rusty." Handing the Greek New Testament back to its owner, C.E. leaned back in his chair, smiled a little and thought, *This young pastor will be a joy to observe.*

Michael located his favorite verse—James 1:12. He began reading, translating as he went. "Blessed is the man that endureth temptation: for when he is tried, he shall receive the crown of life, which the Lord hath promised to them that love him."

C.E. found it difficult to keep from grinning. Not one of the other candidates had read from the Greek.

"Just out of curiosity," C.E. asked, "why is that your favorite verse, Jenson?"

"Well," Michael began, "Life's taught me I can't predict what events might come my way. Nor can I know for certain how I'll respond." He closed the New Testament and placed it in his coat pocket. "This verse says to me the Lord forever keeps His promise to me of the crown of life—no matter what happens—because I'll always love him. It's that simple."

"Well spoken, Jenson. I like your style!" C.E. finally allowed himsef to grin at the younger man as he gathered the sheaf of papers together and signed them, promoting Michael G. Jenson to the official rank of pastor of the Norwegian Lutheran Church, serving in northern Minnesota.

They prayed together, rose from their chairs, and, as Michael turned to go, C.E. took an envelope from the top of the desk and handed it to him. "I see by your papers you're just turning thirty, Jenson—the same age as Jesus when He started His ministry."

The young man nodded and smiled. C. E. continued. "When you've been in your call three months exactly, open this envelope. Read it and see what you can make of it. Then answer that call as well."

Very curious, Michael took the envelope, carefully folded it, tucked it in his inside jacket pocket, and patted the place where it lay. "I look forward to reading it. And I'm excited to receive a call to any church where you think I can serve."

Then he was gone, his steps once again echoing down the distant, darkening hall. C.E returned to his chair by the window. Once again the cigar whirled. All at once the words of an old story about being a pastor came to mind. He repeated it to himself.

The first pastor was standing on the bank of a river, preaching to his people who were all floundering in the river as it flowed by. "Come up here where I am," the pastor cried as his flock struggled in the current before him. "Be like me—warm and dry!" The people continued to struggle. The second pastor knelt down on the bank of the river, reaching out his arms to his flock as he shouted to them, "Reach up here to me. Take my hand and I will help you!" The people continued to struggle. And the third pastor threw himself down into the river. Splashing about, he beckoned to the others. "Reach out to each other," he cried. "Join hands with me, keep together, and we'll all be able to reach the safety of the shore."

"Pastor Michael Jenson will turn out to be the one who leaps into the river," he said aloud. "I'm sure of that." With a final whirl of his cigar, C.E. turned once again to the desk and the numerous papers awaiting his attention.

Cloquet will be the place for Michael Jenson, he thought, *and the area to watch will be the Island.*

ಔ9ಣ
The Call

THE CITY OF CLOQUET WAS arranged in a very clear geometric design. The main street, Cloquet Avenue, ran east and west across the length of the crest of land rising from the southern bank of the river. The fronts of the shops and businesses along this street looked out over the river, the Island, the horse barns, the train depot, and the huge canyons of cut lumber stored—as far as the eye could see—on the flat lands below the crest.

Streets running east and west were positioned a proper distance from Cloquet Avenue reaching back to an area called Pinehurst Park. The streets running north and south bisected these streets. All streets and avenues formed a neat pattern of square lots on which the homes of the residents of Cloquet had been built.

One block was where the Brush house had stood for many years (and the smaller house behind it), and where the Lutheran church had been built in the early 1900s. Once a permanent pastor had been called to serve what came to be the Norwegian Lutheran Church, a parsonage was constructed right next door to the church, providing housing for the pastor and his family. The imposing Brush home occupied the largest lot on the northeast corner. The lovely but smaller, more modest home, built to accommodate the pastor, his wife, and his usually large family filled the middle of the block. The church itself, with its classic stained-glass windows, soaring steeple, and bell tower, occupied the remainder of the block.

The parsonage mirrored the construction of the church—white sideboard, dark shingles, a welcoming front door surrounded by shrubs and flowers. Eight rather steep steps led to the heavy oak door at the front of the church, while only four steps led to the porch and the front door of the parsonage. Many people, finding themselves in need, climbed the steps of the church or the parsonage for help. Each pastor had been instructed to administer the "Good Samaritan Fund" provided by the congregation for such emergencies. The church members took pride in the accommodations they provided for the flock and for the shepherd called to lead them down the path of righteousness.

ON JUNE 14, 1917, the new pastor for the Lutheran church arrived in Cloquet. With some confusion as to the time of his arrival, the welcoming committee was not aware he would be arriving on the afternoon train from Duluth, not the evening train as they assumed. Thus, no one was there to meet him when he stepped down from the passenger car onto the platform by the depot. Earlier in the day, he had boarded the train in

Minneapolis and rode north to the depot in Duluth, where he changed trains for the last leg of his journey to Cloquet. This short run from Duluth was usually crowded with women returning home from a holiday of shopping and men returning from money-making business lunches in the bigger city. The car echoed with friendly banter, comparisons of purchases, desserts enjoyed, and business deals completed.

The June heat caused the ladies to dab their dainty lace-trimmed hankies at their brows and necks, trying to stem the flow of unseemly sweat that stained their organdy dresses and ruined their fancy hairdos. Men had it a bit easier. They removed their suit coats, rolled up their sleeves, and wiped their faces with a monogrammed handkerchief.

Soon the train arrived at Cloquet. After stepping down from the passenger car, the female passengers adjusted their hats and, laden with parcels and packages, fluttered by the unfamiliar man in the dark suit. Hoisting their satchels, men puffed their cigars and reluctantly put on their suit coats. No one spoke to or paid any attention to the disheveled young man in their midst. The men and women quickly dispersed, until only the rumpled man in the black suit remained, standing alone on the depot platform.

Pastor Michael Jenson was unfamiliar with Cloquet. C.E. had seen to it Michael would be the replacement for the previous pastor, who had to leave due to illness. Michael's superiors at the seminary assured him he'd be a wonderful match for a church that size. After classes in Greek and Hebrew, he was prepared to share the Word with lumberjacks and loggers. He'd be welcomed with open arms, they said, and taken into the hearts and homes of the parishioners.

And here he stood—alone. Reverend Michael G. Jenson was perspiring heavily as he collected his small trunk, the battered leather suitcase, and a bulky rectangular object wrapped in a scrap of old blanket and secured with twine. He stood in the hot afternoon sun, his one and only black wool suit damp with sweat. Removing his jacket and wiping his face with a white handkerchief, he gazed up the hill, trying to recall the directions he'd received earlier in the mail from a deacon of his church. Flies buzzed around him.

Wiping his brow again and replacing his dusty, travel-worn hat, he tucked his suit coat under the belt holding the suitcase together. He hoisted the small trunk onto his left shoulder and tucked the blanket-wrapped object under his arm. With great determination he retrieved the suitcase. He glanced about, looking for a clue as to which road to take. Sweat again trickled down his forehead and clean-shaven cheeks. Flies continued their eager buzzing around his head.

With determination, he started up the dusty road leading to the buildings up the hill. Smiling, he knew he must be a sorry spectacle to anyone who saw him, trudging along in the dust, with a colony of flies circling his hat. He spoke to himself in a playful manner. *I like it here. Yep! I really like it here!* And he—and the flies—headed toward the street signs that read Avenue A and Arch Street.

HENRY LARSON HAD JUST completed his daily deliveries of baked goods. The wagon was empty, and Henry was all set to climb into it and coast—"fly," he preferred—down the hill toward the bridge and the horse barns. The afternoon sun was warm on his back. He had one knee in his wagon all set to push off, when he heard someone call out to him.

"Hey there!" came the voice. "How about I hire you and that wagon for a short trip?" The voice was friendly and the word "hire" sounded intriguing. Henry turned toward the depot and looked into the face of Pastor Jenson for the first time.

Removing his knee from the wagon, Henry headed toward the man in the middle of the hot, dusty street. He had a smiling face, rumpled clothes, and a load on his back and under his arm. Henry could see he'd certainly benefit from the use of his wagon.

The stranger reached out his right hand. "I could really use your help, young man." A wide smile filled the face of the man in the black suit. " I think I might be lost!" Both the stranger and Henry laughed as they stood there, shaking hands like two old friends.

"My name's Pastor Michael Jenson. I just arrived and need to find the Lutheran church," the man said. "I feel quite unprepared. I don't even know where it is." He laughed. "Quite the way to start my first call!" Again, warm laughter and another pump of his hand.

Henry felt comfortable with the man. He returned the smile. "I'd be happy to guide you and carry your load in my wagon." Henry stood tall, confidently measuring his wagon against the load in front of him, knowing the parcels would fill it to overflowing. He thought, *I always knew this wagon would come in very handy!* "I know just where you want to go. Until just a few months ago I lived right down the block from the parsonage," Henry explained. "You'll see where my old house used to be before the city tore it down. It sat right next to the alley, just behind Mrs. Brush's house."

Pastor Jenson and Henry agreed meeting each other in this dusty, hot spot was quite the coincidence. After loading the wagon, they started up the hill toward town.

Turning left on Cloquet Avenue, Henry led the pastor down the main street of the town. Henry pointed out various places of interest as they headed down the wooden sidewalk. The mills in the distance, smokestacks belching smoke, the canyons of cut lumber, the assortment of businesses and shops they passed as they progressed block by block—this fascinated the new pastor The main street was a busy thoroughfare in the afternoon, filled with horses and buggies, newfangled automobiles, pedestrians on both sides of the street, and children hurrying home for dinner.

All eyes turned to Henry and the man beside him. No one had seen the man before, but Henry was known to everyone.

Pastor Jenson smiled, nodded, and tipped his hat to everyone they passed. He had a wonderful smile that filled his entire face, creasing his cheeks with lines there from constant use. He chatted away with Henry, and—as they turned right onto Carlton Avenue—he clapped him on the shoulder and said, "I can feel it! We're almost there!"

And Henry pointed up the street to the next corner where, through the dense leaves of trees lining the boulevard, they could see the bell tower of the church on the left side of the street. White and stately, the church was surrounded by budding trees and shrubs.

"See where the city dug up the alley to make it wider?" Henry pointed. "Well, that's where our home used to be. Now we live on the Island." He looked up at the pastor. "You'd like the Island. Some people think it's a bad place, but I really like living there."

Mrs. Brush's lovely home graced the corner opposite the church. Henry assured Pastor Jenson that Mrs. Brush would be a wonderful neighbor. "She makes the best coffee and cookies. And she's a great chess player. And she has hundreds of books!"

Pastor Jenson smiled down at the eager boy beside him. "Well, I'll certainly look forward to meeting her after that excellent recommendation!"

Once they turned the corner and passed the steps leading to Mrs. Brush's front porch, they could see the walkway leading to the parsonage. Henry and Pastor Jenson noted a group of people clustered about the porch and on the front steps, preparing the parsonage for Pastor Jenson's early evening arrival.

Michael retrieved his suit jacket. "Give me a hand here, Henry. I should try to look a little respectable when I meet my flock!" Henry tried to smooth out the wrinkles across the back of the coat, to no avail.

With his hat covering his disheveled hair, Pastor Jenson brushed off the front of his suit, unloaded the wagon on the sidewalk, and boldly walked to the front steps. "Hello, everyone!" he called out. "I'm Pastor Jenson. I'm very happy to be here."

Taking two steps at a time Pastor Jenson advanced toward the members of his parish gathered on the porch and inside the parsonage. They were surprised and embarrassed once they realized he had come in on the earlier train rather than the final run of the day that arrived at seven—and—God forgive them!—no one had met him. Excuses poured from their lips.

"My goodness! There's evidently been faulty communication! How in the world could that have happened?"

"Can you ever forgive us that no one met you when you stepped down from the train? Who in the world was responsible for being there when the train pulled into the station?"

The men and women on the porch and in the front yard glanced from one to another, dismayed at the event that seemed to tarnish the first impression their new shepherd would have of his congregation. Apologies continued. They wanted to get to know him, hoped he'd enjoy his new flock, the cleaned, polished place of worship, the community eager to clasp him to its bosom, the lovely parsonage, and, of course, his congregation would not fail him again! Ever!

Pastor Michael Jenson shook hands all around. The men thought he had a strong handshake and a bold look in his eye. He seemed eager to smile and called each person by name as soon as they had introduced themselves. Mothers with grown, unmarried daughters appraised him as a possible conquest. He needed some sprucing up, they mused, but perhaps he would clean up well. There was always hope.

Then Mrs. Berg was introduced as they headed to the dining room. A "light supper" had been prepared by the ladies of the church for the group getting the parsonage ready. Mrs. Berg seemed to be the "grande dame" of the church, if there is such a thing. She seemed in charge of the women, if not also the men. Her husband had given up the ghost several years ago. Quite often at the mention of Adolph, she'd tear up, reach into her ample bosom for a hanky and proceed to dab her eyes. Her critical eye investigated the young man standing before her, his hand outstretched. They shook hands in greeting. Mrs. Berg had a very firm grip.

Mrs. Berg automatically put herself in charge of setting up the parsonage in a way appropriate for a bachelor pastor. This was a first for this congregation. *Now this Pastor Jenson arrives, possessing nothing of his own—not one stick of furniture with which to furnish this lovely parsonage,* she thought. Mrs. Berg vowed that she, and she alone, would put together a parsonage furnished top to bottom with the very best.

Pastor Jenson was pleased by the welcome he received, by the smiles and best wishes heaped upon him by the men and women milling about in his new—empty—home. He set down his cup of coffee and molasses cookie on the makeshift serving table, spread his arms to quiet the visiting flock, waiting until it was quiet. He smiled broadly while looking into the many faces before him. He felt he had come to the place he was destined to be. And so he spoke, as he often did, what he felt deep inside. "Thank you so much," he began. "You'll never know how much your warm welcome has meant to me. I know I must have looked a sight when you first saw me, but you looked beyond the rumpled, dust-covered man before you and saw me for what I am—a servant of the Lord who comes to labor in the vineyard, side by side with you." Another wide smile lit up his face as he commenced shaking hands with each person in the room.

Guests lingered over their coffee, then headed to their homes and farms in the city and the outlying area. Individuals had promised an amazing array of furniture to be delivered as soon as possible. A bed was coming within the hour so the pastor would at least have a place to lay his head when the sun went down and this auspicious day came to an end.

The last person to take her leave, Mrs. Berg promised to be back in a jiffy with linens, blankets, some dishes, a pillow, and a warm quilt. "Pastor Jenson, you can always depend on me!" she told him as she headed down the steps. He somehow believed that to be true.

After his welcoming committee dispersed, Pastor Jenson brought his trunk, suitcase, and wrapped package into the dining room. All his worldly possessions were contained in these three objects. Taking a seat on steps leading upstairs, he set down his trunk and opened it to reveal his limited wardrobe. He only owned one suit, two shirts, extra collars, basic undershirts and long underwear, regular underwear, winter boots, heavy woolen winter clothing, a bulky fur hat, gloves and mittens, a top coat, the hat he had on earlier, an extra pair of shoes, warm flannel pajamas, shaving equipment, toiletries, his robe and cassock, and his pastoral collar—not the fancy ruffled type but the plain white collar that circled the neck of his clergy shirt. Making his way up the stairs, he found a closet in the larger bedroom with an assortment of hangers to accommodate his meager possessions.

He opened his suitcase and unpacked his treasured library, collected from friends and professors—his Greek New Testament, biblical commentaries, Hebrew textbook, many packets of notes taken in his favorite classes, his well-worn Bible, full of notes and markers. Some books were treasures from his childhood, when reading was his pleasure and escape. He put the books on a shelf in the dining room in order of use and function—devotionals, books on sermon preparation, ones by favorite theologians and philosophers, recreational reading, and books he'd like to share with others with like interests.

Immediately he felt more at home. He ran his fingers over the spines of the books, some of the only familiar objects in his new life. His favorites were the books his mother had collected over the years and shared with him. They were all he had left of his childhood.

His final chore was to hoist the wrapped parcel onto his lap and untie the twine. He gently folded away the faded blanket that once covered his childhood bed, and there it was—the photograph of his family. A chipped, worn frame surrounded the sepia photo.

He was a small child in the photo. Wide eyes looked out from the photo, face serious, and hands folded in his lap. Seated on his mother's lap, her arms circled him and held him close. His mother, slender but strong, usually worked from dawn to dusk with Michael at her side. Michael concentrated for a moment on his father, a large man with a stoic expression. Thick, unruly gray hair cascaded down his cheeks to a full but neatly trimmed beard. No smile in his eyes nor on his lips, only a challenging look that told the world, "Try anything! You will never defeat me!"

This photo was his treasure. It pained him to look at it, but he needed to study the photo occasionally, just to ground himself in the earth from which he had sprung. He regretted that he had been part of a family for only a brief time. He decided to hang the photo in the dining room once the promised furniture arrived.

By the time the sun slipped toward western hills, a small bed and nightstand arrived and were set up in the downstairs bedroom. Mrs. Berg, true to her word, came with bedding, a casserole, buns, and a jug of milk, plus dishes, cups, glasses, and silverware. Once the bed was made, the food enjoyed, and with his earthly possessions surrounding him, Pastor Michael G. Jenson was ready to call it a day. He emptied his suit pockets of change and the folded envelope he had carried since his visit with the district president. The change he put on a stand by the bed, and the letter he placed carefully under his Bible in the single drawer of the nightstand.

It was time for him to fall asleep in a stranger's bed, in an unknown town, not knowing what the morning would bring. He crawled between the sheets provided by Mrs. Berg and stretched out on the mattress, his hands behind his head. He closed his eyes and recalled this special day.

And then, suddenly, he sat bolt upright. What had become of Henry? He had never had a chance to thank him, to pay him for the use of his wagon, to invite him and his family—whoever they were—to come to his church.

First thing tomorrow he'd find Henry and make amends. Of course! He'd ask his neighbor, Mrs. Brush, if she knew where Henry lived. Plan established, Pastor Jenson rolled to his side and pulled the sheet up to cover his shoulders. The quilt, too warm for a summer night, lay folded at the foot of the bed. At the moment, he was very grateful for the overbearing, but generous, Mrs. Berg.

JENSON'S FIRST DAY AS PASTOR of the Norwegian Lutheran church began with the shrill mill whistles calling workers to their jobs. He dressed quickly in the same black suit, but with a clean shirt and clean white collar. Checking his chin, he decided that, unless a person were nose to nose with him, his beard was hardly noticeable. A couple of passes with a brush and his hair was under control, at least for him. He'd never been a stickler for appearances. He was usually too eager to begin each day to bother much with his toilette. And today he was on a mission.

Knowing it was early, he took the risk and knocked on the front door of Mrs. Brush's stately home. He waited a brief time before deciding perhaps the hour was too early for normal people. Turning to go, he heard the latch open and saw the door swing wide.

Before him stood a slender woman, elderly, yet straight and tall. White hair hung over her shoulders in two braids. She wore a soft floral-print robe. Two bright, lively eyes gazed up at him, crinkling at their edges when she smiled. She reached out a hand twisted with arthritis. He took her hand carefully, gently. Her grip was firm, more than he expected.

"Come in, come in," she held the door open wide, and he stepped into the cool interior of the elegant older home. "You need not introduce yourself, Pastor Jenson. I was a witness to your celebrated arrival yesterday." Smiling warmly, she motioned for him to follow her into the parlor where he was soon seated comfortably with a cup of steaming coffee in hand. She seated herself, poured a bit of cream into her cup along with two lumps of sugar, stirred her coffee carefully, and raised her eyes to meet his.

"I'm here for some information," Pastor Jenson stated. "I hope you can help me." He went on to explain his unannounced arrival by train yesterday and his struggle to bring his meager belongings to the parsonage. He spelled out in great detail his fortunate meeting with Henry Larson, how the boy and his wagon assisted him in bringing his few belongings from the depot to the steps of the parsonage.

As the pastor went on, the smile on Mrs. Brush's face grew wider and wider. "Henry, such a fine young man."

Taking a sip of fragrant coffee, the pastor continued. "I learned so much about the community during the walk up the hill and through town. Henry pointed out all the places of interest, as far as the eye could see."

"I'm not surprised." Mrs. Brush spoke with conviction. "Henry and I have been friends since the day he was born. The Larson family moved into town eleven years ago. We've been family to each other all this time." She added one more sugar lump to her coffee and stirred again. "You'll be fond of the whole family once you meet them."

Michael confessed his great oversight, his becoming so distracted by the people awaiting him, that he totally overlooked the young boy and all his assistance. "By the time everything settled down—that's when Henry came to mind. Henry had slipped away before I could properly thank him." He savored another sip of coffee. "I'm very sorry about that!"

"I'm certainly the one to help you find the Larson family." She smiled. "They lived behind this very house for eleven years." She hastened to tell the pastor some of the details that had recently disrupted the Larson family, turning her tear-filled eyes away when she spoke of Hank's accident and resulting disability that prompted their move to "the Island."

Michael had no idea what " the Island" represented. He recalled Henry had also mentioned it, but let the phrase pass without comment.

"I love them as though they were my very own children." She wiped away the tears. "I'm pleased you'll meet them now."

With promises to visit again and directions to the Larson home, Pastor Jenson took his leave of Mrs. Brush and walked briskly through the awakening town. The streets and businesses were slowly coming to life, the sidewalks only moderately crowded at this hour.

He was more aware of his surroundings on this second journey down the main street. Three mills, made very visible by their large smokestacks, belched a smoldering haze above the city. Millions of board feet of lumber stacked like huge canyons, Henry's description, were piled everywhere, covering all available space not occupied by homes or businesses.

He walked down Arch Street, noting the stables off to the left. Huge workhorses grazed on the grassy meadow. He skirted the two slab piles, then turned toward the Island. At the red bridge, he halted and took time to take in what he could see of the Island.

The river was crammed with logs making their way to the mills, where they'd be sawed and planed into millions of board feet of lumber. Fresh lumber was in heavy demand as the country moved west, new houses and businesses sprouting wherever people settled.

Making his way across the bridge, it dawned on him he hadn't seen one saloon or tavern in his trips through Cloquet. Yet here on the Island stood one saloon after another. He noted the large corner building, whose sign boasted "The Northeastern Hotel—fine dining, fine liquor!"

Taking a quick count of the buildings facing St. Louis Avenue, Michael Jenson counted at least fifteen saloons facing the river. He stepped from the bridge and continued his way up Main Street. He saw more saloons, as well as tobacco shops, a shooting gallery, boarding houses, and a mercantile.

He was intrigued. How did a family as fine as the Larsons, according to Mrs. Brush, manage to survive in such surroundings. He noted the rustic house at the end of Main Street where he'd been told the Larson family would be and hurried toward it. He'd try not to ask too many questions or make judgments.

He passed the boarding house to his right where a young girl was busy sweeping the porch and steps. As soon as she noticed him, she stopped and stared opened-mouthed. Evidently men in black suits and clerical collars were not seen too often here.

He tipped his hat in her direction, greeted her with a warm, "Good morning!" and gave her his best smile. She responded with a nod, quickly closing her mouth. He turned up the path that led to the front of the only house left on Main Street and knocked.

Daisy Larson had started her bread earlier than usual that particular morning. She couldn't sleep when sunlight streamed into the bedroom. Slipping from bed, trying not to disturb Hank's sleep, she quickly dressed, braided her hair, and put on her apron.

Henry was still asleep on his little cot in the storeroom. Soon she'd awaken him. Maggie needed help weeding the large garden behind the boarding house. Henry was always happy to work for Big Jack. Maggie, in turn, would help later in the day when the baked goods came fresh and hot from the oven. After loading the fragrant loaves in his wagon, they'd deliver them across the bridge to their waiting customers.

The dough had already been mixed. Now came Daisy's favorite part. She put the mound of dough on the light layer of flour covering the enamel top of the small table in the kitchen. Flour puffed up, dusting her apron and cheeks as she worked the dough—push and turn, push and turn. The dough yielded under the pressure of her hands.

She returned the ball of dough to the large bowl, gave it a final pat as she set it on the counter to rise, and covered it with a muslin towel. It could rest until it was time to punch it down once more in an hour or so. Just as she turned toward the bedroom where Hank waited for her to help him shave and dress, she heard the knock. Wiping her flour-covered hands on her apron, she opened the door.

Daisy saw a young man in a dark suit standing with his hat in hand. Taller than most men she knew, he had a strong, energetic manner. A breeze ruffled his hair, even as he ran a hand through it to calm it down. Pastor Jenson gazed down upon a petite dark-haired woman dusted with flour. She had smiling eyes, curly hair, and appeared ready—even eager—to welcome any person who came to her door.

Pastor Jenson took the initiative by introducing himself, explaining as best he could why he was there. "Your son was very helpful when I arrived yesterday. I don't know how

I would've managed to get my belongings to the parsonage if it hadn't been for Henry and his wonderful wagon."

He laughed in a warm and friendly way, making Daisy smile. "I wanted to reward him for his good service and for introducing me to the fair city of Cloquet." He smiled down at her. "Plus, he told me how much I'd enjoy Mrs. Brush, my neighbor. I received directions to your home earlier this morning as I shared a cup of coffee with her. And Henry was right—she is delightful!"

After realizing this young man was the long-awaited new pastor, Daisy relaxed, reached out to shake his hand, after which she opened the door wider and invited him in.

For the second time in less than an hour, Michael found himself seated across from a charming woman with a hot cup of coffee in hand. Visiting came easily for Pastor Jenson, and Daisy Larson responded quickly to his comments and questions.

A deep voice called from the bedroom. "I'd like to come out and join you two for coffee." Pastor Jenson assumed that voice belonged to Hank, who, Mrs. Brush had told him, had been seriously injured in the mishap on the river earlier that spring. Daisy excused herself and slipped into the room from which the voice came. Michael could hear her explaining his presence, his relationship to Henry, and his position in the community.

Pastor Jenson was conscious of the effort Daisy was making to prepare Hank before he could come into the parlor to meet him. He could hear the rustling of bedding, the sound of feet moving slowly across the floor. He could almost imagine how Daisy was getting Hank up from the bed and prepared for the day and the pastor. As he waited, Michael sipped his coffee and looked out the window toward the buildings that covered the island to the south.

The front door flew open and the biggest man Michael had ever seen entered. This burly man nodded to Jenson and quickly stepped into the bedroom. A moment later three people emerged—Daisy on one side of a handsome, smiling man, her arms about his chest as if to hold him upright and Big Jack on the other side, basically carrying Hank all by himself, supporting both Hank and Daisy in their short journey to the rocker by the window.

Big Jack let Pastor Jenson know he was in charge of preparing Hank's legs to work again. "My strength will be his strength," Big Jack said with conviction. "Hank's legs are going to be strong some day soon, if I have anything to say about it. By God, we'll work hard 'til we get power back into those skinny old legs and damaged muscles!"

Hank laughed through the whole procedure. "I don't think I have skinny legs, Big Jack. Not everyone can be a giant like you!" They all laughed. And Michael had no doubt, from that very moment, that Hank was in good hands—very large, strong, good hands.

Once Hank was comfortable, feet resting on a stool, a mug of hot coffee in his hand, all three men introduced themselves and made small talk about the lovely day, the early morning activity on the Island, the fine boy Hank and Daisy had produced, life in the logging camps, and what was occurring at the boarding house just down the street.

WHILE BIG JACK STIRRED his coffee, he observed Pastor Jenson as he visited with the Larson family. *Seems like a good man*, he thought . Never before had Big Jack had the opportunity to visit face to face with an actual "man of the cloth." Suddenly words exploded from Big Jack's lips. "Why don't you stop by my boarding house for dinner one night soon, Pastor? I could introduce you to my boarders and give you a chance to convert them—if you wanted to!" He laughed at the thought of it, and the others joined in. "They curse and swear and fart and belch and have no manners whatsoever. What do ya think?"

Michael took a last bite of cookie and smiled broadly at the large man. "You know what, Big Jack? Your boys sound like most of my friends. I'd be honored to dine in your establishment—any time!"

As Big Jack took his leave, he stretched out a hand as large as a griddle and enveloped Michael's hand to seal the deal. "I'll be waiting for you, Pastor! It'll be my pleasure to introduce you to my rowdy boys."

Pastor Michael Jenson felt comfortable and at home with his new-found friends. He always pictured himself a common man, not a philosopher or a theologian or a professor. He loved people just the way they were—sinners and all. He always had. He'd grown up dealing with the "haves" and "have nots" of his home town.

Pastor Jenson studied the injured man, seeing great strength in that broken body. Broad hands, thick fingers. Cords of muscles rippled in the lower arms. Hank's shoulders were wide, and his chest deep and defined. His broad face had strong bone structure. An unruly head of blond hair covered his forehead, most of his ears, and trickled down his cheeks in a thin tracing of whiskers. His spirit of life and strength belied his condition.

But the legs—it was difficult to look upon the still limbs. No motion, no sign of life. Michael swallowed hard, vowing he would be there for this family. He felt destiny had brought Henry into his life. And because of him, Michael was led to the Island and the rest of the family, especially Hank, whose clear blue eyes looked out on the world from the window, longing to return to life as it had been such a short time before.

Before Pastor Jenson took his leave, Henry sleepily emerged from the storeroom and grinned widely when he saw his new friend sitting in the parlor visiting with his parents.

"Henry saved the day for me yesterday," Michael said. "I had no idea where I was or where I was supposed to go. I can't thank him enough! You have a fine son here!"

Henry blushed, warming quickly to the praise heaped upon him. He tried to refuse the silver dollar pressed into his hand to repay him for the use of the wonderful wagon, but the pastor insisted. Henry kept the dollar.

Pastor Jenson shook hands all around and, with sincere thanks, took his leave of the Larsons. Walking briskly by the Riverside Boarding House on his way home, Michael saw Big Jack tending to a broken post on the front porch. Michael paused for a moment, turned, and then decided to ask Big Jack for a favor.

"If I come back to have a meal with you and your boys, and if you have some free time, would you give me a tour of the Island? I've never seen anything quite like it."

Big Jack threw back his head and laughed loudly. "So you want to see the Island, the place the town wants to keep all its sinning! I'd truly enjoy showing you around and introducing you to all the sinners that roam this insignificant island!" No date was set, but Pastor Jenson was intrigued, and promised to return soon.

He crossed the bridge and found himself once again in the bustle of Cloquet. He briskly walked up the hill toward the parsonage, eager to begin preparation for Sunday, when he'd preach his first sermon to his new flock. He searched his mind for a Bible verse appropriate for a new beginning for himself and the people of his parish.

He turned the corner by the church. Several wagons were parked in front of the parsonage. Five strong farmers quickly carried furniture up the front steps.

Mrs. Berg, in the middle of the porch, directed the men who labored beneath her critical gaze and commanding voice. "Put that over here! Take that upstairs! Careful! Don't break anything! I told you that large chair belongs in the parlor! Pay attention!"

By late afternoon the parsonage had undergone a mystical change. Two comfortable chairs and a large, worn leather couch anchored the gently worn, deep-red floral area rug in the living room. Two end tables supporting two lamps were stationed near a chair and one end of the couch. A well-used but sturdy oak dining table rested on a somewhat worn green carpet with an oak scroll and leaf design. A wide, heavy fringe edged the rug and gave it an elegant air, even though it had been used for many years in another home in the parish. Four heavy oak chairs with cracked leather seats surrounded the table. Two chairs of a different design sat on either side of a bookcase/writing desk against the wall opposite the kitchen.

Kitchen furnishings consisted of an icebox left by the previous pastor and a small table by the window with two bow-backed chairs flanking it. A small pottery crock with a healthy, green plant centered the table. Anchoring the wall opposite the windows was a vintage kitchen cabinet that bore evidence of years of use—scratches in the finish, drawers that no longer closed flush, dented enamel kneading board, missing pieces of hardware.

The two large drawers at the bottom of the cupboard were clean and ready to hold at least sixty pounds of flour, according to Mrs. Berg. She took great pleasure pointing out to her bachelor pastor that the top drawers and cupboards were full of mismatched dishes and utensils, ready for the new pastor to fend for himself in the kitchen.

"You'll eventually have to do some of your own cooking. We can't feed you every day," she warned him. Opening a small drawer under the kneading board, she indicated a muslin apron he could use. "You wouldn't want to get spots on your only suit now, would you!"

The miracle continued. Pastor Jenson followed Mrs. Berg's ample frame as she laboriously climbed to the second floor. When entering the master bedroom, Michael was speechless. An old iron bed frame took up most of the room. The decorative scrolls of the headboard and footboard overpowered the meager size of the spring and mattress. Mrs. Berg had taken it upon herself to bring another set of sheets, fresh from drying on her clothesline. They were tucked in with fine square corners. Pastor Jenson sat on the edge of the bed and the spring let out with a loud squeak. He quickly stood once again.

A ponderous quilt covered the bed and fell nearly to the floor. Pastor Jenson was sure he'd find it difficult to turn over in bed with such a heavy quilt on top of him. Two plump handmade goose-down feather pillows, stuffed into hand embroidered cases, crowned the head of the bed. A chiffonier topped with an adjustable mirror stood against the wall to the left of the bed, while the small nightstand stood to the right. A kerosene lamp and a pack of matches waited on the stand, and—much to Pastor Jenson's surprise—his very own Greek New Testament, evidently selected by Mrs. Berg from the bookcase downstairs, lay next to the lamp. He smiled. Mrs. Berg did not miss a trick.

Pastor Jenson, amazed, thankful, bewildered, and beholden to the many people who had come with a gift and left with a warm handshake, sat that evening in a comfortable old reed rocker one of his members had brought over and set on the front porch. His Bible lay open on his knees as he searched for the appropriate scripture to center his message—the first of many, he hoped—for his first Sunday service. There were many possibilities: a new beginning, responding to the call, stewardship, fostering togetherness, the mission to the community. Then he came upon Matthew 10:40-42.

Christ says to his followers, "He who receives you receives me, and he who receives me receives him who sent me. He who receives a prophet because he is a prophet shall receive a prophet's reward, and he who receives a righteous man because he is a righteous man shall receive a righteous man's reward. And whoever gives to one of these little ones even a cup of cold water because he is a disciple, truly, I say to you he shall not lose his reward." The verses were perfect, just what Michael had experienced.

The commentary on the Gospel of Matthew said: "There is no distinction as regards the reward going to those who receive the prophet. A cup of cold water is a proverbial expression for a minor service. Matthew concludes an important doctrinal section by emphasizing the need for practical loving kindness. This is the final result and test of discipleship."

And Pastor Michael G. Jenson had just reaped the reward of the loving kindness so generously given by the members of his flock. He quickly moved inside, where he set out his paper, pens, Bible, and commentaries, and began to write. The title of his first sermon would be, "A Cup of Cold Water, a Houseful of Furniture—All Given in Christ's Name."

As the summer days passed, the whole community warmed to Michael's exuberance. Reports circulated of his lively visits to the ill and homebound. "That new pastor stopped over for a visit one afternoon," an elderly gentleman commented to his friends. "He even offered to play checkers with me and any of my old cronies who wanted to challenge him." The old men chuckled at the thought of their approaching games and easy victories over this youngster. "We'll show him a trick or two," they promised each other.

And sure enough, more often than not, the older gentlemen won, although the game always came down to the final few moves. Michael would shake his head in disbelief and rise from the table, stretching his arms and legs after sitting so long.

With satisfied looks, the grizzled old men reassured their pastor, "You keep playing with us, young man, and we'll get you in top shape in no time!" After numerous handshakes and slaps on the back, Michael went on his way, a wide smile on his face.

He was a welcome visitor of the aging widows. The often lonely women always broke into a smile when Pastor Jenson turned up at their front door. "Well, look who's here," they'd croon as they took his hat and ushered him to the kitchen table. He'd sip coffee—or tea, if necessary—and carry on a conversation while admiring their knitting, crocheting, embroidering, or darning, all the while nibbling cookies baked especially for him.

"I was hoping you'd stop by. I heard from my neighbor you visited her last week," he'd sometimes hear. There was often a slight pause before the elderly woman brought back all her coquettish charm. "I was certain you wouldn't forget me!" she'd say as plump cheeks lifted in a wide smile.

"Did I hear right? Is your favorite a molasses cookie?" At his nod, the woman settled herself in the chair opposite the young pastor, passed him a plate of molasses cookies, and was ready to hang on his every word.

Baked goods usually accompanied him as he made his way home at the end of the day. He felt sure he'd gained weight since his arrival. It was an occupational hazard.

On his days off, Michael might, in everyday work clothes, swing an ax in the back yards of some members too ill or unable to maintain their woodpile. No one could believe the pastor actually enjoyed splitting kindling. He'd tell anyone who commented on his unusual behavior that physical labor reminded him of his boyhood on the farm. He would smile and add that physical labor helped him keep in shape after enjoying all those baked goods.

He was also seen, his sleeves rolled up, his only suit coat on a lowerbranch, in Mrs. Brush's back yard, balanced on a flimsy ladder, trimming the giant lilac bush hindering the entrance to her screen porch. Sweat stained the underarms of his black clergy shirt.

Mrs. Brush sat in the shade by old Syd, who chewed and spit and gave constant advice: "Take another foot off that top branch. Keep the lower branches even with the ground." Syd took a moment for a spit and another chaw. "Hey, you're getting too close to the porch!" Michael ignored his directions and kept cutting. A pitcher of ice cold lemonade sat on the table, ready to share with the pastor when his work was done.

Most members loved that Pastor Jenson was so involved in serving the members of his church in these unusual ways. But, of course, there were always a few who criticized him for his "non-pastoral" behavior.

"Shouldn't he spend more time in prayer?"

"Shouldn't he be more particular about his appearance?"

"Shouldn't he purchase another suit? The one he always wears really looks worn."

"Shouldn't he call on the wealthier members of the church who could afford to add money to the annual budget?" Most of the congregation paid no attention to the "shouldn't he" critics. In their eyes he was their shepherd—and their friend.

But there was one thing about Pastor Jenson no one in his congregation could bring themselves to criticize: his preaching. Each Sunday he strode to the pulpit, arranged his Bible and notes, and invited the congregation to join him in prayer. Then he'd raise his head, place his hands on either side of the pulpit railing, and gaze out upon his flock. He scanned their faces, smiled, then let the words flow from his heart and his mind.

People often came out of the church feeling as though he had preached directly to them. "How does he do it?" they wondered. "How could he know of *my* struggle, *my* grief, *my* transgression?" After the service, as Pastor Jenson stood by the door with the summer breeze rumpling his thick, unruly hair, his handshake was firm for the strong and gentle for the weak. And there was always the smile.

ঙ৹10ଔ
Back to the Island

JULY HAD ALMOST COME to an end before Pastor Jenson returned to the Island and the promised tour with Big Jack Swanson. Daisy and Henry Larson had been constant visitors to Mrs. Brush's house next door, so Pastor Jenson was able to visit with them and gain information about Hank's progress. Daisy remained positive and prayed for the best. Henry often pulled his wagon through the neighborhoods delivering the treasures of Daisy's kitchen. Maggie came along to keep him company.

Occasionally Daisy had Henry set a loaf of fresh bread wrapped in wax paper on Michael's reed rocker. He'd find it waiting on his return home. He'd carry the loaf into the kitchen, unwrap it, and admire its perfect shape and golden color. Cutting into that perfect loaf with a sharp bread knife was like opening a gift. Spreading a slice with freshly churned butter and Mrs. Berg's homemade chokecherry jelly was like receiving ambrosia from Mount Olympus. The gift of bread always made Pastor Jenson feel very well cared for, in a practical and also a scriptural way. *The bread of life*, he'd reflect as he enjoyed a fresh, thick slice or two.

After a busy day working on his sermon, calling on the sick, having coffee with Mrs. Brush on her screen porch, and meeting with the Women's Mission Society, Pastor Michael Jenson set out for the Island. He looked forward to seeing Big Jack again, as well as Maggie, and perhaps even the Larsons. After all, Big Jack had invited him to drop in for a meal any time. The day was warm, too warm for a long-sleeved shirt and woolen suit jacket, so Pastor Jenson hung his jacket and hat on the clothes tree in the hall, rolled up the sleeves of his shirt, and headed out his front door.

Sometimes, if he were traveling a distance, Pastor Jenson would rent a horse and buggy from one of the two livery stables. He was comfortable with horses and enjoyed the time spent on the dusty back roads finding the members of his flock who lived a distance from town. Going to the Island didn't warrant a buggy. The walk would be good for him, and the sun would soon descend behind the tree-covered western hills. He hoped for a cool breeze by the time he headed for home after one of Big Jack's famous dinners.

Walking down Cloquet Avenue was a totally different experience for Pastor Jenson now that he'd been a part of the community for just over one month. "Hey, there, Pastor," people would call out as he passed their shops. Many drivers and passengers of autos and buggies on the road called out to him, waving through the cloud of dust they created as they passed. He enjoyed feeling that he was at home in this place.

He turned down Arch Street, passed the depot, crossed over the tracks and made a right turn in front of the Duluth Brewery and the Minneapolis Brewing Company buildings, enjoying the aroma of beer and hops. Heading north over the bridge, he was again on the Island.

He paused a moment in front of the Northeastern Hotel, noting the comings and goings of mill workers and men in dark suits who negotiated business deals for their wealthy employers—the lumber barons. Nestled close to the hotel were four saloons, built so close that a person in one could open a window and pass a beer to someone in the next.

To his left stretched a long block of saloons. Their front exposure faced the southern arm of the river and the town beyond. Pastor Jenson smiled. Whoever planned the layout of the Island surely placed those saloons to tempt those across the log-filled river.

People stared at him. He didn't fit in with the usual Island people. Neither lumberjack nor executive, he was a curiosity, a fish out of water. Some acknowledged him with a nod or a tip of a hat. Others, perhaps recognizing him as a pastor, quickly looked away.

He passed tobacco shops, grocery stores, a shooting gallery—he'd have to try his luck someday—several more saloons, and another hotel on the corner of Main and Central. This hotel was smaller and more rundown that the Northeastern.

On his right, across from the small Svea Hotel, stood Big Jack's boarding house. A freshly painted exterior with large half barrels full of red geraniums near the steps welcomed boarders. Pastor Jenson saw strapping young men come and go.

He followed three young men into the dining room, where they sat at the long plank table and waited to be served. He sat down as well. Eyes were on him, but no one said a word in welcome or rebuke, instead continuing their conversations as if the pastor hadn't arrived. Michael smiled and nodded in each direction, trying to meet the eyes of the dozen or more hungry men waiting to eat.

Then Big Jack burst through the swinging door of the kitchen, platters and bowls stacked in his large arms and hands. He spied the pastor. After setting down the first of many platters of food, he strode over to him, raised him from his chair and clamped his large arm across Michael's back. "Hey, boys!' he called out over the laughter and talk at the tables, "I want you to meet my new friend, Pastor Michael Jenson."

He let go a laugh. "I bet this is a first for most of you, having supper with a preacher!"

Again he laughed. A few boarders laughed with him and nodded. "Be nice to him—for my sake! And for God's sake, don't cuss!" He headed back to the kitchen for more food.

At first the men looked in Michael's direction with curiosity, a pastor in his shirtsleeves, sweat stained and rumpled. Michael reached out to everyone within arm's length and shook their hands. Large, muscular hands reached back in welcome, and Michael grasped each with as much strength as he could muster, trying not to flinch.

He filled his plate as the serving dishes were passed, then reached for the gravy dish, the breadbasket, the butter bowl, and the pickles. Mashed potatoes drenched in gravy, large pieces of crisply fried, oven-baked chicken, boiled carrots—freshly plucked from Big Jack's garden—it was a feast by any standard. By the time Michael took samples of everything, his large plate could barely contain it all. Passing completed, the room grew quiet as the men gave the meal their full attention. Then came uncensored belching and burping—certainly a sign of the diners' deep appreciation for the fine food.

Maggie smiled at Michael and began clearing away dishes. The diners sat back in their chairs, toothpicks working away in their teeth, waiting for the dessert that followed each meal. Henry circulated with a coffee pot almost as large as himself and filled outstretched mugs, beginning with Michael's. He grinned at Michael and moved on to the next logger.

Contentment dropped like a blanket over the men. Henry and Maggie carried in large trays with big pieces of chocolate cake. *One piece,* he thought, *could surely feed an entire family.* Still, he found himself consuming the whole piece, even picking up each crumb from his plate and licking frosting that clung to his fingers. He smiled as he looked into the faces of these hard-working men; they smiled back. Michael felt grateful.

One by one the men left. Some went upstairs to their rooms where they slept, two beds to each room, sometimes two men to a bed. Others rolled cigarettes, struck a match on their jeans, lit up, and inhaled a long drag, despite Big Jack's rule against it.

Several of the men introduced themselves. Pastor Jenson responded warmly. "I'd like to invite all of you to church on any Sunday you'd find convenient." With a final pump of their hands he added, "Church starts at 10:00 a.m.—but you're welcome to drop in at any time." The men laughed.

He didn't receive many firm promises, but a few said, "I hope to see you again." Perhaps that was progress.

While sipping coffee, he listened to the friendly banter coming from the kitchen. Big Jack was definitely the boss, and he ran a tight ship. Tomorrow's breakfast was already in progress, as were the numerous meals he packed for the men's lunches the next day.

Big Jack, issuing orders over his shoulder, came into the dining room. Tossing his stained apron on a bent-wood chair, he waved Pastor Jenson out of his chair. "Let's go!" he called and strode to the front door. A few men still sat on the porch and the front steps, visiting before calling it a day—or heading down St. Louis Avenue for drink or women.

"I'm taking the pastor on a tour of the saloons," Big Jack said with a grin. "He needs to see where his sheep come to gather on occasion." He took Pastor Jenson by the elbow and set off at a brisk walk down Main Street.

"We'll stop at the Larsons' on the way back," he said. "They'll still be up."

Pastor Jenson could hear the laughter of the men still on the porch. "A pastor touring the Island. How strange is that!" someone said. He even smiled as Big Jack propelled him through the crowds on the wooden walkways leading to the saloons. Nothing at the seminary prepared him for this. He felt like Jesus, invited to the home of Matthew, the tax collector, as he entertained his rowdy friends.

Big Jack knew almost everyone by name. He'd either worked with them in the mill, the logging camps, or served them at his boarding house. Michael acknowledged each person he met, hoping he'd remember faces and names. They paused at the corner of Main Street and St. Louis Avenue. With a broad gesture, Big Jack indicated the short block to his left that housed the Northeastern Hotel and four saloons, each building crammed tightly against the next. They quickly walked past the buildings, looking into the open doors as customers came and went. They turned back and stopped again before the hotel.

The Northeastern was the showplace of the Island. The two men peeked into the fancy etched-glass doors to see a spacious, well-furnished lobby. The hotel owners claimed they had the handsomest dining room in the city. Well furnished with solid oak tables and chairs, each table was enhanced with a linen tablecloth, fine white china, and polished silverware.

On the second floor the businessmen could retreat to the guest rooms. The building stood two stories high and was lit by electricity, that incredible invention. Being under the American plan, the charge for room and meals was one dollar a day. Located just a stone's throw from the Union Depot, the hotel was very convenient for train travelers.

The bar was furnished with dark wood trim, the customary brass foot rail stretching across the base of the bar, large paintings of rustic scenery, only one of a plump nude woman, reclining on what appeared to be a bear skin, on the walls. This hung to the right of the mirror behind the bar. Shelves lined the front of the mirror, each holding as many colorful bottles of liquor as possible. Glasses and mugs lined up on the counter under the mirror, ready to be filled and sent sliding down the length of the bar.

All was quiet this evening. Only a large crack in the top right corner of the mirror indicated that times were not always so peaceful.

Big Jack led Michael west down the longer block to the more concentrated area of the Island. One after the other, saloons lined up—different heights, different colors of paint on the façade, different liquors and beers advertised in the windows, a different class of patrons, a different atmosphere once a person entered through the swinging doors.

"I'll show you the Moose Saloon," Big Jack shouted over the din of the street. The two of them entered through swinging doors of a well-worn wooden building crowded between other saloons .The façade included a fake second floor. Written on the top of the building in large black letters, was THE MOOSE SALOON AND RESTAURANT, with a worn, heavy, drooping canvas awning below it. Just in case customers missed the sign at the top of the building, SALOON was printed across the front of the awning.

Pastor Jenson observed the lively atmosphere of "The Moose," as it was called by patrons. Big Jack wandered to the bar to greet logging friends. Michael watched him gesture in his direction. The lumberjacks stared, turned back to face Big Jack where they gestured—some making the sign of the cross—then resumed grinning at Michael, who grinned back, putting his hands together as though in prayer. Big Jack and his friends broke into laughter. Michael laughed with them.

The saloon was furnished with rustic oak fixtures, one heavy plate-glass mirror above the bar, and a battered upright piano. Each wall held a gigantic rack of moose antlers at least five feet across. A huge dusty moose head, with its typical drooping snout, hung on the wall across from the bar and was visible in the bar's mirror.

Two tipsy men complained loudly and profanely, "Why the hell can't ya hang a plump naked floozy over there instead of that flea-bitten moose head?" Taking a loud gulp of beer, they wiped their bearded lips and continued. "We'd sure as hell enjoy our drinks more if we had a fleshy gal with big tits to look at in the mirror!"

One of the men turned and came face to face with Michael. "Hey, you there!" he said, grabbing Michael by the front of his shirt and spewing beer foam in Michael's face. "What do you think, young fella?" Both men held up their mugs. "Wouldn't ya drink more if you were looking at a naked woman, rather that a damned old moose head?" Both men gazed expectantly at Michael, waiting his verdict.

Big Jack burst into laughter and waited to see how Michael would handle this deeply philosophical question. Firmly removing the man's hand from the front of his shirt, Michael seemed to give the question deep thought. "Well, now that I think about it, I suppose I'd rather look at a fleshy young nude than that shaggy old moose head," he replied, then added, "but maybe a shaggy old moose head is better than a droopy old nude in the long run! Nothing too droopy looks good after a while—even a nude."

Michael was once again aware that no one at Seminary had taught him how to handle this subject. Big Jack was still laughing as he took Michael by the arm and led him away from the bar and his two inquisitors.

"What'd we tell you?" the lumberjacks shouted. "Even the young guy agrees with us—if the gal's not too droopy!" They grinned broadly and raised their mugs to Michael.

The bartender rolled his eyes. Men clustered at the bar to drink, nude or no. He winked at Michael. "After they get enough beer down their gullet, even that dusty, old moose looks like a nude to them," he confided.

Someone with little talent pounded out a tune on the piano. Mill workers and townspeople sat or stood as they talked, shouted, swore, or argued with anyone within hearing. The atmosphere was rowdy; the smell of sweat and liquor permeated the air.

The Moose Saloon was crowded. Michael, needing fresh air, turned to the door and accidently bumped into two very large lumberjacks, causing beer to spill over the sides of their mugs. They didn't look pleased. Big Jack quickly ran interference, shaking hands with the men he'd known from his years working in the camps and saying, "I want you guys to meet Pastor Jenson, my new friend." Throwing his arm across Michael's shoulders, he said, "Bill and Wilbur Martin—they're brothers—this is Michael Jenson."

Large, muscled hands enveloped his as he shook their hands. Gritting his teeth to the crushing pain he felt when they pumped his hand, Michael forced a smile.

"We all worked in the cook shack of the camp north of town," Big Jack explained. "We peeled a million potatoes a day and scrambled a thousand eggs—at least!" The three of them laughed at the memories they shared. "Then Agnes took sick and I came to town to take care of her—and Maggie." His smile faded somewhat as he spoke.

Big Jack's friends thumped him on his back. "You did the right thing, Big Jack," they said. "We were all proud of you. But we sure missed you when you were gone!"

Michael could tell the older men were fond of Big Jack, and that they had been great support for him when his wife had passed away. At the moment, however, they seemed a bit surprised Big Jack had escorted Pastor Jenson into the Moose Saloon.

Wilbur said, "Damn it anyway! What in the world is a pastor doing in a place like this?"

Michael started to laugh. Then both men joined in, and summed up the night's activity in a few concise words. "I 'spose you're looking around for new members," Wilbur said seriously, "to keep the church running in the black!"

Michael tried to keep his laughter under control. "That's a great idea," he said. "Maybe we should have services here. One beer, one dollar in the offering!" Big Jack's friends caught the humor and gaffawed, spewing beer everywhere.

They invited Pastor Jenson to Lumberjack Days, held in August, celebrating the logging industry and the skills that kept everything running smoothly. Michael was very intrigued. "I'll be there cheering for both of you. What skills?" he asked.

"We take part in the two-man sawing contest," they proudly announced. "Last year we almost beat Big Jack and his partner. This year, since Big Jack's partner can't take part, we're determined to come in first." They pumped their fists in the air. "No doubt about it!"

Big Jack just smiled. He had a new partner, young Samuel Berg. The competition would be exciting. Big Jack caught Michael's eye and slowly shook his head. Michael interpreted the motion as saying, "Not a chance in hell of their beating us!"

The level of noise was increasing and the crowd got thicker. Pastor Jenson stepped outside, took a seat on a bench and breathed in some fresh air. He noted the change in the talk and laughter as liquor flowed from the cup to the brain. He remembered his childhood. His father drank far too much and far too often. He loved his father, especially the kind and gentle man he knew when he wasn't drinking. Michael had become wise for his age, having learned early that liquor builds a wall between people who should love, be kind, and not hurt each other. The sad memories came less often since his father died and Michael had grown to manhood. The passage of time was a good teacher, and he had learned, to some degree, how to deal with the events of his past.

Part of his answering the call to be a pastor was born from the desire to ease the pain people carried and often tried to drown in alcohol. As a pastor, he always tried to show that each person was a gift, a special creation. Having God's love within them could give them a sense of being valued, according to Michael's thinking, a sense of having merit no matter how many mistakes they made along the way.

Michael stood, shook off his memories and stepped into the street. He plunged his hands into his pockets and walked through the milling crowds to the edge of the river where the logs floated, waiting their turn for the sharp teeth of the saws in the mills. After a few minutes, Big Jack joined him. "Have you seen enough?" he asked. "This is about what goes on here every night, only on the weekends the crowds are bigger."

Michael spread his arms wide, as though he could embrace the entire Island. "This is quite the place. I've never seen anything like it." Smiling slyly, Michael thanked him for introducing him to his friends. "Are you really going to beat them in the two-man sawing competition?" he asked. "They looked really strong to me."

"Are you kidding?" Big Jack said. "You just wait until you see for yourself what a champion two-man team looks like!" Michael laughed and slapped Big Jack on his very broad back as they made their way back down St. Louis Avenue.

Main Street was much less congested as they walked toward the Larson house. The sun had totally disappeared behind the trees across the bend in the river, leaving the evening sky a deep crimson. The sunset, reflected in the river, made it seem as though the logs floated in a sea of molten gold. The air was cooler and a breeze followed the river as it cradled the Island—a perfect summer evening.

Michael loved being in his shirtsleeves and feeling the summer breeze through the cotton shirt. *It'll be hard to put on that woolen suit coat again*, he thought with a grin.

Within a minute of their coming into the Larsons' home, the coffee pot was percolating. Oatmeal and sugar cookies appeared from the large crock on the counter. Both were equally delicious, as far as Pastor Jenson was concerned.

Hank sat in his rocking chair, buoyed up by pillows, his feet resting on a cushioned footstool. His appearance had improved greatly since Michael had last visited. After sitting out in the yard in the sunshine every chance he could, Hank radiated a healthy tan.

Each day Daisy positioned chairs by the front door—maybe two or three—and the chairs would fill throughout the day with men stopping by to visit. Daisy loved to listen to the masculine voices and hearty laughter as one logger followed another.

Big Jack continued to work Hank's damaged legs, always trying to strengthen the muscles and restore them to their former use. Day after day Big Jack exploded through the door and cast an aura of hopefulness through all their hearts. Hank was only too willing to press and pull and push and extend those muscles that at first were hardly able to move in any direction. Doctor Thompson stopped by regularly and was pleasantly surprised. His prediction from the beginning had been that Hank was strong, stubborn and determined to recover. Dr. Thompson saw definite progress.

Pastor Jenson quietly observed the Larsons as he sipped the coffee and reached for another cookie. Hank was a master at bringing everyone into the flow of the conversation. He asked questions and replied to each subject as it was raised, always coming back to the initial speaker for another viewpoint or another related topic. Henry listened carefully, ready to jump into the fray if he had a comment or two. The adults welcomed his participation. Henry smiled often. Michael could see Henry entering the open door to his becoming a man. And he had such fine examples in Hank and Big Jack.

Daisy stayed in the kitchen, working at the counter, always stirring or cleaning or preparing food. She smiled constantly, enjoying the boisterous conversation.

When she had an opinion to offer, she stepped into the parlor and gracefully put the men in their place with her feminine wisdom. She loved to do that. And the men enjoyed the new perspective she offered. The climate of the Larson home was open and loving. No wonder so many felt welcomed when they stepped through the front door.

The topic of discussion that evening was Pastor Jenson's voyage to the streets of the Island. All agreed that never, in all their collective memories, had a pastor ventured to the Island and walked the length and breadth of St. Louis Avenue.

"Did the men really know you're the pastor of the Lutheran Church?" Hank asked. Big Jack assured them Michael was introduced as a real pastor.

"I wish I could've been there to see for myself," Hank said. "Funny thing is you don't look much like a regular man of the cloth—no insult intended."

Michael laughed as he replied, "I'm sure I gave my identity away when I was the only man on the Island without a mug in my hand."

Big Jack's grinned. "Jenson, I really like your style—pastor or not! You even handled the nude and moose head problem in great form." Big Jack related the story to the Larsons—with a few embellishments—and everyone had a good laugh. Especially Henry.

Michael smiled, listening as they commented on his foray through the swinging doors of the saloons on the Island. "I met some very nice people, thanks to you, Big Jack. I was bumped and pushed by some of the biggest men I have ever seen." He paused and added with a grin, "I was careful not to push back!" Everyone laughed.

As the laughter quieted, Michael grew more serious. "I experienced the side effects of alcohol when I was a young boy. I doubt there's anything new you could show me about the effects of alcohol and heavy drinking. My father taught me well."

He paused, looked down into his coffee mug, and concluded, "It's not easy to love someone who so often hurts and disappoints you, but it is possible. So, that's why I'm here. Some people are just harder to love than others." And then, of course, he flashed that wide, irresistible smile.

He rose, shook hands all around, and felt the returning strength of Hank's grip as their hands locked. Daisy had a small bag of cookies ready for him to take with him and enjoy later. As Pastor Jenson stretched out his hand for one final handshake from Big Jack, the man pushed the hand aside and wrapped his arms around him, nearly lifting Michael from the ground. "You're a good man!" Big Jack said. "A good man, and a good pastor."

Henry walked Pastor Jenson as far as the red bridge. The street lamps lining the road cast a pale silver glow over the rowdy crowds. Henry liked this pastor and promised to stop by the parsonage whenever he came to visit Mrs. Brush.

From the bridge they could see the red barns and hear the neighing as the horses. "If you want," Henry said, "I'll take you to the horse barns some day and show you the horse I call Samson." Henry looked up into the pastor's kindly face. "I've kind of adopted him."

Pastor Jenson heartily agreed. "I took care of four horses when I was about your age, Henry." He smiled down into the face of the eager boy at his side. "I loved them. I'm sure I'll love your Samson as well."

The man and the boy said goodbye, then parted ways. Pastor Jenson crossed the bridge, turning briefly to look back toward the Island. He watched as Henry hurried through the shadows on Main Street toward home. Then Michael took a cookie from the paper bag and munched it as his feet turned toward the parsonage. He savored the cookie's sweetness, replaying the evening in his mind.

ഇ11ര
The House in the Woods

A RUSTIC BRIDGE, JUST BEYOND the Larsons' home, connected the north side of the Island to the hillside beyond. An orderly white house was tucked into the midst of a large grove of evergreens, and both the grove and house were set back from the gravel road up the hill leading to the pine forests. An air of quiet mystery surrounded the structure.

In the spring of 1912, when construction of the house began, curiosity prompted people to watch carpenters and workmen come and go across the north bridge, bringing supplies and equipment to the pine grove. Another saloon? Another hotel or boarding house? The townspeople thought there were already enough dens of iniquity on the Island.

Then the news exploded. People couldn't believe it. Rumors spread like wildfire. Someone had heard from a "very reliable" source, according to the bearer of the shocking news, that the new building was going to be a brothel! The owner of the brothel would arrive in two weeks. The townspeople were speechless! Scandalized! Women gasped and raised their hands to their breasts to still their wildly beating hearts.

Disbelief intensified. Crowds lined the shore, scanning the comings and goings from the evergreens. Rumors spread like poison ivy as townspeople thought they spied the owner. Reports claimed it was a mobster from New York City or a madam—the most expensive one from Minneapolis—looking to expand to their hallowed ground and the waiting loggers and lumberjacks. People were ready to believe anything.

By late June, the house was completed, and, just like magic—before anyone could discover how the newcomers had so quickly settled into their recently constructed place of business—a small, tasteful sign with artistic lettering appeared in front of the evergreens, right by the road: PEARLS OF GREAT PRICE. Nothing more.

A wave of disgust and disbelief swept the town. What gall! To take a quote from the Bible and create the sign designating where naughty ladies plied their trade. Was there no end to the owner's blasphemous disrespect of the moral values of the town?

A woman named Pearl—no last name—was behind the construction of the house in the pines. She hailed from Floodwood, a small town up the road from Cloquet. Having come upon hard times after the "unfortunate," but opportune, death of her husband due to a logging accident, Pearl decided go into business for herself.

With limited options, her reputation already sullied beyond redemption by her drunken husband who offered her unwilling services to his equally drunken friends, Pearl was ready for change. Reports—some true, some much exaggerated—circulated through the community. After her husband's sudden death, the people of Floodwood offered her little support. No one would hire a woman with her reputation.

Pearl decided she needed a fresh start for her business, a brothel she would own and operate as she saw fit. Since this was the only option she felt open to her, Pearl decided to set up her business close the lumber mills in Cloquet. She selected the site with great care. The location was private, well concealed, close to the loggers and mill workers, and the long-established reputation of the Island concentrated her customers.

The house was two stories with four medium-sized bedrooms upstairs for the girls and one large private suite at the rear of the first floor for Pearl. She entertained no customers. She'd had no control over any part of her life before; now she'd be in charge and could set the standard for what took place in the white house.

As the summer of 1912 progressed, the townspeople scrutinized the comings and goings from the white house on the hill. Travelers from the north described the vibrant flower gardens surrounding the white house, how rose bushes clustered against the long, narrow front porch and provided a gentle fragrance. They told of lace curtains in the windows and handsome green shutters trimming every window. Most interesting was their description of the young women, often seated on the porch in what looked to be comfortable rockers, waving as the travelers passed by. Of course, the travelers swore that they quickly averted their eyes and, of course, they certainly did not wave back.

Rumors circulated that Pearl ran a tight ship. She'd broken a wine bottle over the head of one man who stepped over the boundary of behavior she'd declared as proper. The man appeared later that evening at one of the nearby saloons, holding a bloody cloth to the side of his head. The men at the bar admired the young man's daring and Pearl's hefty swing.

Some "visitors" reported the girls to be quite young, shameless as they were. Other "patrons" claimed the ladies had "been around the block a few times and were almost ready to be put out to pasture." Beauty, evidently, was in the eye of the customer. In fact, the young women were local girls, farm born and bred, eager to escape the drudgery of their country life. They were robust young women, corn fed and sturdy and used to hard work. When Pearl invited them to join her, they had been quick to respond.

No lack of gossip circulated about the white house in the pines and the women who entertained the men. There also was no limit to the embellishments added to the lusty accounts spun in the saloons as men exchanged stories of their nocturnal visits to Pearl's place and the hours they spent in the plump arms of the harlot of their choice.

Reports of the transgressions going on at the white house flew across the river to the town proper, and from housewife to housewife. Tempers flared, tears flowed, promises were pledged—and, in most cases, were soon broken. Women of the city rose up in anger and came together in defense of their men and their marriages.

In the early fall of 1912, Mrs. Berg found herself thrust into leadership of the crusade, intent on obliterating the festering blight north of town. She was, even at this time, a pillar in the Lutheran church. She felt empowered to declare her intent to rid the area of the festering problem in the pines. Husband or no husband, she still had a grown son to watch over. Samuel didn't have the sense he was born with, according to his mother. Thus Mrs. Berg took charge of the attack. Her plan was daring, purposeful, strategic, and full of enough fury to light a blazing fire under all the proper women of the city.

Reports of Mrs. Berg's mission flew across town, woman to woman. Her words ignited a passionate reaction in the hearts of the wives, mothers, and girlfriends of the weak, spineless men of the area. To a women's study group at the library on a Wednesday afternoon, Mrs. Berg laid out her strategic cleansing mission. Mrs. Berg—resolute, undaunted, and impervious—said, "My dear friends, we will show the entire town—and the Island—that we have set a standard to uphold." The women clapped. "We will band together and march across the bridge to the Island!"

Her cheeks flushed. "We can assume the clientele will be engaged in their dastardly deeds in the house. They'll be totally unprepared. Hopefully we can, without any violence or loss of blood, put the fear of the Lord into our men carousing with those harlots."

Several young women, feeling slightly faint at the mention of violence—and blood—grew pale and began to fan themselves with their hankies. Finally, their scheme was determined. The women would gather this coming Friday night behind the public library, a block or two south of the red bridge. Once at full strength, they'd cross the bridges and storm the hillside. Like wildfire, the plan spread from one indignant woman to another.

The attack was set for ten o'clock in the evening—a proper time for wives and mothers, after the children had been tucked in bed and the kitchen straightened after supper. At least forty women vowed they'd gather under the cover of darkness behind the library. All were expected to carry a weapon of some kind—brooms, shovels, hammers, axes, rakes, buggy whips, hoes, even hat pins—items they could use in the battle. No one knew exactly what to expect, yet the women were sure they'd be a righteous force to be reckoned with.

The night arrived. In the shadows behind the library, Mrs. Berg called everyone to attention. "We don't really want to hurt anyone," she shouted over the women's excited chatter. "We just want to show that we care about our husbands, our sons, our city, and family values!" The women raised their "weapons" to the darkened sky above and cheered.

All of them were eager to storm down the hill and across the red bridge. Some had never before set foot upon the Island. They were curious, giddy with excitement, and of course, emotion was seasoned with purity of heart. The ladies began their march down the hill, weapons brandished. One woman started singing "Onward Christian Soldiers," and soon all the women joined in the familiar hymn.

Saloon lights shone as they strode down the hill, clattered across the bridge and mounted the shore. They momentarily paused, unfamiliar with the layout of the Island streets. Mrs. Berg noted the street lamps that lit the way to the north. She waved on her companions. "Follow me!" she shouted, pointing her hoe in the direction of their attack.

The men, up to that moment comfortably seated on the porches of the saloons sipping their liquor, heard the commotion as the army of women appeared. Their mouths fell open as the light of the street lamps fell upon the faces of the crusading women, and the men recognized their friends, neighbors, girlfriends, wives—even a grandmother or two—in the crowd that flowed northward up Main Street.

"I'll bet they're heading for Pearl's place!" one man shouted. Suddenly the men were galvanized into action. Beer spilled, chairs tipped, saloons emptied, streets filled as the men ran to out-pace the marching, singing women. The men—husbands, sons, lovers, friends—were filled with dread. The women—and the weapons—looked serious.

Cutting through back lots, the men arrived at the north bridge before the women. The men joined arm in arm, three rows deep, and stood crouched, ready to deflect the attack that seemed sure to occur as the women marched up to them.

"Move aside!" commanded Mrs. Berg. "We come to drive away the sinners!" She made a move to the center of the line of men, threatening them with her garden hoe. From behind a slightly tipsy man in the front row, a strapping young man stepped forward. Everyone recognized him as Samuel Berg, Mrs. Berg's only son. He was young, having dropped out of school a year earlier at age sixteen. He took a job at the mill, moved away from home, and had, in his mother's eyes, taken a turn to the wild side. She wasn't shocked. He had grown up to be just like his father—spineless, weak, easily tempted. Just a chip off the old block, as she liked to say. She resisted the impulse to swing her hoe right over the crown of his head. He was her son, after all.

He walked up to her, the odor of cheap beer surrounding them. "Mother, what do you plan to do with that hoe?" he asked, attempting to remove the weapon from her hand. "We're all sinners! That's what you've always told me." He smiled weakly. "I was always a sinner, according to you." Her hoe again hovered close to his head. He stood fast.

The men behind him had by this time sighted a woman or two familiar to them—wife, mother, sister, employee, student—and, selecting the ones they knew best, began to pacify the unruly crowd of women. An arm about a shoulder, a kiss on the cheek, a tender clasp of the hand—began to dismantle the explosive nature of the army of women.

The mayor of the city materialized from the rear of the crowd of men and shook his fist in the direction of the somewhat deflated women. "Any more commotion, and I'll have all of you women put in jail!" He glared into their faces as he paced unsteadily back and forth before them, looking like he meant what he said—if he didn't tip over. The women lowered their weapons.

Mrs. Berg stood nose to nose with her son. Standing this close, she thought he looked surprisingly well—even without her constant care and fine directions as to how he should live his life.

"Give me the hoe, Mother. Don't hurt anyone." He gently unwrapped her fingers from around the handle and took it from her. "Let me walk you home. It's dark. It'll be hard for you to find your way."

Mrs. Berg suddenly deflated, allowing her son to take her arm.

The tension defused. Then two women swung their rakes while attempting to untangle themselves from the group. The long handles smashed the glass on one of the street lamps illuminating the porch of Big Jack's Boarding House.

At the sound of breaking glass, Big Jack burst suddenly through the front door, stood on the porch and made a quick assessment of the tense situation. A huge smile slowly evolved over his face. He laughed his contagious laugh and slapped his knee like he had just heard—or seen—the best joke ever. "Well, look who's here!" His eyes swept the crowd. "Looks like the start of a great party! Inside, everybody!" he shouted in his booming voice. "Coffee and cookies all around—on the house!"

The women hesitated, wondering, if by entering the boarding house they'd be participating in an immoral act. Curiosity finally gained ground, and their resistance melted away. Even Mrs. Berg walked up the steps on her son's arm.

Big Jack ushered everyone through the front door of his establishment and seated them at the long, worn dining tables. Some men returned to the saloons to finish what they had left on the bar, but others followed their women into the dining room and found seats. Big Jack and one of his boarders came through the kitchen door, coffee pots in hand, large molasses cookies on a gigantic tray.

Moving quickly through the crowd, they soon had a cup of hot dark coffee and a large cookie in everyone's hands. Big Jack saw to it everyone was served. Some couples were having more conversation that night, in Big Jack's boarding house, than they'd exchanged in months.

Shortly after eleven, Big Jack's dining room emptied. The women had gathered up their tools—no longer weapons—thanked Big Jack and crossed the red bridge back to town. Their "weapons" would soon be returned to sheds, pantries, barns, and hats. Many men accompanied their women through the dark night. Some couples even held hands as they wound their way through Cloquet streets.

The women felt somewhat vindicated, having put action to their concerns. The men were impressed by the valor and spirit the women had shown. Conflicting stories would be told for years related to the events of this very memorable night.

Mrs. Berg walked home with her son. She felt safe, pleased Samuel didn't seem to be cut from the same cloth as her deceased husband after all. He must have inherited some of her sterling qualities. Perhaps she'd extend him an invitation to Sunday dinner soon. He hadn't been home for a good meal in a long time. She missed having him about the house.

A smile played about her lips. She had enjoyed the events of the night. Being involved in community activities could sometimes turn out to be very exciting.

Across the river to the north, a solitary figure had observed the drama evolve. Pearl, in her rocker, hidden by the shadow of the porch roof, had heard the commotion and recognized the indignation and passion in the singing, shouting army of women. Knowing this moment would come sooner or later, she'd been prepared. She'd easily recognized the distaste in the expressions of the people observing the construction of her home. Those faces told her that she and her house were not welcome. Yet she continued to pursue her plan. She had no other options, now that her capital was invested and her business underway.

The woman in the shadows had been molded by hardship and trial, making her strong yet vulnerable. A person might see her as a modestly attractive woman in her late thirties or early forties, might notice she was somewhat on the ample side, sturdily build with a modest double chin and hands that displayed hard work. Her thinning hair had definite streaks of gray she tried to hide; her waist line rebelled at being confined by a corset. She wasn't a beauty by any means, but she exuded an air of comfort and well being.

Not exactly a sexual figure, she was a nurturing one. Over the years she'd learned sometimes a man needed that as much as seduction. At this point in her life, Pearl was only too happy to nurture. She allowed her girls to seduce. The arrangement worked well.

Positioned on her porch, she had her left hand in her lap, her right in the pocket of her robe, holding tight to her small pearl-handled Remington Derringer just in case. Her eyes were trained on the Island, watching the drama play out on the opposite shore.

The lamp at the end of the Main Street lit the scene like on a stage. Men stood with their backs to her, arm in arm, facing off the women ready to do heaven only knew what damage to her house and person. She'd sent clients home at the first sign of trouble. Two girls wanted to sit with her, but Pearl ordered them to their rooms. If anyone would be hurt that night, she'd be the only victim. No one else. So she waited.

She could make out some conversation as it filtered over the river and through the branches of the pines. The anger subsided, the singing halted, and men's voices raised and lowered as they subdued the wrath of the women. She took note as the weapons stopped waving and were lowered. Then she heard the sharp sound of the glass lamp as it shattered.

She sat up straighter, her hand tightening on her weapon, wondering if the violence would continue in her direction. Then a deep, infectious laugh floated across the river. Of course. Big Jack. She listened to his resonant voice but could not make out the words. After a few moments, most of the crowd disappeared into the boarding house.

Once again the night was quiet. Pearl relaxed, sat back in her chair, and breathed a sigh of relief. Evening sounds once again grew calm. Remaining on the porch, she soon became chilled by cool autumn breezes. The waning moon and a few stars appeared briefly through the nearby branches, still chased by clouds. As she watched, small groups of men and women left the boarding house and headed down Main Street toward the red bridge.

Voices muted by the breezes whispered through the pines. Pulling her crocheted shawl snugly around her shoulders, she closed her eyes, resting her head against the pillow at the back of the rocker. She removed her hand from the Derringer, thankful she'd had no need for it. The crisis had passed—for now.

SINCE THAT EVENING, five long years had passed with an uneasy truce hovering between the women of the town and the white house in the pines. Never again would there be a march of women armed with weapons. Still, some watched with annoyance and condemnation as Pearl made her weekly excursion from the pines to the bank on Cloquet Avenue.

With Pearl seated in her 1908-model phaeton, the horse would clatter over the red bridge. Pearl gently flicked her with a slender whip as she climbed the hill to the main street. Casual observers often commented that, if they earned what Pearl did (and no one knew for sure how much that was) they'd certainly purchase one of those noisy, newfangled automobiles. However, Pearl stayed faithful to her comfortable old mare.

Just for spite, Pearl dressed to perfection when she ventured out in public. People might think her a fallen woman and want to cast stones, but she'd look her best as they flung them.

Season after season, for five years, people watched as she pulled up to the bank, entered the large carved door and walked confidently to the desk of the leering bank president, where she made her deposits. How the public would've loved to know the exact balance of her account! To the bank's credit, no one divulged how much money she had saved—and invested—over the years.

But no one on the street acknowledged her. No one complimented her, asked about her health. As the years passed, no one cared enough to notice the subtle physical transformation consuming Pearl before their uncaring, judgmental eyes.

ᔥ12ᐅ
Summer

HENRY HAD NEVER ENJOYED a summer vacation as much as the first summer he and his family lived on the Island. The days flew by, each more exciting that the last. Best of all was watching his father regain more of his strength as each day passed. His next favorite activity was time spent listening carefully to the stories told when Hank's friends stopped by. Thus, Henry became familiar with the workings of lumber camps.

The men reminiscenced about their days at the logging camps. They told yarns about hard work, freezing cold, great cooks who heaped platters of nourishing food on the tables until they groaned under the weight, giant trees that refused to fall where directed, pranks and amusements the men concocted on Sunday—their only day of rest—when they had opportunity to bathe, wash their clothes, trim their hair and beards, play cards, or just take a nap. A great feeling of camaraderie bound the men together. They laughed and commiserated about their labors in the woods. In more serious moments they spoke soberly of the men who'd died or been injured.

Most of the men in the front yard of the Larson home had lost part of a hand to the sharp teeth of the saw at the mill or in the camp. A newcomer from upriver, Harold, was welcomed to the group one warm summer day and sat with the other men in the late afternoon sun, visiting and enjoying the fruits of Daisy's labors.

Hank said, "Henry, I'd like you to meet my old friend Harold. I met this crazy guy way back before you were even born. Harold, this is my son Henry."

Henry reached out to shake the man's hand. Harold did the same, but there wasn't much left of Harold's hand, only the thumb and partial chunk of the palm. Henry was shocked. Looking first at mutilated hand, Henry raised his eyes to Harold's grizzled face.

Harold smiled. "Don't worry, kid. After all these years I'm used to that look. Just grab onto the thumb, and we'll shake like old friends." He laughed. Henry had to smile as well. Like he was grabbing the end of a broomstick, Henry clutched the thumb and the two shook hands with great energy. "See. What'd I tell ya, kid? It's not as bad as it looks."

Henry held on to the mutilated hand a moment, turning it over to inspect both sides. Being curious, he asked, "How in the world did this happen, Harold?"

Harold sat down, filled his pipe with tobacco, tamped it down with his heroic thumb. "Well, Henry, I was working on the planer one cold autumn day. Shouldn't have been wearing mitts, but I was—leather mitts." Taking a drag on his pipe, Harold held the smoke a short time before exhaling in a series of rings. Henry was very impressed by this feat. "The leather cuff of the mitt caught on the bar holding the plank and took my hand right through the saw. Bled like a stuck pig, I did." Harold extended his muscular thumb for all to see.

"I have a 'magic thumb.' You'd be surprised how handy I can be with just a thumb!" To demonstrate, Harold reached for the cookie basket and plunged his thumb through the center of a large oatmeal cookie. He raised his thumb, held it to his bewhiskered lips and took a large bite. "Yep! I have a magic thumb."

Harold's story led to a chain of stories concerning the danger of saws, knives, and axes. Each man had an episode or two to regale the other roughhewn men.

"I was working the table saw, pushing the board with my right hand. I reached across the blade with my left to pull on the board—and, *bam!*—off went two of my fingers!" Hank's friend Alvin laughed as he recalled his encounter. "My God! Blood squirted everywhere! Didn't even think to look for what was left of my fingers before I went to the doctor. My buddy found 'em and put 'em in his pocket." The men laughed, then laughed harder when the storyteller added, "He forgot 'em in his pocket with his cigarettes until the next day! Pretty stinky!"

Henry loved to listen to the men's deep, guttural laughter. According to the men, just about every part of a man's body had been severed at one time or another by a saw or an ax—even the private parts, which Henry didn't want to contemplate.

Over the course of a couple weeks, Hank's friends designed a traveling chair tailor-made just for him. They knew how difficult it was for Daisy and Henry to transport him to and from anywhere.

One man cut boards, shaped and curved them to fit Hank's contours. Another adapted two bicycle wheels to fit the dimensions of the chair itself. Smaller wheels at the front came from an old wagon. The body of the chair, with the high curved back and padded arm rests, fit perfectly on the base that contained the axle, wheels, and a frame forged from metal scraps from the machine shop at the mill.

They finally delivered the extraordinary chair. Looking out her kitchen window as she washed the supper dishes, Daisy noticed a procession of men making their boisterous way up Main Street toward her house. *Now what are they up to?* she wondered. The delegation proudly marched up to the front door, pushing something before them—she wasn't quite sure what it was.

Hank, seated in his usual spot in front of the house, watched his friends arrive. "We've come to take you for a ride you'll never forget!" they laughed and stepped aside to reveal Hank's wondrous new chair.

Hank was speechless. The men watched his expression go from surprise to appreciation. He stroked the smooth wood and rough fabric. "What in the world have you crazy guys put together?" He looked up at them, gratitude in his face. He thanked them, reaching out to shake each man's hand.

Daisy stood in the door, watching, smiling and trying not to cry at the same time. She dearly loved these big, rough men with such generous hearts.

"Well, Mrs. Larson, what do ya think? Can we take Hank for a stroll in his new throne and check on the Island?" Big smiles all around. "We promise to have him home before bedtime!" This comment brought loud laughter, Daisy's included.

Hank, using the strength of his arms, was able to raise himself from his chair, but his legs were still undependable and could give out when least expected. With one husky logger on each arm, they lowered Hank into his new vehicle. Hank settled back and was amazed at how soft the chair was and how it was molded to his body.

With a hearty "Let's go see what's going on!" the men headed down the street toward St. Louis Avenue. Frank Shaw, Hank's newly "adopted" son, who'd been the instigator of the idea and the designer of the vehicle, stepped behind the chair, and they were off.

The group marched down the street, talking and laughing. The chair rolled as if it on a polished floor rather than a bumpy gravel road. Daisy, watching from her doorway, was sure a new era in Hank's recovery had just begun. She returned to the kitchen, checked the clock, and wondered what time the men would return with her now fully mobile husband.

Frank Shaw still battled guilt over Hank's injury while saving his life. How could Frank ever repay him? Hank and Daisy reassured Frank time and again that his good health was reward enough. His friendship was a gift to the whole family. A bonus was the arrangement between Henry and Frank. If they caught any fish, Frank would help Henry clean them and stay for supper. Frank was only too happy to comply.

Henry and Maggie fished together as well. These they had to clean themselves. Together they constructed a small dock using the broken wooden crate that once housed the wonderful stove now serving them so well. The dock jutted into the north branch of the river, right behind the Larsons' home.

Some nights Henry and Maggie lay on their backs on the dock, looking up at the stars. They could point out many constellations that spread across the black velvet sky.

When the temperatures climbed into the nineties, they'd get a running start on the dock and propel themselves into the river. Both learned to swim that summer and were cautious and confident as they splashed and kicked their way through the hot summer days.

BLUEBERRY SEASON ARRIVED. Henry and Maggie headed across the north bridge to the hill where the blueberry crop was reportedly abundant. Before this summer, Henry had never had the opportunity to experience this backbreaking, bug-infested chore.

Women from town tried to be inconspicuous as they headed across the north bridge and into the woods. Crossing the Island was bad enough, but coming so close to the white house was even worse. However, the lure of fresh blueberries proved too much. As news reached Cloquet that the blueberry crop was extraordinary, the parade of women began.

Carrying baskets and bowls, the women fanned out over the hillside. Bent over in the sun, large brimmed hats shading their faces, their ample derrieres thrust skyward, they raked the berries from the branches with gloved hands into their containers.

On one hot summer day the two youngsters were just completing their second picking of the day when a great commotion arose close by.

A young woman picking berries a short distance from Maggie and Henry had tired of bending over the bushes to coax the blue jewels into her containers. Noticing an old rotted stump nearby, she had a great idea. With a great sigh, she lowered herself onto the stump, leaned forward, and commensed to pick while seated. Her rear pivoted slowly across the stump and, unknown to her, she disturbed a multitude of large black ants.

Before long all the pickers on the hill heard a sharp cry of pain. Looking around for the source of the scream, they saw the woman leap up from the stump and begin jumping in all directions, scratching at her legs, her belly, her bosom. Her hard-won berries flew in all directions as she upset her baskets and began tearing at her clothes. Her shirt came off and was thrown aside, then her skirt left with reckless abandon.

The shocked observers then saw the large black ants as they marched up and down the entire body of the agitated woman. There was no escape from their painful attack. Everyone watched in fascinated silence as the frantic woman danced around, all the while shouting "Ants! Ants! Ants! Help! They're biting me everywhere!"

Her friend, picking berries nearby, finally leaped up and hurried to her side. "Please! Please! Don't take any more of your clothes off, Emma!" she shrieked, whisking aside as many of the ants as possible.

By now the ant-covered woman had loosed her breasts from her corset and was heaving them up and down to rid herself of the pain from the bites. Too numerous to count, the vile insects marched around her fleshy bosom, across her ample belly still encased in her corset, down her back, over her legs, and even into her hair.

Quickly covering the flailing woman with the tablecloth on which they had enjoyed their lunch earlier in the day, Emma's friend took charge. With her arms about the hysterical woman, she led Emma down the hill and back across the bridge. Once upon the Island, everyone watched as the woman plunged into the river, much to the fascination of a few lumberjacks getting an early start in the saloons.

Henry and Maggie were totally enthralled by the performance. Once their surprise subsided, they laughed so hard they had to sit down on the ground—never on a rotting stump, of course. Henry especially was quite taken with the event. "So that's what a lady's boobies look like," he said with a bit of awe in his voice. He looked at Maggie's not-quite-flat chest and pondered what women did as their bosoms expanded.

"Do you look forward to having all that stuff hanging over your chest?" he asked her. "When does it all start to pop out?"

Maggie laughed so hard tears came to her eyes. "Henry Larson! I can't believe that you of all people are talking about a lady's boobies." She raised her hands to her as yet-undeveloped chest while commenting on his question. "I'll need them if I'm ever going to be a mother. For now, my biggest question is, if I start to get bigger, where do I put my hand when I recite "The Pledge of Allegiance" in school?"

"That might be a problem for a girl," he said. "Never really thought much about it."

They gathered up their bowls and baskets of blueberries and started for home. Each time one of them mentioned the plight of the ant-infested woman, they burst into laughter. By the time they reached the north bridge and crossed the river to the Island, there was no trace of the woman and her friend. They could hardly wait to get home and share the story with Hank, Daisy, and Big Jack.

Early every morning during blueberry season, Henry and Maggie headed across the bridge and up the hill. The sun made its appearance over the eastern horizon and the breezes flowing down the river were cool and fresh. They carried several containers they hoped to fill as the morning wore on. As the hours passed, the hill became more crowded. Maggie picked berries for her father. His blueberry pie was famous in all corners of the county. Henry picked for Big Jack as well, but he also filled a basket or two for his mother and Mrs. Brush. What could be better than fresh blueberries in a deep bowl, liberally covered with rich whole cream and several teaspoons of sugar?

The best part of Henry's day was when he took the bowl filled with berries to Mrs. Brush's back porch. More frail of late, her face always lit up when she saw him at her door. His arrival was often the highlight of her day. Within a moment he was ushered into her kitchen, where she seated him at her table. After quickly preparing him a cup of coffee, heavy on the cream and sugar, she carefully washed the berries and prepared three bowls of ambrosia, as she like to call the berries—one for Henry, one for old Syd, and one for herself.

Then the three sat together in the sunny kitchen, enjoying each other and the delicious fruit. Henry regaled them more than once with the story of the ant-covered berry picker. Old Syd and Mrs. Brush laughed until tears ran down their cheeks. Henry loved sitting there, being treated like an adult. He especially enjoyed seeing Mrs. Brush laughing so hard she had to wipe away her tears with the lace-trimmed hankies she always kept tucked in the pocket of her apron.

As the summer days passed, Henry found his way, as often as he could, to the company horse barns just across the river. Heading home after making a baking delivery, he'd pull his wagon as close as he could to the fence surrounding the pasture. When not hitched up to the heavy wagons, transporting loads of cut lumber from the mills to the storage areas, the horses were curried, fed, and allowed to graze there.

Henry would stand in his wagon to get some height so he could lean over the top fence rail. By now Samson recognized the young boy. A few sugar lumps on Henry's outstretched hand, and Samson responded with a shake of his shaggy mane and a loud whinny as he pressed his head into Henry's chest, nearly knocking him out of his wagon.

Henry would hold Samson's head in his hands. They'd almost be nose to nose as Henry whispered to the animal. As weeks passed, the horse would stretch out his neck and all but lay his head on the boy's shoulder. Henry loved the feel of the horse's hot breath on his neck. Henry occasionally did not make it home on time for their evening meal.

Mr. Ivor Keller, the man in charge of the barn workers, noticed the boy and horse at the fence. Mr. Keller had also been a horse lover as a boy. He approached Henry and invited him to come into the barn any afternoon.

Henry jumped at the chance. In the late afternoon of any given day, he was welcome to enter the barn and assist with Samson's care. He'd brush down the horse after a day of heavy hauling. He helped with the feeding and providing water. Of course, the less attractive part of the deal was being asked to assist in cleaning Samson's stall.

Hank was acquainted with Mr. Keller and approved the arrangement. Henry would stop by the stables when he found time. No money changed hands. Yet Henry was overjoyed at the opportunity to be so involved with the big old horse he'd come to love.

Over time, Henry grew more comfortable around horses as he performed his few responsibilities. Then, on a warm summer afternoon when the stable chores were finished for the day and Samson was contentedly eating his oats, Henry decided to brush Samson's coat one more time. Henry enjoyed the physical act of brushing Samson and the pleasure the animal seemed to experience. Acting on a impulse, Henry put down the brush, climbed up the stall gate and threw his leg over the back of the large work horse.

Mr. Keller had often warned Henry that workhorses used to harnesses and pulling did not take kindly to anyone mounting them and had forbidden Henry from climbing up on Samson.

Once Henry was seated on Samson's broad back, he waited to see if the horse would explode and throw him. Samson moved about the stall slowly. Henry could feel the horse's muscles flex beneath him. As Samson's head nodded up and down, Henry stroked his thick mane. Finally Henry lay his head down on Samson's neck and wrapped his arms around the neck of the tranquil animal.

For several minutes there wasn't a sound in the stall except the heavy breathing of the big horse. Henry felt safe, at peace. He felt Samson's strength flow into his lean, young body. Henry desperately wanted to be as strong as Samson for his family.

He wanted to remain with his cheek buried in the horse's heavy mane for a much longer time, but he could hear other workers approaching the stable. Sliding off the horse's back and giving Samson one final pat, Henry left the barn and grabbed his wagon. Pulling it across the bridge, he heard a horse's whinny. Pausing, he listened carefully, and he was sure it was Samson bidding him good night.

ක13ෙ
The Banker's Family

MAGGIE AND HENRY SPENT part of each summer day delivering the warm, fresh bread straight from Daisy's oven. The two children scuffing through the dust of the streets in their bare feet became a familiar sight.

At first, they took turns pulling the wagon and traded off carrying the fragrant loaves to the doors of families awaiting them. Their constant hellos and visits with people in the yards they passed got them friendly greetings from just about everyone they met on their travels. Then they met Oscar.

Oscar Lund lived two blocks west of the Lutheran church. Henry recognized the house and the name. Oscar's father was the president of the bank—the financial wizard who initiated the sale and destruction of their little house on the alley. At first Henry found it difficult to acknowledge Oscar as they passed his house. Often Oscar would be seated alone on the front steps of his elaborate home. After being the fifth grade with Oscar, they always greeted him with a wave and a "Hey!" Most of the time he gave only a cursury response.

Then one morning as they completed their delivery route, Henry and Maggie initiated a connection with the dejected boy. There he was, sitting on the third step, his arms hanging limply over his knees and his head bowed to his chest. Oscar presented a very sad image to the two children. They thought they could hear him crying. Parking the wagon, the two friends approached Oscar. Both Henry and Maggie had known sorrow, and recognized the symptoms in the weeping boy.

Oscar was not aware of their approach until they stopped at the bottom of the steps and softly spoke his name. He raised his head and looked at them a long moment. His eyes were red and his nose ran. He reached into the back pocket of his knickers for a white handkerchief and gave a mighty blow. Then Oscar came to stand before the two children that he, and other students from school, had previously called "Island Trash."

"Hi," he said, sniffing and gulping. "Sorry to be such a cry baby." He blew his nose again and worked not to start crying again. "I'm glad you stopped. I see you walking by my house all the time. I really hoped sometime you'd stop."

He gestured to the steps, and all three sat on a step in the shade of a large birch tree whose branches stretched over the porch steps. "You always seem to be having such a good time together." The tears began once again.

"What's the matter? Can we help?" Henry asked, feeling sympathetic toward Oscar.

Oscar wiped his tears away, and then his troubles spilled from his lips. Maggie and Henry listened, caught up in Oscar's sad tale. Partway through, Maggie reached out to take his hand. The gesture encouraged him and the words kept coming.

"The problem," Oscar said, "is my father. He's not nice to me or my mother." Oscar told of numerous trips to the basement where his father took the razor strap—or his belt—to his bare back. Sometimes Oscar wasn't even aware what he had done.

"I get sent to bed without supper if my school work's not perfect," the boy said. According to Oscar, his father thought everyone else was far down the social ladder, and his wife and son had failed to measure up to the perfect family. Oscar and his mother were under a constant barrage of criticism and physical abuse.

The two friends listened. Their experience with parents had been completely different. "I can't believe a dad would treat you like that," Henry said, thinking of the love and encouragement his own father, wounded as he was, gave him every day.

Oscar, encouraged by the interest of his two new friends, continued his tale of sorrow. He often worried about his mother. She was "ill," had a "problem," and he didn't know what to do about that. He turned to Henry and Maggie and hesitantly invited them into his home. Henry fetched the wagon up to the front steps next to the peony bushes bordering the porch. Oscar motioned for them to be very quiet. Together they tip-toed through the front door and into the ornate entry beyond. The entry was dimly lit and the stale inside air was much cooler than outside. A floral rug covered the oak floor, making the Island children's bare feet feel as though they stood on a velvet sponge. Oscar led them through the parlor, crowded with ornate settees, tufted chairs whose arms and backs were covered by antimacassars, round tables draped with fringed tablecloths hanging to the floor, and sideboards filled with valuable china and glassware.

Henry and Maggie followed Oscar to the sunroom that angled out from the formal dining room. All the windows in the rooms were covered by heavy velvet drapes, preventing much of the sunshine from brightening the room.

As they proceeded through the crowded, darkened rooms, Maggie became aware of a strong, familiar odor. Liquor—she was certain of that. Many times, she was awakened by sounds and voices in the wee hours of the night. Peering out her bedroom door, she often saw Big Jack caring for the men who didn't seem to "feel very well," who were "ill." Maggie was sure she knew what awaited them when they finally found Oscar's mother.

Oscar led them to a chaise lounge in the darkened corner of the sunroom, and there she was—Oscar's mother, Anna Belle. She lay sprawled across the lounge, her head against the arm of the chair, one arm across her eyes and the other draped toward the floor. Her fallen hand held a large crystal glass, now empty, which Maggie surmised caused the large spill on the floral rug on the floor beside her. There was also a dark spot of wine on the front of her gown. Her hair fell loosely about her face and over her slender shoulders.

Oscar smoothed her hair back from her forehead and removed the empty glass from her limp hand.

He turned to look at the two shocked youngsters behind him. His face was full of anxiety as well as love for his mother. "I never really know what to do for her," he said softly. "I'm afraid for her most of the time. I don't want my father to see her like this. She started drinking so early this morning—I just wasn't prepared!"

He lifted her fallen arm and gently placed it over her abdomen, then retrieved an afghan from a nearby chair and covered her. The youngsters stood silent and anxious. "Our maid comes in at noon." Oscar swallowed. "She always tells my dad—and then we're in trouble!"

Maggie said quietly, "I know what to do—I think. If we hurry and work together we can awaken her, clean her up, dress her, then feed her something to give her strength." At the incredulous looks on the boys faces, she added, "My dad helps people who are sick like this all the time at the boarding house. I could go get him to help us!"

Oscar vetoed that idea immediately but was in favor of the their attempting to remedy the situation themselves. Maggie started giving directions, then they started to work.

"Oscar, where does your mother keeps her robes?" she asked. He trotted off to find a clean robe. "Find some slippers, too, if you can. We need to make her look beautiful again."

Oscar said, "I know just where to look," as he took the stairs two at a time.

Then, taking a quick look about the sunroom, Maggie set Henry to the task of cleaning up the stained rug and any other blots or smudges on the furniture. "Quick! You might need a bucket with warm water, soap, and a scrub brush."

"I can do that!" Henry was gone like a flash, heading for the back hall where he figured cleaning supplies would be kept. Maggie could hear the sound of water running from the pump and the rattle of pails and brushes as Henry followed her instructions.

Maggie went to the kitchen, stoked the fire and brought water in the tea kettle to a boil. After locating the crock containing coffee grounds, she prepared a pot full of strong, black coffee. While it percolated, she filled a large bowl with warm, soapy water, picked up two dishtowels, and returned to Mrs. Lund's side. After soaking one towel in warm water, then wringing it out, she used it to wipe away the soil and smell of the spilled liquor on Anna Belle's face and breast. Lifting one of the still, limp hands at a time, she gently cleaned them and dried them with the soft towel. She removed the combs from Anna Belle's hair, loosened her long braids, and then smoothed the tousled locks before once again braiding them and tucking them back into the control of the decorative combs. Mrs. Lund slowly opened her eyes, surprised at the gentle touch of the unknown girl hovering over her.

"You'll be fine, Mrs. Lund," Maggie softly reassured her. "I'll just get you freshened up a bit." The woman smiled slowly and once again closed her eyes.

By this time the coffee was ready. Oscar had secured another dressing gown from the closet upstairs, a lovely robe of blue velvet, and had it ready when Maggie was ready to exchange the sour, foul smelling gown for the fresh one, whose fragrance had been reinforced with a bit of toilet water from Mrs. Lund's dressing table.

Finished with his cleaning assignment, Henry took charge of preparing toast with butter and jam for Mrs. Lund to eat with the rich, dark coffee. Henry added a bit of cream and two sugar lumps to her cup just like Mrs. Brush had trained him. He thought the makeshift breakfast looked quite appetizing.

Maggie and Oscar gently removed the soiled gown and replaced it with the fresh, fragrant one. "I think you should destroy this robe, Oscar. You wouldn't want your dad to find it." Oscar agreed, hastily gathered it up and headed for the back door.

When he returned, empty handed, Oscar looked pleased. "He'll never, ever find that robe. I put it down the hole in our old outhouse. Nobody looks in there anymore."

Mrs. Lund was now sitting up on the chaise lounge, legs outstretched before her, the afghan across her lap. She was fully awake and quite mystified by the actions of the three youngsters.

Maggie gently held a large mug of hot coffee to her lips. "Here, Mrs. Lund. Sip on this and I know you'll feel better." Breathing in the aroma alone made Mrs. Lund feel as though she would survive the despondency she had felt earlier in the day.

Henry brought her the plate of buttered toast to complete the morning repast. Three pairs of eyes watched her sip the coffee and nibble the toast .

She smiled a sad but lovely smile. She knew what they'd done for her, and she was very grateful. "I can't tell you how much I appreciate what you two young people have done for me," she said in a very soft voice, "and for Oscar." She turned her head away.

Then she spoke in a stronger voice. "Hopefully I can now make it through the rest of this day on my own, and the days yet to come. I have to be in full control of myself, when Mr. Lund comes home for dinner," she paused as a sad smile filled her eyes. "He always expects a full report of how Oscar and I have spent the day." She raised her hand to stroke her brow. "He must never know I once again lost control," she whispered. "I need to be strong—for Oscar's sake."

From then on, Oscar joined the bread delivery crew. He would be waiting on the corner as Henry and Maggie turned up the street from Cloquet Avenue. He always offered to pull the wagon. Henry allowed him to do so occasionally. The bread, cookies, and rolls were precious cargo, and, after all, he was the sole owner of the wonderful wagon.

Sometimes the three of them sat in the shade and divided the treats Daisy included for them. Oscar tried to go barefooted like his two friends but discovered his feet needed toughening before that would happen—and that took time. The sunshine burnished Oscar's pale cheeks, and soon he looked as healthy and robust as his two companions.

Once or twice a week the trio would stop by Oscar's home and were invited in to visit with Mrs. Lund. Most of the time she was seated in the sunny parlor working on her embroidery or her knitting. She was always pleased to see her son's two friends, and seemed to be in better control of herself.

"Please stay for tea," she'd often say with a wide smile, and all four of them would sit at the round, cloth-draped table for tea and biscuits with jam served on fancy china.

Maggie was always impressed. Big Jack had only heavy-duty dishes that could survive the rough treatment of the loggers. As she held the delicate handle of the rose teacup, Maggie extended her little finger gracefully as Mrs. Lund did. Mrs. Lund appeared to be fine during their teatime visits, yet there was a sadness and a longing evident to her two young guests, as well as her son. Only on one rare occasion did she seem to be somewhat "ill," but never as extreme as when they first met her.

Oscar occasionally was allowed to travel to the Island for a brief visit, but his father was to never to know about his forays across the red bridge. He was very impressed with Big Jack, who, when shaking his hand, almost lifted him from the ground.

The three children occasionally took time to give Big Jack assistance peeling potatoes for the evening meal. Peelings flew wildly in all directions, accompanied by much laughter, and Big Jack laughed as well, not at all caring about the extra mess.

Oscar also met Henry's father. Hank greeted the boy with a warm smile and a handshake—one not quite as exuberant as Big Jack's. Henry had explained his father's physical condition to Oscar. As soon as he met Hank, Oscar saw past the man confined to his wonderful chair. His welcoming eyes were full of kindness and affection.

The frightened knot that so often constricted Oscar's chest when confronting his own father never materialized.

Even as young as he was, Oscar saw the difference in his contact with Big Jack and Hank, and with his own father.

Daisy, her apron covered in flour, embraced Oscar. She carried the fragrance of chocolate and cinnamon and freshly baked bread. He breathed it in and hoped he'd remember it for a long time. After seating Oscar, Henry, and Maggie at the parlor table, she served them glasses of fresh milk and chocolate drop cookies fresh from the oven.

Oscar looked about him and saw contented families, not perfect families, but ones where love and affection were a top priority. He so longed for that.

ஐ14ை
Lumberjack Days

AUGUST ARRIVED, BRINGING with it a hint of autumn and the realization that the end of warm summer days loomed on the horizon. The mills kept up hectic schedules of sawing, planing, sanding, and stacking. The number of logs waiting in the river diminished as mechanical jaws plucked them from the water and sent them up the conveyor belts to the waiting teeth of the saws. The logs were stripped of their bark and sliced on all four sides so they could be ripped into boards. The whistles and bells called the men to work in a never-ceasing rotation of shifts.

August also brought Lumberjack Days, an event all the loggers looked forward to. It was a day when the entire city celebrated the best of the best in strength and logging skills.

Big Jack's favorite event was the two-man sawing competition. Even though he'd been a cook when at the logging camps, Big Jack was skilled and strong. Alvin, his former partner, had lost part of his left hand in the mill accident earlier that year. He'd never grasp the handle of the giant saw ever again.

Big Jack, however, was still entering the competition. His new partner would be Samuel Berg, Mrs. Berg's strapping son. Big Jack had been coaching him for months.

When they practiced, loggers gathered around to cheer them on and give advice on how they could improve their technique. Rumors even filtered across the river to Mrs. Berg that her son was a champion sawyer in the making. Against her will, she was proud of Samuel.

After pushing Hank's new chair across the dusty street, Henry positioned it so he could watch two friends practice. Hank had never competed in the single or double sawing competition, but he knew how much skill was required.

"Looks good, Big Jack," Hank would shout. "Keep the pressure even! Concentrate, Samuel! Don't take your eyes off the saw! Maintain your rhythm!"

The two-person cross-cut saw was the mainstay in logging. Affectionately called the "misery whip," arm muscles tired fast as the saw was forced back and forth through the dense, heavy logs. The giant saws could be five to seven feet long. Loggers practiced their technique—never push, always pull—so they didn't buckle the saw as it passed through the log. In the contest, loggers were given a one-inch starting cut, then had to saw the rest of the way through the log. The first slab to hit the ground determined the champion.

Other competitions attracted loggers with other skills. The one-person cross-cut saw drew loggers with broad backs and massive arm muscles working a somewhat smaller saw alone. Strength and unflagging pressure often determined who was a true champion.

Perhaps the public's favorite event was logrolling, or "birling." Two men mounted a floating log and, using their weight and the quickness of their footwork, spun the log. The challenge was to maintain balance while trying to unbalance the other logger.

River pigs, who worked the logs as they came down the river each spring, always received the loudest cheers from the hundreds of people filling Pinehurst Park. Sometimes the duel on the log lasted only a few seconds before one of the men was dumped into the pond. When expert birlers competed, the log could spun for up to twenty minutes without either man hitting the water. Then the log was exchanged for a smaller one and the two men went at it again. If neither one plunged the other into the water, it would again be replaced by a still thinner log. The smaller the log, the faster it spun. Few men, even the most expert birlers, made it past the third log.

Log rollers could make birling look easy, but it was exhausting. These men needed to be strong, agile, and fast, and these skills needed to be combined with great balance and a mind that could quickly execute clever strategy. In the contest, men who lost got wet; in riding logs downriver, falling among hundreds of other logs could claim a man's life.

The ax throw demanded deadly accuracy. Winning that competition was a source of pride for a working logger. Using a double-bit ax, the 'jacks had three throws at a stationary target, a large tree across a wide open area, aiming for a three-point bulls-eye cut into the bark of the target. Crowds watched as mighty men took aim, stepped back, wound up and let fly. The ax rotated through the air and hit with a deep *thunk*. Loggers handling the heavy axes looked like characters from Greek mythology—Zeus casting lightning bolts from atop Mt. Olympus.

Each year as August approached, the Island became a training camp for contestants. Every night men discussed the prospects of events and money changed hands as they wagered on who would be the best of the participants. As contestants came from many towns, there was always the possibility winners might not be a local hero.

Debates at the bars got louder and more confrontational as the big day approached. In the two-man saw contest, Big Jack and Samuel soon became favorites. Almost a decade had passed since anyone had beaten Jack and his former partner. Now the odds had changed. Samuel had never competed. Reports differed about his strength and skill. Crowds gathered in back of the boarding house as the two perfected their skill.

Working diligently, Samuel wanted to prove to Jack he wouldn't let him down. He was young, strong as a bull, and worked with the two-man saw all winter at the logging camp. But brute strength wasn't enough. There was a rhythm to it, a kind of dance. The two men had to move and breathe as one.

But this team had an accidental physical advantage—Big Jack was right-handed and Samuel was left-handed. The strength and pressure applied at each end of the saw grew more equal because of this.

The log rolling competition was of particular interest to Hank. He had been the best of the best birlers for the past several years. Loggers sought his opinion about the men who now had to rise to the challenge if they were to keep the champion local.

For the past few weeks Hank had watched the men and boys mounting the logs floating in the river in front of the saloons as the logs made their way to the mill. Legs pumping, arms flailing, bodies splashed into the river. Just about everyone fell within the first few minutes of their attempts. The observers spent most of their time in raucous laughter. Birling was not as easy as an expert could make it appear.

Only one young man gave Hank hope the championship would stay in the Cloquet area—Frank Shaw. However, reports spread through the men in the saloons that Frank wouldn't take part in the birling competition because he had been the cause of Hank's injury. Rumor said Frank's confidence and spirit had been weakened by guilt.

"I can't do it," he'd tell the inquisitive. "I keep seeing Hank with that huge log riding his legs. It was all my fault." He'd shake his head and walk away. "Nope! Can't do it anymore!"

Hank was relentless in urging Frank that he was the only man who could stand against men coming from other logging camps. "Frank, you're like a son to me! Of all the men I know, you're the only one who can beat those guys. You're the best—we all know that." Leaning forward in his chair, Hank put his hands on the muscled forearms of the young man. "Do it for me, Frank," he said quietly. "Give me the gift of watching you up on that log, knowing you're there for me—and for yourself." Hank grabbed Frank's shirt collar and pulled him down until they were face to face. "You need to do this to show me you're healed of the guilt you don't need to carry. I forgive you, Frank. I've always forgiven you!" With one more tug on the collar, Hank said, "Now it's time for you to forgive yourself!"

Hank's words cut through the guilt and sadness Frank carried. Soon afterward, word came that Frank had begun training for the competition.

Rumors flew that Frank had a secret location on the river north of town where he practiced to reach the high level of skill he desired. Then rumor had it Frank had a serious relationship with the girl who distracted him on the day of the accident. Her family lived on the river property where Frank trained. The rumor mill went into high gear. Betting became brisk, some claiming a girl would ruin him, others saying he'd win for her. Two facts fed rumor and betting. First, the girl, Katherine, was always on shore cheering him on. Second, her father, George Ackerman, had been a fine log roller and had been the champion some years ago. George, Frank's coach, aimed to perfect his technique before Lumberjack Days. George, a fine birler, had gone to a third log in contests a few years back.

Frank was now eager for his debut. Hank and George both felt he was a champion in the making. Hank was confident Frank was receiving good instruction from George— plus the finest affection from Katherine.

Henry and Oscar and other young boys often came to Hank for advice on how to spin a log. Hank parked his chair as close as he could to the river and kept a close eye on the youngsters who tried to spin logs—and often failed. "Keep your feet moving!" he'd call to them. "Use your arms for balance! Feel the movement of the log under your boots!"

Oscar maintained his balance only a second or two. He'd laugh every time he, with flailing arms, landed in the river. He'd probably never be a birler, but he loved trying. His biggest challenge now was explaining to his dad why he was soaked to the skin. Daisy often hung his shirt and trousers on her clothesline while Oscar and Henry sat in the sun, wrapped in towels, and played checkers. Some days Oscar was a bit damp when he arrived home, but no one seemed to pay any attention.

Maggie watched from the shore, a bit envious. Not one girl ever came down to the river to attempt birling. After hearing reports that women near other logging camps had learned the skill and could spin an opponent into the drink, she approached Hank one afternoon as he watched boys practice on logs. Standing quietly behind his chair, she whispered in his ear, "Would you ever help me become a birler?"

Surprised, Hank turned his chair and looked into her eyes. He could see she was serious. He decided he'd take part in her quest and smiled into her young, eager face. "I'd be delighted to teach you how to be a champion birler." Her face lit up. "We'll begin training after this year's competition is over. We'll have a big surprise for everyone by next summer's celebration. I promise you that!"

"Really, Hank? You'd do that for me?" She threw her arms around his neck. Then she clapped her hands in anticipation.

"You bet," Hank laughed. They shook hands to seal their pact.

Maggie skipped back to the boarding house. Big Jack looked up from the roast he was seasoning when she came in. "Maggie, my sweet, what put that big grin on your face?"

"Ask all you want," she replied playfully, picking up a potato and the paring knife. "It's a secret. I can't tell even you!"

Big Jack studied his daughter. "Well, then, I guess I'll just have to wait for you to surprise me, won't I?" he said, rubbing seasoning onto the other side of the roast.

Hank enjoyed it when his son and the other boys came to him for advice, even as he grieved for the life he no longer had. He was determined to work his damaged legs at least until he could stride up to Daisy, scoop her into his arms, and walk outside to look at the moon and the stars or stand beside Henry, cast an arm around his maturing shoulders, look him straight in his eyes, and tell him how proud he was to have such a fine son.

THE MORNING OF LUMBERJACK DAYS dawned with the promise of a perfect day—clear with just a few soft clouds casting brief shadows on the town while drifting overhead.

The temperature would be a perfectly normal day for August. By midmorning Pinehurst Park filled with workers finishing preparations for the competitions to come.

All the logs were in place. The pond was equipped for the birling. Targets for the ax throw were firmly attached to three distant trees, ready to receive the sharp axes. Tables were set up in shady spots. Families came early to lay claim to a table, or even just a spot in the shade.

The streets and roads to the park were filled with families coming to cheer their favorites and enjoy a day with friends. The women's dresses created a quilt of color. Parasols bobbed over their heads to protect porcelain complexions. Blankets were spread on the ground when the tables filled. Children ran around like puppies let off-leash, always hovering within shouting distance of a parent and the picnic baskets filled with the treats.

The men, the sleeves of clean, everyday shirts rolled up, greeted their friends and shook hands full of calluses and scars with their own large hands, also familiar with the rigors of the lumberjack life. The day became a reunion, a celebration of strength, skill, and survival of those who spent their hard working days in the mills or at the camps.

They reminisced about the champions of the past, those men who symbolized the heights of strength and endurance achieved in past years now remembered in mythical stories passed from logger to logger. They speculated on who would be added to those auspicious ranks after this year's contests were over.

Soon, Old Syd and Mrs. Brush had driven across the red bridge and parked the carriage in front of the Larsons' Island home. The plan was to settle Hank, Daisy, and Henry in the wagon and take them to the park at midmorning. Everyone in town wanted to arrive early. Old Syd had crept into the park at dawn and placed a tablecloth on a table in a prime spot, weighting the cloth with a rock on each corner and setting a rather large food basket right in the middle.

After loading the Larsons' lunch basket and Hank's chair, Henry and Old Syd assisted Hank onto the front seat of the wagon. Henry sat in the back, tucked in between his mother and elderly Mrs. Brush. Grateful that the ride would be short, Henry thought ahead to the great day he'd have with Maggie and Oscar.

Old Syd's selection of a shaded table was perfect. After parking the horse and wagon, the group made their way to the center of the park. The tablecloth and picnic basket remained untouched. Setting up a folding chair, Mrs. Brush arranged herself comfortably. Hank navigated his chair to the opposite end of the table, set the brake, and looked forward to a tall glass of lemonade before the contests began.

Daisy and Old Syd, sitting on either side of the table, organized the lunch that would be served later. Henry was eager to be off to find Maggie and Oscar and be in the thick of the activity taking place throughout the park. So, with his parents' permission, he set off at a run to find his friends, ready for the excitement to begin.

Suddenly, the crowd's attention shifted to the park entrance. A hush fell over the milling crowd. Everyone watched in fascination as Pearl and three of her girls entered the picnic area. Young, healthy looking, dressed in the high fashion of the day, the girls were lovely. They wore broad-brimmed hats decorated with wide, colorful ribbons and flowers to match their dresses. Their hair was tucked beneath the hats with only an occasional curl cascading down in a beguiling manner onto their necks and shoulders.

Their colorful summer dresses were immediately condemned; the hemlines were scandalously higher than acceptable, revealing at least three inches more leg and ankle than decorum allowed. The body line of the dresses was softer than the current corseted look and belts gathered in their waistlines and emphasized the natural flow of their ample bosoms.

Nonjudgmental eyes saw the women as lovely, but that wasn't the view for most people—especially the older women. Their eyes went directly to Pearl, the nemesis they had hoped to destroy. There she stood, sedately attired in a navy-blue dress that hung loosely on her frame. A straw hat of modest proportions sat atop her upswept hair, one red flower being the only ornament. Taking their time, the four women made their way across the park to a table situated under a canopy. Here, while everyone watched in stunned attention, the women seated themselves and settled in to watch the events of the day.

Pearl took a moment to peruse the crowds of people. No one met her eye. No one greeted her. Her girls had been unrelenting in wanting see the events. They were flushed with excitement, eager to cheer on some of the young men who frequented Pearl's place. Pearl was determined she would try to enjoy the day.

From across the park, Daisy watched as the group of women took their seats. Being sensitive to the exclusion she knew Pearl must feel, Daisy stood suddenly and, while her companions watched in disbelief, walked through the crowds toward the canopy.

A moment later Pearl felt the gentle touch of a hand on her shoulder and, looking up quickly, found herself looking into the smiling eyes of Daisy Larson. "Hello, Pearl. I'm happy to see you."

Since the Larsons had moved to the Island last spring, the two women had met occasionally when Pearl made trips back and forth to the bank. As she drove by the Larson home, Pearl soon became conscious of the delicious aroma of baking bread and pastries.

One day, on impulse, she stopped the carriage in front of that house just as Daisy was taking down the laundry from the clothesline stretched from tree to tree in the rear of their house. While they chatted in the summer sun, Pearl commented on the delicious aroma of freshly baked bread she always detected as she passed.

"Let me get you a loaf," Daisy offered, putting the dry linens and towels in a basket before hurrying to the kitchen. Pearl protested. Daisy insisted. Since that day the two women had visited on occasion as the phaeton passed by on the dusty road. Occasionally Pearl contracted for an entire batch of bread and rolls—and she rewarded Daisy very well.

In another setting they might have been good friends. Pearl knew that was impossible and didn't want to inflict any discomfort or embarrassment into Daisy's already difficult life. They remained comfortable with each other, but never close.

Daisy knew people watched as she chatted with Pearl. She really didn't care what any of them thought—or whispered to one another. Her heart went out to Pearl who, in Daisy's eyes, was the loneliest person she had ever met. Even in the short time she'd lived on the Island, Daisy could see Pearl wasn't well, growing paler and more fragile as time went passed.

"You look lovely today, Pearl," Daisy said. "I hope you have a wonderful day."

Pearl responded warmly and took a moment to introduce the young women seated beside her. "Daisy, I'd like you to meet Judith," and Daisy shook hands with an ample blond with a big smile. "And here's Lenore," Pearl said, indicating a slender brunette with a shy demeanor. "And this is Beatrice, my adopted daughter." Beatrice was a lovely girl who didn't look a day over sixteen.

Daisy shook hands all around and appreciated their smiling faces as they responded to her. And finally, with a touch of their hands, Daisy smiled down into Pearl's eyes, then turned and walked back through the curious crowd to her family and friends waiting for her in the shade of the pine trees.

As she took her seat at the picnic table, Mrs. Brush smiled and said quietly, "I'm proud of you, my dear."

By this time Henry had collected Maggie and Oscar. As soon as possible, Oscar escaped the stern looks of his father, who only attended the festivities in order to relate to the depositors frequenting his bank. "Never ask permission" was Oscar's new motto. His father always said no to any request, so Oscar found it more expedient to slip away undetected and blend in with the other young people watching the events.

Suddenly, a long loud blast came from an old fashioned gabrel, a slender tin horn five to eight feet long that had been used in lumber camps of the past to awaken the men in the darkness of the morning or call them in from the woods for the evening meal. The horn was affectionately called "the Gabriel" in honor of the angel who, scripture said, would one day blow it to call humanity to the gates of heaven. Former military buglers in the area found they were adept at making music on the gabrel, their lips having been conditioned by bugling during their time in the Army. Events were about to begin. Quickly, the spectators positioned themselves to watch the competitions.

Large men with assorted axes, saws, and other necessary equipment for their contests milled about, moving toward the area of the competition in which they'd be involved. The city band struck up a medley of lively tunes, prompting people to sing along and dance.

The locals took pride in picking out those men from distant localities taking part in the day's events. Several robust men, reported to have come from Moose Lake, were not modest in their claims to roundly defeat the local men. Another group from up north boldly claimed their intention to claim championships, letting everyone know they would crush the hometown boys. The louder the bragging, the more the hometown crowd cheered on the local favorites, causing everyone to catch the excitement and set the stage for the battles of strength and skill soon to take place. Money changed hands in bets.

Henry, Maggie, and Oscar, flushed with excitement, ran from station to station, wherever qualifying matches were taking place. Starting with the younger, less-experienced men, some were quickly eliminated, but some went on to compete again and again. The trio cheered loudly at the ax-throwing competition, where they watched as a group of younger, boisterous men strutted up to the line.

Each contestant appeared certain of his victory. However, looks weren't everything. Posing and waving to their fans, the young men did not concentrate as they should, and more often than not, the ax went flying but didn't hit the bull's eye. Some missed the tree altogether.

The crowd cheered, sometimes laughed. The young men not eliminated focused harder.

The competition came down to two men—one young man and a middle-aged man, the champion for several years running. The young man looked like a champion as he stepped up to the line, flexed his muscles, spit in his palms and readied the ax for its flight to the tree.

With a mighty heave and all the brute force the young man could muster, the ax left his muscular hand and flew across the open space. Transfixed, the crowd held its breath as the ax seemed to rotate in slow motion until, with a loud thud, it struck the tree and hung there, vibrating from the impact. To the naked eye the ax had hit the direct center of the target. Quickly the judges ran to the tree with their measuring equipment. "Off to the right and an inch below the perfect center of the target," came the judges' official decree.

By the time the final contestant stepped up to the line to throw his ax and win or lose the contest, Henry and his friends had found a perfect vantage for the final throw of the day. Henry was shocked to see his friend from the horse barns, Mr. Keller, step up to the line and ready his ax. According to spectators around Henry and his friends, Mr. Keller had been the ax throwing champ for as long as anyone could remember.

Henry suddenly saw Mr. Keller in a new light. Before today, Henry had thought of Mr. Keller as being short. He now changed the adjective to "compact." Mr. Keller rolled up his sleeves and revealed well-developed arms, and Henry instantly thought of the word "brawny." Henry had never noticed how broad Mr. Keller's back was. Henry always had focused on Samson. Today he concentrated on his friend.

Mr. Keller removed a cloth from his back pocket and carefully wiped, almost caressed, the blade of his ax. The local crowd cheered wildly for their friend as he readied himself for the mighty throw. Suddenly, the shouting subsided and all eyes pivoted between the man about to throw and the target across the green field.

Positioning himself toward the target, with a mighty thrust of his arms and entire torso, Mr. Keller stepped forward and brought the ax around. He let it fly, end over end, toward the target. No one breathed. With a sharp crack, the ax embedded itself in the tree, penetrating so deeply the ax handle hung there, still as death.

For a split second the crowd stared, breathless. The judges measured carefully, conferred among themselves, wrote in their notebooks, then turned to the crowd. Mr. Laurila, the chief judge, announced in a loud voice, "The winner of the ax throw for the year 1917 is Mr. Ben Keller, with a perfect hit. It's his seventh consecutive championship!"

The crowd exploded into cheering and applause, Henry clapping wildly. Maggie and Oscar did as well. They didn't know Mr. Keller, only what Henry had shared about him. Eagerly the three youngsters made their way through the crowd to shake Mr. Keller's hand.

Next they headed across the park to where the one-man sawing contests were already working their way through the younger contestants. One of Maggie's friends from the boarding house—a young Finnish lumberjack named Toivo Hentila—was said to be the heavy favorite. Maggie had been teased constantly by Big Jack and Henry, for, whenever Toivo sat down at the tables in the boarding house, Maggie seemed to materialize out of thin air to stand beside his chair and serve him whatever he desired.

Toivo, tall, blond, and young, was a local favorite, known for his great strength with the ax and the saw. His hands were as large as Big Jack's, his shoulders and back developed mightily from work in the camps and the mill. Young as he was, the men respected him and encouraged him in his development as a top notch worker and competitor. Maggie ran ahead, wanting to find a vantage point that would allow her to see her friend, motioning to Oscar and Henry to follow her.

By the time the three friends were situated, Toivo was two away from his turn at the saw. People shouted, cheered, and cursed, creating an atmosphere of raucous enthusiasm for each contestant. A man from Carlton was reported the one to beat, but when Toivo mounted the platform and proceeded to prepare his saw for what lay ahead, his fans from the Island erupted.

Old-timers preached the benefit of wiping the saw blade with a coarse rag soaked in kerosene. According to them, the kerosene helped keep the blade free of pitch and tar that sometimes collected in the teeth. Toivo followed the advice of those elderly men who had spent their entire lives with a saw or ax in their gnarled hands and stood with a ragged, kerosene-soaked cloth in his gigantic hand, gently going back and forth over the length of his well-used one-man saw.

When ready, Toivo placed the blade of his saw in the prepared slit in the top of the log and set his feet and legs to provide the best leverage and pressure. The timer bell clang, and the crowd went crazy. Sawdust belched from the log as the saw bit into the pulp of the tree. Toivo developed a perfect rhythm, becoming one with the saw. First the thrust—

not too forceful, which would cause the saw to buckle—and then the pull—where the man's whole body leaned back against body of the log. His left hand pressed into the top of the saw handle, forcing the teeth as deeply as possible, the right hand controlling the back and forth of the saw.

For a brief moment Toivo moved in perfect sync with the city band as the music floated over the boisterous cheering of the crowd. Toivo's back and shoulder muscles convulsed with the strain, his face flushed but calm, even as the breeze tossed his blond hair. Maggie cheered with all her might. The boys jumped up and down as the victory seemed imminent. Toivo was now their hero as well.

Once the cheering subsided and Toivo's victory was announced, the Carlton contingent, miffed at their defeat, complained to the judges. "He wiped his saw with kerosene!" they shouted and claimed it gave unfair advantage. The judges waved at them and told them sawyers had been doing that to their saws since time began.

"If you think it makes that much difference," one judge shouted over the din, "next time try it yourself and see if it gives you the championship!" The crowd broke out in laughter and another cheer. And that was the end of that. Toivo was the champ. He smiled and waved at the three youngsters as they stood in awe of his accomplishment.

When the city band played a medley of old-time waltzes, couples rose from the tables and picnic blankets and waltzed across the grass. As the music continued, Daisy invited the children to take a plate, fill it with whatever they wanted, and find a place in the shade.

By now it was well into the afternoon and the finals in the two-man sawing and the birling contests would start soon. Mrs. Brush sipped lemonade and savored a date-filled cookie. Hank manuevered his chair to a circle of men nearby and discussed the results of the contests so far. Old Syd sat at the foot of a oak tree, head against the trunk, his spindly legs stretched before him. Hands crossed in his lap and cap pulled down over his eyes, he was sound asleep, a half-eaten sandwich balanced precariously on a knee.

The band finished the last waltz and began some popular Sousa marches. The level of anticipation rose as the time for the finals of the two most popular contests approached.

Oscar thanked Daisy for lunch and quickly ran to find his parents. He wanted to share with them all the excitement he had experienced so far this most extraordinary day. Even a sullen glance from his father would not diminish his spirit. He found his parents near the bandshell and embraced his mother as she sat beneath her colorful umbrella, sipping a lemonade. He expected to see disapproval and blame in his father's face, and wasn't disappointed. But Oscar didn't give his father's expression time to register. Instead he relayed in animated detail the new experiences he'd had, the people he'd met, the contests he'd witnessed. His father was a bit taken aback by the outpouring from his usually somber son. Before Mr. Lund could say a word to dampen the exquisite pleasure of his day, Oscar said he'd return soon and share with them the results of the last two contests. Then he was off, dashing through the crowd as he wound his way back to the Larsons and their comfortable spot in the shade of the pine trees.

Henry and Maggie were waiting for him. Hank was primed and eager to maneuver through the throngs of people to the final two-man sawing competition. Maggie just returned from spending a moment with her father, telling him she knew he'd win. Big Jack hugged her close and, with final tug of her long chestnut braid, he and Samuel disappeared into the crowd that pressed close to the area of the final sawing rivalry.

The two men, one mature and the other young, clapped each other on the back and hoisted their equipment. The crowd parted like the Red Sea as they made their way to the site of this final test. Samuel searched the crowd for Beatrice, the young girl from Pearl's place who filled his dreams. He did not see her at first, but then he found her standing on the fringe of the boisterous crowd, her smile willing him to do his best. Shyly, she raised her hand to him. Samuel smiled back.

The three friends were able to secure a spot where Mrs. Brush could place her chair and the rest of their party could stand and easily see what was about to take place. Big Jack had friends from the Island park Hank within shouting distance—in case Big Jack and Samuel needed expert advice at a moment's notice. Hank was sweating from the warm sun and excitement as the two men mounted the platform.

The log the men had to cut was twenty-four inches in diameter, and the finalists would each saw off a two- to three-inch disc of wood from the same log.

Hefty men from the crowd volunteered or were called up to straddle the log to weigh it down, keeping it still as the sawyers bent over their saw. The heavier the man, the better. Big Jack noticed Pastor Jenson near the front of the crowd around the trailer. After a word to one of the judges, Big Jack motioned to Pastor Jenson, inviting him to climb up and join the stocky men already sitting on the log.

Pastor Jenson smiled broadly, leaped onto the platform and threw a leg over the far end of the log. All was ready. The timer would clock the seconds from the starting bell to the crashing of the slab of cut wood as it hit the platform.

The first contestants in the final round of the two-man saw competition were from Floodwood and had been contenders for the past two years. Both years Big Jack and his partner had won by a second—or even a fraction of a second. The two burly men stood ready for combat, caps pulled low, arm and back muscles pumped and ready, legs positioned to obtain the best leverage. The crowd was familiar with them and cheered wildly as the men flexed their brawny arms in preparation for the contest.

Men from the Island countered the cheer with defiant shouts for Big Jack and Samuel and soon the two competing crowds were close to starting a brawl before the sawing even began. The judges threatened to stop the whole affair if order wasn't restored immediately. Slowly the tumult ceased and the sawyers took their places—one on each side of the waiting log, the five-foot saw separating them.

The bell rang, the cheering became deafening, and the two men bent to their task as they quickly cut through the log as though it were a stick of butter. As the disc of wood crashed to the ground, the head judge raised his hand as the three judges peered at the stopwatch in his outstretched hand. "An impressive time of nine seconds!" shouted the judge over the din of the crowd. The men from Floodwood smacked each other on the back and waved their arms in a victorious gesture. With great bravado the two sawyers shouldered their equipment and descended the steps to their waiting fans.

Big Jack and Samuel Berg now mounted the platform. Because of his background, Big Jack had been explicit in his directives for the challenge. They wore comfortable clothes, clothes most often worn to their jobs, none of the fancy duds some men donned to impress the girls coming to watch the contests. Jack had noted that strong men held back if in new clothes and new shoes with slippery soles. At times they triumphed, but when they didn't Jack felt they'd lost their edge not being their natural self, in their natural habitat, so to speak.

Thus, Samuel stood, saw in his large, calloused hand, dressed in his oldest denim work trousers, a worn flannel shirt with the sleeves cut off at the shoulders, and a pair of suspenders that looked as though they might snap at any moment under the strain that lay ahead. His feet were comfortable and secure in his old, studded work boots. There would be no slipping on his part. Samuel removed his hat, and, sure enough, his hair was slicked back and held in place by an application of Macassar, a hair oil guaranteed to control a man's hair through rough weather and tough competitions. Samuel would move, but his hair would not.

Big Jack doffed his hat to the crowd, causing them to cheer wildly. Always a crowd favorite, he loved to excite the masses that watched. He, too, wore comfortable work clothes. He never forgot an early match where his opponent was supposedly far superior to him, but, in the height of the duel, the other sawyer's foot slipped ever so slightly, messing with his balance and equilibrium. He did a little jig to the music of the city band—they now played popular music of the day—and his fancy footwork brought another cheer from his fans. Samuel smiled, though he was nervous.

Their saw sharpened, the handles securely attached, the blade carefully polished with kerosene, they cast aside their leather gloves. The men needed to feel the vibration of their saw as it flashed back and forth through the log. They carefully placed the center of the saw on the mark made in the top of the huge pine. They looked at each other across the saw, each willing his partner to perform his very best.

The crowd went crazy. Big Jack was a known quantity. Samuel had yet to prove himself. They were almost equal in size and strength. It was an intriguing combination. The two men clasped the saw handles in their mammoth hands. The judge checked the timer and, with a flourish, rang the starting bell.

The men exploded with ferocious zeal. Their saw cut through the rings in the log, blasting through the multitude of years the white pine had grown and flourished in the forest. Sawdust erupted and curls of wood spun from the depths of the log as the saw gnawed its way through the wood. The two sawyers were as one. Neither man slipped, lost their balance, buckled the saw, or broke their perfect rhythm.

When their round hit the floor of the platform, the crowd knew for a fact these two men were in a class by themselves. Years later, the old-timers would harken back to the celebration when Big Jack and young Samuel Berg brought the house down with a cutting time of seven seconds. Unheard of! Impossible! A new record!

Big Jack and Samuel stood proud as the judges announced their unbelievable time. Pastor Jenson leaped from his perch. The log had vibrated beneath him as he clung to it. He clapped Big Jack on his sweaty back, shook his enormous hand, and shouted like a school boy. But Pastor Jenson was brushed aside by the two burly sawyers from Floodwood. They threw their arms over the shoulders of the two men who had vanquished them. Even they were conscious of the amazing feat accomplished by the two men from the Island.

Samuel wiped his face with his red hankerchief and scanned the crowd, hoping for another glimpse of Beatrice. She stood to the left of the trailer in the shade of an oak tree. Their eyes met. Shyly, she again raised her hand in greeting, then turned slowly and returned to her group clustered beneath the awning. He was elated, her wave reward enough.

After gathering his equipment, Samuel turned to descend the steps into the crowd. There stood his mother, her face flushed, her hat askew. She dabbed at the beads of sweat cascading down her cheeks with a lace-trimmed hanky. She threw her arms about him and kissed him on his sweaty cheek. He could see her pride, and he was pleased.

The final event—and everyone's favorite—was the birling competition. People made their way to the pond in the center of the park, circled around the shoreline, and awaited the test of strength, endurance, and agility soon to take place. The long, slender log quietly floated in place, and the officials were situated in a row boat near the shore, ready to deliver the contestants two by two to the waiting log.

Hank, Daisy, Mrs. Brush and old Syd had a great view of the action. Having been the birling champion for the past few years, Hank was given special recognition as he took his place beside the officials' table. The crowd gave a thunderous cheer for Hank, he responded with a wide smile and raised his arms in a general salute to his fans.

Daisy was touched by how much the crowd's accolades meant to Hank. His eyes were bright, his cheeks flushed with excitement, and he leaned forward in his chair as though he could leap out of it at any moment. Henry stood behind his father.

The first two men were rowed out to the floating log. In a loud voice the judge repeated the rules of the competition, with one final direction: "Any man who spits tobacco juice in the eyes of his opponent will be disqualified! Play fair!"

Very carefully the men mounted the log as the boat with the judges moved away. Then the excitement began. The timer began. Feet flying, arms waving, the men spun the log one way, then the other, bouncing it and churning up the water. The men stopped, started, and reversed the turns of the log beneath their nimble feet. Seven minutes elapsed, and to the wild cheering of the crowd, one of the men splashed backwards into the water.

Pair after pair of rivals mounted the log as the sun descended toward the tips of the western trees. One pair lasted eleven minutes before one man plunged into the water. Three pairs of birlers survived their first and second attempts on the churning log before their opponents hit the water within seconds of each other.

At last a great cheer erupted from the crowded shore when the Island favorite— Frank Shaw—stepped into the boat along with a birler from Superior, Wisconsin, who had held the championship there for the past two years. The roar grew deafening as the two men stripped off their shirts and mounted the awaiting log. The officials drew back as the signal to begin was given.

George Ackerman stood on the shore, barely able to breathe. Having coached Frank for the past few months, he could feel the very movement of the log beneath Frank's studded boots. Noting the flexing of Frank's thigh muscles and the ripple across his bared torso, Mr. Ackerman prayed Frank would remember the cardinal rule of logrolling. "Repeat it over and over," Mr. Ackerman drummed it into Frank's head: " Never take your eyes off your opponent's feet!"

The other young man was prepared as well—a match in height, weight, and age— and with a mighty lunge the great log began to turn.

Arms extended for balance, the men started, stopped, reversed, ran, paused, jumped, all the while trying for some degree of intimidating eye contact with their opponent. These expert birlers could make the sport look easy to the casual observer, but it was a grueling match of endurance. Strength, speed, balance, and agility—not to mention a devious degree of mental strategy—were essential qualities needed to endure in this taxing sport. Both young men seemed equipped with all the necessary traits. George willed his strength and expertise to the young man who had so diligently trained under his expert direction. He held his breath and watched—and waited.

Time passed. Neither man fell into the pond. At the ringing of the bell notifying the competitors and those on shore that the first timed match had elapsed, the officials halted the log rolling and called for another log, this time one with a smaller diameter, which would make the birling more difficult. Once the new log was in place, Frank and his rival again mounted the waiting log, the bell rang, and the log began to spin.

George took a deep breath as the fierce competition resumed. Anyone in the crowd who had ever been a log roller or a river pig knew that, by then, the leg muscles were burning with exersion and the contestants were having difficulty drawing a full breath. Still the two young men continued, consumed with the desire to defeat the other. A third log was called for, and the two exhausted men mounted that log for the grand finale.

Then it happened. Starting their time on the final log, when the lungs and the muscles of both men were on fire, Frank saw that his opponent seemed to work his feet in smaller, more hesitant steps. Taking a risk, Frank increased his speed on the slippery log, then maneuvered it into a reverse flow.

Suddenly Frank, with his feet still flying, came down on the log, his studded boots firmly planted. The log held still for only a fraction of a second, but it was enough. His rival, not prepared for such a sudden move, catapulted backwards off the log.

The two young men had mesmerized the crowd by their daring antics for the past twenty-seven minutes. They were both champions in everyone's mind, but Frank was the hero of the day. The crowd on shore erupted thunderously, cheering, tossing caps, striking one another on the back. George Ackerman was pleased but, because he was a somber man, tried to hide the wide grin that fought to cover his entire face. The Island lumberjacks had done themselves proud. Frank made him proud.

On shore another monumentous moment had taken place, understood only by those who stood beside Hank. He cheered, shouted encouragement, shook his fists, leaned forward, his hands on the arms of his chair, and pressed himself toward the battle. He remembered the thrill of the rivalry, the strain of the muscles, the will to win that rose in his chest as he had pressured his opponent with all the skill he could muster. In the heat of the moment, Hank stood and stepped boldly toward the shore of the pond.

Then he heard Daisy shout, "Hank! Look at Hank!" Turning his head away from the celebration before him, Hank looked down at the grass, surprised to find himself standing several steps from his chair. Feeling sturdy and strong, he glanced down at his legs. How long he had been standing there he did not know. Hank had surprised even himself, not to mention all his cheering friends who surrounded him. Stepping back, he slowly lowered himself once again into his chair, a wide smile covering his face as Daisy threw her arms around him and kissed him repeatedly on his cheek.

Later that evening the entire Island reverberated with cheers, repeated toasts to their lumberjack friends and heroes, and shouted to one another as they elaborated on the events of the day. Those who had competed in the events were elevated to Olympian heights as accounts of their victories were told again and again, growing more spectacular each time. Glasses were raised in their honor. Big Jack and Samuel Berg, Frank Shaw, Mr. Keller from the barns, and especially for Hank Larson.

It was difficult to believe Hank had stood by himself and walked unaided as he cheered for the success of his young friend. A jubilant spirit of celebration and hope for Hank's recovery spread through the vast crowds that milled about the Island on this very special night. No fights errupted, no one threw anything at anyone, no one argued over who would pay the ever-rising tabs for drinks, no mirror was broken by a tossed mug. Even the saggy moose looked good to the men at the bar. Surely this day would live in the memories of these hard-working men for a long time to come.

Hank had arrived home earlier, propelled in his chair by Big Jack and Samuel Berg. The two men implored Daisy to let them take Hank to the Moose Saloon for a nip or two. "Hank needs a chance to be there, Daisy," they begged. "We'll give him a chance to celebrate with all his friends, and they'll all celebrate with him!"

"Come on, Daisy," Big Jack implored. "We'll watch him like a hawk."

She was helpless before their exuberance and their wish to share the evening with Hank. "Oh, go ahead and hit the saloons if you must!" Smiling, she shook her head and kissed Hank on top of his messed up hair. "But don't you dare bring him home drunk!" Laughing, she gave him a swat where she had just kissed him. "I mean it! You guys behave!"

They went, *like three school boys,* she thought as she watched them head down Main Avenue toward the milling crowds of filled St. Louis Avenue.

As she straightened the kitchen and readied her equipment for the morning's baking, Hank filled her mind. She had seen him rise from his chair, walk forward, and stand there, legs firmly spread beneath him to support his weight, the only thought in his mind at that moment to encourage young Frank. He had no consciousness of his own limitations at that moment.

How she had prayed for his recovery! How Hank and Big Jack had worked on those wounded legs! How Hank had struggled to keep his spirits high and his disappointments at bay! Her mind held on to the vision of Hank, on his feet while slowly stepping forward, looking as though he could take on the world. Healing was taking place, the strength of his muscles could be restored. God really did hear—and answer—prayers.

Pastor Jenson had shared one of his favorite scripture verses with her during one of his visits. "Don't be afraid! Only believe"—the words Jesus said to Jairus, Mark 5:36, as they set out together to heal Jairus's dying daughter. Pastor Jenson explained how Jairus risked his position and reputation to come to Jesus. Jesus must have seen the deep need in Jairus's eyes as they set out for Jairus's home. Before they arrived, the news that the little girl had already died reached them. That was when Jesus spoke said to the grieving father, saying, "Don't be afraid, only believe!" And they kept on going.

That was not the end of the story. Not to be deterred, Jesus placed his arm about the shoulder of the grieving father, and they pressed on until they arrived at Jairus's home where the mourners met them at the door. Weeping and wailing, they blocked the door. Yet Jesus, with Jairus still at his side, brushed them aside and entered his house.

Going straight to the girl's room, Jesus saw the twelve-year-old pale and lifeless on her couch. With the parents weeping behind him and his three companions off to the side, Jesus moved closer and took the girl's hand in his. After a moment, he gently called to her, "Little girl, I say to you—arise!"

Her eyelids fluttered, then opened. Curiously she looked at those who surrounded her. She raised her head from her pillow, then sat up. And—miracle of miracles—she came back to the parents who loved her. Daisy could picture it all in her mind and treasured the account of this event in the life of Jesus.

How desperately Daisy wanted healing for Hank, not to make her life easier, but to give back to Hank the life he had so loved and enjoyed. What such a miracle would do for Henry and Big Jack and Mrs. Brush and Maggie and all the friends who lifted Hank up day after day. Daisy hung onto that verse for dear life, only occasionally finding herself afraid—for Hank, for Henry, even for herself.

She stepped outside, pulled her crocheted shawl about her and breathed in the cool fresh evening air that foretold of cooler months to come. The lights of the Island's main street illuminated her view as she looked to the south and the town beyond. These past months on the Island had been a blessing in many ways. More friends than she could number had come to their aid. Henry was thriving on the work at the stables and with positive influences surrounding him.

Most of all she loved observing the interaction between Henry and his father. Hardly a day passed when they didn't spend time together, one teaching, the other listening and learning. What a gift it was for a young boy, soon to arrive at the portals of manhood, to learn the ways of the world from a man with such strength and character.

And Mrs. Brush was Daisy's constant friend and advocate, a surrogate mother in many regards. Even though the elderly woman was frail and growing more dependant on Daisy and Henry's help, she infused them with confidence and good advice and encouragement. Each time Old Syd drew the carriage up to the little house and helped Mrs. Brush into the big rocker in the Larsons' living room, Daisy felt a great sense of relief that someone truly cared about their family and loved them unconditionally as Mrs. Brush did. Daisy needed that sense of security. The loss of her family still pained her in ways that she found difficult to explain, even to herself.

Daisy gazed above her where stars shone in brilliant relief against the black velvet night. Henry came up the road from the boarding house, where he had been working in the kitchen. Whistling as he scuffed his bare feet in the dust of the road, she waited for him, listening. When he came alongside her—almost a head taller than she was—he put his arm about her shoulders. Together they entered the little house that had become such a warm and secure home for the three of them.

Daisy readied herself for bed and prepared a snack for Henry before he entered the storeroom for the night. Then, wrapping herself in a quilt, she settled herself in the big rocker to await Hank, ready to hear the tales of the adventures the three men encountered as they joined in the celebrations all over the Island.

Still awake—barely—she heard them, laughing and talking, making their way up Main Street and through her front door. They sounded very pleased with themselves, and that made her smile.

∞15∞
Autumn

LUMBERJACK DAYS HAD BEEN wildly successful. Reports that all outstanding events had been won by local lumberjacks were on everyone's lips for many days afterwards. Paul Bunyan was swiftly brushed aside as a legendary hero while Frank Shaw took his place, along with Samuel Berg and Big Jack Swanson—hometown men who had made their mark in the annals of loggers of the past. Not every day was a legend created.

"Could you believe it? Did you see Hank stand up by the pond? All by himself!" Hank's friends could not stop talking about his moment of accomplishment and what a difference it seemed to make in his attitude as well as his view of the future.

The doctors who had examined Hank after his injury came over to the Island, wanting to observe just what had taken place. Their early diagnosis of an injured spinal cord seemed to fit the healing that had taken place. Hank was only too happy to demonstrate the growing strength in his legs.

"Mr. Larson, we can't tell you how pleased we are to see your marvelous recovery."

Hank no longer hesitateed to try to stand by himself. Sometimes he looked very secure as he rose, and on other attempts Henry was there to steady him if he appeared unable to feel secure by himself.

Autumn was in the air. Golden patches of birch leaves were set like jewels among the deep green of the pines. The sun continued to warm the days, but the nights brought coolness with more than a hint of fall. The Island still swarmed with mill workers and loggers as the sun closed the day earlier and earlier.

Oscar often visited the Island. He, Henry, and Maggie liked fishing off the small dock north of the Larson home. Now that Oscar had become a regular visitor at their home, Daisy saw changes in his demeanor. A calmer, more self-possessed attitude began to emerge. Laughter seemed to come more easily now as he and Henry listened to Hank's wild tales about days in the woods. A smile suited Oscar's young face.

Daisy noted a wistful expression slip onto Oscar's face as he looked from one laughing logger to the next. The men were rough but kind, unkempt but appealing, strong yet gentle. Daisy guessed Oscar longed to have a father something like one of these men, for they often would include him in conversations and always appreciated the occasional comments he would add. They treated him like a "young man," and that is what he desperately tried to be.

One evening in late August the three young fishermen stayed longer than usual on the dock and came in with several fish that Frank helped them clean. By the time the fish were cleaned and in the ice box, Oscar started out for home much later than usual. Henry and Maggie were given permission to accompany him to the bridge to see that Oscar made it safely to the shore of the town.

The Island was alive with activity. Flickering lights over the doors of the saloons cast shadows down the steps to the dusty street below as customers filled the saloons and sat or stood on the wooden walkways beneath the canvas awnings. The volume of talking, singing, hollering, and cheering was high.

As the three young people neared the bridge, they prepared to bid their friend good night. Maggie suddenly halted and stood still. "Listen!" she said. "Do you hear that? Someone's calling for help!"

They paused, listened carefully, and determined that whoever was calling was near the shore. Carefully they made their way over the railroad tracks leading to the large canyons of stacked lumber stored on the east end of the Island and then through the long grass covering the southern shore. The call was weak, but became clearer as they neared the river.

With the lights of the saloons behind them, darkness surrounded them as they combed through the matted grass, finding nothing. The call seemed to melt away in the night, and then Oscar excitedly called to his friends. "Look!" He pointed. "There's something floating in the river!!"

Within a fraction of a second the three youngsters discerned a body, a man caught in the flowing current of the river, his arms grasping for a hold in the tall grass growing near the river's edge. Henry leaped into the river to steady the man while Oscar and Maggie each grabbed an arm and began pulling the man onto the shore, where they placed him gently on the grass.

"Help me!" the man implored weakly. "I've been stabbed!" He indicated a slash through the fabric of his wet, clinging shirt, where blood now stained his arm and covered his chest. Oscar stood up quickly and set out at a run for the nearest saloon.

Maggie and Henry stayed with the man. "Help's coming! Hang on and we'll get you to a doctor," they told him. The blood continued to flow from the wound in his chest as the man slowly closed his eyes and let his head drop into the grass.

"Don't die," shouted Henry. "Keep breathing!" The two children looked at each other with fear in their eyes.

Within minutes Oscar returned with several men who quickly took charge of the situation. The police chief soon arrived and demanded to know what had taken place. He listened intently to the explanation given by the three young people and commended them for their quick response.

"If you three hadn't come along when you did, this guy would probably have floated downriver," he said. The chief patted the three "heroes" on the back. "Good work!"

Loggers from the saloons chimed in, relating an account of an earlier fistfight between the injured man and a bar customer with whom they were not acquainted. The stranger was thought to have come from a camp some distance northwest of town.

"Never saw the guy before!" commented one logger. "Not from these parts—I'm sure of that!"

Another tipsy saloon regular chimed in, waving his mug to make his point. "He was one hell of a tough looking character! Scars on his face, so he must have been used to fighting with a knife!"

Several more witnesses added information for the chief of police. It appeared that both men had been drinking heavily and took to insulting each other. That led to physical confrontation, and things quickly got out of control. Becoming annoyed at the ruckus, the crowd at the bar told the two men in no uncertain terms to stop fighting or leave.

Thus, no one paid much attention when the men took their fight into the street. Not one bystander was able to give witness to the actual stabbing. The injured man was a familiar patron of the saloon, according to the lumberjacks now clustered about the river shore. The attacker had evidently taken flight over the north bridgee.

The injured mill worker, Willard Scheibe, called out in agony. He twisted in pain and gasped for air. As the men wrapped him in a blanket and loaded him into a wagon to take him to the hospital, he slipped into unconsciousness. Others remained by the river. They were puzzled and wondered who the missing violent man could be. No one seemed to know him or recall ever seeing the mysterious attacker before.

Soon the onlookers wandered back to the saloons to refill their glasses and recreate the events of the night in a multitude of scenarios. The three young heroes stood there, cold and damp, plus somewhat in shock. The reality of what had just occurred flooded their minds. How would they explain their muddy, wet, blood-stained clothes to their parents? Oscar was in turmoil. How could he justify being so close to the saloons at this late hour?

Henry and Maggie would be fine. He, however, would be in big trouble once his father got a look at his soiled clothes. Not only was Oscar late, but here he was on the Island in the middle of an attempted murder. In his father's standard of proper deportment, this fell off of the bottom of the page. A knot of anxiety began to fill Oscar's stomach.

After the saloon patrons left, the three friends stood anxiously at the bridge. The night had quieted. "Do you want us to walk you partway home?" Henry asked.

Oscar refused their kind offer and assured them he would be fine. "I can run like the wind," he told them, "and be home in a flash. I'll be just fine."

Maggie hugged him, while Oscar and Henry did the manly thing and struck each other on the back. Then Oscar took off running, crossing the red bridge and mounting the hill beyond. His two friends tried to watch him as he raced through the glow of street lamps.

Henry and Maggie started down the dusty street in front of the saloons, then broke into a run up Main Avenue, knowing warmth awaited them in their own homes. The lights of the Island glowed behind them as they plunged into the darkness of the northern shore of the Island.

All three parents were waiting in the shadows at the northern edge of Main Street, gazing intently towards the commotion erupting on St. Louis Avenue. Their children should have returned home by then. Big Jack was prepared to head down the street and find out just what was going on. Then, through the glow of the single street light illuminating the gravel street leading to their homes, they could see two figures running toward them. The parents waited, then enfolded the anxious children in their arms, and all of them entered the warmth of the Larson home.

The events of the night spilled from the two children. Both fathers knew Willard Scheibe and thought well of him. Neither had any idea of who the assailant could be. They commended their children, still noticeably upset from their ordeal. Hank placed his arm about Henry's shoulders. "You did a fine thing tonight, Henry. I'm very proud of you!"

Maggie's father's stroked her head, smoothing the wisps of hair loosened during her crawl through the brush and her wild run home. She lay her head upon his wide shoulder.

Daisy set a plate of brownies in front of everyone and in a flash they disappeared. The Swansons soon headed across the street to the boarding house and the Larsons readied themselves for sleep. Henry washed away the mud and blood. It was a relief when he crawled into his bed, where he fell asleep as soon as his head hit the pillow.

Daisy retired, adjusted the lightweight quilt over her body, and nestled close behind Hank. He made her feel warm and safe, even though she felt apprehensive about the events of the night. He rolled over to face her, folded her slender body into his strong arms. Together they thanked God that no harm had come to their beloved son.

Oscar, on the other hand, made it home and immediately crept up to the garage to see if his father's car was inside. Thank God, it wasn't there, so Oscar was safe for the moment. Silently opening the back door, he removed his shoes and proceeded up the back steps, being careful to skip the steps known to creak. His mother's light was out, and he could hear her even breathing from the hall. Taking only a moment to remove the telltale bloodstained clothes, he shoved them under his mattress.

I'll take care of them in the morning. Right now I have to get in bed and look asleep before my father climbs the stairs. He smiled as he pulled up the quilt. *What a crazy night! We were heroes!* The smile quickly faded. *I hope the man doesn't die from that bloody wound!*

Suddenly, he heard the garage door open. He covered his head, hardly breathing until all was still.

Before the sliver of a moon disappeared and the morning sun broke over the tops of the pines, reports of the attempted murder had traveled over the Island and through

Cloquet, as well. By all reports Willard Scheibe had barely survived the attack and was now being treated in the hospital. Rumor had it Pastor Jenson had been awakened in the middle of the night and made a pastoral call on the severely wounded man.

While Willard's friend Carl waited in the lobby of the hospital, Michael stood at the bedside of the wounded man, who lay pale and still, bandages covering the side of his head where he had received a blow with a blunt object, and his upper chest and shoulder where the knife had cut a long, jagged gash. The nurse smiled quietly at the young pastor, indicated a chair near the bed and left the room on silent leather soles.

Michael pulled the chair closer, putting him nearer the wounded man, and spoke softly into his ear. The pastor looked at the man, a person in need, a sinner like all the rest of humanity, redeemed by the love of Jesus Christ who gave his life as "a ransom for many." He reached out, gently resting his hand on the lean-muscled forearm. The eyelids opened slightly and clouded eyes met Michael's gentle eyes and held a brief moment. Willard saw a man, much his same age, with a kind, earnest face and large hands. Silence filled the room, and a sort of peace washed over him. He closed his eyes and waited.

Michael said, "Your friend came to me because many people care about you. They're thinking of you this very moment and will soon come to your bed and support you as you recover." Michael paused and took out his Greek New Testament, where he turned to a particular section of well-worn pages. "I'd like to read these verses to you and let you know that as you lie in this bed and struggle for recovery, you're never alone. Will you listen?"

The pain-filled eyes closed briefly, then opened. Michael's hand still rested on his arm. He said, "Here's an invitation from Jesus himself—just for you. Listen carefully. 'Come unto me, all ye that labor and are heavy laden, and I will give you rest. Take my yoke upon you and learn of me; for I am meek and lowly in heart; and ye shall find rest unto your souls.'" Pastor Jenson leaned closer to Willard's ear. "Lean back in the strong arms of Jesus Christ and let his rest and peace and healing fill your body and soul."

The pastor's hand moved down to the wounded man's, carefully taking it into the warmth of his own as he prayed for healing, peace, forgiveness. Then it grew quiet, their hands still joined. The wounded man felt the pressure of the pastor's hand and responded weakly. "Thank you," he whispered softly. "Help me—help me to live," and Pastor Jenson reassured him he would certainly do that—and he would return soon.

The hand relaxed and the eyes closed, yet Pastor Jenson remained beside the bed until he was sure Willard was peacefully asleep. Then he carefully slipped his hand away and placed the Greek New Testament back in his pocket

By mid-morning more accounts of the night's adventure had spread. "Did you hear three kids found the guy? Where were the parents? Why weren't they responsible and keeping track of their children? Those Island kids are nothing but trash!"

"Willard was one lucky son of a gun those three kids found him. Otherwise I bet we would have found his body floating somewhere down the river after a week or so!"

"I heard more murders take place on the Island, but the sheriff's paid to keep them under cover! I wouldn't step foot across the red bridge if I were paid to do it!"

"Can you believe that Mr. Lund, the president of the bank, was called on the carpet by the police because his boy Oscar was the one who ran to the saloon and called for help? I'll wager Mr. Lund, who thinks he is better than everyone, took a strap to that son of his!"

"I hear Willard was almost dead when those kids found 'im. I'd be thankful they were out at that hour. Otherwise so long, Willard old buddy! They should have a reward!"

"Poor Hank Larson, as if he doesn't have enough to worry about, crippled and all. Now he has to deal with a son who chases around in the middle of the night with Big Jack's daughter! Girls have no business chasing around the Island in the middle of the night!"

The attempted murder was all anyone could talk about during the bank hours the next day. Mr. Lund was speechless when he heard the news. "Your son was practically a hero, Mr. Lund!" In the minds of many of the bank employees, Oscar deserved a medal. To them, saving a man's life was not a small matter.

Mr. Lund bit his tongue and said nothing during the course of the day as rumors swirled when customers came and went. The Island and its blight had once again darkened the purity of their fair city. And Oscar Lund had been right in the middle of it.

The bank president smiled grimly while catering to his depositors. Deep down, he grew more and more outraged and as the hours passed, mentally planned the vengeance he'd administer to the back of his son. *No one, especially my son, will bring shame to my name or put a blight on my fine reputation. No one will ever say I spared the rod and spoiled my child!* He slammed shut the ledger on his desk and ushered the final bank customer out the door. Banker's hours had finally come to an end.

Mr. Lund's "teaching" moment for his son took place in his darkened basement that very evening. Arriving home earlier than the usual hour and wasting no time, Mr. Lund stood at the foot of the ornate staircase and called for his son. "Oscar. Come down a moment. I'd like to talk to you about your recent adventure on the Island." He paused. "I heard all about it today. Many of my customers were impressed with you." He choked over the words as he said them, lies that they were.

Sensing a conciliatory tone in his father's voice, Oscar closed his book, rose from his desk, tucked his shirt neatly into his trousers, and descended the stairway to the hall below. His father waited there, his hand resting on the banister, his eyes riveted to the slender form of his approaching son.

Suddenly Mr. Lund's hand reached out, grabbed the collar of the boy's shirt and thrust him ahead of him down the narrow wooden steps to the dark, damp cellar. After pushing Oscar to the floor and standing over him, Mr. Lund removed his finely tailored suitcoat, lay it carefully across a chair, and rolled up his shirt sleeves. Oscar, berating himself for having even an ounce of trust in his father, soon stood shirtless, clutching the thick oak support beam that stood near the door to the fruit cellar. Soon he bore the marks of his "education"—made with his father's finely tooled leather belt. This was not the first time with the belt. But as the belt cut into his skin, Oscar vowed it certainly would be the last.

After the lash came the hurtful words. "You don't deserve to be my son! You made me a laughing stock in the community!" The belt struck, then struck again. "What am I to do with you and your shrinking violet of a mother?" More lashes cut into Oscar's back. "Is there no release from the likes of you two?" His arm tired, beads of sweat covering his brow, Mr. Lund finally stopped. The fine leather belt was returned to the tailored trousers.

Oscar slipped slowly to his knees, tears of anger and pain flowing silently down his cheeks. Mr. Lund adjusted his shirt sleeves and checked his cuff links. After slipping once again into his finely tailored coat, he turned and leaned over the boy huddled on the floor. "I hope you've learned your lesson. You will *not* associate with that Island trash ever again! Do you hear me?"

No movement of the boy's head gave the slightest assent to the command.

Mr. Lund turned and ascended the steps, where he found his wife kneeling by the basement door. Taking her arm, he led her to her fainting couch in the parlor where he roughly set her down, poured her a drink, and placed it in her trembling hand. "Now— that is the end of that! Tell the maid to serve our dinner. I've worked up quite an appetite!!"

And silently they sat, still as stone. Sitting leisurely in his leather chair, Mr. Lund drew heavily on his cigarette and, with the aromatic smoke circling his head, gazed casually out the nearby window. Unable to even look at her husband, Mrs. Lund slowly sipped her drink and tried to hold back her tears, while waiting to be summoned to the dining room.

In the basement, Oscar wrapped his shirt about his wounded shoulders and rose. The welts smarted and bled. He sought the refuge of his room where he could tend to his back. As he slowly climbed the stairs to the main floor, just hearing his father's voice in the parlor made him sick to his stomach. Slipping quietly through the pantry, keeping out of sight of the maids in the kitchen, Oscar headed for the stairway to the sanctuary of his own room.

He was ashamed of his weakness, wished he were bigger and stronger, that he could put into words all his thoughts and feeling and smash his fist into his father's face.

After washing and drying his back, he slipped on a soft well-worn flannel nightshirt before climbing into bed. Of course he'd had no supper. Food would have to wait until morning. Lying on his stomach, to spare himself the pain of the wounds on his back, he thought of his friends, certain they'd been better received into their homes than he had.

Oscar had not had contact with Henry or with Maggie since he'd run home the night before. He vowed he'd be out of the house in the morning before either of his parents awoke. No matter what his father said or how much he was punished, Oscar would be with his friends. In the warmth of the Larsons' kitchen—that's where he wanted to be. Then he would feel better.

The headline, in bold print, covered the front page of the local newspaper two days later: BRAVERY OF LOCAL YOUNGSTERS SAVES LIFE OF LOCAL MAN. The article that followed extolled, in great detail, the valor and quick thinking of Henry, Maggie, and Oscar, how they'd found, rescued, and secured help for the wounded man. Suddenly they were heroes to everyone—with the exception of Mr. Arthur Lund, president of the local bank. If anyone commented to him on the bravery of his son, he quickly waved them aside and buried his head in his accounts and investments. He never mentioned the incident to Oscar again. And Oscar stood resolute as he came and went to and from the Island as he willed. All in all, the whole affair turned out to be a positive thing, except perhaps the memories of the beating that Oscar constantly pushed to the back of his mind.

SCHOOL STARTED THE FIRST WEEK of September. Days were still warm, almost too nice for youngsters to sit inside stuffy classrooms to learn grammar and solve math problems. Garfield Elementary School was the destination for Henry, Maggie, and Oscar—*just like the three musketeers,* thought Henry, who still read books from Mrs. Brush's library. They seemed to have safety in numbers this year, as the three friends entered their final year of elementary school.

They felt confident. All three were bright, motivated and eager to learn. Plus, after just recently being hailed as heroes and rather enjoying their moment of fame, they were ready to prove to the community that "Island trash" was not an option for them. Even Oscar, who didn't live on the Island, had been put in this category by his fellow classmates because of his association with Henry and Maggie. The "Three Musketeers" set goals for themselves while making plans for the coming year.

Miss Thoreson was to be their teacher. Former students from her class told about her sense of humor. They listed the interesting projects she planned for her class. While her strictness was always tempered by fairness, she would not stand for a smart mouth or disrespect. All in all, this school year might be an outstanding year for all three of them.

So the day came when Henry bid his parents goodbye, picked up his lunch pail, and started up the road where Maggie waited for him in front of the boarding house. Both students wore their best everyday clothes. Henry's shirt was tucked into his knickers, his hair parted and combed to the side. However, this only lasted a short time as the breeze caught at his hair as soon as they reached the bridge. Having run barefoot all summer, his feet complained about being confined in thick socks and new, heavy, laced-up boots.

Maggie had pulled back her long, dark hair and fashioned it into one thick braid down her back. Henry had to subdue his surprise when he first saw her on the porch—in a dress. Maggie wasn't exactly a "dress" kind of girl, but her father had insisted she put away her overalls for school. She put her foot down at the prospect of a ribbon at the end of her braid. That was just going too far, she told her father.

As she stepped down from the porch, she, too, walked gingerly, her freedom-loving feet tucked into slightly more feminine black lace-up boots. Together they set out to meet Oscar on the corner nearest his home before the three of them made their way to the waiting doors of Garfield School and sixth grade.

September and October brought beautiful weather. Trees lining the river turned brilliant shades of scarlet, russet, gold, and umber. Even the avenues of the town were gilded with vibrant color. The Indian summer of 1917 was exceptional.

✺16✺
Parish Life

B Y EARLY SEPTEMBER, the fall schedule of the Norwegian Lutheran Church was in high gear and eagerly embraced by Pastor Jenson. Numerous house calls had been made on potential new members. Michael always enjoyed face-to-face contact with the people. And once the families joined the church, they were left with the feeling that both the pastor and the congregation were warm and welcoming.

Michael also enjoyed contact with long-time members. He still turned up in backyards in his work clothes, the proper tools in hand to meet the needs of those living there. He raked leaves, cut kindling, washed and hung storm windows. Sometimes the elderly men would protest, but they were soon quieted by Michael's assurance that he enjoyed the work and would certainly appreciate a cup of coffee when the chore was completed.

Church attendance had grown. He loved preparing for the mornings he most often spent alone in his office. Shaving, washing up, dressing in the freshly pressed shirts provided by Mrs. Berg, drinking a large glass of milk, cutting a hefty piece of Daisy Larson's homemade bread—and he was ready. After closing but never locking the front door of the parsonage, he briskly walked to his office where he stored his ever-growing library.

As was his custom, he started the day with a healthy dose of scripture, since he was working his way once again through the Bible. Having just completed his journey through the Old Testament (where there was much sinning, killing, worshipping idols, prophecies of death and destruction), he took pleasure in studying the words and actions of Jesus Christ as He traveled the dusty roads of Palestine, preaching and healing and loving everyone those many centuries ago. He paid special attention to the vital aspects of Jesus' ministry. He wrote them down and always kept that list, his "Necessities for Ministry," in his vest pocket.

1. Always look at people with eyes that see them in a positive light and desire only the best for each individual.
2. Never be afraid to stand up for what you believe and do the right action called for at any given time.
3. Be willing to forgive anyone who seeks your forgiveness after wronging you by word or deed.

A short, simple list, but one that would be a challenge for even the best of Christians.

Way back in June, when he first arrived at the church, Michael had placed his sealed letter from the district president under the lamp on the desk when he first organized his office. Three months passed quickly by the time he remembered the envelope. Curiosity had often tugged at him, but he held true to his promise and left the envelope unopened. Suddenly, it was already September—time for him to read the letter.

This morning, however, Michael needed a quiet moment to contemplate an event that occurred at the close of service the previous Sunday. The memory troubled him, and he desired to deal with it in the most positive and nonjudgmental manner. He felt anger rise, though. And it wasn't a righteous anger. He felt for his list, trying not to settle on a reaction.

Michael always enjoyed his visits to the Island, either at the Larsons or at the boarding house. While he visited with them, he always invited them to Sunday services. Hank didn't yet feel secure with the sanctuary steps, and Big Jack was always in the midst of serving breakfast, but Henry and Maggie told him they'd be in church the following Sunday.

When Michael entered the sanctuary, his gaze swept over the rows of expectant people before him. In the back pew he saw the two smiling faces of his young friends. A grin spread over his face, to which the entire congregation seated before him responded, each taking it personally and smiling back at their well-loved pastor.

The service went well. The organist only hit a very few sour notes and the hymn singing was enthusiastic. Michael preached on the moment in Jesus' ministry when the disciples tried to keep children from approaching Him. "Let the children come unto me!" was the theme of the service, for Sunday School classes would now meet after the church service and continue for the school year.

At the close of the service, the Sunday School children followed the volunteer teachers down the aisle to the basement classrooms. Michael, at the front of the church, shook their eager little hands as he directed all the energetic young students down the stairs.

Members visited inside and outside the church. The autumn day was perfect—the sun warm, the breeze fresh. Michael could see Henry and Maggie as they waited for him to stop by the last pew. Taking his time, he visited with several members while making his way to the final pew. There, he grinned widely at his two young friends.

His grin disappeared. Maggie had her head down and tears cascading over her cheeks. Henry had his arm about her shoulders and was speaking gently into her ear. His face was flushed and his eyes, when they looked up were hard and angry.

"What's happened here? Why's Maggie crying?" When neither answered him, Michael took the youngsters' hands and led them up the aisle and into his study at the rear of the church. Once seated across from his desk, Michael demanded to know what was wrong. "I need to know what's making you cry, Maggie. And what in the world is making you so angry, Henry?" He leaned toward them, speaking firmly, and asked once again. "What happened back there to upset both of you? This is my church, and I need to know."

"Maggie and I planned for days that we would come to the church service on the first day of Sunday School. We were looking forward to the singing and hearing you preach." Henry paused before he continued with his sad tale. "We loved being here in your church," he said, "until that lady—I don't know her name, but I've seen her when we made deliveries—came up to stand in front of us. We both looked up, expecting her to talk to us like you talk to us—friendly like. She was a pretty lady, kind of young, but she had tears running down her cheeks. Then she leaned across the back of the pew in front of us and talked right into Maggie's face. She talked so loud it made her spit land on Maggie's face!"

Michael knew anyone leaning over the pew would have been nose to nose with Maggie. "Tell me what she said," the pastor said quietly.

Henry swallowed. "She said, 'You two can get all cleaned up, curl your hair all you want, put on a fancy dress with a red sash, but inside you'll always be Island trash, and you'll never be good enough to be a member of this church!' Then she stood up, fixed her hat, and walked out the door." Henry looked squarely into Michael's eyes. "I thought Christians were supposed to love one another."

Pastor Jenson felt the pain and disappointment of his two young friends long after they had left his office. Even three days later, he still felt his anger rise when he thought of the woman who had inflicted such an insult onto undeserving children. He knew he had to deal with his own anger before he could confront the person who spoke such unkind words in the Lord's sanctuary. Finding it difficult to concentrate on the task before him, he grabbed his jacket and took a walk.

He knew exactly who had uttered those biting words. In fact, he could visualize her just as if he'd been eye witness to the affair. He had noticed her in the back of the church last Sunday as he was helping students find their way to the church basement. She was usually by herself and seldom shared fellowship with other members after service. Bertha Ness. He had often sought her out as people exited the church, wanting to make sure she had felt welcomed and included in the mix who lingered to visit. She always seemed in a hurry to leave but was usually seated in her "family" pew by the time the service was to begin.

He had heard about Miss Ness from Mrs. Berg, who was only too happy to fill in the personal details pertaining to anyone within a five miles of the town. At times Mrs. Berg was very helpful; other times she trespassed on other people's lives, causing him to raise his hand to halt her discourse, much to her dismay.

According to Mrs. Berg's narrative and his memory, Miss Ness lived alone in a lovely home once occupied by her parents. Both her siblings had married and moved away. The man she was to have married this past June, Mr. Joshua Rajala, had been employed as a bookkeeper and cruiser of standing timber at a nearby logging camp. While estimating the board feet of a load of logs being stacked on a sleigh, he was killed in a logging accident.

Josh Rajala, an expert at his job, was able to quote the number of board feet contained in a large load or stand of timber just by taking a few measurements. He always carried *The Woodsman's Handbook*, by Henry Graves, in his back pocket, and referred often to the charts and formulas there.

A rumor circulated through the camp and city that the four loggers responsible for chaining down that particular load of logs had been drinking on the job. Their judgment wasn't what it should have been. Josh Rajala had been standing by the sled as it was being loaded, his record book and pen in hand, when insufficient chains suddenly snapped or pulleys malfunctioned or the lumberjacks made an error in judgement, causing the load to explode off the sled and roll in all directions, crushing the man with whom Bertha Ness planned to spend the rest of her life.

Bertha took to her bed for a week after being notified of his death. Only the desire to be at his funeral brought her to her feet. Still grieving, Bertha carried Josh Rajala's copy of *The Woodsman's Handbook* in her handbag.

The final report by the director of the logging camp confirmed the crew operating the sled and lift had been "impaired." The men were promptly fired and sent to the Island, without pay, to fend for themselves for the remainder of the winter.

Residents of the Island were held in great contempt by Miss Ness because of this, and with Lumberjack Days recently celebrated, the sad event was fresh in her mind, and she had lashed out at the innocent children she knew to be from the Island.

Pastor Jenson soon found himself standing on the porch of Bertha's imposing two-story home. As he raised his hand to knock, the door suddenly opened, and he faced a tall, slender woman. Opening the door wider, she motioned him to enter and said quietly, "I'm pleased to see you. I have expected your visit."

No one ever knew what transpired behind the ornate oak door. Neighbors were curious, of course, for a pastoral call was always of interest. A casual observer might have noted Bertha and Pastor Jenson as they came out onto the porch a while later. Pastor Jenson took Bertha's hand, as though a pact—or a covenant—had been made. He descended the steps and set off down the street with a broad stride. Bertha remained alone on the porch, watching the pastor leave. Then she went back into her home and closed the door.

After one more call, Michael returned to the church and once again seated himself behind his cluttered desk, feeling he had accomplished two monumental achievements. Second in importance was seeing how well it was working for Willard Schiebe to be boarding temporarily at the home of Mrs. Berg. Being Samuel's friend had been the stimulus prompting Mrs. Berg to invite Willard to stay at her home until he was well enough to return to the Island and his room at Big Jack's boarding house.

The slash along his upper chest and shoulder was healing slowly. The less he used his arm and shoulder, the quicker it would heal. Willard's assailant had never been identified.

And Samuel seemed to growing fonder of his usually straight-laced mother, especially as he watched her care for his injured friend.

When Pastor Jenson visited there shortly before returning to his office, he found Willard propped up in Samuel's former bed. Mrs. Berg had sponged off his face and hands and fluffed up his pillows. She insisted she be allowed to give him a shave and even entered the room with the shaving cup, brush, and razor freshly sharpened. After one glance at the shiny razor, Willard thought she looked just a bit too eager to come at him with such a sharp object. "I sure do appreciate your caring for me like this, Mrs. Berg," he said, raising a hand in defense of his whiskers. "But I'll just call this growth a bit of a head start on the beard I'll need in the woods this winter!"

"Really! Well, I don't want to force anything upon you." Shaking her head, she deferred to his protests and left with slightly hurt feelings, only to return with a bowl of steaming hot oatmeal swimming in cream with a healthy dose of brown sugar sprinkled on top. Willard's right hand and shoulder were bandaged, so Mrs. Berg pulled up a chair next to the bed, covered her ample lap with a towel, and proceeded to spoon the oatmeal into his protesting lips. He soon quieted as the warmth of the oatmeal flowed into his belly.

Michael had to work hard not to grin as he observed the whole procedure. Mrs. Berg had gifts that came as a surprise to him the longer he knew this interesting woman. One more week of Mrs. Berg's careful attention and Willard would no longer be treated like a royal visitor. He would be back on the Island in his room at Big Jack's.

His earlier visit to Bertha Ness, too, felt as if Jesus Christ had led him in the proper response to what she had done. His heart was touched by her realization of how the words she had uttered had cut at the hearts of the two young people. With tears in her eyes, she confessed she hadn't known how to go about asking for forgiveness—and then Michael had knocked at her door.

He sat at her kitchen table observing her as she moved about her kitchen. She moved with precision and purpose. Her curly hair had an auburn cast and escaped from the braid and combs trying to restrain it. When she spoke she looked him in his eyes, never glancing down in shame or contrition. She knew exactly how cruel her words had been.

He had never called on her before this and was sorry he'd waited so long. As they visited, Michael found it evident how deeply she still grieved Josh Rajala's untimely death. Knowing she was past her prime, being over thirty years old, Josh had came into her life like a gift from God. He, too, had not yet married and was approaching forty. Miracle of miracles, the two of them looked forward to a future as man and wife and, perhaps, even with the gift of children.

Then, that dream had been taken from her. She had nowhere else to place blame for that reversal until she focused on the life style of the lumberjacks who frequented the Island and worked in the logging camps.

As she entered the church the previous Sunday, she recognized the children in the back pew from the recent article in the paper. She knew they both lived on the Island. Reports through town told of the wild, intemperate behavior of those who flocked to the Island.

"I don't know what came over me," she said softly. "Suddenly, the children symbolized the behavior of everyone on the Island. All I could see were the drunken men responsible for the death of my beloved Joshua." While she poured out her heart, tears coursed her cheeks. She tried to staunch them with a lace hanky. "I truly loved my Joshua—and he often told me how much he loved me."

She paused to compose herself. "We so wanted a family!" She took a deep breath. "And those little children you sent down to Sunday School," she choked on the words, "I won't ever be able to have such lovely children." She buried her face in her hands.

Michael was touched by her grief. Inspiration came. He took out his Greek New Testament and turned to Mark 9:36-37. "May I share some scripture with you?" he asked.

She nodded, and he began. "And Jesus took a child, and set him in the midst of them; when he had taken him in his arms, he said unto them, 'Whoever shall receive one of such children in my name, receiveth me; and whosoever shall receive me, receives not me, but Him who sent me.'"

Michael paused, then commented, "When we care for another person when they are young—like a child—or are incapable of caring for themselves, we're literally caring for Jesus Christ. As adults we're responsible to care for those who cannot fully care for themselves. A child is a perfect example. They need our example, instruction, our love and care. Perhaps we can do nothing better with our lives than to receive a child in Christ's name."

She slowly reached for his hand and together they prayed—and the plan that was to change Bertha's life began to take root in Pastor Jenson's mind.

Michael leaned forward in his desk chair and began preparation for next Sunday's sermon. The designated text for that particular Sunday would be set aside and the verses he had read to Bertha would be substituted. A pastor could never spend too much time speaking about children or how they were formed into loving, dedicated Christian adults. Suddenly his mind was full of ideas. He loved when the Spirit filled his mind with possibilities. Smiling broadly, he readied his paper and dipped his pen.

Later, Pastor Jenson walked briskly through the cool autumn afternoon down the main street, over the red bridge, up Main Avenue. He soon came to the Larsons' front door. He knocked. Hank opened it, standing alone, supported by a single cane. He looked wonderful. Michael couldn't restrain himself from giving the man a masculine hug. They both laughed, parted, and Michael seated himself in front of Hank's comfortable rocker.

Very little small talk elapsed before Hank brought up the insult the two children had endured in church. As a father, Hank's heart was troubled when his son was sad. Michael began to explain what had taken place and the emotions behind the verbal attack.

After Michael talked about Bertha and her loss, Hank looked intently at Michael. He rose from his chair and turned to the window. "Josh Rajala and I often worked together in the logging camps. Big Jack was his friend, too. We loggers become close marooned in the woods an entire winter. Josh was a very smart guy, honest as the day was long, and a great friend." He paused. "I knew he was engaged to be married come spring. He spoke of his bride-to-be often, and how much he looked forward to starting a life with her. I'd never met her, but looked forward to getting together with them after they were married."

He turned to face the pastor. "Then after my accident I lost touch with many of the men I knew from the camps. I couldn't go to the visitation or the funeral. I just didn't have the strength." He sat down once again in his chair and held his head in his hands.

Daisy joined them, wiping her flour-covered hands on her apron as she took a chair next to Hank. Seeing how distraught he seemed to be, she gently placed her arm about his shoulders. She looked inquiringly at Pastor Jenson, wondering what was going on.

Hank said, "We must do something for Bertha Ness to help her deal with Josh's death. I'm so sorry I haven't gone to see her. I just didn't know her—but I should have been there for her, for Josh's sake. He was my friend and I didn't reach out to his family or loved ones. I'm ashamed of myself!"

Pastor Jenson related the details of his visit with Bertha Ness. Michael had formed a plan to bring forgiveness and healing to all the people involved in this unhappy incident. Before he could describe his solution, Daisy interrupted him. She clasped her flour-covered towel to her breast and said, "Could we invite Miss Ness to our home? We would be grateful to meet her and introduce her to the Swansons. She could get to know all of us. Most people seem to like us," she added with a grin.

Michael threw back his head and laughed. "That was my plan exactly!" And thus the pain and anger of the whole event had been transformed into an act of reaching out and sweetening the air with forgiveness.

Hank said, "I'll feel much better if I can meet Bertha and tell her how much Josh meant to me. I have stories I can share with her. Some should make her laugh!" Just thinking about them brought a smile to his face.

Thus the plan was put in motion.

Big Jack and Maggie were informed, and both agreed they'd love to help plan the dinner. The day was set—next Sunday evening. They'd come over as soon as they were free of supper clean-up at the boarding house. Daisy would set the table and prepare the main dish, and Big Jack would bring his famous pies for dessert.

Pastor Jenson would be in charge of bringing their invitation to Miss Ness and assuring her these families—on the Island—would be honored to have her as a guest. Michael thought he might have the most difficult task. He knew if Bertha would come, she'd feel the love and forgiveness that flowed from these people.

Soon Pastor Jenson found himself again before Bertha's ornate oak door. He held out an invitation meticulously written in his best handwriting that spelled out the details of the dinner planned especially for her.

She read the card. She looked up into his face. She read the card a second time. When she looked up again, he saw her eyes had filled with tears. Her hand trembled, and she brought the card close to her breast where she held it with both hands. "I confess I've never set foot on the Island, yet, I'm honored to be invited to the Larsons' after my ill-mannered behavior. Please give my regards to these two families. Tell them I eagerly await my visit. Their hospitality is exceptional."

She smiled, and they made arrangements for the following Sunday. The pastor would call for her at 6:30 p.m. She'd have a carriage ready so he could drive them over the bridge to the Island. That would certainly give the neighbors something to talk about!

Michael returned to his office just as the sun began its descent, alive with reds and purples and golds. He gazed at the magnificent sunset before entering the silent church and making his way to his office. Inside he lit the lamp and returned to the task of finishing his sermon for Sunday. He felt on the verge of a real epiphany about the text for Sunday—Mark 9: 36-37. He read them again. His *Biblical Commentary* said, "What this meant to the early church doubtless included the admonition to hospitality. Such charity rules out all thoughts of greatness. The highest possible social achievement will be to receive a child in Christ's name." The words flowed, mind to pen to paper. "Hospitality"—how perfect!

THE CHURCH SANCTUARY seemed to hold more and more worshipers as the weeks passed. This Sunday was no exception. Mrs. Berg sat in her usual place—second pew on the outside, next to the aisle. Samuel was there as well. Between the two sat Willard Schiebe.

Michael smiled observing his regular church members as they put themselves forward to shake hands with the two young men, making them feel welcome. Willard had become a celebrity of sorts since being attacked.

Michael usually stood by the front door of the church to personally welcome families and individuals as they climbed the steps. On this warm autumn day, he waited by the door a few seconds longer than usual, hoping Maggie and Henry would come. At last it was time to shut the door and go to the altar area where he would begin the service. Then he saw them running down the street trying not to be late. He brought them inside, where they slipped into the pew in the back of the church.

Striding to the altar, he gave the welcome and opening liturgy. His voice caught. Bertha Ness silently slipped into the church and took the outside seat of the last pew—right next to Henry and Maggie.

Michael spoke the familiar words that cleansed the sinner and spread the love of Jesus Christ to everyone. "Beloved in the Lord! Let us draw near with a true heart, and confess our sins unto God our Father, beseeching Him, in the Name of our Lord Jesus Christ, to grant us Forgiveness. Increase in us true knowledge of thee and of thy will. He hath given his only Son to die for us, and for his sake forgiveth us all our sins. Help, save, pity and defend us, O God, by thy grace."

During his sermon, Michael had all the younger children come to the front of the church. He stepped down from the pulpit and stood behind the little ones. "We all love these children. And when we receive them—when we love and care for them—we literally love and care for Jesus himself. That is what Jesus instructed us to do.

"Now imagine that those we are to love and care for are all grown up—and not as appealing as these beautiful children." He paused and his eyes swept the congregation. "In fact, these grown-ups might be downright difficult to love, much less care for. The command is still a command, even if the recipients are different. We are to love and care for others as though we cared for Jesus Himself."

He stretched out his arms as if to embrace all before him. "Again I repeat the words of Jesus—'If you have done it onto one of the least of these, you have done it onto me!' The key is how we look at the people who come into our lives. We must learn to see Jesus in the faces of people who need our help."

After the service, the little ones scrambled downstairs to Sunday School. Families milled about, talking to friends and catching up with events in the community. Michael always enjoyed this part of the day, where conversation flowed easily and the very atmosphere was hospitable. He made his way to the entry. The autumn breeze caught at his hair and his alb. He felt refreshed. He loved shaking hands—gently with the women, especially the elderly, and vigorously with the men who always clasped his hand as though they were wrestling one another. He could handle those farmers, mill workers, and lumberjacks.

Finally the last members had descended the steps and set off for home where they would enjoy their traditional Sunday dinner. Mrs. Berg had invited him over to share pot roast with Samuel, Willard, and herself, but he had declined. He wanted to focus on the gathering later that evening. After hanging up his gown and putting his sermon notes in his file cabinet, he stood for a moment looking out the window toward the Island.

He often thought the Island figuratively wore a "scarlet letter" blazoned across its shore. People were people, sinners all of them, and certainly the Island did not have a monopoly on the sinners of the area. During his short time serving this parish, Michael had met a great variety of "sinners," himself included.

Not living on the Island did not guarantee a person's "purity." He smiled while putting on his suit coat. He truly loved these people—the "publicans and the sinners"—and counted himself fortunate to live among such a diverse group of believers and non-believers. Challenges were never hard to find. Tonight would be no exception.

LATER THAT AFTERNOON, when the sun began its descent, a stiff wind tossed the remaining leaves into the air, fluttering them from yard to yard. Michael held onto his hat.

The horse and carriage were already parked in front of Bertha's house. She must have seen him coming, for she stepped out on the porch and closed the door behind her. She wore a blue silk scarf covering her braids, saving her hair from flying in all directions. A brightly colored shawl across her shoulders would fend off the cool night air. A black handbag hung from her arm. The bag appeared to contain more than its usual contents.

He took her hand and helped her to be seated. Bertha insisted Michael drive and, with a snap of the reins, he started the buggy toward the main street and the red bridge. Both of them knew that, even if they saw no one on the street, many eyes watched their departure and would fabricate tales about the pastor driving off with the maiden lady from the big house on the corner. All would have gasped in shock had they known their destination.

Much later, with moonlight shimmering on the dark river, Pastor Jenson and Bertha Ness clattered back over the red bridge on their return. Lamps from the saloons contrasted with the soft darkness of the town beyond.

After seeing his guest to her front door, Michael returned the horse and carriage to the livery. The stable hand was sound asleep on a bale of hay and not pleased to have his sleep interrupted. Seeing it was the pastor, he swallowed the swear words poised to spill from his lips and jumped up to be of assistance. Michael smiled and thanked him for his help.

With the wind at his back, Michael's walk home was brisk. He had given up on his hat and clutched it under his arm while his hair tossed about. A smile played about his lips, recalling the evening and the assortment of people positively affected by being together around a table. Taking the parsonage steps two at a time, he entered the dark, silent house.

Glowing lamp in hand, he climbed the stairs and made ready to close this Sabbath day with a final reading from his Greek New Testament. He really did love to read the scriptures in the Greek. He felt calmed by the mental discipline and the flow of the always unusual words. Plus, he always felt at peace once he completed his evening regimen, knowing a sound sleep would soon follow.

Meanwhile, Bertha prepared herself for bed. Nightgown on, she sat down at her vanity, undid her braids and began to brush her hair. She watched herself in the mirror and, for once, had to smile at what she saw reflected there. She tried to imagine what the Larsons and the Swansons had thought when they met. She replayed the entire evening in her mind as she brushed her auburn hair for at least one hundred strokes.

Her first shock of the evening occurred when the carriage crossed the red bridge and looked as though it was heading directly toward the Moose Saloon. Still early, not as many loggers and workers milled about as there'd be later in the evening. She was revolted those men still lived and drank when her beloved had been killed by such behavior. Some of the men waved to the pastor as he drove down St. Louis Avenue; some even came down the steps of wooden walkways and to shake Pastor Jenson's hand.

Word had spread through the loggers that Pastor Jenson had ministered to Willard Scheibe while he was in the hospital. Samuel Berg often spoken highly of the pastor as well, so Michael's "fame" had spread through the saloon community. He was held in high regard. Bertha watched in fascination as Michael reached over, shook hands, and made small talk with the rough men on the street. Michael politely introduced Bertha to them. "This is Bertha Ness, who was engaged to Joshua Rajala—I'm sure you remember Josh."

Bertha felt uncomfortable at mention of Josh's name. Then, suddenly the men moved to her side of the carriage and began to speak of their friendship and their admiration for Josh, of their sorrow at his passing. Looking into their faces, she realized they truly meant what they said—that they had known and had cared for Josh. She had never considered that possibility. Tears come to her eyes, and she attempted to blink them away. Suddenly the men, as if acting in concert, removed their hats while they stood silently before her.

"Thank you for your concern," she said quietly. "I can't tell you how much your words have meant to me." She looked from one rugged face to another, trying to smile in appreciation for their attempts at consolation. "God bless you—and keep you safe!"

Michael tipped his hat and flicked the reins. Within a moment, they pulled up before a small, well-kept house on the northern edge of the Island. A garden and chicken coop filled the fenced-in backyard. Hardy blooms by the front door welcomed them even though the frosty nights had taken their toll on most of the remaining blossoms.

Bertha continued brushing her auburn hair, recalling meeting the two families. In spite of her cruel remarks, they seemed to hold no malice, no ill will. Their smiles were sincere and friendly, their hands outstretched in greeting.

Maggie took her scarf and shawl. Henry showed her to the table, where he directed her to be seated. Big Jack went to the kitchen to aid Daisy in the serving of the meal. Hank found his way to the head of the table, and Michael sat down between Henry and Maggie. Big Jack would be seated next to Bertha once the meal was served. Daisy would hover over all of them, tending to their every need during the course of the meal. Once dessert was served she'd also sit next to Bertha.

The face in the mirror was attractive in an unusual way, slender and angular, with a slightly pointed chin and a high forehead. A widow's peak accentuated her hairline and caused her hair to flow back from her face. Her narrow nose was just a bit too long for true beauty, yet it seemed to suit her face because her eyes were large and luminous. Looking at herself, she recalled the previous hours and how she had longed to have the Larsons and the Swansons think highly of her and find her worthy to be their friend.

The meal had been delicious—meatballs in a rich, delicious gravy, white and fluffy mashed potatoes, freshly baked squash with brown sugar, thick slices of Daisy's homemade bread covered with butter and strawberry jam. Bertha thought she wouldn't be able to swallow even a bite but found the food irresistible.

The final touch to the evening was a piece of freshly baked apple pie, compliments of Big Jack. Bertha's corset had all it could do to contain the expanse of her satisfied stomach.

She still brushed—and counted—now up to ninety-five long, slow strokes of the brush. Her auburn tresses shone like polished copper. As she brushed she recalled the moment when a strained silence seemed to descend like a pall over the group . She knew it was time for her to speak her piece and beg their forgiveness. She took one more sip of coffee, replaced her cup on its saucer, and reached under her chair for her handbag.

She removed two wrapped packages, placed the gifts on the table before her and began to speak. She gave no excuses for her behavior. Their warm acceptance of her even after such behavior to their children was a pure gift from God. "I can't begin to tell you what a difference all of you have made in my life," she said. "Your hospitality and welcome has shown me there is still a life for me in this world. Even visiting with the lumberjacks on my way to your home tonight taught me a lesson in forgiveness and hospitality." She smiled and those large, brown eyes of hers seemed to truly come alive before them.

She placed one of the gifts on the table before Henry and the other in front of Maggie. With a nod she indicated the gifts should be opened, and the children complied.

Henry was speechless. His gift was a fine antique gold pocket watch, complete with a black leather watch fob. "That was my father's," Bertha said softly. "When I was growing up, I saw him put it in his vest pocket every morning as he prepared for work at the hardware store. He was a kind, loving man, and I miss him." She smiled at Henry and added, "I've kept his watch for such a long time, hoping I'd find a person I thought worthy of carrying it. And now I have met you, Henry. I know it'll be carried in the vest pocket of an honorable person. May God bless you, Henry, and give you a long and happy life."

Maggie slowly folded back the tissue paper that surrounded her gift. Her face lit up with surprise when she saw what it was. Everyone at the table watched as she picked up a heart shaped locket hanging from a slender golden chain. Bertha could not help but smile as she noted Maggie's pleasure. Bertha reached over to help place the lovely necklace around Maggie's slender neck. As she adjusted the clasp, Bertha explained the background of the necklace. "My grandmother received this necklace when she was a young girl. It was passed to my mother, and then to me." Her face lit as she spoke of those people who had been so significant in her young life. She adjusted the chain and centered the heart-shaped locket on the front of Maggie's dress.

"There you are, Maggie. The locket has no photo in it now. Someday perhaps you can place a photo of someone you love in the locket and carry it close to your heart."

Bertha observed the attention the parents gave the children and their gifts. She was pleased she had thought these two items as an offering to the delighted children. Finally the excitement of the gifts passed, and all eyes focused again on Bertha. She took a deep breath and spoke the words that needed to be said. "Please forgive me—please help me wipe away the stain of the awful words I uttered." She gazed from face to face and, as the seconds of silence passed, all she saw in the eyes of those who looked back at her was love and caring and—most importantly—grace.

They adjourned to the sitting area where Hank and Big Jack regaled everyone with tall tales of days at the logging camps. Hank's remembrances of Josh Rajala and their years of friendship were like a balm on Bertha's sorrowing heart. Both men seemed to know Josh well and appreciated him as a friend and as a professional logger. For the first time in months Bertha laughed, and the laughter came from deep in her wounded soul.

Unknown to Bertha and the rest of the party sitting there, Big Jack had taken a secret pleasure in watching Bertha as she threw back her head and laughed when he told his tall tales of the logging camp and his escapades with Josh. Her smile and her wistfulness had captured his attention and made him smile as he watched her from across the room. Bertha had no idea she was being admired.

She finished her one-hundredth brush stroke and reached around to braid her hair before going to bed. If she did not restrain her hair, it drifted over her face while she slept and often caused her to awaken too early. The lamp dimmed, she walked to the window and looked out over the sleeping town. Her eyes glanced to the north where she now was acquainted with human beings who lived and worked on the Island.

What a change this evening had brought to her heart and mind. Her entire life she had been told to stay away from the Isand. Now one of the most enjoyable evenings of her life had been spent in that very place. Darkness covered the town. She went to her bed, pulled open the quilt and slipped beneath its comfortable warmth. Very soon she was asleep.

On the Island, not one of Bertha's dinner companions had been able to close their eyes in sleep. Henry lay in his store room bed, moonlight his only light. In his hand he held the wonderful watch from Bertha Ness. He had a new appreciation for her. It wasn't just the gift; it was mostly hearing her tell of her sorrow and loss. He could understand, even though he was young. He had been so afraid he'd lose his father when he was hurt.

Loving someone's really risky, he thought.

One last time he read the name on the face of the watch—Plymouth Watch Co. He traced the shape of the eagle with its outstretched wings engraved on the lid. He quietly opened and closed the lid. He loved the Roman numerals of the watch face that were almost visible in the soft light filtering through the window. He had mastered his school lessons on Roman numerals and felt very intelligent recognizing those that appeared before him when he flipped open the cover. He consulted his watch one final time—twenty minutes past eleven—very late for Henry. In the darkness, he could hear the steady ticking of the watch that now belonged to him. It finally lulled him to sleep.

Across the street at the boarding house, Maggie was also having trouble falling asleep. Big Jack had wanted her to take off the necklace and place it in a safe place before she crawled into her bed. She resisted. He relented, and now she lay on her left side, quilt tucked around her shoulders, the heart held gently in her right hand.

She'd never had such a lovely piece of jewelry. Feminine items were scarce in the Swanson house since her mother had passed away. In fact, she'd try to find a small photo of her mother and father and see if she could fit them into the locket. She smiled at the thought of her beloved parents sharing space in her locket, being always together in her heart.

Henry and Maggie didn't know the reasoning behind those generous gifts. Since the passing of her parents, Bertha had kept these two treasured items in hopes she'd be able to pass them on to children she and Joshua might someday have. She realized this dream would never materialize, yet the gifts could still be given and appreciated by these two children. Her heart had been warmed as she watched their excitement opening her gifts. Both children looked up into her face as they carefully held her gifts. They smiled with warmth and affection, not just because of the gifts, but because all three of them knew she was forgiven. Bertha slept this night with peace in her heart—at last.

Big Jack worked in his kitchen before turning in. He measured water into the large kettle for the next day's oatmeal and set it on the stove, then measured the oatmeal itself, enough to fill the bellies of the hungry men who'd soon descend to his dining room. Bacon, pancakes, scrambled eggs—all would be steaming hot and ready to be wolfed down before the men left for work. Lunches for the next day had been prepared before he and Maggie had left for the Larson home.

Finally, he sat at the counter and held his head in his hands. *I must be crazy*, he thought. *This can't be happening! I was really attracted to Bertha Ness!*

Most of the time he was immune to eager husband seekers that had followed him around after he lost his beloved wife. He had a child and a business and no time for anything else. Years had passed and he was fine with life and how he and Maggie lived. Now he felt he'd betrayed himself by enjoying Bertha's company during the course of the evening.

Was it sympathy he felt? She wasn't a girl anymore, he told himself. On the other hand, that was part of what appealed to him—she was a mature woman. She was grieving, and he could resonate with those feelings. After all these years, he missed his lovely Agnes. Maybe a person never truly recovered from the loss of someone they loved. On the other hand, perhaps there was still a source of love that could be nourished and grow again to include yet another person.

He rubbed his hands through his thick, unmanageable hair and wondered how she had seen him. He grimaced, recalling when he dished up her apple pie and, in spite of her refusal of a dollop of whipped cream, he had placed—with a dramatic flourish—a large helping of whipped cream on her piece of pie.

She looked at him with those guileless brown eyes—first in surprise and then with good humor—and he watched as she devoured the pie—and the cream—to the very last crumb. She voiced her warm appreciation for the generous helping of whipped cream.

Big Jack looked in on Maggie, watched her sleeping peacefully. He saw she still cradled the heart necklace. *Bertha Ness*, he thought, *you did wonderful things tonight.*

He partially closed her door. The sun would soon rise over the treeline to the east. He'd try to get some sleep before his boarders began clomping down the stairs, ready for their ample breakfast. The thought crossed his mind that maybe tomorrow he should start shaving his scruffy beard more often. He wasn't sure when he might meet Bertha Ness again, but was sure she wouldn't ever be attracted to the unshaven man he saw in his mirror.

On the Island, the crowds on St. Louis Avenue were still going strong. Their shouts and laughter floated over the autumn night to the Larson home. Hank and Daisy had cleared away the dishes, stored the leftovers in the icebox, and cleaned the kitchen. Hank sat on a chair, drying the dishes, pots, and pans as Daisy washed and rinsed them.

Soon everything was in place, and husband and wife sat in the parlor, smiling as they recalled their evening. Daisy's heart had been touched watching Bertha as they spoke of Joshua Rajala. Daisy knew with certainty how Bertha felt. Memories rushed back to the day Hank had been crushed by the log and no one knew if he would live or die.

The two of them sat quietly in the lamplight, Daisy just watching as Hank took out his bag of tobacco and made a smoke. She loved his large strong hands that could force a saw through a log or handle the fragile cigarette paper and the small bag of tobacco. She loved his smile and the joy of living it now displayed as he grew stronger every day.

She treasured Hank's relationship with Henry, how the two of them grew closer and more alike as the years passed. She felt tears well up as she realized the blessed gift of having someone to love, someone with whom to share life. The truth came home with stark clarity this evening as she observed Bertha tell of trying to live without her beloved.

Hank looked at Daisy, the end of his cigarette glowing in the soft light of the kerosene lamp. He drew deeply on it, and slowly allowed the smoke to escape his lips. Their eyes smiled at each other across the room.

Daisy said, "I truly love you, Hank Larson." She walked to him, knelt and placed her arms about him. Her head rested on his chest. "You are my dearest friend!"

Hank snuffed out the cigarette in the nearby ash tray, then took her in his arms. He tipped her head slightly so their eyes met. He said softly, "My beloved Daisy, you and Henry are my life, my reason to live. Thank you for loving me, cripple that—"

She hushed him, not wanting him to dwell on the negative. Their lips met and, for a moment, the world was a perfect place. Daisy stood and reached for Hank's hand. They blew out the lamp. In the light of the autumn moon they found their way to the bedroom. Hank removed her pins and combs and watched her dark hair fall about her shoulders. He ran his hands though the curls as he had done all those years ago when they were young and knew so little of what lay ahead.

Soon they lay beside each other in their old brass bed, she holding his hands as his arms encircled her slender body—"bundling" they called it. For more than twelve years this was how they met the night. Soon he'd turn to the window and she to the door. Yet their physical presence reassured them both that the coming day could be dealt with.

MONDAY MORNING DAWNED clear and bright. October was Michael's favorite month. The air seemed clearer, the sunshine brighter. After completing a task at the office, he thought he'd make a call on Mrs. Brush, who always seemed determined to feed him, and he looked forward to whatever she placed before him. During the conversation at the table last evening Daisy mentioned that Mrs. Brush seemed to be ailing. He'd stop by and check on her.

Before he left his office, he needed to tend to a task that had been on his desk for some time and was lost under a multitude of papers. As his head hit the pillow last evening, the memory of the envelope given him by the district president during his interview flashed in his mind. His brain snapped to attention, and he counted the months he'd lived in Cloquet, June to July to October. He'd gone past the three-month date set when he left the office. His reply was one month overdue. How was he going to explain that?

Each time he entered his office, he gazed at the disorganized mess scattered over his desk. Somehow he knew approximately where an item was whenever he had need of it. Now he needed to locate that particular envelope given him just before he left the seminary and arrived in Cloquet. Now where could it be?

He put books back on shelves, then sorted through his sermon notes and illustration ideas used in his recent writing. He had a file for each sermon he'd written and the materials used for that particular text. With the desk top visible, he searched for the envelope.

Finally his eye fell upon a corner of white envelope barely showing from beneath his lamp stand. Yes, he remembered putting it there so it'd be safe. The words "TO THE PASTOR CALLED TO SERVE" were penned with a flourish in large letters. He carefully tore off the end of the envelope and removed the letter.

> To whom it may concern:
> Should you be fortunate enough to receive the call to Cloquet, you must know it comes with an extra addendum. Reports have come to me regarding a disconnect between the residents of Cloquet and the people inhabiting the Island; this is troubling to me. I personally challenge the person receiving this call to cross over the bridge with the express purpose of bringing the Gospel to those who frequent the Island's establishments.

Always remember that Jesus was "a friend of sinners" and the book of Romans states that "it is God's will that ALL men be saved and come to the knowledge of the truth." Therefore, you are to offer no less than that to everyone within your realm of influence—city, county, and Island equally. God bless you as you tread where few men of God have trod before.

Sincerely in Christ,

C.E. Hanson—Norwegian Lutheran Church President.

Michael threw back his head and laughed out loud. He quickly took out pen and paper and began to write a letter to C.E. Beginning with his first trip across the bridge to find Henry Larson, he wrote in great detail of his introduction to people on the Island. All the faces of those he had met and conversed with over the past four months caused him to write quickly and fluently of the friends he now possessed connected to the Island and the saloons: Willard Schiebe, Samuel Berg, Big Jack, Hank Larson, and the nameless men he'd met because of his ministry to Willard.

Then he told of his relationship with Henry, Maggie, Daisy, and Bertha Ness. All came alive in his account of times spent on the Island. Words flew from his pen in his eagerness to share his ministry up to this point with his superior.

In conclusion he impulsively issued an invitation to C.E. Hanson: "Come to Cloquet at your convenience and visit the town, the church, and the Island." He smiled as he visualized the two of them walking down St. Louis Avenue. "Together we can stop by the many saloons, greet the men I have come to know over the summer, and maybe have a beer—if you so desire."

He smiled again as he signed his name with gusto, folded the letter, and, after placing it in the already addressed envelope, he grabbed his hat and set out for the post office. He would love to see C.E.'s face as he read this letter.

On the way back to his office, he stopped at Mrs. Brush's lovely home. He knocked once, twice, then the door opened. Mrs. Brush stood before him in her colorful blue floral dressing gown. Her white hair curled in wisps about her face and hung over her shoulders in two long braids. She seemed more fragile than when he had last visited. A paleness now lay over her face instead of the blush of health that previously brought a touch of youth to her aged cheeks. Yet a smile appeared, defining her many wrinkles, when she looked up into his eyes. "Come in! Please come in!" She stood to one side of the entry and motioned him through the door.

He couldn't resist giving her a very gentle embrace as he came up to her in the hallway. Suddenly he became conscious of just how frail she had become. She stood for just a brief moment with her head resting on his chest, then she turned and, once again in charge, led the way into the sunny kitchen. He picked up the aroma of freshly brewed coffee.

When seated at her enamel kitchen table with a large white coffee cup in his hand, he began to tell her about Bertha Ness and their evening on the Island. Mrs. Brush listened intently, eyes wide with amazement at the amount of forgiveness that surrounded and filled the people who'd sat around Hank and Daisy Larson's oak table. "I've known Bertha since she was a child and had been close friends with Bertha's now deceased parents. I must say, I'm so proud of all of you—you, Bertha, the Larsons, and the Swansons." She stirred another cube of sugar into her coffee. "Some people would have preferred to carry a grudge and never allow grace to wipe away Bertha's pain or the hurts of the children. You're a good shepherd, Pastor Jenson—just what every pastor ought to be." She reached out once more to pat his hand in a motherly fashion, a gesture that Michael always found most touching.

Finishing his coffee and the date-filled cookie Mrs. Brush had placed in front of him, Michael was about to take his leave. Walking him to the front door, she paused and said, "I'd appreciate it if you could come by some afternoon and assist me in planning my funeral."

The shock that crossed Michael's face made her smile. "None of us goes on forever, as you well know, and I can feel the tug of eternity on my soul." She laughed her infectious laugh, and Michael had to appreciate the ease with which she greeted her final adventure.

"There is no one I'd be happier to help plan for their transition to heaven than you, my dear Mrs. Brush." He gently placed his hands on her slender shoulders and smiled into her face. "You and I will put our heads together and plan one fantastic funeral service, one that the people of Cloquet will never forget!"

They stood on the porch in the cool morning air, smiling at each other, celebrating the bond of friendship that had been forged between them in the few months they'd known each other. Pastor Jenson took the steps in one large leap, then turned to wave farewell before heading once again to the church office where he would take time to read his Greek New Testament.

Mrs. Brush held her robe close about her shoulders, watching Pastor Jenson stride down the street. She dearly loved him and, at times, would imagine that if she and her husband had been blessed with a son, he might have been just like Pastor Jenson. She smiled as she retreated to the warmth of her kitchen where she would wait for Old Syd to come. They, too, would have coffee before she gave him the list of things to do around the yard.

After lunch Daisy would come to help with the care of the interior of her house. Daisy was the dearest person she had ever known, and Mrs. Brush constantly grieved over the Larsons' move to the Island. The three of them had been like the family she had never had. Having them right in her backyard had been such a blessing.

Now she would dress. Something warm, with a shawl to cover her shoulders. She had always loved clothes made of fine fabrics with varieties of lace and buttons for stylish trims. Long ago she had refused to wear the customary corset that was the base of any well-dressed woman's apparel. She had tired of being laced in and thrust out, as was the mode of the day.

Looking for comfort and simplicity, she covered her almost nonexistent bosom with a soft cotton lace-trimmed corset cover that attached to a bloomer/petticoat combination. A comfortable house dress made of a soft rose cashmere slipped easily over her head and shoulders and fell to the floor. She was not as yet willing to accept the new, shorter styles. A dark gray sash fitted the dress to her ever-diminishing waistline.

Next, her hair would need tending. Usually Daisy came just in time to fix it. Today after the pastor's visit, Mrs. Brush felt so energized she did it herself. Taking a seat before her vanity mirror, she loosed the braids and combed out her hair. Making a braid on each side, she eased in the illusive strands of hair that constantly slipped from the braids. As usual she wound both braids about her head, securing them with dainty combs on each side and several tortoiseshell hair pins.

She had always been proud of her hair. Her mind often slipped far back into the past and remembered how her husband had sometimes offered to brush her hair as they made ready for bed. She'd loved his strong yet gentle strokes. Even now as she aged, her body seeming to crumble before her eyes, her hair remained thick and full of life.

Oh, well, she thought, *one can't have everything. Hair is good.* She certainly did not want to become bald, as was the case with some of her elderly friends .

With a touch of rouge, she felt ready for the day. As she carefully descended the stairs, she could hear Old Syd come through the back door and make his way to the kitchen. There were many outdoor chores before winter blew in upon them. She would be the manager, and Old Syd the worker. They both functioned well in this order. He had been her right-hand man for more years than she could remember. Giving her braids a final pat, she called out his name as she entered the kitchen.

‰17 ∞
Winter

THE GLORIOUS DAYS of the Indian summer of early October quickly departed with the arrival of November. Area residents worked diligently to prepare for the weather ahead.

Woodpiles grew larger and closer to back doors. Garden produce had been harvested, stored, canned, or hung in cellars. Warm woolen clothes were plucked from the cedar chest, brushed off, and hung on clotheslines to disperse the smell of moth balls. People got out their warm underwear, longjohns in most cases. Style gave way to warmth and comfort.

Chimneys were cleaned to prevent fires that could result from soot deposits. Coal wagons traveled from house to house, the driver so black with coal dust only the whites of his eyes showed.

Chicken coops were banked with hay bales, and a rope was tied from the back door of the house to the door of the coop or barn, just in case of the sudden onslaught of a blizzard, so they could find their way to gather eggs or milk cows.

Many townspeople kept livestock in small barns at the rear of their lots. Bales of hay were positioned near the barn entrances, and sacks of feed were stored in shed corners, in the hopes the supply would suffice until spring.

The manure that accumulated over the winter months would be applied to garden plots once the snow disappeared. The pungent odor filling the air after these applications made nearby residents' eyes water until the ground was tilled. The resulting bounty of garden produce was worth the smell and the endless work needed before the harvest.

Pearl, dressed in a warm fur coat with a woolen scarf around her head, still took time to sit on her porch. Watching the change of seasons from week to week and day to day always spoke to her of the extreme swiftness of the passing of her life. Her eyes wandered to the vegetable garden that had filled the yard south of her house. What had once been lush and green with abundant growth lay stripped and lifeleess. She missed the growing things recently harvested, leaving behind weeds and stalks flung into piles of waste.

Pearl had always been a compulsive gardener. From childhood on she had a natural affinity for the earth and what she could coax out of its blackness. Any time she could find by herself, on her knees in the sunshine, was counted as a time well spent. No matter what the residents of the area thought of her and her brothel, no one ever drove past the white house beyond the bridge without admiring the expansive gardens that surrounded her property.

Blooms of all descriptions spilled out of window boxes and large urns, abundant vines trailing down to the ground below. The area surrounding the house itself was filled with flowering shrubbery from distant places and perennials of all varieties and colors. Near the backyard fence she had apple trees. Once the picking was complete, the crimson fruit provided the makings of delicious pies and tart apple cider.

To Pearl, the growth of her vegetable garden was a joy. Somehow watching everything grow to maturity fulfilled an inner desire to create something she could point to and display with pride. Every time she donned her wide-brimmed hat, knelt in the dirt, felt the warmth of the soil beneath her bare knees and the sun upon her back, she felt pure. She and God Himself had brought this beautiful garden to life. This was as close as she had ever felt to having given birth to something worthwhile.

But once again the season had come to an end. Fall and the beginning of winter always brought about great sadness to her. And this year, 1917, was no different. Her business would soon diminish drastically when the lumberjacks and mill workers left for the logging camps north of town. This was not always a negative event, for she appreciated the quieter lifestyle she and her girls could maintain over the winter months. And earlier this year she had come to the painful conclusion she needed to distance one of her girls from the sordid reputation surrounding the white house. The young girl, Beatrice, had become like Pearl's own child as the years had passed. She needed a new beginning.

Beatrice, now seventeen, had lived with Pearl since she was orphaned at eleven. Beatrice's father, Matt Laurila, had been a logger and a friend of Pearl's since she lived in Moose Lake. One wintery day he stopped by to talk to Pearl before leaving for the logging camp. Matt was desperate. His wife had recently passed away, and his daughter had no place to live while he was making a living at the camp. None of the mother's relatives would care for her child over the winter.

Pearl looked at the frightened child, then at the distraught father. Immediately she opened her home and her heart, agreeing to keep Beatrice until the log run was finished in the spring and Matt returned to town.

The following February, a brief message came to Pearl from the camp. Matt Laurila was dead. He had died in a logging accident. Accidents were not uncommon as the dangerous work continued through weeks of bitter cold. Little by little the details arrived, giving a somber account of his death. A pine tree landed in the wrong place, and Matt was crushed beneath it. A few relatives had shown up for the funeral, but not one of them had any interest in the heartbroken little girl who clung to Pearl's side.

Beatrice had become the cook over the past few years, separating her from the more sordid activities of the house. Always keeping her eyes lowered as she completed her chores, Beatrice paid no attention to the men coming and going. No man ever made a move toward Beatrice, knowing he'd have to answer to Pearl.

Then, about a year ago, one unfortunate customer couldn't take his eyes off the lovely, youthful Beatrice as she came and went from the kitchen. His brain, clouded by drinks previously downed at a saloon, forgot Pearl's number one rule of the house. Waiting for a moment when the object of his desire was away from other guests, he made his move.

Moving stealthily toward Beatrice as she carried clean linens down the hall, he followed her into the pantry off the kitchen. He grabbed her from behind, causing Beatrice to drop the linens. Taken by surprise, Beatrice struggled as he forced her against the wall.

"Stop it!" she cried. "Keep your hands off me, you pig!"

He pressed his bearded face to hers, Beatrice beat his chest. "Help me, please help me!"

The kitchen door flew open, and Pearl stood in the dim hallway. Her eyes met those of the attacker and a sardonic smile slowly crept over face. "Well, my goodness, Olaf Schmidt, what in the world's going on here?"

As Pearl approached, Olaf loosened his hold on Beatrice and retreated toward the parlor. Frantically picking up the scattered linens, Beatrice fled into the kitchen and slammed the door shut behind her. Pearl, smiling, approached the cowering man.

"You know the rules of the house, Olaf." Pearl's voice was smooth, almost seductive. "Why in heaven's name would you want to play with a girl when you could have a real woman?" Her smile intensified as she advanced, her eyes hard.

Olaf's mouth went dry even as the sweat broke out on his brow. "I didn't mean no harm, Miss Pearl," he stammered. " Too many drinks at the saloon, I reckon!"

Those in the parlor listened, waiting to see Olaf's outcome. Pearl drew closer, disgusted by his foul body odor and liquor-laden breath. Pearl pushed him against the wall. Her right hand rested in the pocket of her muslin apron. Violence was a byproduct of her trade. She carried her Derringer for just such an occasion as this.

All at once, Olaf's eyes widened in shock. Something very hard pressed into him as Pearl forced the cold steel barrel of her gun into his groin.

"I can pull the trigger and blow your trouble-making organ completely out of sight! How do you feel about that?" She whispered in his ear. Olaf knew she'd do it.

Without warning, Olaf lost control of his bladder, soaking his heavy woolen trousers. Aware of what had taken place, Pearl threw back her head and began to laugh.

"Good grief!" She could hardly talk because she was laughing so hard. "Take yourself out of my house and don't ever come back!" She pressed the barrel once again even harder, for added emphasis, then stepped back as the frantic man made a hasty retreat, stumbling back to the parlor and out the front door.

The patrons—and the girls—in the parlor had watched the entire exchange, some laughing and some seeing Pearl in a whole new light. Applause broke out spontaneously as the front door slammed shut, and brothel discipline was much improved once the news of this confrontation circulated through the saloons.

After that, all men knew Beatrice was not ever to be trifled with. She cooked and cleaned and organized the parlor, attended to the dining room when a dinner was served, and did laundry. The other girls depended on her for fashion and make-up advice, counsel in their various love affairs, and providing general friendship in this very segregated setting.

And then, last summer, Samuel Berg came on the scene. He was tall, clean cut, strong as an ox and hardworking, according to reports that had filtered into Pearl's ever attentive ears. Coming from a good family well-established in town, Pearl was surprised to see him at the brothel. Yet there he was, striding right through the front door of her establishment on a warm summer evening in early June, headed straight for Pearl.

Standing calmly before her, hat in his hand, Samuel spoke practiced words.

"Pearl, I realize you don't know me or my family," he began. Pearl stifled a smile as she thought of his militant mother. "So I want you to know I come here with good intentions. Your girl, Beatrice, has caught my eye, and I'd really like to get to know her."

His large hands squashed his hat in his nervousness. "For some time, Beatrice and I have passed each other in front of Big Jack's boarding house. Sometimes I'm coming out just about the same time she's walking by—on her way to do errands for you." He grinned, and Pearl was suddenly smitten with the young man. "I think we liked each other right away, even if we only said 'Hello' to each other as we passed."

"I'd really like to meet her in the proper way." He blushed, smiled at Pearl, and continued his request. "I've heard she is like a daughter to you, and not one of your . . ." He stammered to find the proper word. "Well," he shrugged. "I figured I couldn't lose anything by coming right to you."

Under Pearl's intense gaze and with his confidence slowly ebbing, Samuel make one final point. "We've seen each other in passing, but we've never had a chance to talk or get to know each other. I'd really like to have some time to—well—to visit with her."

Pearl tried not to smile. Visit—well, that was a whole new approach in the brothel.

All at once, Beatrice came through the door, and a blush bloomed on her cheeks when she noticed Samuel Berg. She stood looking up at the tall young man. Pearl became acutely aware of just how mature Beatrice had become in the past months. She had grown into a lovely young woman, petite yet substantial. Blonde hair—part of her Finnish heritage—billowed about her face.

Pearl saw the attraction between them. Since they had never been formally introduced, Pearl said, "Beatrice, this is Samuel Berg. He says he'd like to . . ." Pearl paused, ". . . visit with you." Pearl turned to Samuel. "Mr. Berg, I present Beatrice Laurila." Neither Samuel nor Beatrice moved. "For heaven's sake," Pearl laughed, "shake hands with each other!"

Then Pearl said, "Samuel, remember that Beatrice is like a daughter to me. So, I give my consent for the two of you," again the pause, "to visit." Pearl laughed again, and the young people smiled as they reached forth to shake hands in a formal greeting.

Samuel Berg became a regular visitor. Pearl often seated them in the backyard under the stars and brought them lemonade. Crickets serenaded them from the rose garden while the two visited. As the weeks passed, the visits grew more frequent. Pearl—and Beatrice—grew fonder of Samuel. Pearl soon came to the conclusion that he was indeed the type of young man that a " respectable" young woman should desire to marry.

Of course, Pearl still had a vivid memory of that night a few years ago when the women of the town crossed the bridge with vengeance in their hearts and weapons in their hands. She knew Mrs. Berg, Samuel's mother, was the leading figure in the attack and had carried a hoe as a weapon. She also knew Samuel had been the voice of reason that had helped disperse the mob.

The townspeople would assume Samuel's purpose in coming to her house was something other than exploring a marriage option, but Pearl began to believe marrying Beatrice was the only thing on Samuel's mind. Occasionally they'd be seen in the late summer moonlight, holding fast to each other in a passionate embrace, their lips silently telling of their love for each other—again and again. The more seasoned girls watching from upstairs windows reported theirs as a "virginal" relationship.

Over time, Samuel helped Beatrice, carrying in wood for the stove, shucking corn with her, picking produce from the garden. The two filled basket after basket of rosy, red apples, ready to be turned into pies, apple crisp, or cider.

Beatrice and Samuel seemed to enjoy each other—no matter the activity they shared. Pearl saw that Mrs. Berg certainly had taught her son well about morality and the proper behavior with a person of the opposite sex. Some day, if the opportunity arose, Pearl hoped to compliment her on her fine son, and, maybe, the two of them could speak calmly of honorable things. Perhaps Mrs. Berg would come to her home for a visit (it would take a miracle!), and she would arrive at Pearl's front door without her hoe.

Suddenly, what should happen came clear to Pearl. She would pay a call on Pastor Jenson—and the sooner the better. Rumors often reached her that the pastor was willing to visit with all people, to accept any one who had need of his counsel—no matter what heinous sins hovered in their past. Pearl was determined to give Beatrice—and Samuel—an opportunity to live the sort of life together that had seemed so unreachable to herself.

Her mind made up, Pearl walked to the kitchen. Only in the last week had one of those newfangled telephones been installed. After the telephone line had been strung across the river to the Island, then to her establishment, one of her "guests" offered to install the phone if she ordered one from the Sears and Roebuck Catalog. The cost was high, ten dollars, but, reportedly, were easily installed. *Why not go with the modern trend?* Pearl thought.

Pearl had only used the telephone a time or two, and she still worried she'd be electrocuted by it. She hesitantly lifted the receiver from its cradle on the left side of the oak box containing all the paraphernalia necessary for her voice to travel wherever she wished. She turned the crank on the right side of the box and asked the operator to connect her to the church. She stood on her tiptoes in order to speak clearly into the transmitter—then she heard the pastor's voice.

"Pastor Jenson speaking" said the voice, sounding just a bit unsure.

She took a deep breath and introduced herself. She realized the pastor most likely knew who she was, yet they had never spoken face to face. She bravely made her request. "If you could spare a small portion of your time, I would very much appreciate coming to the church to visit with you. Or you could come here." She paused. "Perhaps coming here isn't a good idea, and I fully understand if you choose not to see me or talk to me. I know how the town feels about me, and I wouldn't want to make trouble for you."

"Pearl, thank you for calling." His voice sounded friendly. "I welcome you and invite you to join me in my office. I'll make a cup of tea for us, if you like."

Pastor Jenson consulted his calendar and, within a moment or two, the appointment was set—10:00 a.m. on Friday. After thanking him profusely Pearl replaced the receiver in its holder and pressed her hand to her breast. My, how fast her heart was beating!

She had done the deed, and she was proud of herself. She returned to the parlor, where she poured herself a small glass of wine and settled into her comfortable chair by the window, her fashionable shoes resting on the footstool at her feet, her head resting on the antimacassar that covered the back of her chair. Looking out on the early winter landscape she felt the wine warm her from the inside. A smile slowly flowed over her face; she had always hoped for a fairy tale ending somewhere in her life. Maybe this was as close as she would ever be to becoming the heroine of a story.

∞18∞
Miss Thoreson

THE SIXTH GRADE, under the direction and encouragement of Miss Thoreson, was proceeding far better than the "three musketeers" ever dared hope. Miss Vivian Thoreson was a born teacher. Taller than most women and sturdy from her youth on a nearby farm, after completing the two-year teachers' training program, she had been hired to teach at Garfield School in Cloquet. For the past fifteen years, she awakened every day eager to open the door to her classroom. She loved every day, standing before her students and opening their minds to learning. Her goal was to fill all of them with knowledge and a large dose of curiosity.

A quick glance measured Vivian Thoreson as plain, ordinary. Closer inspection saw her as having warmth and winsome charm. Her eyes, bright blue, were as eager as a child's. Needing spectacles only for small print, her face was framed by light brown, wavy hair done in braids wrapped together at the nape of her neck and secured in a bun with large pins.

She often wore a colorful apron over her modest dress. The large pockets always contained some interesting object pertaining to the subject for the day. Students always remembered their time in Miss Thoreson's sixth grade class.

Once school began, reports circulated about the stabbing on the Island. Most students had seen the headlines on the *Pine Knot*, telling how Oscar, Henry, and Maggie were involved in helping the injured man. This created awe and wonder in their classmates. *How exciting,* they thought.

The three friends saw changes in their classmates' attitudes even on the first day of school. No one called them names, no one shoved Oscar in line. Henry and Maggie didn't have to defend themselves because they lived on the Island. Their classmates came up to them and commented on their bravery.

"Did you ever find the knife?"

"I bet there was lots of blood everywhere!"

"Did you get any of the blood right on your clothes?"

"Wow! I would've been scared the bad guy was still there!"

"Which one of you ran up to the saloon and got help?"

"Could you see what was going on inside the saloon?"

"Did you see anybody you knew from town?"

"Were you scared?"

"What did your parents say when they found out you were by the saloons?"

The questions went on and on. After the first week of school there had been so much conversation among the students and the three "heroes" that any previous social walls had now crumbled completely.

Oscar was pleasantly surprised to be chosen third or fourth instead of last by the leader of the boys' kickball team. Henry always fared better than Oscar in that regard, so Oscar felt he had definitely made social progress. Whenever Miss Thoreson posed a question in class, Oscar's hand shot up boldly. He loved feeling confident and he loved being enthusiastic about all the knowledge he had tucked away. Some days he just could not wipe the smile from his young face.

Since the first day of school, Maggie was constantly accused by her peers of being Miss Thoreson's "pet." She denied it, but down in her heart she loved that Miss Thoreson called on her for assistance. Maggie often passed out papers to the twenty students of the class. At times she was in charge of monitoring the organization of the class, seeing that all five rows of desks were straight and orderly, checking for any litter under the desks, and erasing the blackboards when Miss Thoreson finished her lecture notes.

She passed out books, worksheets, penmanship papers, ink wells, art supplies, and assignment sheets. When the time was right, Miss Thoreson motioned to her, and Maggie collected the assignments ready to be passed in for the teacher's inspection.

From all of this attention, Maggie felt a strong desire growing within her heart—she would dearly love to someday become a teacher just like Miss Thoreson and make students feel just as excited about learning as she did in this year of the sixth grade.

Miss Thoreson often smiled to herself as she observed Maggie blossoming into an outgoing, confident young girl. The shy, withdrawn look often on Maggie's face slowly disappeared under the deliberate warm attention lavished on her by Miss Thoreson.

And Henry—what a year he was having! Miss Thoreson dearly loved all twenty of her students and felt her calling was to encourage each of them to do their best while enjoying every day they spent in her class. Yet Henry stood out from the rest of the class since the very beginning of the year. He first caught her attention when he quoted from books and authors a sixth grade student would rarely be familiar with. One afternoon, Miss Thoreson planned a trip to the library where each student would check out a least one book to read. She held up several examples of books that might appeal to her students—*Call of the Wild, Little Women, Around the World in Eighty Days, Alice in Wonderland.*

Miss Thoreson addressed her class. "There is a poem by one of my favorite poets that explains to the reader what is possible when we open our minds and think about what we read. I'd like to take time to share that with you, so pay close attention." She took a small book from her apron pocket and opened it carefully.

Henry's hand shot into the air, almost throwing him from his desk. "I bet I know that poem, know it by heart from reading it so many times with my friend Mrs. Brush. It's one of her favorites, too!"

Surprised by his confidence, she smiled patiently and said, "Well, Henry, let's hear this poem you think is the one I intend to share." She motioned him to stand beside his desk. He smiled broadly, rose to his feet, cleared his throat, and began.

"There is no frigate like a book
To take us lands away.
Nor any coursers like a page
Of prancing poetry;
This traverse may the poorest take
Without oppress of toll;
How frugal is the chariot
That bears the human soul!"

"This poem is by Emily Dickenson, who lived in the 1800s," Henry went on. "Mrs. Brush really likes her poems. She explained to me we can get carried away by the words to many different places." And, with another big smile, he sat down.

Once she recovered from the shock of her student quoting poetry, Miss Thoreson had to admit Henry's vocabulary and literary background was extensive for a boy his age. "Thank you, Henry, for sharing that poem with the class. Please tell Mrs. Brush she is certainly leading you down the proper path." Suppressing a grin, Miss Thoreson closed her book, put it back in her apron pocket, and focused the class on their trip to the library.

At the close of each school day the three friends gathered up their books and lunch buckets and headed out. They stopped by Oscar's home and visited with Anna Belle Lund, who eagerly awaited the children as they burst through the front door, laughing and talking. On her good days she'd have milk and graham crackers waiting for them. The three would relate the events of the day while Mrs. Lund listened and laughed, a quiet smile lingering on pale lips.

Occasionally she would be "indisposed," and the children would find her on the lounge by the dining room window. The late afternoon sun usually flooded the room and warmed her fragile body as she slept. On rare occasions, an empty glass lay overturned on the rug beside her, whatever liquor it had contained staining the oriental rug.

The children restored everything to order. Maggie often brushed back the unruly locks that had slipped loose from the decorative hairpins. Every time she did so Maggie got a vision of her long-departed mother. She'd love to have had a mother. In her heart she had now "adopted" Mrs. Lund, as well as Daisy Larson, and wanted to help Anna Belle Lund.

The maids were usually busy in the kitchen preparing dinner, which was served promptly at 6:00 p.m.—or whenever Mr. Lund burst through the front door. They did not pay much attention to the mistress of the house. They did the work they were hired to do and when they were done they packed up their supplies and left for home, where they would cook another meal for their own families.

Oscar knew, without a doubt, he had to check on his mother before the maids began serving the evening meal. Once he was sure his mother was safe, Oscar and his friends set out for the next part of their daily schedule—the bread and baking delivery.

After a quick trip over the red bridge and an efficient packing of the wagon, the three friends hastily crossed the bridge again. Daisy's baking business flourished, and families eagerly waited to receive their orders. With the three youngsters working at top speed, they could make the home deliveries before the sun slid behind the hills to the west.

Oscar would be home way before his father came to his room to check on him, as he always did. Maggie often left the two boys before they were quite done because she knew Big Jack depended on her to serve the meat, potatoes, and gravy to the tables and pour the coffee into waiting cups.

Once the baked goods had been delivered, Henry always breathed a sigh of relief. Then he felt he had a moment or two to stop by the stables before he went home for the evening meal. His parents often held supper to a later time knowing his love for the stables and Samson.

Henry would miss the time he spent at the stable brushing Samson and any other horse Mr. Keller felt needed attention. Mr. Keller had risen very high in Henry's opinion ever since Henry had seen him throwing the ax at Lumberjack Days. Henry had learned not to judge a person by appearance alone. Being on the stocky side and older than most other competitors, Mr. Keller's expertise with the ax was quite the surprise for Henry.

Feeling at home in the stables, Henry often perched on Samson, his hands and face deep in the dark mane cascading over his neck. Mr. Keller occasionally walked past the stall, aware Henry had ignored his directions. Yet he never criticized Henry for mounting the horse, even when he looked Henry full in the eyes as he lay across the back of the large horse. "You be careful, Henry," he'd say. "Some horses ain't as calm as Samson."

Samson was strong. He seemed indestructible. Henry soaked in the horse's strength and stored up the sensation of the quivering muscles he felt beneath his legs as he sat astride the broad back of the patient horse. Soon the stables would empty as the horses traveled north to the logging camps, with only a few horses left behind to accommodate the reduced workload at the mills during the winter. Henry would have to wait until spring for Sampson to return. After one final stroke of the brush, Henry put back the equipment, checked the water bucket and feed box, put on his jacket and cap, and headed out into the twilight of the early winter evening.

Waiting for him in the shadows of the stable, a light dusting of snow covering the cloths and empty boxes, the wagon was almost invisible in the dusk. He knew his mother and father waited for him at home, supper warm and ready on the table. Leaving behind a trail of footprints and wagon tracks in the snow, he headed once more across the red bridge, toward the light that shone from the window of his home at the far end of Main Street.

ക19ര
Flivvers and Tin Lizzies

O VER THE PAST FEW YEARS the number of newfangled automobiles seen churning up the dust on Cloquet Avenue had greatly increased. Horses drawing carriages were constantly spooked as the autos chugged by them on the street, their drivers cursing under their breath as they tried to control their horses.

All the men at the highest positions in the mills drove automobiles. Many well-known businessmen of the community proudly motored up and down the streets of the town with their families. The passengers, wrapped in scarves, hats, goggles, and long coats to protect them from the exhaust and the mud bounced through the dirt and ruts of the unpaved streets.

By 1917, Henry Ford was building a Model T in less than ninety minutes. With such an increase in production, the cost had been lowered to under $400.00. The automobiles flew off the assembly line and into thousands of garages across the country. So it was to be expected that Mr. Oscar Lund, president of the bank, ruler of his family, pillar of the community, would deem it necessary that he should present himself on the roads of his community in a classy "Flivver," as they were sometimes called.

Since early August, Mr. Lund had worshiped his auto as it quietly rested in calm dignity in the refurbished garage at the rear of his property. In years past, the building had housed horses and small livestock. Now, however, with his elevation in society by being the owner of a shiny new auto, Mr. Lund created a home worthy of his latest acquisition.

New garage doors with a substantial lock heightened security. A new roof repelled the elements, and the floor was thoroughly cleaned before Mr. Lund drove his auto into his yard. Oscar and his mother watched in nervous agitation from the dining room window, aware that there was now one more object in their lives that could cause them anxiety.

Mr. Lund immediately set the ground rules:

1. He alone would be in charge of the polishing, cleaning, and maintaining the auto.
2. No one else would be allowed to come in contact with the body of the auto unless specifically invited to accompany Mr. Lund on a jaunt about the town.
3. There would be no food within the body of the auto itself.
4. All passengers would have to be dressed appropriately and were required to check their shoes for dust, dirt, mud, or any general sources of soil.
5. There would be no exceptions.

Oscar and his mother knew there would be hell to pay if either of them transgressed the "Ford's commandments," as they called the rules.

Mr. Lund dusted the fenders and the hood of the car every morning before he started the motor. As soon as the car shone like new he would don his long coat, hat, and goggles. Oscar and his mother always breathed a sigh of relief when they saw the auto back out of the garage, make the turn onto the street, and proceed toward the bank in a billowing cloud of dust.

Mr. Arthur Lund held himself in very high regard. As the years passed he came to the realization he had married beneath his station. Anna Belle had been a beauty when he first took note of her, was from a well-to-do family, and led him to believe she'd be an appropriate partner as he scaled the ladder of success. Too late he realized she'd never be equal to the task of keeping up appearances in a manner befitting the social state he so deeply desired. Angry, he let her know in clear and ringing terms she was a grave disappointment. Taking perverse pleasure in watching her wilt before his eyes, he constantly censured her every move. Things grew even more distasteful to him once their son was born.

Being a caring, nurturing father was not on his list of priorities. The baby was fussy. Anna Belle's milk wasn't abundant enough to satisfy the infant. He'd slam the front door as he left his weeping wife and crying child behind him.

There must be a woman somewhere in this Godforsaken town to appreciate a man such as myself, he thought bitterly. He wanted to stop for an occasional visit, a sip of fine wine, and maybe an occasional rendezvous. Cursing, he lamented the cards life had dealt him— a drunk for a wife and a son incapable of rising to the standards he'd set.

He toyed with the idea of creeping over to Pearl's under the cover of darkness, but that seemed beneath him, too base, too vulgar. Besides, someone was sure to recognize him. He required a woman set apart—one eager to submit to a man of his stature and high repute.

He found such a woman—one trying to appear younger than her years, who taught piano lessons to youngsters. After being introduced to the piano teacher in August of 1917, he approved his wife's request that Oscar be exposed to a more cultured life, and was only too happy to bring Oscar to the lessons each Thursday at 7:00 p.m.

The teacher, Wilma Rud, lived alone on the southern edge of town in a small house previously belonging to her parents. A large upright Beckwith Piano took up most of her small living room. About two dozen students came weekly to sit before its eighty-eight keys and receive her instruction.

Oscar rebelled. Not gifted in music, he only took six weeks of lessons before facing his father's wrath for being a quitter. Oscar held his ground, even under threat of his father's belt. He wanted to stay home with his mother, have time for his drawing, his reading, and work on his studies. This time Oscar was victorious, allowing Mr. Lund to eagerly embark upon his new career—that of a first-rate adulterer.

Time was passing Wilma by. Only too conscious of aging—the random gray hairs she discovered, the crow's feet beside her eyes—she, too, had needs. Any chance for passion—and/or money—was quickly passing her by.

In just under six weeks, she had trapped her quarry. Wilma lost a student when Oscar quit, but gained a generous monthly stipend for the frequent attention she lavished on his father. Mr. Lund's evening "business obligations" ultimately became more demanding as the months passed.

The townspeople took note of his shiny black Ford often heading toward Carlton, perhaps to advise a client needing a business loan, they mused. They were impressed with his devotion.

On their intimate evenings, Wilma often played a calming sonata while Mr. Lund listened, leaning back in a comfortable chair. He sipped a bit of wine to settle his spirit after a particularly stressful day dealing with the hoi polloi at the bank. Breathing in the bouquet of his wine, feeling the tension flow from his body, he knew for certain this was the life a man of his stature truly deserved.

Neither Anna Belle nor Oscar felt neglected when Mr. Lund left on "business" evenings. In fact, they both seemed to relax a bit, reading to each other and laughing together while Oscar shared his school day. They'd be in bed before the Model T chugged once again into the yard and was safely parked in the garage. The less time they shared with Mr. Lund, the better they felt. Neither wife nor son was under any illusion about the "work" Mr. Lund so diligently pursued so late into the night. Oscar may have been young, but he wasn't stupid. He had felt the uncomfortable, unnatural relationship developing between his father and the piano teacher. In his young, uncomplicated mind, his father and Miss Rud deserved each other.

Anna Belle seemed to feel better and drink less each day Mr. Lund didn't harass her about some trivial misdeed, some flaw in her appearance, or a shortcoming in her social behavior. She realized she was making progress toward being a better mother.

The two of them faced the world together now. She looked forward to the time she visited with Oscar's friends, and had even invited Daisy Larson in for tea when Daisy accompanied the children one day as they made their deliveries. Occasionally, she even felt like a perfectly normal woman, a good mother—if not an adequate wife. The bottle became less and less a necessity when she rose from her bed and greeted each new day. What ever it was that took Mr. Lund away from them, it was a blessing.

෨20෨
The Meeting and the Battle

FRIDAY MORNING DAWNED in the midst of snow showers and a blustery wind that howled about the corners of the church. At the church early, shovel in hand, Pastor Jenson cleaned off the sidewalk in front, then swept the steps to the front door. Once inside he hung up his coat and hat. The church felt colder than usual at this early hour, probably because of the bitter wind seeping through rattling windowpanes and under doors.

Once the fire crackled in the potbellied stove in his office, heat immediately radiated through the room. He put a kettle of water on top of the stove to make tea.

The seminary had not probed deeply into the possible personal situations that might confront an inexperienced parish pastor. Preaching—he'd covered that in several of his classes. Bible interpretation—his favorite classes. Liturgical choices were few and far between in the Lutheran Church, but he could sing and recite the entire selection of liturgy from memory—forward or backward, if necessary. Yet personal conversations with total strangers, dealing with situations where there was no common ground, knowing how to confront the sinner without giving off the strong odor of condemnation—he felt like a novice even after all his interactions with the unique mix of people he had come to know on the Island.

And now he was to minister to and advise the infamous woman who ran the local brothel. Was there no preliminary instruction for this? No preparation or questionnaire to fill out? He almost started to laugh at himself. Instead, he ran his hands through his hair, praying for divine help in setting the course to be taken during this morning's visit.

Then, suddenly, the perfect confrontation in the Gospel of John, chapter eight, forced its way into his consciousness. Of course! Jesus had already been in this predicament in His earthly ministry and set the standard for those who followed. Who better to set the tone than the Son of God who went to the cross for the sins of all the world—Michael's sins as well as Pearl's. A great expectation surged within him.

Suddenly he heard voices. Someone opened the front door of the church. For a brief moment Michael regretted not asking Pearl to park her carriage in the rear of the church, but he quickly dismissed that cruel and judgmental thought.

Michael stood, smoothed his rumpled hair, and entered the sanctuary. Pearl stood alone in the narthex, snow clinging to her cashmere scarf and generous fur collar. She stepped hesitantly into the aisle of the church, removed a glove and reached out her hand in greeting. "Thank you, Pastor Jenson, for setting aside this time to visit with me." A shy smile crept across her face. "I'm sure you would have found it quite difficult to make a personal call on me."

He returned the smile. "That's probably true, but I'm glad you called, Pearl. I'm pleased you could take the time to visit me here." Taking her slender hand in his large one, he led her up the aisle, around the white-painted altar and communion rail, toward his office located at the back of the church next to the sacristy.

The altar painting—the one he walked by every time he made his way to his office—depicted Jesus standing before the empty tomb, His pierced hands reaching out to Mary, who knelt weeping before him. It flashed through Michael's mind that many biblical scholars had come to the conclusion that Mary Magdalene might have been a prostitute.

Once in the office, Michael helped with Pearl's coat and scarf, hung them on the coat tree, and invited her to be seated in the comfortable chair near the desk. The small wood stove had outdone itself. The room was warm and inviting and the kettle hot. Pearl had settled herself in the chair, her heavy perfume permeating the room.

"Welcome, Pearl. I've been looking forward to our visit. Thank you for coming." He made tea and, with her assent, poured them each a cup. Small talk came easily to them.

Then with deep longing in her voice, she asked, "Can I be totally honest with you? I have a list of topics I would like to cover in our visit this morning." She extracted a folded paper from the pocket of her frock. Carefully unfolding it, she referred to it, then again raised her eyes his. He could see her list of words covered the paper.

"I'm hoping you can help me find my way to settle all the troubling items I have written here." With both hands she attempted to erase the creases in the sheet of paper as it lay in her lap. "May I begin? " she asked.

Pastor Jenson was intrigued. No one had ever come to him with a list before, one neatly written out on a piece of tablet paper. He set aside his mug, leaned forward, and said, "I'm at your service. Please, Pearl, tell me how I can be of help."

Two hours flew by. A loud knocking at the front door interrupted them. Excusing himself, Michael hurried through the church to open the door, and found Max, Pearl's recently hired driver, shivering on the top step. "How much longer should I wait?" he asked.

"Good grief, Max," Michael said as he took his arm and ushered him into the sanctuary, where he settled Max comfortably in a pew. "Come in! Come in! Let me get you some hot tea to warm you up!" Within a minute or two, Michael came back down the aisle with a steaming cup of tea in his hand.

Max lifted the mug in salute and made himself comfortable. Soon the warmth of the tea lulled him to sleep, his eyes drooping as his chin fell to his chest.

Abruptly, Max was awakened from his nap by the sound of the office door opening and closing. Pulling himself upright and trying to look attentive, he watched as Pearl, supported on the pastor's arm, came out and proceeded to the front of the altar. Pearl leaned heavily on the pastor, his strong right arm surrounded her, holding her steady as they paused, both facing the altar painting before them.

The pastor placed his hands gently on Pearl's shoulders, turning her so he looked directly into her eyes. Then he spoke. "You must remember always the freeing power of forgiveness and the gift of being able to start anew." She leaned into his chest, and Michael enclosed her in a warm embrace. The sound of her quiet weeping echoed softly through the empty sanctuary. Max turned away, finding it difficult to see Pearl in such an emotional state. He had never seen her shed a tear.

Pearl regained her composure, straightened, and adjusted her scarf about her face as she pulled her fur collar up. She turned and the two of them proceeded to the pew where Max now stood waiting. "Thank you, Max, for being so patient." Her face was stained from the blend of tears with her cosmetics. Slipping her hands into her fine leather gloves, she smiled a wan smile at both the men. "I think I'm ready to return home now."

Max tucked her arm securely around his elbow as Pastor Jenson opened the front door. Cold air swept into the narthex, bringing in a swirl of snow. With Max on one side of Pearl, the pastor on the other, they descended the steps to the carriage.

Pearl settled into the carriage, her head resting upon the tufted leather seat, while Max made sure the heavy woolen quilt was tucked securely about her. Max then removed the blanket on the horse. The horse snorted and shook his head, making the bells on its bridle ring, as if to say, "Well, it's about time!"

Michael reached into the buggy once more to take Pearl's gloved hand. "I have your list. I know your heart. I won't rest until you're at peace!" She did not open her eyes, but acknowledged him with a slight nod. Michael stepped back from the carriage and Max snapped the whip and set the black phaeton with the rich green trim heading across the bridge, past the Island and over the river to the white house on the far shore.

Rubbing his hands together, Michael bounded up the steps and securely shut the front door against the cold and snow.

When he entered his office he was thankful for its warmth. The stove needed to be filled again. The kettle retained enough water for one last cup of tea.

Again settled behind his desk, Michael warmed his hands on his teacup, his mind full of all the topics he and Pearl had covered in the course of the morning. In his dealings with people of the parish, he was constantly amazed by the amount of pain and suffering hidden behind the eyes of the people he had come to know and love. And now Pearl, having shared her story, craved help and forgiveness for the torturous events of her past life.

He placed his head in his hands, elbows resting on the desk, and came to the conclusion the entire list of the Ten Commandments had been spelled out and disobeyed, in one form or another, throughout the course of her life. She had been a victim and a perpetrator. She had lived in innocence and trust and had committed vile deeds.

As Michael so often did, he reached for his Greek New Testament and thumbed his way to a verse he had shared with Pearl over the course of their visit—I John 1:9. He read it silently, and then he read the familiar words one more time aloud, giving emphasis to the words he found so moving. "If *we* confess *our* sins, He is *faithful* and *just* to *forgive* us our sins, and to *cleanse* us from *all* unrighteousness." Two points always impressed him. The sinner had to initiate the process—"if *we* confess," and the totality of the promised forgiveness—"cleanse us from *all* unrighteousness." Who could ask for more?

Pearl seemed to take great relief from this verse. Noting her reaction, he copied it down on a piece of paper for her. She read it carefully, folded it, and placed it in her dress pocket. He also gave her a Bible of her own, with a bookmark placed at this verse.

Her list remained on the desk. He turned it about and looked over the careful notations. She had some impressive tasks to accomplish in the approaching months. Now it was his turn to make a list for himself. Taking pen in hand he began:

1. Contact an attorney, possibly Mr. Fessenbeck.
2. Check with Mr. Skemp, a real estate and insurance agent.
3. Make an appointment for Pearl with Dr. Sewell.
4. Set up a meeting with Mrs. Berg and Pearl.
5. Arrange for a baptism.

The fifth would probably be the most difficult. He thought perhaps the baptismal service could be held at Hank and Daisy's home. He would invite her Island acquaintances and see if Big Jack and Daisy would serve a meal following the service. There! That should keep him busy for a time.

By evening the snowfall had diminished and the wind declined enough to allow the snowdrifts to remain undisturbed. Michael returned one last time to the church, where he made a final attempt at clearing the stairs and sidewalk leading to the front of the church. The night was beautiful. Pausing to look up as he made his way home to the parsonage, he was dazzled by the clear skies, displaying the stars like diamonds scattered across a black velvet cloth.

The day had been full, and tomorrow would certainly be no different. He prepared himself for bed, and once he had settled under the warm quilts he felt the stress and tension flow from his body and his soul. Then, suddenly, the sound of his telephone shattered the stillness and his peace of mind.

Dashing down the stairs, a quilt clutched over his long underwear, Michael found his way to the dining room, where he quickly lit the lamp on the buffet. He picked up the receiver and, before he even placed it close to his ear, he could hear the sound of someone weeping hysterically on the other end of the line. "Hello! Hello!" he shouted into the transmitter. "Who's calling? What can I do to help?"

The sobbing person seemed to rally, taking a deep breath in an attempted to regain control. Michael still didn't know who was on the other end of the line. Then, a slight intonation of the voice at the other end of the line brought a person to mind. "Mrs. Berg? Is that you?" The sobbing continued. "Mrs. Berg, let me help you. Do you want me to come over? Do you want to wait to talk until morning?"

"Please! Please! Come now!" Another volley of crying. "Please come now!"

"I'm coming, Mrs. Berg! I'll be standing on your front porch in a few minutes." Taking the steps two at a time and tossing the quilt back on the bed, within a minute or two he was dressed and galloping down the stairs, and out into the inky blackness of the wintery night.

A few minutes later, he charged up her front steps. The porch light came on and the front door flew open. There she stood—the intimidating Mrs. Berg—rumpled, tear-stained, deflated, looking like a child whose heart was broken. She reached out to him as he entered. The door shut firmly behind him, and the porch light was shut off.

Before a half-hour had passed, the porch light again came on and Michael stepped back outside, framing Mrs. Berg in the doorway by light from her living room. She looked as though she had almost regained control of her emotions, though her eyes were still red and swollen from weeping. Michael embraced her briefly before turning to leave.

She reached after him. "Please! Please tell Samuel I didn't mean what I said." Her voice caught and she could barely speak. "Everything was sin-filled. If I could, I would take all the words back!" Leaning on the door frame, she cried, "Dear God, please give me another chance. I'll never call anyone a slut again!" Turning slowly, she returned once again to her home. "Never again, I promise!" The door closed behind her and the porch light went dark.

Mrs. Berg's sad laments behind him, Michael set out through the shadows with determination. Once down the block, he turned at the corner and began to run, silently putting a dark and deserted Cloquet Avenue quickly at his back. As he passed the bank, he noticed the clock on its wall read almost eleven thirty. Soon he reached the red bridge, crossed over the river, and quickly found himself in the middle of a Friday night on the Island.

Aware the Island nightlife was just getting started, Michael wasn't sure how he'd be received at the saloon where young Samuel Berg had gone to drown his anger toward his mother, his disappointment in the social order, and his sorrow for the girl he loved.

Hurrying in the direction of the saloons, Michael shook his head. How foolish humans could be, how hard-hearted toward even those they loved most. Fragments of his conversation with Mrs. Berg echoed as he hurried to find the broken-hearted lover.

Mrs. Berg had spelled out in frank terms what had transpired with her son, and she was ready to bite her tongue off in regret for her hurtful words. Her relationship with Samuel had been refreshed since her kindness to his friend Willard. She had been proud at Samuel's expertise on Lumberjack Days. He had warmed to her less critical opinion of him and that of his friends. He wasn't perfect, but he always told her he was trying to be the son she always wanted—at least in some modest degree.

That night he came home to confess his love for Beatrice and share with his mother that he and Beatrice would like to be married before he left for the logging camp. "We want your blessing, Mother," he had said. "I'd love to bring Beatrice home to meet you."

Full of hope, he continued. "I know you and Beatrice will grow fond of each other. Beatrice hasn't really had a mother for a long time. She never had any family until Pearl took her in and cared for her like she was her own daughter."

At the mention of Pearl's name, Mrs. Berg's cheeks flushed and her eyes narrowed.

Filled with happiness, Samuel was unaware of the storm brewing. "We'd love to have a church wedding. I thought you could speak to the pastor on our behalf. I know how much you like him." He looked at her, smiling, with childlike anticipation his wishes would be granted.

She exploded in righteous indignation. "Samuel, you can't be serious! The girl is a whore! She lives in a brothel, for heaven's sake! That woman, Pearl, has trained her up to be just like she is—a slut! What are you thinking!?"

Her words battered against the love in Samuel's heart. Before he could justify his love for Beatrice, his mother told him in no uncertain terms that a "woman of that sort" would never be welcome in her home. She continued, growing more vehement as her anger overtook her common sense. "Stop talking like that, Mother!" Samuel's voice was soft, so soft the words his mother continued to fling at him were all she could hear. "She's pure, Mother—kept from sin by Pearl, who wanted her to have a better life."

His mother paid no attention. Her tirade continued.

"Listen to me!" Samuel spoke firmly and rose from his chair. "She's pure as any young girl can be! And I love her all the more because of that!"

Words like "slut," "Island trash," "tramp," and "whore" continued to thunder against his ears. Samuel lost his temper. Striding over to his mother, he roughly took her by the shoulders and yelled, "You never listen to me!" Tears suddenly filled his eyes. "You can't talk about her like that! I swear I'll never enter this house again—ever. I'll go to the saloon and drink until I'm fall-down drunk and can wipe you and your damning, hurtful words from my mind. Forever!"

With one final look of contempt toward his mother, Samuel grabbed his woolen jacket, slammed the door as he left, and disappeared into the darkness of the street.

Mrs. Berg suddenly realized what she had done. She had ruined the progress she and Samuel had made toward being a parent and a child who could care for each other. Once she realized how she had alienated her beloved son—her only son—her heart seemed to break. Collapsing on the couch, she buried her head in her hands and let the tears flow.

So, she called her pastor—a man as young as her son—and wept on his shoulder as the words spilled from her lips. "He became so angry! For a moment I was afraid when I saw the effect my words had on him!" She buried her tear-stained face in his jacket, sobs wracking her shoulders. "He shouted that he couldn't live without Beatrice, whether I accepted her or not. He paced the floor and shook his fist in my face."

Disbelief flooded her face. She stepped back, eyes wide with apprehension. "He hasn't been drinking at all since last summer. I realize now he'd changed his ways ever since Beatrice became a part of his life. And now he swore he'd drink himself into a stupor!"

She covered her face with her hands and again collapsed into a chair. Tears choked her voice as she entreated Pastor Jenson, "Please find Samuel! Beg him to give me one final chance to be the mother I so want to be!"

She pressed her lace-trimmed hanky to her lips, "Help me be someone who can love unconditionally and not judge so quickly. Dear God, I will truly love Beatrice."

The wind from the north carried the sounds of the revelry taking place on the Island. By the time Michael turned the corner at the end of Cloquet Avenue and headed toward the horse barns and the red bridge, he was chilled to the bone. No scarf, no gloves, thank goodness he had grabbed a knit hat as he flew out the door. He broke into a run, concerned for the events taking place in a saloon and also to warm himself.

Once he crossed the bridge, the Island spread out before him. To his left and to his right the saloons were brightly lit and humming with business. Most patrons sought a warm place on a night like this, and few loggers walked about on St. Louis Avenue. Michael stopped to help an elderly man who came tumbling down the steps into the street. Setting him firmly on his feet, Michael pointed him in the direction of the hotel on the corner and watched as the man walked unsteadily toward the door.

Now came the difficult part of his mission—choosing which saloon would have been the choice of the heart-broken young man. The only one that caught Michael's eye was the Moose Saloon, where Big Jack had taken Michael last summer when they toured the Island.

Just as he was about to enter the Moose Saloon, the door flew open and a man crashed into Michael. Both fell, and when they stood brushing the snow from their clothes, Michael recognized Max, Pearl's carriage driver, who appeared anxious and upset, eager to be away.

Max clutched Michael's arm. "God must have sent you, Reverend! They're beatin' him to a pulp!" He motioned wildly inside the saloon. "Samuel's in big trouble with some of the rowdy boys on their way to the camps. He was drinkin' heavy and got real nasty with some of them loggers that just came in from Carlton. It wasn't pretty!" He shook his head in disbelief. "I'm on my way to get Big Jack!" Max shoved Michael through the door of the saloon and took off running up the street as fast as his crooked old legs could go, yelling for Big Jack at the top of his lungs.

For a moment the brightness inside the saloon blinded Michael. Then the sounds and odors of the saloon swept over him—the stale odor of cigarette smoke, the spats of gnawed and chewed plugs of tobacco dotting the floor in every direction, the sweat of hard-working, unwashed bodies, the burning wood, the liquor spilled and ingested and vomited on occasion, the cussing and shouting and arguing. Michael was suddenly overwhelmed.

Once accustomed to the light, Michael saw three young men brawling right in the middle of the saloon, tipped tables and chairs scattered across the floor in all directions. The men engaged in battle were surrounded by a circle of onlookers. The spectators kept right on drinking and smoking and chewing and cheering loudly for Samuel—or for no one in particular.

"Hit him in the gut, Samuel!"

"Keep moving! Don't let 'em get a hold of ya!"

"Kick him again! One more time—in the face! Way to go!"

"Poke his eyes out! Hell, then he won't be able to find you!" Much laughter followed.

"Grab his hair and pound his damn head on the floor! That'll put an end to him!"

The atmosphere of the Moose Saloon was charged with the violence of battle going on. As the moments passed, the fight seemed to take an even more violent turn.

Samuel was taking the brunt of the battle. Evidently he'd held his own at first, which was impressive considering how drunk he'd become. Everyone knew Samuel was strong, but two against one was hardly fair.

With blood running from his nose and lips, Samuel warily circled the room, fending off the attacks by one—or both—of his adversaries. Michael saw in a moment that Samuel seemed to be having trouble drawing a full breath and the strength of his arms was draining away as the two aggressive men continued to rain their blows upon him.

From the looks of things, not one man in the saloon seemed ready to come to Samuel's defense, but they took great pleasure in watching—and cheering. Michael knew he couldn't just stand there, doing nothing, while his friend was being hammered. Suddenly, throwing off his coat and hat and, without thinking about the results of his actions, Michael—the pastor—leaped into the fray.

He could hear the surprised voices around him. "Hey! Ain't that the pastor from town? What the hell is he doing out here on the Island?"

The entire saloon focused on the new man entering the fight. Michael knew this would not be his finest moment, but there was no way he could just stand by and watch. "I'm here, Samuel!" Michael shouted as he quickly rolled up his sleeves. "You take one, and I'll take the other!"

Michael's voice and presence seemed to infuse Samuel with new vigor. Straightening, Samuel began throwing punches in all directions, being disoriented from alcohol and the blows to the head. One or two lucky connections knocked one of the assailants on the side of the head, causing him to crash to the floor. Recovering quickly, the man regained his feet only to be smashed in the face with a lucky punch from Samuel's hammer-like fists.

He instantly fell to his knees, holding his broken nose, as Samuel collapsed on top of him. Both men momentarily lay on the floor of the saloon, still as death.

Michael, in the meantime, took a flying leap and landed on the back of the second assailant, who was aiming a kick at Samuel's head. Michael's right hand clutched the face of the logger, his left arm surrounded the logger's chest, and his legs encased the logger's hips. Holding on for dear life, Michael almost laughed out loud as a vision of what he must look like—wild pastor in a saloon brawl. Who could have predicted this moment?

Reaching back, Michael's assailant grabbed onto Michael's hair with both hands and gave a powerful tug, a tug that wrenched Michael's head and neck. Michael felt his neck snap, but he held on—tighter than ever.

The trapped logger stumbled across the saloon floor, slamming Michael into the front of the bar, scattering glass mugs, bottles, and the cheering bystanders as he tried to loosen Michael's grip. Even though it felt as though he might have a broken rib, Michael was not about to let go. His technique wasn't pretty, but it was all he knew how to do. His mind slipped back to his younger days on the farm, when he wrestled livestock and broke horses for the neighbors. He may have been a pastor now, but hidden under his robes and collar was a man who knew how to hang on and ride to the finish.

The bar customers were cheering wildly. After all, Samuel was one of them, and they had known him since he was a boy. And now this crazy young pastor had turned up on the scene, so they decided to cheer for him as well. A groan went up from the crowd of onlookers as Michael's back and head were smashed into the wall by the front door.

Stunned for a moment, Michael lost his grip and crashed to the floor. Once the logger was free of him, he turned to the fallen man at his feet and delivered a well-placed kick to the head. Instantly, Michael rolled over on his stomach, using his arms to protect his face. When he was just about to receive another kick, the front door flew open.

A cold wind swept into the saloon as Big Jack stood framed in the door, large and intimidating. He hesitated only a second, assessing the situation. His attention quickly zeroed in on the man about to administer a nasty kick to Michael's back.

"I wouldn't do that if I were you," Big Jack spoke quietly, but with an implied threat.

The logger looked up briefly and saw Big Jack advancing toward him, a menacing look in his eyes. Retreating slowly, as he appraised Big Jack's size and strength, the logger came to the quick conclusion that surrender was the better part of valor. He meekly raised his hands in surrender. "I give up! Don't hit me!" he gasped, blood streaming down his face. "I'm all done with this crazy fight!" he muttered as he dropped to his knees. Thus, the evening's entertainment had come to an end.

Big Jack grabbed the logger by the shirt collar, dragged him to his feet. When they were nose to nose, he told the quaking man in no uncertain terms to pack up his gear and leave—*now!* Both loggers staggered to the door and were handed their packs by the cheering saloon customers. They were roughly shoved out the door and into the street.

Big Jack watched from the door of the saloon as the injured men hesitated a moment, glancing up and down the street, trying to decide where they could go for shelter. Suddenly crowds of men spilled out of other saloons, having heard a dandy fight was going on at the Moose Saloon. They were too late.

Big Jack shouted to the two brawlers, "Walk up Main Street. I'll let you have a room for the night in my boarding house!"

Max headed out of the Moose Saloon, ready to guide the men to a warm bed for the night. Big Jack always tried to live by the unwritten code of ethics shared among lumberjacks: to watch over and protect a fellow lumberjack whenever necessary—even if he picks a fight with a friend.

The two men followed Max, limping up the darkened road.

Big Jack was still left with two more casualties on his hands. Samuel, totally inebriated and on the floor in a pool of his own vomit, had initiated the attack by pouring a pitcher of beer over the heads of the two boisterous young men sitting at a nearby table. According to witnesses, Samuel had told them in no uncertain terms to "shut up!" and dumped the alcohol on them when they didn't listen.

The two seated men, dripping with beer, had leaped to their feet and advanced menacingly toward Samuel,who started swinging. By the time Michael burst through the front door of the saloon, Samuel was barely able to stand upright. Michael, a man of the cloth, became the hero of the evening.

When Samuel came around, two of his friends, one on each side, helped him off the floor, out the door, and into a carriage that would take him to the boarding house. Big Jack would take care of him and make sure he survived the night.

Pastor Jenson, on the other hand, needed medical attention for a gash on the side of his face where his assailant's boot had connected and slashed open the skin. Setting some of the chairs upright, two men lifted Michael from where he sat on the floor and placed him on a chair near the bar. Everyone could see that the pastor was bleeding profusely from the cut on his cheek, even with the bartender holding a towel tightly to the wound to stem the flow of blood. Michael felt dazed on the one hand and, on the other hand, felt like he might erupt in unrestrained laughter.

Big Jack clapped Michael on his sore shoulder and couldn't suppress a wide grin. "Well, Reverend Jenson. This is a first for any of the saloons on the Island." Big Jack shook his head in disbelief. "You son of a gun! I'm damn proud of you!" Still shaking his head, he couldn't contain his grin. "Where did you ever learn to fight like that?" A loud chuckle escaped Jack's lips. "You were the Avenging Angel, if I've ever seen one! This fight will be one of the stories people will tell over and over about the Island!" Then, still laughing, he stepped out onto the boardwalk and headed up the darkened street toward the boarding house.

The men in the saloon were eager to help the pastor as well. "Can you believe it? A pastor coming into the saloon and getting into a fight with a couple of loggers?" The regulars at the saloon were puzzled by his aggressive behavior, but even more impressed by his willingness to stand up for his friend.

One man brought Michael another towel for his cheek. Two somewhat inebriated observers brought him a shot glass full of whiskey—for medicinal purposes, of course. They held it to Michael's lips and down it went with a sting and a bite. Michael was surprised; the drink actually did make him feel better. Two men he recognized from their occasional church attendance offered to take him to the doctor. He agreed, and the two men helped Michael from the chair and, with one on each side, they headed for the door.

Just as they were to take leave of the saloon Michael paused, turned his head to address the men hovering around him, and said in a slightly shaky voice, "Well, men, our church service begins at 10:00 a.m. Sunday. You are all welcome!" He paused for a moment and then grinned with his battered face. "I'd love to see all of you there!"

All the men broke into laughter and clapped him on the back as he made his way through the door, across the boardwalk, and into one of the men's carriages. "Our first stop has to be Mrs. Berg's house," Michael told his good Samaritans. "She needs to know Samuel's okay and being cared for by Big Jack." The two men agreed, and off they went into the darkness.

The carriage clattered over the red bridge and turned east on Cloquet Avenue. The clock on the side of the bank now read 12:35 a.m. *What a difference an hour can make in the course of the day*, Michael mused. They turned the corner and parked in front of Mrs. Berg's home. The light came on immediately, and Mrs. Berg drew back a curtain, peering out into the street. One of the men went to her front door where Mrs. Berg now stood in her robe, silhouetted in the porch light. Upon hearing that Samuel was going to be fine and was in the care of Big Jack, she grasped the bearer of the good news to her bosom in a warm embrace.

"Oh, dear God! Thank you! Thank you!" Her encompassing embrace grew even tighter. "Bless you, my dear man! Bless you!"

"Well, I never!" the man repeated over and over as he returned to the carriage and they headed off to the doctor's house.

The doctor cleansed the wound and stitched Michael's face back together. Finally home, he bid his new friends good night

In the course of his dreams that night, someone might have heard the pastor shout, "Take that, you Philistine!"

ഇ21രെ
After the Battle

SATURDAY MORNING DAWNED clear and cold. The Island swirled with activity as the loggers collected their gear and readied themselves for the winter months ahead, when they would live in the logging camps up north. The stables and storage barns were full of teamsters working to outfit some of the wagons with sturdy wooden runners, reinforced with iron bands. The early transportation to the camps would be by wagon, jolting over the impossibly difficult roads, loaded with building supplies, equipment, barrels of food, and anything else the boss decided was a necessity.

Then the snows came, and the wagons would struggle over the snow-covered roads on runners. Experienced teamsters looked forward to traveling on the smooth surface of the frozen rivers once the ice was thick enough. Some winters were too mild and the river roads never materialized. When the winter weather did cooperate, the teamsters and horses appreciated the much smoother, faster route to the camps.

Pearl's house was nearly hidden by the snow-covered pines. On this particular morning Pearl remained in bed, pillows propped behind her while she sipped her coffee and contemplated the activities of her day. Yesterday's visit to Pastor Jenson had been exhausting. By the time Max had driven the carriage to the front door of her establishment, she was in no condition to share any of her experience with Beatrice or Max.

The three of them sat in silence, warming themselves in front of the fire in the parlor. Refusing the light meal Beatrice had prepared for her, and before the sun slipped behind the naked boughs of the apple trees to the west, she took to her bed and remained there until morning arrived along with her customary cup of strong, black coffee with a dash of cream. After two sips, she was ready to deal with the consequences of yesterday's decisions.

Pearl had known for some time she was ill. She felt her strength ebb away day by day. Yet today, she felt full of life and determination. She relived the moment yesterday when she had gone to her knees, weeping so intensely she could not catch her breath, after baring her soul to Pastor Jenson. Never before had she spoken of the deep, hidden blots on her soul and the pains that had followed her from her youth. She felt she had breathed out the vile parts of her soul and breathed in freshness, newness, and cleanness.

Pastor Jenson had raised her up from her knees and helped her to the chair in front of his desk. She could still feel his hands resting on her bowed head and recalled his voice as he prayed for her absolution, separation from her past, and a new beginning.

How she had loved the sound of his words—that she could be the child of God, who loved her just as she was. She had felt a rush of peace and tranquility, like a calming breeze, fill her inner being. She felt it still. She held her warm cup with both hands and closed her eyes. "Thank you, dear Lord!" was all she could say.

Soon Beatrice entered to help Pearl with her wardrobe. Settling herself on the bed, Beatrice breathed in the heavy aroma of fragrant perfumes that always surrounded Pearl, while gently stroking Pearl's unruly hair.

How Pearl adored this lovely girl! And now, thanks to all they covered yesterday, Pastor Jenson had given her a plan that would prepare Beatrice for a better life and give Pearl the satisfaction of knowing that at long last she had finally found a path to peace and atonement.

With help from Beatrice, Pearl selected her attire for the day, a process she always enjoyed now that she could pick and choose from the lovely clothes that filled her closet. Today she would wear something in blue, a frock to symbolize the peace in her heart.

Meanwhile, in the parsonage, Michael opened his eyes to a throbbing headache. His stitches ached and his head felt like it would soon explode. Easing himself into a sitting position, he placed both feet on the cold wooden floor and reached for his robe. Trying not to bend over or move his head, he slipped his bare feet into a pair of worn slippers and aimed himself toward the bathroom. Not everyone had an indoor toilet. Michael was very thankful to the trustees that he did.

As he painstakingly descended the stairs, he was surprised to hear someone in his kitchen. Slowly he opened the door to the kitchen. Warmth radiating from the wood stove greeted him, quickly bringing a sense of comfort and wellbeing. And there, frying hot cakes on a big black skillet, stood Mrs. Berg. A pot of coffee percolated away on the back burner and the table was set for two. Michael's eyes widened. He pulled his robe more closely about his long underwear and ran a hand through his hair. Mrs. Berg turned to him with a smile.

Her cheeks were flushed, her braids a bit askew, and a flowered apron covered her ample bosom and waist. Scrambled eggs stood at the ready in another pan set to a rear burner, and bacon sizzled in a cast iron pan. Everything looked delicious.

"Sit down!" she ordered as she bustled back and forth from stove to table. "I hope you don't mind I took it upon myself to enter the parsonage and prepare breakfast for you." Three round, golden pancakes were flipped onto his plate, followed by a helping of eggs and four slices of crisp bacon. Maple syrup and butter awaited him.

"I heard what took place on the Island last evening." Tears filled her eyes as she continued. "I don't know what would've happened if you hadn't come to Samuel's defense." Coffee and cream nearly overflowed his cup. "After you and the two men left my house, I walked all by myself through town—yes, I did—across the bridge, up the street on the Island, to Big Jack's boarding house."

She laughed. "I knocked on the door and, when he answered it, I introduced myself to Big Jack." She again chuckled, and her bosom shook with levity.

"I can tell you, he was really shocked, so I left him standing at the door with his mouth open and just continued inside until I found my son. Of course, Samuel thought I was a bad dream. He was speechless!" She sat down opposite Michael, who finally realized how famished he was and began to eat.

Five pancakes and two cups of coffee later, Michael felt he had some idea of what Mrs. Berg had wanted to accomplish on her clandestine journey to the Island. He admired her for her grit. How many women her age would have had the courage to cross the boundary between the town and the Island to seek her son? He admired her grace when she relayed the conversation with her son, when she pleaded for his forgiveness and another chance to meet and come to know the girl he loved so much.

She asked Michael, "Pastor Jenson, would you consent to serve as the minister at Samuel's marriage to Beatrice sometime in the near future—hopefully before Christmas?" Tears suddenly filled her eyes. "I would consider it your gift to all three of us!"

Michael was only too happy to comply, as he helped himself to another strip of bacon. "Tell them to come in for a visit so we can make some plans for the service," he managed to say.

Mrs. Berg walked around the table to plant a warm kiss atop his messy hair.

"You go get ready for the day. I'll clean up," Mrs. Berg ordered. She took hot water from the stove and poured it into the dishpan, where she began an attack on the dishes.

"When I'm finished I'll just head for home." She looked into his somewhat battered face and raised her hand to pat his wounded cheek. "You're quite the warrior for the Lord. I'll never forget what you did. God bless you always!" She pulled Michael against her, his face planted in her bosom, which smelled faintly of talcum powder.

After one last sip of coffee, Michael headed upstairs, where he tenderly shaved the part of his face not covered by bandages, dressed, and prepared for a busy Saturday. He needed to be ready for the Sabbath. Suddenly he realized that his face felt somewhat better after such an excellent breakfast, and hopefully by tomorrow it would even look better as his congregation saw him for the first time as a wounded warrior.

Soon he heard the front door open and close and, looking out his bedroom window, he saw Mrs. Berg walking briskly down the street toward her home. Michael smiled as he watched her bundled-up figure disappear around the corner. On an impulse, he decided he would pay one more visit to Big Jack's before settling into the work waiting for him at his office—just in case Samuel needed him.

SAMUEL AWAKENED TO LOUD VOICES and the tramping of hobnail boots on the wooden floor of the hall outside his room. What time was it, anyway? For a moment he couldn't quite remember where he was, why he felt so poorly, and how his face and body had become such a source of pain and suffering.

And his stomach—without warning he had to vomit. He leaned over the edge of the bed to find a bucket waiting, already containing a large amount of whatever it was he once had in his stomach. Retching once again, he then lay back on his pillow. He was covered with sweat. The sun streaming in from the nearby window hurt his eyes. He forced his mind to return to his vague memories of the previous evening.

He had been very drunk. He recalled drinking heavily before ending up in a knock down, drag out fight, but he couldn't remember who he had been fighting. Either he was seeing double as he recalled the night, or there had been two hefty loggers involved.

Then the image of another man materialized out of his dim memory. He could recall the man's shout of encouragement and the sight of his rescuer flying through the air, finally crashing onto the back of one of his assailants. Then Samuel's memory skipped to waking up in this room, wherever it was, and feeling like a chunk of rotten meat. He hung his head over the edge of the bed and aimed once more for the foul-smelling bucket.

The door suddenly flew open, and Big Jack strode in carrying a basin and a towel. "You're quite a sight, my friend," he said. "I'm here to clean you up and then get some food and coffee into your empty gut before I send you home to your mother's house."

Big Jack set the bucket in the hall and pulled up a chair to the bed. Samuel began to protest the sponge bath and the possibility of a trip to his mother's house as Big Jack applied the soap and warm water to Samuel's face, arms, and chest as he explained the events of the previous evening. While drying Samuel off, Big Jack chuckled at the reports being circulated on the Island, of Samuel being so drunk he was swinging blindly.

"There you were, throwing punches in all directions, not necessarily connecting with anyone!" Big Jack laughed. "Back and forth, you were tossed like a ball between those two loggers." He soaked the washcloth and wiped down Samuel's arms and hands. "You were so drunk you could hardly stand, much less fight with anyone."

He laughed even harder as he told Samuel about his "savior"—the man who came through the front door of the saloon and leaped onto the back of the logger about to beat Samuel into unconsciousness. "Pastor Jenson, believe it or not, was like a bat out of Hell!"

Samuel's jaw dropped in disbelief. Big Jack pushed Samuel's mouth closed and began to apply shaving soap with a well-worn shaving brush. "I didn't see it for myself, but I heard tell from everybody there that it was a sight to behold."

The straight razor in Big Jack's large, steady hands glided up Samuel's throat and down his lean cheeks. "He saw you were in trouble so he waded in," Big Jack said. "He held on for dear life, rode him like a cowboy on a wild horse."

He wiped the remaining soap from Samuel's face and neck. "I guess we don't usually expect that from a pastor. Max came running for me when the pastor seemed to be having trouble. I came through the door just as the pastor hit the floor and was getting a well-placed kick to the head. The brawl ended before I could knock heads together." He laughed.

"I even invited the two brawlers to spend the night here. They both took a beating, too." Big Jack shook his head. "Not bad guys, really. I'd met them before. Too much to drink and then someone—namely you, Samuel—poured a pitcher of beer over their head."

A touch of aftershave lotion was Big Jack's final touch for Samuel. "You need to smell good, cuz you sure don't look very good. What if Beatrice should wander by?"

Big Jack surveyed his work and nodded approvingly. "You got the whole fight started, Samuel. God, you guys in love are foolish, foolish men!" Big Jack put the cork back in the aftershave bottle. "Those two guys got up early this morning, grabbed a pancake or two, and hightailed it for the camps." He smacked Samuel on the side of his head. "They looked as bad as you do—almost!"

When Big Jack placed his equipment and the basin out in the hall, Samuel said, "The pastor came to my rescue?"

"I can't believe it, either," said Big Jack. "He took a kick to the face and had to be taken to the doctor for stitches." Big Jack shook his head. "I never saw the like!"

Samuel was shocked. "But . . . how in the world did he know I was in the Moose Saloon? Why would he come defend me in the middle of a drunken brawl? I don't get it."

Big Jack responded to a knock at the door. Maggie had an armful of clean clothing for Samuel. She waved shyly when Samuel lifted a hand in greeting. Then Big Jack closed the door, and Samuel rose unsteadily to his feet and began to change clothes.

"The pastor came because your mother was worried about you," Jack said. "I guess she was so distressed about your argument she called him just before midnight." Big Jack helped tuck in the back of Samuel's shirt. "And shortly after two o'clock this morning, I went to the door," he paused for effect, "and there, on my front step, in the cold and snow, stood your mother herself, all bundled up like an Eskimo. She pushed right by me, walked past all the loggers in their long underwear, and found her way to this room. She cleaned you up a bit, cried over you, said she was sorry a hundred times, and tucked you in for the remainder of the night. Then she turned around and headed for the door, refused a ride, and walked back home in the dark, past all the drunks on the Island." Big Jack shook his head in wonder. "Your mother is quite the woman."

Samuel sat down on the bed, head in his hands. Now he could remember what he first thought was a bad dream, a hallucination. He vaguely remembered seeing his mother's face floating unsteadily before him. .

He recalled hearing a still, small voice far back in the recesses of his mind saying, "I will love your Beatrice, I promise!" That must have been his mother.

Samuel quickly pulled on his boots and his knit hat and walked unsteadily down the hall to the dining room for some breakfast. Max was waiting for him near the front door, the horse and carriage outside, already tied up to the hitching rail. Samuel flung open the front door and stepped outside onto the porch of the boarding house, where he collided with Pastor Jenson as he bounded up the steps two at a time. The two men, not quite a match in height and body weight, ricocheted off each other.

Once they regained their balance, they embraced each other. Samuel was overcome when he saw Michael's bruised and bandaged face. Soon Michael and Samuel were laughing uproariously, while the loggers coming and going from the boarding house quickly joined in with back-slapping and good-natured pushing and shoving.

Samuel pointed to the carriage. "Come with me, please. I'm going to Pearl's to get Beatrice. Then I'd like the three of us to go to my mother's house." He paused, considering once again the plan he had devised. "I'm not completely sure what will happen when we get there, but I think we're ready to see each other face to face."

Michael helped Samuel into the carriage, then climbed in beside him. Max flicked the whip and off they went toward the north bridge and the white house beyond. "I'll be at your back, Samuel, if you should need me. I know your mother is ripe and ready for what you and Beatrice desire."

Michael had no doubt about the result of today's visit. His inner gauge of right and wrong was firmly in the positive. The world appeared to be in a better place—"And God saw that it was good!"

ᔥ22ᔧ
The Sabbath

THE NEXT DAY DAWNED bright and clear, a lovely November Sabbath. Michael slipped from the warmth of his bed earlier than usual. He'd need time to change his bandages and try to make himself look presentable before setting foot outside. Before long he had dressed, attended to his bruised face, made coffee, eaten a bowl of oatmeal, had a second cup of black coffee, and now felt ready for the day.

Today's church service would be like no other. He was sure reports of his altercation on the Island had flown across the town. He was also certain details had become more violent and more sensational as the tale was repeated.

He turned to his sermon. He opened his Bible and scanned his notes. Psalm 119 was the basis for his sermon. He would begin with the first eight verses, emphasizing verse six: "Then I shall not be put to shame, having my eyes fixed on all thy commandments, I will praise thee with an upright heart, when I learn thy righteous ordinances." He would finish with verses 169-171: "Let my cry come before thee, O Lord; give me understanding according to thy word! Let my supplication come before thee; deliver me according to thy word. My lips will pour forth praise, that thou dost teach me thy statutes."

He loved the idea of having no shame, of learning how to live right, of being able to cry out to God, and that God would hear and give the seeker an understanding of His word. Finally he would close with the concept of praising God for teaching all of them the right way to live in this mixed-up world.

He'd be standing before his flock with a black eye and a bandage over half his face. He smiled wryly as he pondered what the seminary professors would say about that.

Later, at the church, Michael checked his robe and collar, put his notes and Bible in order, and looked up to heaven, imploring God to help him through the approaching service. The organist played her prelude with gusto, if not perfection. Michael stepped out and faced the altar, bowing his head. Above him was the painting of Jesus Christ with his arms outstretched to Mary. On this particular morning, the congregation could almost see the compassion on the Lord's face as His servant, their pastor, stood before Him and His flock.

Pastor Jenson faced the congregation, beginning the liturgy, "In the name of the Father, the Son, and the Holy Ghost. . . ." Words failed him. Silence echoed loudly as Michael's unbelieving eyes scanned the faces of people literally overflowing the pews. The sanctuary was full. People who only attended occasionally were seated with men he had met on his strolls through town visiting shut-ins and women who worked in the stores or in households. The Larson family sat close to the door for Hank's easy access and Mrs. Brush sat between Henry and Daisy. Big Jack and Maggie sat next to Bertha Ness. Across the rear wall loggers stood, leaning against the wall since there were no more seats. The men looked ill at ease— rough-hewn men in work clothes, bewhiskered, and some with whiskey still on their breath. Michael recognized them from his nocturnal visit to the Moose Saloon. As though in unison, they all removed their caps and ran hands through their unruly hair. Two of the men managed to raise a hand in greeting, as much as to say, "You invited us and here we are!"

Every eye was trained on Pastor Jenson. Everyone in the church had heard the account of their pastor's rescue of Samuel Berg, a boy most of them had watched grow into a man, a man who seemed to lose his way for a time but now was found.

The regular attendees had never seen such an outpouring of new people, people they never would have contemplated inviting to a service. The silence lasted only a second or two, but it seemed like an eternity to Michael as he totally lost his place in his *Book of Occasional Services*. Turning to the organist, he called out, "Let's have a rousing hymn. How about 'Just as I Am Without One Plea,' number 296."

And the organist let out all the stops and played like a concert organist in Westminster Abbey. Everyone rose to their feet and sang with gusto, and almost everyone was on the same note. Michael blinked hard to keep tears from overflowing his eyes.

Suddenly the doors to the sanctuary opened with a cold gust of air. Heads turned, still singing the familiar hymn. Then, one by one the shocked onlookers stopped singing and focused disbelieving eyes on the four people who slowly made their way down the aisle to a pew at the front of the church. Finally the only person who remained conscious of the music was the organist, but finally she, too, turned to see what was happening.

Silence reigned, except for the footsteps on the wooden aisle. Michael was surprised in an "I should have known this could happen" sort of way when he saw who had come through the door. Four children were quickly turned out of the first pew and directed to the front of the church, where they settled themselves comfortably on the edge of the communion kneelers.

The imposing Mrs. Berg stood in the middle of the aisle, her arm about the shoulders of the lovely Beatrice. Samuel, behind his mother, had his arm about Pearl's stooped shoulders. Samuel quickly ushered the three women into the seats now available. When he himself was finally settled, the organist once again recovered her zeal and turned her attention to the closing stanza of the hymn. All their voices rose together, singing, "Now to be thine, Yea, thine alone, O Lamb of God, I come, I come."

Afterwards, no one could quite recall the specific topic Pastor Jenson addressed in his sermon. They did, however, remember the atmosphere that settled over the sanctuary when he mounted the steps into the pulpit. They remembered the rapt attention of the worshipers that focused on him as he looked out over the crowd, opened his Bible, and checked his notes. Placing one hand on each side of the pulpit railing, for a long moment Michael let his eyes move over the crowd of people that sat looking up at him in silent expectation. He smiled, and then he began to preach.

Yet all of them would remember far into the future the vision of a fine young man, a man who had come to live with them, minister to them, and work with them—and had stepped out to defend one of their own. In their minds, they carried away not only his words, but also the care and concern he had shown to so many of them. He had let them know that this business of being a Christian was not an easy task—but it was a journey into righteousness, one step after the other.

After the organist pounded and pumped out the final hymn, the congregation rose slowly from the pews. All the youngsters followed their teachers to the Sunday School rooms downstairs as the sanctuary went from temporary silence to the hum of congenial visiting. Many of the regular members took the time to seek out the new visitors who stood self-consciously in the aisle, not quite knowing what to do next.

A group of businessmen shook hands with loggers still holding up the back wall. One logger had just gnawed off a fresh chew of tobacco and had it tucked in his cheek. He struggled mightily to hold the juice in his mouth while he kept up his end of the conversation, shaking hands with the owner of the town's mercantile.

And, miracle of miracles, Michael noted three women slowly making their way to the front pew where Samuel and the women with him stood quietly. Michael had all he could do to restrain himself from running over and hugging all three of them. But then, of course, he noted that Mrs. Berg had all three of her friends clutched to her bosom in a warm embrace before she introduced them to Beatrice and then—to Pearl.

Hank, Daisy, Henry, and Mrs. Brush waited for Michael by the front door of the church. "If you have no plans for Sunday dinner, we'd love to have you join us," said Mrs. Brush as she extended her gloved hand. "We'll be at my home, and we'll eat at any time convenient for you. The Swansons and Bertha will also be our guests." Mrs. Brush smiled widely as Michael accepted. He slowly helped her down the steps, where faithful Old Syd waited to walk her down the block to her home.

Big Jack surprised Michael when he reached out to take his arm. "Well, Pastor, I think I'll have to give you some boxing lessons if you are going to get into any more fights in the saloons!" he said. All the members within hearing distance started to laugh, and before long everyone standing in front of the church was having a light-hearted moment at Michael's expense.

And Michael laughed the hardest of all.

‮ℬ‬23‮ℛ‬
A Baptism, a Funeral, But No Wedding

THANKSGIVING HAD COME AND GONE. Most families still enjoyed the remains of the turkey, potatoes and gravy, *lefse*, and even a piece or two of the pumpkin pie, while the men who worked in the camps had already packed up and headed north.

Food staples, building equipment, cooking utensils, coal stoves, medicinal supplies, various items of clothing, and footwear for the company store, pipe tobacco plus the makings of cigarettes, and anything else that might possibly be needed were secured and checked off long lists in the hand of the job foreman.

On his way to school, Henry paused to watch as the procession of carts and wagons climbed the hill to the north and disappeared over its crest. Long rows of men walked behind the carts, struggling like a retreating army through the drifts of early snow. Each one carried a backpack of personal equipment tucked away inside—extra woolen socks, heavy canvas trousers, a handmade sweater lovingly knit by a wife, daughter, or sweetheart, a brush, comb, and straight edge razor with a chunk of soap wrapped in a towel. Each man also carried his personal stock of liquor, for " medicinal purposes."

Hank would not be making the journey this winter. Even though he was healing well, the doctors advised he remain at home this season to give his back muscles time to heal more completely. Daisy and Henry were grateful to have him safe at home.

Hank, however, was eager to find something to occupy his time. When a representative from the mill called on him to see if he would be interested in writing and editing some of the reports sent down from the camps, Hank was thrilled. Not only would he feel productive, but he would earn a salary to help support his family.

Daisy and Henry were recruited to help with his penmanship and spelling. Hank had the background and the experience to summarize the numerous reports delivered to the offices of the local mill. He'd itemize the figures and put the information in order. The papers eventually found their way to the desks of the wealthy lumber barons who dictated the ebb and flow of the logging business. Hank was eager for the challenge.

The Larson household was busy as the first Sunday of December approached. Pastor Jenson had approached Daisy to ask for a favor. Sitting with Hank in the parlor, a cup of coffee in one hand and a large molasses cookie in the other, Michael stated his idea.

"Pearl would like to be baptized into the Christian faith, and," he paused, "I thought it'd be meaningful if all of us surrounded her, like family, and made it a memorable occasion."

Michael set his cup down and smiled at Daisy. "Would you consider preparing a meal for eight to ten people to share, celebrating Pearl's becoming a child of God?"

Hank and Daisy eagerly agreed to be part of the planning committee. Daisy said, "Oh, Pastor Jenson, I'm thrilled to be asked! I've always thought of Pearl as a woman sorely in need of a friend—I'd be more than happy to be that friend."

A somber look crossed her face. "Hank and I know what it is to be shunned and judged—and excluded from family. I won't let that happen to Pearl, not if I can help it!"

The baptism service would take place on Sunday in the Larsons's living room at 3:00 p.m., followed by a celebration of Pearl's adoption into the family of God.

Big Jack, Maggie, and Bertha were also invited, along with Mrs. Brush. Pearl, Beatrice and Samuel, who was leaving soon for the lumber camp, would round out the guest list. Daisy contemplated inviting Mrs. Berg, but decided she would talk that over with Hank first. And finally Pastor Jenson would be there, both as the pastor and as a friend.

With only three days for preparations, Daisy had a long list of things to do. Big Jack donated a large, fresh venison roast for the dinner. Daisy would add potatoes, carrots, onions, and squash. Also on the menu were freshly baked buns, with apple pie for dessert.

Sunday dawned bright and clear, the winter sun spilling its muted brightness over the snow-covered town and the Island. Pearl awoke earlier than usual, eager for the day. Still she lingered beneath her quilt. Rising each morning had become more difficult.

The physical preparations needed to ready her to meet the day had become more and more demanding. Some mornings Pearl fought the nagging thought that the easier path would be to just quietly let herself slip away from the pain and bother of her present existence. Then she'd think of Beatrice, and Pearl tossed aside the covers, slowly rose, and began getting ready for the day.

Tears welled up as she gently removed a cloth covering her left breast and cupped it in her palm. An open sore—red, raw, and oozing pus—covered the side of the breast closest to her left arm. She had watched the wound evolve over the past years—from the small lump she had felt nearly six years ago to the odorous, weeping cancer that had eaten its way through the very meat of her breast. Now, with the skin having been devoured, the cancer threatened her life. Pain radiated through her ailing breast.

Most of all she loathed the stench of the cancer. She tried to wash away the pus as it continuously oozed from the open wound. And yet the odor followed her everywhere— the sweetly fetid smell of rotten fruit, something putrid, something dead. Attempting to conceal the cancer from Beatrice, Pearl bathed herself constantly and doused herself often with the perfumes and toilet water she ordered from the catalog—Eau d'Espagne, White Carnation, Hyacinth, Lily of the Valley, Bourjois Manon Lescaut. Still, she was not sure she could escape the reeking cloud that seemed to hover about her.

In all the years she'd dealt with the demon of cancer, she never possessed the courage to take her carriage to any local doctor. She could just imagine what a doctor or his nurse might say. But now she knew the cancer had gotten out of hand. After sharing her fears with Pastor Jenson, he offered to talk to a young doctor he knew. Dr. Sewell soon arrived at her door with the pastor at his side. The doctor conducted a cursory examination.

"I can't bring you any good news or hope for the future," The doctor had to tell Pearl. "I can give you something to help with the pain, but that's all I can do at this point." Shaking his head, he added, "I do wish I could call for a miracle and make the cancer disappear. But that is not my department." He smiled at Pastor Jenson and added, "I think that's in your department, Pastor."

Pearl was not surprised; she knew what awaited her in the near future. Yet, she was grateful for their visit and told them so.

Now, on this very special Sabbath day, Pearl forced the pain and fear from her mind and began to ready herself to be "washed clean," to prepare herself for what lay ahead. Leaving her gown in a heap at her feet, she walked to the commode where a pitcher of water stood waiting beside a towel, a washcloth, a bar of soap, and a medium-sized wash bowl.

In the final moments of her daily bathing regimen Pearl concentrated on her cancerous breast. The soap stung the open sore as she applied pressure to take away the dried blood and pus that surrounded it. She cradled her wounded flesh in her hand and did her best not to cry out. When she felt she had done the best she could, Pearl gently dried the area with a soft towel. Finally, she splashed a small amount of her best whiskey over her breast to purify the area. The resulting pain always made her weak, and she sat down.

If the cloths used to cover the weeping wound were stained enough so the traces of the seepage could not be rinsed away, Pearl opened the door of the small wood-burning stove heating her room, tossed them into the coals left from the evening's fire and watched them burn, wishing it were that easy to rid herself of the cancer.

Poor Beatrice! Pearl thought. *She does not have to carry this burden of mine. No signs will give away my secret, if I have anything to say about it!*

Beatrice always knocked on the bedroom door just about the time Pearl finished her bathing and had slipped into her undergarments. Forsaking the corset that so many women wore to rein in their abundant bosoms and bellies, Pearl now chose to wear a warm winter undergarment made from a blend of cotton and wool. The fitted undergarment sufficiently covered the clean cloth serving as a bandage on her breast and also held it firmly in place. The only aromas now circulating in the room were mixed, smelling heavily of perfumed soap, whiskey, and Lily of the Valley toilet water. Together they masked the putrid odor of the cancer.

Pearl guarded her secret well. Yet Beatrice noted the physical changes slowly occurring to her beloved guardian as the months slipped by.

Beatrice secured the knitted underskirt about Pearl's waist, then slipped a soft, rose-colored dress over Pearl's head. The dress was tailored, with long sleeves and a tucked bodice trimmed with a row of delicate pearl buttons down the front. The full skirt, constructed with seven gores, also had button trim in two rows on either side of the front panel. The long sleeves had matching pearl buttons on the cuffs. Fine black cashmere hosiery with elastic tops would warm Pearl's legs and feet when she ventured out into the wintery day.

Both Pearl and Beatrice enjoyed the morning regimen, and before the hour had passed, Beatrice had worked her magic. Make-up brought health to Pearl's cheeks; her coiffure enhanced her thinning hair and handsomely framed her face. Beatrice stepped back and returned the smile she saw in Pearl's eyes, reflected in the mirror before her.

Now Pearl was prepared to encounter her friends. Beatrice selected La Dore perfume—Heliotrope—and applied one last touch behind both of Pearl's ears. "Now you are perfect, my dear!" Beatrice said, slipping her arm about Pearl's shoulders and placing a kiss atop her head.

"Then all I need is another cup of your delicious hot coffee, and I'll be ready to face my Savior and be welcomed into His fellowship!" Pearl laughed quietly to herself. "Oh, dear! I truly hope heaven is ready for a sinner such as I!" Arm in arm, the two women walked slowly to the parlor.

LATER THAT EVENING, with a velvet-like darkness wrapped about the Island, lamps had been lit in the Larsons' kitchen, and Daisy stood alone at the sink after sending Hank and Henry off to bed. The hour was late, but she wasn't tired yet. And she wanted to put her kitchen in perfect order before Monday morning dawned, when the baking orders needed to be filled once again.

As she finished the dishes used for the baptismal celebration she recalled the events of the day. Twelve people had gathered in her parlor to share the meal she had prepared with Big Jack's help. The aroma of venison lingered in the room, even after the leftovers were safely stored on the back porch—except for one last piece of apple pie Daisy intended to enjoy all by herself. This had been a wonderful day.

At last she removed her apron and hung it next to the stove. After blowing out one of the lamps in the kitchen, Daisy took the other lamp and moved into the parlor. Carefully putting the lamp on the table Pastor Jenson had used during the service, she settled herself in Hank's chair. Savoring the final bite of her pie, she allowed her head to rest back on the cushion of the chair, closed her eyes and recalled special moments of the day.

Once their guests had all arrived, Daisy had been so pleased by the sounds of light conversation, soft laughter, and friendly banter flowing from friend to friend. She recalled that Henry and Maggie, seated on the floor near the door to the kitchen, turned their full attention to look at Pearl as Pastor Jenson called her to step up to the table where the towel, the bowl of water, and the Bible had been placed.

Both children watched Pearl rise from her chair and make her way to the table where the pastor waited. Kneeling on a small footstool, she shyly raised her eyes to his and smiled. Everyone seated in the small living room became aware that Pearl was trembling, and suddenly realized how important this moment was to her.

Daisy watched from the kitchen, a dishtowel in hand. From where she stood she could clearly see Pearl's face. Watching transfixed, Daisy was aware of one emotion after another playing over Pearl's features as Pastor Jenson voiced the words of the baptism service—joy, sorrow, expectancy, remorse, release, acceptance—culminating with tears mingling with the waters of baptism being poured over her bowed head.

Daisy could still envision Pastor Jenson's large hands as they scooped the water three times from the bowl, allowing it to flow gently over Pearl's head and brow. "In the name of the Father," the water spilled over her head, "and the Son," then it trickled down her neck, "and the Holy Spirit!" Now the water flowed over her cheeks and even onto her lips. Taking the linen cloth from the table, Michael reached for Pearl, lifted her head, and gently wiped away her tears plus the remnants of the cleansing water.

For a moment there was no sound in the room. Pearl remained kneeling, hands folded on the table, until Beatrice helped her rise, then enveloped her in her arms. Pearl leaned into her. They stood, quiet and at peace, for a moment. Then everyone stood up, smiling, visiting, and sharing the significance of what had just taken place. A soul had just been welcomed into the gates of Heaven.

A smile slipped over her lips as Daisy recalled how Henry, Big Jack, Maggie, and Bertha then came to the kitchen to put the finishing touches on the meal that was ready to bring to the table. Big Jack, handsomely clean shaven, carved the roast, while Daisy made the gravy. Bertha dished up the squash. Maggie cut the bread, and Henry mashed the potatoes. Mrs. Brush had contributed cranberry sauce and freshly preserved pickles. Mrs. Berg brought enough jams and jellies to feed the multitudes. Two large apple pies, made from apples from Pearl's orchard, were Daisy's finest and lay waiting on the counter.

The table had been pleasantly crowded with ten people. The children were good sports and sat on the floor with their plates on a bench. No one minded. Daisy smiled contentedly to herself as she remembered how the mood had been one of celebration and affection.

Conversation swirled about the room until Samuel brought it to a sudden halt by standing up, saying he had a special announcement. Daisy came in from the kitchen to hear the news—whatever it was—and the guests paused with forks and spoons on the way to their lips as they turned their attention in his direction. Even now, at this late hour, she felt she might cry just thinking about what occurred next.

Samuel blushed as he reached down for Beatrice's hand and raised her to his side. "I've spoken to Pastor Jenson and to Pearl and," he hesitated a moment before he finished, "and to my mother" and another pause, "and of course to Beatrice." Everyone laughed.

"And we'll be married next Sunday in the church, before I leave for the lumber camp." He smiled broadly and looked from face to face, waiting for their affirmation.

Everyone responded with joy, congratulatory handshakes, and best wishes. Then, Samuel wrapped his arms around Beatrice, kissing her. He stepped back a moment as though waiting to be disciplined, then kissed her again. Everyone clapped and rose from the table to embrace the young couple while wishing them their very best regards. Everyone, even Mrs. Berg, thought it a perfect conclusion to a most meaningful day.

Daisy, still in Hank's chair, was filled with love for her family and all their lovely friends. Finally, she rose, carried her plate to the sink, and set out the large bread bowl to be ready for the morning. She stoked the stove, blew out the lamp and went to bed.

Meanwhile, in the white house in the woods, Pearl lay awake in bed. The house was quiet, her girls upstairs sound asleep. The wind tugged at the window shutters. Pearl watched shadows dance on the ceiling. Her hands lay calmly across her chest, pressing down, refusing to give in to the sharp pain she felt in her breast.

She breathed deeply, realizing she indeed felt like a new person, as though the old air—her past, her mistakes, her transgressions, her painful memories—had been expelled, and the fresh, clean air of a new beginning now filled her heart and soul. She felt lighter, cleaner, childlike in the delight of the moment.

So this is what being a baptized child of God feels like, she thought. No wonder the pastor shared the words, "Come onto to me, all ye who labor and are heavy laden, and I will give you rest." She truly felt the rest, the peace, the tranquility wash over her. Finally, when she slipped off to sleep, she continued to inhale deeply the beginnings of her new life. Her left hand, rising and falling slowly with each breath, rested on her cancerous breast, absorbing the pain and willing it away.

For a short time she slept, then woke suddenly. Her chest felt as though it were being crushed by a giant hand, her left arm and neck radiated pain, and she knew at once this had nothing to do with the cancer. She struggled to breathe, to call out for Beatrice, but no words came. She raised her eyes to the shadows on the ceiling and surrendered to the pain now pulsing through her body.

And then she saw it—a bright light that seemed to fill the room, radiating from the shadows and becoming brighter as it neared her. The light reached out to her, filling her with peace and tranquility. It seemed only natural to raise her arms to meet the light as it descended over her.

Two long, deep breaths escaped her lips, then her arms fell back, her body relaxed, her breathing ceased. The muscles of her face softened, removing the ravages of age and pain. The room remained still, dark shadows still moving over the ceiling. Only one thing had changed. Pearl's left hand no longer rested on her cancer-filled breast. Both hands lay quietly at her sides, palms up, as though in one final act of supplication.

By morning the wind had increased and chased itself down the alleys and around the houses of the town. On the Island large snow drifts blocked St. Louis Avenue and hindered the progress of the parade of vehicles leaving town for the camps to the north. A few stragglers, just lately hired, trudged through the drifts, following the tracks of sleds and wagons.

Just at dawn, Beatrice awoke, her thoughts on Pearl. Since coming to live in the white house, she had loved her little room, always the warmest room in the house because of the kitchen. From the very beginning she felt safe with her beloved Pearl. Smiling, she threw back the covers and quickly dressed in her warm, everyday clothing. After tucking a woolen shawl across her shoulders, she stepped onto the porch to gather an armful of wood to keep the fires going.

At seventeen years of age, she was engaged to be married and would soon become Samuel Berg's wife. She smiled at the thought of him and the love they shared. She filled the wood box to overflowing, seeing the day would be blustery. When the fire in the parlor stove once again flared and burned brightly, she stoked the kitchen stove and turned her attention to the preparation of Pearl's breakfast tray.

Since yesterday had been such a busy day, Beatrice decided to allow Pearl to rest a bit longer than usual and surprise her by serving her breakfast in bed. While she worked in the kitchen, Beatrice's imagination put plans together for the next big event in her life.

Arrangements for her marriage had been made, as well as for a brief honeymoon (one night) at the Northeastern Hotel on the Island. Then Beatrice would remain at Pearl's house until Samuel returned from the lumber camp in the spring.

A mug of steaming hot coffee with a small pitcher of cream, two slices of Daisy's bread—toasted, with butter and Mrs. Berg's strawberry jam generously spread on top—along with a three-minute egg in a small saucer, removed from the shell, mashed, and sprinkled with salt and pepper completed the tray. Everything looked appetizing and would tempt Pearl to eat well. A colorful red napkin to the side of the plate gave a festive look to the tray.

Beatrice walked down the back hall and knocked softly on Pearl's door. No answer. Balancing the tray in one hand, she quietly turned the doorknob, pushed the door open with her hip, and walked into the still-darkened room.

Beatrice knew immediately something was not right. A strange odor met her. Usually she was met by the fragrance of perfumed soaps and toilet water and whiskey, but today was different. This morning she inhaled a sickening, repugnant smell, one she had never been conscious of before. The lamp had not yet been lit, leaving the room shrouded in the gray of an early winter morning.

Placing the tray on the trunk by the door and quickly lighting two lamps near the bed, Beatrice saw Pearl lying on her pillow, eyes closed, motionless and pale. Beatrice carried one lamp over to the table next to the bed, set it down, and leaned over the still body under the floral quilt, arms and hands outstretched on top of the quilt. She found no pulse.

Conscious of the repulsive scent, Beatrice carefully folded back the quilt. She was introduced to the wound and the seeping stain covering Pearl's gown over her left breast. She recoiled. How had she not been aware of this hideous wound? Why did Pearl keep her from knowing about it? With trembling hands she replaced the quilt, and stared in disbelief at Pearl's lifeless body.

Realizing Pearl was gone, the young woman crawled onto the bed and curled up beside the still body. Pressing the cold, limp hand to her lips over and over, she wept great, heaving sobs. Finally, exhausted by her grief, Beatrice rose, dried her eyes and straightened her apron. Picking up the tray, she headed back to the kitchen, where she would call Pastor Jenson. There was no need to send for a doctor. Of that she was quite sure.

THE WEDDING PLANS were postponed. Instead, plans for the funeral were set in place. The service would take place at the Lutheran Church, with Pastor Jenson officiating. Some members of the church were vocal with their disapproval—a woman of ill repute being buried from their church sanctuary was more than they could stomach.

Michael was unmoved by the criticism. He responded to them in no uncertain terms. "Who are you and I to judge? Pearl will have her service in the sanctuary of the this church. She believed, was baptized, was saved—just like our Lord Jesus directed. What more do you want?" he challenged them. They had no answer and turned away, only to continue their complaining among themselves.

Mr. Fessenbeck, a lawyer Michael had recommended to Pearl for assistance with her will, made a professional call at the white house to inform Beatrice she was Pearl's sole beneficiary. The white house would now be in Beatrice's name, as would the accounts at the bank and the investments prudently made in the lumber industry, the Ford Motor Company, Standard Oil, the Great Northern Railroad, plus other stocks and bonds. Beatrice felt faint when the totals were revealed to her; she could not even begin to fathom such large sums of money.

Mr. Fessenbeck himself had been shocked at the final totals. "That Pearl must have been some kind of business woman to put such a fortune together without help from any professional," he said. *Perhaps*, he thought, *I should have paid closer attention to Pearl as she came and went from the bank week after week, year after year, rather than looking down on such a soiled and sinful woman.*

Adding up all her accounts, Mr. Fessenbeck realized he might have earned a percentage of her profits had he been willing to have her as a client, to advise her monetary deposits and business investments. Now it was too late, and by the look on Samuel Berg's face, sitting protectively at Beatrice's side, Mr. Fessenbeck knew there was no chance of suggesting any hidden fees at this particular time.

Since the day of Pearl's earlier visit, Pastor Jenson had filed away the directions she had given him for her service. Pearl explained she did not relish the idea of strangers, all those who had dismissed her very existence while she was alive, leaning over the casket, peering at her body. Thus, Pastor Jenson followed Pearl's directions down to the last detail. She had requested a simple pine coffin constructed by one of Big Jack's carpenter friends. It would be nothing fancy, only a place where she could lie wrapped in the handmade quilt that always covered her bed, a quilt stitched by her mother when Pearl was just a girl.

The curious public would be disappointed, of course, to see a closed, plain pine box.

Years hence, many old timers would reach into a pocket or a purse and pull out a small stone. They would open their hand, the stone in the center of their palm as they displayed it to a child, a grandchild, a mate, or a friend. "This is the stone we received on the day of Pearl's funeral service," they would say. "I've kept it with me ever since." And the viewer would lean over to touch the stone before asking about its significance.

Inspiration for his funeral sermon did not come easily to Pastor Jenson. He began working on the message late on the day before the service, but no revelations flashed into his mind, no heavenly voice spoke into his waiting ear. The sun began its descent behind the western hills and faded. Still nothing.

Finally, Michael pushed his chair away from the desk and decided to move around a bit. Perhaps he would think better if he cleared off the front steps leading to the church and shoveled the walk out to the street. After setting aside his Greek New Testament and his commentaries, he slipped on his heavy woolen jacket, turned out the lamp and stepped outside into the cold, crisp December evening. He stood for a short time on the steps of the church, breathing in the frigid air as he watched the lights come on in the homes near the church. Still no ideas.

Even though he worked up quite a sweat, the shoveling didn't help. Eating supper brought no new insights. He desperately needed a hook on which to hang the point he wished to make about Pearl's life—a new beginning, the total forgiveness available to all of his congregation. Finally he gave up and went to bed and lay there, gazing at the darkened ceiling with a multitude of thoughts whirling through his brain.

Suddenly Michael sat bolt upright and threw back the quilts. He wrapped his robe about him, then quickly lit the lamp on his desk. He sat and reached for a sheet of paper and his pen. Chuckling aloud as he wrote, the torrent of words poured out onto the paper, covering first one sheet and then another. "Of course! Thank you, Lord! You illustrated this situation perfectly!" He smiled as he quickly wrote. "I'm going to borrow your words and even add something for everyone to hold in their hands!"

Thus it was that a stone was handed to everyone who attended Pearl's funeral service. Had his neighbors been awake and peering out their windows the previous night, they might have observed Pastor Jenson, bundled up in boots, hat and jacket, shoveling the snow away from the empty flower gardens surrounding the front porch of the parsonage and collecting numerous stones and pebbles hidden beneath the drifts.

Henry, Maggie, and Oscar were enlisted the next morning to wash the stones. Then, at the funeral, the three young people stood in the center aisle of the church, giving one stone to each person as they arrived. Men, women, and children gingerly held their stones, glancing from one to another, puzzled. Occasionally there was a *clunk* as a stone accidently dropped onto the floor or onto a pew where it was quickly retrieved.

The sanctuary soon filled with the curious onlookers, Pearl's friends and acquaintances from the business community, former customers, and "girls" who lived with and worked for Pearl. With furtive glances, the adults in the pews looked about the sanctuary, trying to determine just who each person was and how he or she related to the notorious person in the pine box at the front of the sanctuary.

Just before the service was to begin, Beatrice was escorted to the front pew on the arm of Samuel Berg, with Mrs. Berg close behind. Not everyone knew of the special relationship between Beatrice and Pearl; those with knowledge were only too happy to share their information with others seated nearby. Beatrice leaned heavily on Samuel's arm, weeping as they made their way up the aisle. Pearl had no other people she would call family.

Just before the service was to begin, Beatrice stood and walked to the front of the church, where she stood beside the closed coffin. Her head was bowed, and everyone could hear her deeply felt grief. A tall white candle stood on the table. Beatrice, with hands trembling, tried to light it. Samuel stood, walked to her and wrapped his strong arms around her and lit the candle as Beatrice wept against his broad chest. Together they returned to the front pew. Beatrice sat with her head bowed, her hand tightly clasped in Samuel's larger, stronger hand. Beatrice and Samuel would have been husband and wife by now if Pearl had not passed away, and they grieved for that as well.

The congregation joined in singing "Children of the Heavenly Father." The organist finished with a flourish of notes. Michael stepped to the pulpit, placed his broad hands upon the rail, let his gaze linger on those who sat in the pews. Then he began to speak.

He read Pearl's obituary, brief as it was, and some in the audience were left wanting more details of the life Pearl had led. Pastor Jenson set out three Bible verses for them to contemplate, begining with Romans 3:23—"All have sinned and fall short of the glory of God." He urged the listeners to realize not one person in the sanctuary of the church— or anywhere in the world for that matter—could claim to be free of the bonds of sin.

Not everyone seated in the church that day, hearing those words, was in agreement with the pastor's interpretation of that verse. Self-righteousness was a mantle a devout few seemed to place upon their own shoulders and exclude from the shoulders of their less pious neighbors. Surely a flagrant sinner such as Pearl would, in their opinion, have to pay the price for her iniquities. It was only fair—wasn't it?

Pastor Jenson continued with the second verse he wished them to contemplate, Ephesians 2:8—"For by grace you have been saved through faith; and this is not your own doing, it is the gift of God." He spread his arms wide as though he wished to embrace everyone who sat before him. "We all are able to receive the *gift*—nothing to buy, nothing to negotiate, nothing to barter for, nothing to trade—Grace is a gift! And on the day Pearl was taken from this life, that *very* day, she believed, she was baptized, she accepted the free gift of *grace* available to all of us if we but reach out to accept it. And Pearl reached out for God's grace with her whole heart, body, mind, and soul."

Finally, Pastor Jenson held up his right hand, opened it so the people in the pews could see the stone he held. "One last point needs to be made before we can enjoy our fellowship together as we celebrate Pearl's receiving the gift of grace, and that has to do with the stone each of you holds." Several *clunks* and *thunks* came as stones fell and were quickly retrieved.

"I realize that Pearl was a disturbing presence in the midst of our community. I can understand the condemnation thrust upon her because of the life she led until recently. Yet kindness was always a part of her nature. Reports of her generous spirit were whispered from person to person. She was always a child of God. Thus, when the community stormed against her and violence erupted, we can all be thankful no one was injured. Human nature, in all its multiple facets, was on display that particular evening. We now need to observe the actions demonstrated for us by our Lord and Savior, Jesus Christ. Actions that show love, not judgment."

Pausing a moment to let his eyes take in the upturned faces before him, he continued in a somber tone. "John 8:7, the final verse for your consideration, speaks directly to all of us in this place, all of us who inhabit this community, all who have fallen short of living a perfect life. As he confronts the angry mob who wishes to kill, by stoning, a woman caught in the act of adultery, Jesus looks into the eyes of the accusers and challenges them by saying, 'Let him who is *without* sin cast the first stone!' and one by one the angry mob, each person knowing their own sinful nature, slowly disperses until Jesus is left alone, with the woman cringing at his feet. Not one person remained willing to cast that first stone.

"'Does no one condemn you?' Jesus asks the woman. And when she answers 'No!' he says, 'And neither do I condemn you! Go—and sin no more!'

"The words Jesus spoke to this woman, he speaks to all of us. The woman at Jesus' feet was forgiven and able to begin a new, grace-filled life."

Michael held up his stone. "Look at your stone, the one you did not throw at anyone, the one you could not be so presumptuous as to fling at another human being knowing yourself as you do." The eyes of the people in the pews looked down at the stone they held; they contemplated it silently before folding it once again into the palms of their hands.

"Tuck it in your pocket or purse, and when you come across it sometime in the future, think of Pearl, grace-filled and forgiven. And remember that the same gift of grace also waits for you. We will no longer be throwers of stones. We will be givers of grace. Let us pray!"

The organist pumped the bellows, and the congregation began singing the rousing Christmas Carol, "O Come All Ye Faithful." They rose from the pews and slowly filed by the modest wooden coffin containing Pearl's remains. Some reached out a hesitant hand to touch the box, as if to say a fond farewell to the soul of the person within. Slowly and silently they made their way to the basement and the lunch that awaited them there.

Daisy had outdone herself preparing the baked delicacies served. Trays of pastries and baked goods lay in abundance on the linen cloths covering the modest church tables. The best church dishes, pure white with a slender green trim at the edge of the plate, awaited the guests as they approached the buffet. The serving line slowed as the guests took their time choosing from a variety of cookies, bars, cakes, sweet rolls, coffee cakes, donuts, and dainty sandwiches created with Daisy's famous breads. Daisy monitored the serving table, and Bertha was in charge of the beverages—coffee and tea for the adults and lemonade for the children. Finally, after everyone had made a selection from the display of goodies, they all found a seat at one of the waiting tables.

At first there was little visiting. A certain restraint hung like a shroud over the room. After Pastor Jenson offered a brief prayer in thanks for the lunch—as well as the gift of forgiveness—the volume of the voices rose and soon conversation filled the room.

Townsfolk and Island residents now sat side by side at some tables, eating donuts together, sharing the cream pitcher, passing Mrs. Berg's strawberry preserves from one sticky hand to another, commenting on the weather and the prospects for the blustery winter yet to come.

Beatrice watched the parade of people going by as she sat at the family table. She felt like laughing and crying, all at once. She had grown up, often alone, deserted, cast away from society. Only Samuel, who now sat beside her holding her hand, stood between her and the abyss of great abandonment she carried since her childhood. The white house was hers now; the property surrounding it was also in Beatrice's name. She was poised on the brink of a new life—a life where having enough money would never be a problem for her.

She leaned her head on Samuel's shoulder as she acknowledged the sympathetic glances from all these people she had seldom met before. One by one they passed by the family table with their full plates, their cups of steaming coffee, and their evident discomfort with not knowing what words to say to ease the sorrow they saw in her eyes.

Before long, when the sun began its descent behind the western trees, the church emptied as people hurried home for evening chores. The wind howled around the church, drifting the new-fallen snow across the roads and walkways. Darkness fell over the town and the Island, and soon all the funeral guests were safe at home going about their everyday business. The act of living often gets in the way of contemplating the hidden mysteries of death.

Michael was exhausted from the emotions he had felt as he dealt with Pearl's passing. Now Christmas Eve loomed—two days away. Returning to his office after everyone had departed, he straightened his desk and added wood to the dimly burning stove. A flame leaped and warmth rolled out as he sat at his desk, cradling his head in his hands.

The Christmas Eve service needed to be uplifting, joyous, full of music, appealing to the children as well as to the adults. The Sunday School classes were scheduled to present their memorized pieces before their proud parents. They'd be the stars of the evening, he was sure, for the sanctuary would be filled with proud families.

He needed to have an appropriate sermon to round out the evening before everyone joined in the traditional singing of "Silent Night" as the church lights were dimmed. For the first time in his ministry he'd be able to watch as, one by one, everyone's candle was lit. From the altar, he would watch as each face became illuminated in the darkness when the candle flamed to life. He'd be able to see them all as he stood at the altar for this first Christmas as their shepherd, his candle lighting his face for the congregation to see. Running his hands through his hair, he decided to lock up the church and contemplate the sermon material tomorrow. Right now he needed to rest.

Putting on his woolen coat, his fur-lined hat, and his leather mittens, he extinguished the lamp and shut down the stove. Making his way through the darkened church, he found his key and locked the front door before heading down the church steps and across the snow-covered walk to the darkened parsonage. He knew he'd have to tend the stove there as well, for he had not been home since that morning and the temperature was definitely dropping. Loading his arms with wood from the pile on the porch, he felt he would be prepared to keep the parsonage warm through the blustery night ahead.

The wind continued to blow, quickly filling in the footprints made by his boots in the drifting snow. Once he entered the parsonage he lit lamps as he moved from the front hall to the parlor to the kitchen to the bedroom. Later that evening all the parsonage windows darkened and the wind finally diminished, whispering softly between the houses of the town and over on the Island. Peace seemed to prevail once more.

The days of 1917 marched to their end. The final week of the year proved to be busy for just about everyone. Christmas came and went in a flurry of excitement—with all the entertaining of family and friends, gifts bought, wrapped, and given, holiday cooking and baking, and children's programs at school and at church. Freshly cut Christmas trees, covered with multitudes of candles, gleamed through the front windows of most of the homes and reflected out upon the clean white drifts of snow in the yards. With all that accomplished, everyone took a deep breath and relaxed before the arrival of the new year.

A storm blew in from the northwest on New Year's Day, blanketing the town, the Island, and the hills near Pinehurst Park. With the holiday celebrations over, people returned to their own homes, and life returned to its everyday routine.

Children flocked to the park with sleds of all shapes and sizes. Some were made entirely of wood, some more modern styles had metal runners, some sleds were just a slab of lumber or a sheet of cardboard with a child perched precariously on the makeshift sled as it cascaded down the slippery hill. Shouts of joy and peals of laughter filled the air.

Both youngsters and adults felt the pleasure of the holidays just passed and had eager expectations for the new year. No one had any inkling of the catastrophic events ahead of them. Before the next year arrived and it was time to hang up a new calendar, the lives of every person—in the town of Cloquet and on the Island—would be altered forever in ways no one could now even imagine.

೫24ೢ
1918—The New Year

THE NEW YEAR STEPPED boldly onto the scene. The Great War had been raging for years in countries far removed from Cloquet and the Island. Newspapers brought reports of death and destruction of people and places far away. People shook their heads in disbelief as they read the news articles and were made aware of the carnage taking place in the trenches across Europe.

Several young men from the area had enlisted in the armed forces and were immediately deployed to countries and cities far from the pine-covered hillsides of Cloquet. This new year of 1918 brought reports of local boys being injured, even killed. Before the war was over, more than 500 soldiers from the area had joined the cause.

A little-noticed cut in the United States budget for 1918 would have far-reaching ramifications before the year was done. The U.S. government decreased monies delegated to states to finance the government's ever-increasing cost of the war. Minnesota found it necessary to cut the funding for "track walkers," those men hired to patrol miles of tracks winding through the parched forests, always on the lookout for sparks from train smokestacks, grass fires gone bad, or even lightning strikes.

The area saw extreme heat and drought that summer, not an ideal time to pull funding on track walkers. However, the war was the government's immediate concern.

In 1918, women still strove for the right to vote. Demonstrations filled the streets and caused disruptions in many major cities. Leaders of the movement stood before assemblies of women across the country, proclaiming their right to be heard in the ballot box. Hecklers and protesters tried to force the rallies to a close, and yet the believers in the cause never gave up hope. On June 14, 1919, they claimed success.

Suffragettes were even found in Cloquet, though they attempted to remain somewhat anonymous and not too confrontational. Women stood straighter and looked their men in the eye more often than before. They began to discard their corsets, their long skirts, and their intricate hairdos. Some women even went so far as to cut their tresses and allow people to see them in public with bobbed hair!

More and more automobiles had been purchased and were bouncing over the gravel roads of cities, large and small. Drivers and passengers dressed for driving, wearing large hats, scarves, coats called dusters, and even goggles. Over three million cars were now rattling around the countryside, churning up dust and spooking horses. By 1920, there would be nearly four million cars, and Cloquet, being no different from the rest of the country, had its own fleet of flivvers chugging up and down the streets.

Every time he chugged down the road in a cloud of dust, Mr. Arthur Lund felt like a man prepared for the adventures of the coming decade. Behind the wheel of his Ford, he felt invincible, powerful, dominant. His Ford had worn a track to the edge of town, to the home of his mistress, leaving the troubles of his "unappreciative" wife and "delinquent" son behind him, shrouded in neglect. The auto gave him a sense of reckless abandon each time he slipped behind the wheel. Often he would fantasize about heading out of town with Wilma—even though she was beginning to bore him—and making his way to Minneapolis, where a man of his caliber would be more appreciated.

The first event of the new year would be a marriage—between Beatrice, the orphan girl raised by Pearl, and Samuel Berg, son of the well-known pillar of the community, Mrs. Berg. Pearl's death caused it to be rescheduled for the second Saturday of January.

Shortly before Christmas, Samuel left town with the other men from the mill and was hard at work felling the giant pines with the other loggers. However, with intervention by Pastor Jenson and Big Jack Swanson (who maintained a friendship with the camp boss after years of being one of the cooks), the wedding was on the calendar once again. Samuel was allowed to take a short leave, returning home for four days. Then, after the wedding and a very brief honeymoon, he would return to the camp with the sleds, loaded with more supplies to sustain the camp for another month or two.

After the funeral service was over and Pearl's girls departed, Beatrice found herself alone in the white house. She stoked the stoves so the rooms on the first floor were warm and comfortable. She opened the curtains, letting the brief light of winter fill the rooms.

Later, as the sun set and the light slipped into darkness, she curled up in the large chair nearest the fire. A small knot of fear rose in her breast when she contemplated her future, but she beat it down, preferring to be hopeful. Samuel gave her assurance—and most of all a sense of peace.

One by one the empty days passed. Often sitting in the room where Pearl had drawn her last breath, Beatrice contemplated her treasured memories and made her way to the empty bed. There she sat, hands on her lap. Occasionally she stroked the lace-covered silk pillow that once cushioned the head of her beloved Pearl as she slept. Beatrice often felt very much alone, for the two people who had loved her were not nearby. Pearl was gone forever, and Samuel was hard at work deep in the pines.

Tears came easily, and often she quietly curled up on the bed, her head resting on the lace-covered pillow. She breathed deeply of the lingering scent of perfume that had, for so long, masked the odor of Pearl's illness—Lily of the Valley toilet water and, Beatrice's favorite, White Carnation. At times she eventually fell into a restless sleep even as the tears continued to course down her cheeks, dampening the silk pillow.

New Year's Day dawned cold and clear. Not even a whisper of wind. The snow drifts, a brilliant white, smoothly undulated in all directions over the hills and shrubs of the yard. By late morning Beatrice perceived everything, as far as she could see in all directions, as truly a winter wonderland.

And then she heard a knock. Beatrice was puzzled. Who would be calling on such a busy family day? Up until this time she had encountered no difficulty with former customers approaching the white house. She was grateful to the men in the saloons, acting as her guardian angels, who were dedicated to keeping trouble away from her door. The men spread the word informing former customers that "business" was no longer conducted at the white house, nor would it ever be again.

Before opening the door, Beatrice peered out the glass side panel and stepped back in surprise. There stood a shivering Mrs. Berg, up to her knees in a drift with her face partially covered by a knit scarf tied over her hat and under her chin. In what used to be the driveway before it was lost under the snow, a man from the livery stable huddled against the cold while perched on the seat of a sleigh behind a horse, the best mode of transportation for such snow-covered streets. Beatrice almost felt like laughing, but instead the tears flowed once again as she threw open the heavy wooden door and reached out her arms to embrace her soon-to-be mother-in-law.

Before many minutes passed, the two women were seated at the kitchen table near the comforting heat of the stove, one of Daisy's donuts and a cup of fragrant coffee in hand. The driver had been dismissed, told to return at three o'clock that afternoon.

Mrs. Berg had never ever set foot inside a brothel in her whole life. And here she sat, warm, comfortable but very curious, at ease with the lovely girl seated across the table from her. Looking about her she noted that the house was tastefully decorated with stylish furniture and colorful accessories. The furnishings were not opulent or overdone, as one might expect in a brothel. Everything was clean, as far as she could detect. And she struggled to keep her eyes from straying up the stairway where she suspected the rooms were located where the "dastardly deeds" occurred. She forced her eyes and attention on the young woman at her side. There was a wedding to plan and Mrs. Berg had always been an accomplished organizer. Patting Beatrice's hand, Mrs. Berg officially got about her business.

"My dear Beatrice, we must put our heads together, make plans for your big day, and have everything in order when Samuel returns for the wedding."

She had vowed she would not be pushy, that she would allow Beatrice to speak her mind and set the tone for the celebration. But Mrs. Berg's organizational skills overran her good intentions. "We must make a list and see to it that your wedding to my Samuel will be just as I—I mean you—would desire it!" She smiled at her verbal slip, took a pencil and small notebook from her purse, and was prepared to be the director of the coming event.

Two heads, one blonde and curly, one shaded with gray, bent over the table as the guest list was organized, the food for the reception selected, and the bride's attire considered.

"I'll be happy to call Pastor Jenson and reserve the church for the wedding," Mrs. Berg noted as she began to write this final item on their "to do" list. Gently but firmly, Beatrice reached out her hand and covered the veined hand of her soon to be mother-in-law as she wrote. Puzzled, Mrs. Berg turned her head and looked into the serious eyes of the young woman at her side.

"No, dear Mrs. Berg." Beatrice spoke quietly, with surprising confidence. "I have decided that I want to have the wedding here, in the parlor, where I can feel Pearl's presence around me."

Mrs. Berg's back stiffened in resistance. "You can't be serious," she said. Visions of her church friends filled her imagination, gasping in shock, fainting, when they received the invitation to Samuel's wedding—to be held in the brothel.

"Samuel and I talked it over and we agree this place, Pearl's house, is where we wish to be united in marriage."

Beatrice spoke quietly, but with determination. "I know what some people will say— that this house has been a brothel. How can anyone have a wedding service in a brothel?"

With a deep sigh, Beatrice said, "But I just don't really care. This has been the only home I ever really had, the only place where I ever felt loved." She took a deep breath. "I will be married here—or not at all!"

Mrs. Berg blinked, swallowed, and for once held her tongue. Her wounds were still fresh after hastily spoken words to her son triggered such a disastrous results, and she had learned a good lesson: that she could not always have her way.

Both women agreed—January 14 would be a very special wedding day! And the celebration would take place here, in Pearl's parlor.

๛25๛
The Wedding

BY THE TIME SAMUEL ARRIVED home late Friday, the sun had already descended into lavender clouds. Big Jack met him at the north bridge as soon as the camp wagon crossed over to the Island. Once settled in Big Jack's carriage and headed away from the Island, Samuel was firmly instructed in the proper behavior for a groom.

Big Jack was adamant. When Samuel expressed his desire to see Beatrice, he was told in no uncertain terms, "You keep away from your bride until you see her at the wedding!" Big Jack laughed. "Just mind your mother." Samuel didn't like what he heard.

"I'll deliver you to your mother's house," Big Jack continued, "where you'll be patient and follow instructions. Beatrice can't be seen or contacted by you until tomorrow, the day of your marriage." He shook his head. "There are rules to follow, I guess, and your mother has given me explicit directions." Laughing once more, Big Jack said, "Just do what you're told, and look forward to tomorrow." He threw his arm around Samuel's shoulders. "By tomorrow night, my young friend, you'll be able to see—and enjoy—as much of your bride as you want!"

Samuel blushed, then grinned. With a final swat on Samuel's shoulders, Big Jack drove across the red bridge, headed up the hill through the snow-covered streets of Cloquet, and delivered Samuel into his mother's waiting arms.

As much as he wished to see Beatrice, Samuel realized there was a proper way of getting married, and he wanted to do things exactly right. For once, he headed home to his mother's house without complaining.

Saturday dawned clear and cold, with temperatures plunging below zero, but the sun's bright light held warmth, if a person were sheltered from the wind. The wedding would take place that afternoon in the parlor of Pearl's white house.

Daisy had been busy for days creating a buffet to delight the guests once the wedding service was concluded. She had enlisted help from Big Jack, Maggie, Henry, and even Hank, who sat at the kitchen table and sliced open her freshly baked buns. Henry had invited Oscar to come over and spend the day running errands for Daisy. With permission from his mother, Oscar was delighted to accept, prepared to do whatever was needed to make this a memorable day.

Pearl's treasured hand-crocheted lace tablecloths, polished silverware, linen napkins, crystal goblets, and Rose Leaf Theodore Haviland China adorned the dining room table.

Everything was centered around the Imperial Parlor lamp—rose pink with five-inch pink translucent beads hanging from the shade, which was trimmed with gold-plated brass. Pearl had always loved this lamp; she often claimed the soft rosy glow from it softened her wrinkles and made her appear younger than her years. Her lamp would be the main accent of the table setting and would cast its warmth—and Pearl's love—over the entire celebration.

The grandfather clock standing regally in the front hall finally struck two o'clock. The guests had all arrived and were seated in the parlor, facing the fireplace. A few of Samuel's friends from the Moose Saloon still remained in town and had outdone themselves in preparing for the wedding. Each and every hair had been plastered into place, faces gleamed as a result of a determined scrubbing and energetic shaving, and suits were resurrected from almost forgotten trunks.

Willard Schiebe, the young man who had been stabbed at the close of the summer, had been Samuel's friend for many years. He was pleased for his young friend and was ready to celebrate the union of the lovely couple. However, he had an ulterior motive in his miraculous transformation from a common laborer to a dashing dandy. Her name was Lenore, one of Pearl's former employees and Beatrice's friend. Willard, who had been one of Lenore's most faithful customers, hoped to renew their acquaintance at Samuel's wedding.

After removing his heavy jacket and shaking the snow from his hat and hair, Willard carefully noted the people seated in the parlor, pleased to see Lenore in the second row. He ran a hand over his slicked-down hair and aimed himself toward the empty chair next to Lenore. She turned and gave him a smile of recognition, flavored with a bit of her former art of seduction. "Hello, Willard. I haven't seen you for a while." She smiled at him, her eyes enticing him. He felt his smooth cheeks flush and nodded, returned her smile, and gingerly settled himself next to her.

Suddenly a desperate look spread over his face as he became conscious of the large wad of chewing tobacco he had previously tucked into his left cheek. Looking to his left and right, he searched for an accessible spittoon into which he could spew the tobacco and the brown juice that threatened to overflow his lips.

Lenore turned to him and smiled another warm, welcoming smile. How desperately he wanted to smile in return, but in his mind he could visualize the tobacco juice seeping from between his lips and oozing down his chin. Frantically, he stood, looking greatly agitated as he searched for relief. Not one spittoon was to be seen anywhere.

Unable to step past the people now seated to his right and left, and aware of the quizzical look on Lenore's face, he looked down into her beautiful eyes and thought, *What the hell!* and swallowed the wad and the mouthful of juice it had produced. Willing himself not to vomit, he returned to his seat, withdrew a clean handkerchief from his jacket pocket, and dabbed genteelly at his moist, brown lips. Then he turned to Lenore and smiled, keeping his lips closed, trying not to display tobacco-stained teeth. By the affectionate look on her face, he assumed he had succeeded. Willard nearly choked as she reached over and placed her hand seductively on his knee. He could not suppress a wide grin, and there were those tobacco-stained teeth, displayed for the whole world to see. She looked into his eyes, then at his teeth, and back into his eyes. Her hand never left his knee.

Pastor Jenson had arrived earlier that afternoon to help Big Jack set up the parlor chairs for the ceremony. As the guests began to arrive, he stood at the door to welcome them, taking their coats to a room across the hall. Finally, everyone was seated and a low hum of voices rose as guests visited with the person seated next to them. Michael stood in the dining room, observing the unique mix of people assembled to celebrate the marriage of the two young people who were loved by all their friends.

He found it difficult to suppress a smile as he made a mental note of the guests seated in the well-appointed parlor of the brothel. Mrs. Berg's influential friends from town were seated next to saloon proprietors from the Island. Rough-hewn mill workers shared a row of chairs with sedate members of the church choir. Two of Pearl's former girls sat in the back row beside the town's distinguished mercantile owners and their elegant wives.

The entire back row rose as one and moved to the left to allow Mrs. Brush and Hank to settle into chairs on the edge of the aisle. Hank sat on the end of the row. He walked almost independently, using only a sturdy diamond-willow walking stick for support. Even the chief of police, a friend of Samuel's deceased father, seemed to be enjoying himself as he visited with Judith—one of Pearl's girls who had married and moved to Floodwood a few weeks before Pearl passed away.

Quite the mix! Michael thought. *Rather like the gathering at the home of Zacchaeus when Jesus himself sat in the midst of the motley bunch that came out to meet Him.*

Taking his time, Michael walked to the center of the room and stood before the assembled group. He hesitated to bring an end to the visiting, but knew the ceremony was the most important event of the day. After giving a signal to Mrs. Berg, she began playing the processional on the Story and Clark upright piano that had been so precious to Pearl.

Samuel entered from the hall and walked slowly to the front of the room, where he stood alone, tall and straight, to the right of the elaborate fireplace. Once his thick, unruly hair had been trimmed and his growth of whiskers removed, everyone realized just how handsome he was under his rough exterior. He looked calm as he stood by the pastor, resplendent in a black wool suit with a white shirt and an elegant gray-and-black silk tie.

After motioning the guests to rise, Samuel and Pastor Jenson turned to face the arch through which the bride would enter the parlor from the dining room. Bertha Ness entered, walked slowly to the front of the room, then turned and faced the arch. Many were surprised at how lovely she was, even after her great sorrow. Having become friends with Beatrice over the past months, she was pleased to be Beatrice's only attendant. A moment later, Big Jack came through the arch with Beatrice, radiant and beautiful, on his arm.

She carried no floral bouquet, but held in her hand only a small, worn New Testament that had been presented to Mrs. Berg by her beloved husband when she was a young woman and they were yet courting. Mrs. Berg had carried the New Testament in her hand at the time of her marriage many years ago. A red ribbon marked the location of the verses she had shared with the bride-to-be and which became very meaningful to Beatrice as well. One was I Corinthians 13, known as the love chapter. Verse thirteen read, "Three things remain—faith, hope, and love—and the greatest of these is love." And Beatrice intended to love Samuel forever.

The soft blue of the simple cashmere dress Beatrice chose to wear was reflected in the blue of her eyes. This fashionable dress had been one of Pearl's favorite outfits, and Beatrice had always admired Pearl's exquisite taste in clothes. Mrs. Berg had agreed the dress would be most appropriate to wear at the wedding and would allow Pearl to have a presence at the ceremony. And it fit Beatrice perfectly—not even one adjustment was needed.

The dress was open at the neck and trimmed by a delicate matching lace. Long, fitted sleeves gave it a tailored look, but the slightly flared skirt in the stylish shorter length allowed for a fashionable glimpse of her slender ankles and the dainty black patent calfskin pumps upon her feet. Her narrow waist was revealed by a snug-fitting satin sash, secured by a decorative broach, that defined her slender figure.

Daisy had arrived earlier that morning and assisted with Beatrice's hair—casual curls surrounded her face, while her abundant tresses had been swept up and contained in a stylish bun, held in place by a three-piece set of Pearl's highly polished tortoise combs, embellished with an ornate Japanese fan designed in solid gold. Her only accessory was a simple strand of pearls at her throat, Pearl's Christmas gift to her a year ago. Beatrice had never felt she deserved to wear such a lovely piece of jewelry, so the precious necklace had remained in its satin-lined box until this very day.

Samuel broke into a wide smile as soon as he saw his beloved. Solemnly reaching for Beatrice's hand, he put his other arm gently around her waist, and then both turned to face Pastor Jenson. Big Jack, Samuel's best man, stepped back, joined Bertha Ness and shocked himself by automatically reaching for her hand. Together they attempted to focus on the event before them, while being overly aware of each other's presence.

Michael smiled at the two young people and opened his *Occasional Service* book. He looked out over the assembled group of friends, motioned them to be seated, and began to speak in his deep, resonant voice. "Dearly Beloved, we are gathered here today to join together in marriage this man and this woman . . ."

Minutes later, the formal service over, Beatrice and Samuel were husband and wife. Samuel swept Beatrice into his arms and kissed her for what seemed to be a very long time, while all their friends gave a hearty cheer. Everyone was smiling, visiting, congratulating the newly married couple, and heading for the dining room table where the delicious repast awaited. Oscar and Henry stood close to the kitchen door, ready to replenish the serving dishes at a moment's notice.

Daisy flew back and forth from the kitchen to the serving table seeing that all was as it should be. The three-layer Lady Baltimore cake, with lemon filling between the layers and covered by swirls of absolutely perfect seven-minute frosting, was the centerpiece of the table. Serving plates of small buns filled with egg salad were placed next to trays overflowing with fudge and divinity, plus platters filled with cookies of all descriptions, including several Scandinavian delicacies.

Maggie stood by the sideboard, ready to pour coffee or offer a small goblet of wine to be used later to toast the newlyweds. Willard Scheibe had been her best customer thus far—two refills of coffee (used to slosh about his mouth and clear away the remnants of his chaw of tobacco) plus a glass of wine for himself and one for Lenore, who never left his side. Willard's smile grew wider as the afternoon progressed.

Big Jack also came for two glasses of wine—one for himself and one for his new "friend," Bertha Ness. Maggie loved to watch her father's face as he visited with Miss Ness. She often reached up to the locket that always hung about her neck, the gift Bertha Ness had given her when she apologized for the hurt she had inflicted on Henry and Maggie. Forgiveness came easily to Maggie, and now the locket sheltered a portrait of her mother and father. Maggie had become, over time, very fond of Miss Ness for the smiles she so often brought to her father's face.

The reception was a smashing success. Happiness and good will echoed from wall to wall of the white house. Wine flowed, cake disappeared, coffee pots emptied, and another pot was quickly set to percolating on the stove in the kitchen.

Beatrice had never looked so lovely. Her cheeks were flushed and her smile never left her face. Her hand rested continually on the arm of her beloved Samuel. At last she felt safe and secure.

While the guests visited with one another, they smiled as they observed Beatrice and Samuel circulating among them. Many commented that Samuel was a very fortunate young man and, of course, proclaimed what a fine young woman Beatrice had become. Perhaps they now realized how, over the years, Pearl had nurtured her, sheltered her, protected her, cared for her, educated her, and allowed her to become the beautiful young woman enjoying this special day.

Pearl's presence was certainly felt and very much a part of the day's celebration.

Before long, the winter sun began to dim. Lamps and candles were soon lit inside the white house, bringing the festivities to a close. Carriages, sleds, and autos came and went from the front driveway, delivering the guests to their homes. Chores always had to be done, cows needed to be milked, and chickens awaited the handfuls of corn that would get them through the night. The guests were ever mindful of their stoves and furnaces, sure they would have burned low by now and needed to be stoked up once again before the bitter cold of the approaching winter night descended upon them.

A much smaller group remained, lingering near the fire still blazing in the parlor. Mrs. Berg sat quietly in the large chair closest to the fireplace, looking content and at peace, and a gentle smile played about her lips when she realized that not one of her friends had collapsed when entering the brothel. And best of all, her beloved Samuel was now married to a young woman Mrs. Berg had come to love. She was very grateful.

Hank and Daisy—finally finished with the work in the kitchen—sat together on the sofa. Daisy rested her head on Hank's broad shoulder, weary from such a busy day, but content with the success of the reception. As Hank gazed into the flames, he recalled the sorrow of their break with Daisy's parents and the traumatic early days of their marriage. Placing his arm around Daisy's shoulders, he held her closer, causing her to turn to him and look into his eyes, knowing somehow the thoughts now playing in his mind. Hank bent and kissed her on the top of her head. She squeezed his hand.

Big Jack sat next to Bertha, a bit apprehensive because he did not know if he dared to take her hand or not. Would that be too forward? Would she turn away? What would the others think? And then, suddenly, Bertha turned toward him, smiled up into his eyes and placed her soft white hand on his large, muscular hand. Big Jack had all he could do to suppress a triumphant shout.

Soon everyone noticed the blush slowly covering Jack's face and began to laugh in good-humored encouragement. Henry, Maggie, and Oscar found all this romantic stuff more than they could understand, so they headed back to the kitchen for one last cookie.

Pastor Jenson was the first of this intimate group to take his leave. Sunday would soon arrive, and he needed to be ready for the services. Mrs. Berg would ride home with him, as would Mrs. Brush and Oscar Lund. After quickly packing a lunch for Anna Belle Lund— a piece of cake and an assortment of cookies—Daisy gave the plate to Oscar to give to his mother. Somehow the community seemed to know all was not well in the Lund household.

One by one their friends took their leave while Beatrice and Samuel stood at the door, waving as buggies made their way across the snow-covered bridge, leaving behind tracks that would soon disappear under the blowing, drifting snow. The white house blended in with the snow-covered hillside, and soon the only indication that a building even existed was a sliver of lamplight gleaming from the first-floor bedroom window—Pearl's room.

When at last the young man and young woman were alone for the first time as husband and wife, a sudden shyness came over both of them. Beatrice was still a virgin, not an easy accomplishment in the midst of a busy brothel. Pearl had kept her far removed from the business of the house and had tried to shelter her from the coarseness and uncouth behavior of many of the patrons. Yet, in a knowing and gentle manner, Pearl shared the positive physical and sexual bits of knowledge with her ward.

"I want you to be able to enjoy your moments with the man you come to love," Pearl had told Beatrice. "Sex can be a pleasure—or so I've been told."

More than once Beatrice had witnessed a man bodily thrown out of the house for a crude remark made about her. On the other hand, Pearl had taken time to prepare Beatrice to be a loving, affectionate wife. Pearl herself had been prepared to be such a wife until her husband began his heavy drinking and she suffered the mistreatment that resulted. Great joy always filled Pearl's heart when she thought of Beatrice and Samuel together, becoming one flesh, as it said in the Bible. As the years passed, she herself had longed for that kind of a union, but it never materialized. Watching Beatrice become a young woman, Pearl hoped to be able to provide a gentler kind of love for this girl who had become so precious to her.

Samuel, on the other hand, did not come as a virgin to his marriage. His encounters had been few and far between as he came and went from the logging camps. However, once he had fallen in love with Beatrice, he was true to his pledge to love only her.

As they entered what was now Beatrice's bedroom, he discovered he was sweating. He wanted to be gentle, he wanted to satisfy her, he wanted to be considerate. And now it was time to consummate their vows, and—good grief!—he was the nervous one.

As soon as they entered the bedroom, Samuel gathered Beatrice in his arms, kissed her passionately, then stepped back. Beatrice smiled up at him, caressed his cheek, then lit a lamp and carried it into her dressing room, leaving Samuel behind in the shadows of the bedroom.

With one last glance over her shoulder, she laughed quietly. "Don't go anywhere," she said in a seductive manner. "I'll be right back."

He could hardly breathe as he paced the bedroom, finally sitting down on the edge of the bed. He heard the sounds of her clothing being removed and falling to the floor. For a brief moment, he caught a glimpse of her by the dim light of the lamp on her dressing table and watched in fascination as she set aside her lovely blue dress, then her slip, and finally, her undergarments and delicate silk stockings. Samuel held his breath.

Slipping a robe over her naked body, Beatrice seated herself at the vanity where she removed all the pins from her hair, allowing it to cascade over her shoulders and down her back. Brushing it slowly, her reflection looked straight into Samuel's eyes, and she smiled knowingly.

Dear God! Samuel thought as he watched her, desire rising within him. *It's time!*

Leaping up from the bed and tossing aside his shoes, suit coat, shirt and tie, he stepped out of his trousers. Now he was down to his long woolen underwear and his socks.

Questions filled his mind. Was it too chilly to remove his long johns as well? Would she be shocked to see him naked?

Being in doubt as to what was proper behavior for a newly married man, he climbed into the bed still wearing his woolen underwear. *Is it acceptable behavior for the groom to be totally naked,* he wondered, *when his virgin bride came to bed for the first time?* As cold as it was here in the bedroom, he was aware he was still sweating.

The lamp in the dressing room was extinguished, leaving both rooms dark, the only light being a sliver of moonlight slipping under the shade of one window. He could barely make out the figure of his wife as she walked toward the bed where he anxiously waited.

He cleared his throat. "We can just go to sleep now and wait until morning to— you know—if you're too tired from the busy day we both had." Incoherent words poured from his lips. "Whatever works best for you—if you feel you need some rest before . . ."

Suddenly he heard a soft laugh.

"I'm coming to bed, to sleep with my dear husband. I'm hoping he'll make love to me," she softly laughed once more, "and allow me to make love to him." She paused. "I certainly hope he's not too tired from the events of the day!" She laughed again.

Her voice was rich, playful, and full of love. Then he heard her robe fall to the floor. And there she stood before him, revealed by that one sliver of the moon's gentle light, her loveliness making Samuel find that he could barely breathe in anticipation.

She laughed again, lifted the covers and slipped in beside him. Curling up next to him, she placed her head on his shoulder and her arm across his broad chest.

"Oh, Samuel," she whispered in his ear as she attempted to stifle a playful giggle, "you still have your long underwear on! Please, take off your long underwear tonight, my husband, for I'll keep you very, very warm!"

Then they both laughed until she leaned over him, kissing him long and tenderly on his lips. Suddenly he threw back the covers, sprang up from the bed and, leaping from one leg to the other, struggled to remove his long underwear. Tossing the woolen underwear over his shoulder into the darkness behind him, he bounded back to bed, joining her under the quilts where they shared the warmth of their first night together.

Samuel, surprised by how quickly he put all his apprehensions out of his mind, was totally committed to the process of loving his beautiful, young wife. And before long, the morning sun drove the darkness away and streamed in through the eastern windows where it found the lovers sound asleep in each other's arms—body to body and heart to heart, man and wife from this day forward.

Samuel and Beatrice had previously promised each other that, on this day, the first day of their married life, they would rise early enough to attend church and kneel at the communion rail together as husband and wife. And—miracle of miracles—they fulfilled their promise. Hesitating to leave the warmth of their bridal bed, they finally stepped out into the chilly room and added some wood to the dwindling fire in the stove. They had to rush, but even that was a joy when they did it together.

The congregation was surprised to see the newlyweds enter the church and pause by the cloak room to hang up their coats. Everyone broke into spontaneous applause as

Samuel and Beatrice walked hand in hand down the aisle of the sanctuary. Pastor Jenson added a blessing in his prayers of the day for the newlyweds. The church members smiled broadly and were generous with their congratulations.

Samuel had only the remains of the Sabbath to be with his beloved. On Monday he would once again join the teamsters leaving the Island with their heavily loaded sleds, heading north to the lumber camp. Samuel and Beatrice tried to put the thought out of their minds. They still had the remains of the day, the soft warmth of the night, and the gray dawn of the morning to come.

On Monday morning, Beatrice stood at the window in the parlor looking up the hillside where she had watched the column of sleds disappear into the pines. She wanted to cry, but she was not going to allow that to happen. Since the day was lovely, she made up her mind to take a walk. Daisy always invited her to stop by at any time. So, dressing warmly, she walked briskly through the snow and over the bridge, where Daisy must have seen her coming. As Beatrice approached the Larsons' front door she could see Daisy through the window, holding up a large white mug. Coffee was ready to be poured. Beatrice waved and felt better already.

Several weeks passed before Beatrice suddenly felt an uncontrollable urge to throw up, barely making it to the sink. Food no longer appealed to her, and more than once she retched into the slop pail, the outhouse, or into a bucket close to her bed at night. In contrast to the queasiness of her stomach she had cravings for, of all things, hard to find fresh oranges.

When she told Mrs .Berg about her sudden bouts of vomiting, Samuel's mother threw her arms around Beatrice and whispered in her ear, "My dear, I'll bet my life on it—you and Samuel are expecting a baby!"

The two women laughed together, hugged, and cried with joy.

Nine months would pass as everyone involved looked forward eagerly to the birth of this blessed child. The child would make its entry into the world on October 12, but no one would ever forget the circumstances of this particular baby's birth.

❧26❧
Mrs. Brush

Mrs. Brush loved to read poetry. Sitting in her comfortable chair near the sun-filled front window, she often read from her assortment of favorite poets. Lately, lines written by John Donne resonated with what was in her heart. She read the words aloud, over and over, savoring the intensity of the poet's emotions.

> "Batter my heart, three-personed God; for you
> As yet but knock, breathe, shine, and seek to mend;
> That I may rise and stand, o'erthrow me, and bend
> Your force to break, blow, burn, and make me new."

She often felt overcome by great weariness; perhaps the wintery grayness of the days caused her feelings of ennui, her sensations of discontent. Ever since she had become a widow, she tried to remain strong, but now her heart felt battered. Just living day to day seemed more difficult. She felt she was losing the battle; the light was fading.

Every morning after rising, she greeted the new day with a prayer of gratefulness for still being alive. Determined to "rise" up as long as she was able, she often found the simple act of preparing her mind to deal with the waking hours more difficult as the weeks passed.

Forcing herself to throw back the covers, to sit up and put her bare feet on the floor, she would then slowly and carefully rise to her full height, which had decreased by at least two inches. She would slip into her well-worn robe, then sit in front of the ornate mirror hanging over her dressing table. The face she greeted in the mirror every day seemed to grow more unfamiliar as days passed. Even so, she would continue to wrestle with God until He made her "new." That thought always gave her a focus to live in the body of the stranger appearing in the mirror before her.

After eighty-eight years, every crease and wrinkle was deeply etched into the fine porcelain skin covering the bones of her once lovely face. Every morning she took pleasure in freeing her hair from the braids that kept it under control while she slept. She had always been proud of her thick tresses. She ran her fingers through her hair, wavy from being braided, until it hung full and free about her shoulders. Then she took her favorite brush and proceeded to brush it.

Finally, her hair looked as though it had expanded. White locks floated softly around her face. She loved the sensation of freedom she now felt, symbolized by her flowing hair. Sometimes she contemplated having Daisy cut her hair into the new fashionable style called a Marcel—a haircut that encouraged the waves and spit curls that were so popular with the younger set.

Mrs. Brush leaned closer to the mirror, pleased she never had need of glasses. Her eyes were still full of life and blue as the summer sky. Her skin, however, had become a mystery. She felt as though she dwelled in someone else's flesh. Her cheeks hung loosely toward her neck. The skin about her neck, in turn, drooped wearily about her jaw and fell down to meet her collar bone. Fine creases marched across her lips, and the sockets of her eyes grew more evident as the flesh deserted her face.

To her dismay, her body had deteriorated and seemed to be in a state of even greater disrepair. When she occasionally viewed her naked body before stepping into her enamel claw-footed tub, she was always appalled by what she saw. Her skin didn't seem to fit her anymore. It hung loosely about her breasts, her arms, her belly, and her legs. At times she would laugh, wishing she had a magical needle and thread with which to take a tuck here and there in her outgrown frock of skin.

Yes, she was an old woman. She really did not mind being old; she just did not want to become a burden to anyone, especially Daisy, who had loved her as though she were truly her flesh-and-blood mother. Mrs. Brush desired only to live as long as she was in control of her own personal destiny, as comfortably as possible, without causing a problem.

All Mrs. Brush asked of God, praying about it continually, was that she could just sleep away one evening as she lay, warm and cozy, in her comfortable old bed, under the quilt her mother had sewn for her almost a century ago. Certainly that wasn't too much to ask.

Placing the brush back on the vanity, then catching her long, white hair up in a twist, she temporarily anchored it with a large set of combs. Daisy always told her how much she enjoyed doing Mrs. Brush's hair, and she knew just how to do it to Mrs. Brush's satisfaction. Thus her hairdo was not completed until Daisy arrived on the scene. Mrs. Brush rose from her chair, tied the sash of her robe securely about her, and made her way carefully downstairs to check on Old Syd. Stoking the coal furnace in the basement and getting a toasty fire going in the kitchen were his first and primary jobs of the day .

By the time Mrs. Brush descended the stairway and turned down the hall, she was greeted by the warmth of the kitchen stove and the aroma of fresh coffee. Old Syd, always singing to himself but never for anyone else, was seated at the table enjoying the first of his many cups of coffee of the day. The schedule of these two old friends did not vary much from day to day, and was the foundation of their daily activities. Together the two aged friends would stand side by side for at least one more day and wait to be made new.

Daisy Larson made it a point to arrive at Mrs. Brush's front door every day about the same time, rain or shine. After setting the dough for her bread, roll, and cookie orders, she placed the bowls on the table where the sun could reach them and covered them with a clean, white dishtowel. She made sure Hank was ready for the day and then sent Henry out to meet Maggie at the corner, where they met to walk to school. Finally, she dressed in her warmest clothes and, carrying a basket of fresh goodies on her arm, headed across the bridge to Cloquet Avenue. With a gust of frigid winter air, she entered Mrs. Brush's front door just in time for a very welcome cup of fresh hot coffee.

Daisy was painfully aware of the decline of her beloved friend. Each day that she came and enfolded her friend in her arms, Daisy could sense the changes taking place—always thinner, always moving about more slowly, always a more evident tremor in the veined hands. Often they had spoken candidly of what the future held for Mrs. Brush. Daisy was informed that Pastor Jenson had sole possession of a written note detailing Mrs. Brush's final wishes.

The most important item on the list was the stipulation that, under no circumstance, was Mrs. Brush to be removed from her own home and her own bed as she was dying.

"Let me pass in peace," she would say firmly. "Just pull my quilt over me and wish me a pleasant trip to heaven. Period. End of discussion."

And Daisy had agreed to be the facilitator of Mrs. Brush's very explicit wishes. Much as she tried not to think about it, Daisy mentally prepared herself for Mrs. Brush's prayer to be answered.

As the poet said in the concluding lines of his poem,

> "Take me to you, imprison me, for I,
> Except you enthrall me, never shall be free,
> Nor ever chaste, except you ravish me."

Strangely enough, Mrs. Brush especially enjoyed the poet's choice of the word "ravish." At times she envisioned herself tossed over the shoulder of the Lord Jesus as he carried her away from this earthly life to the splendor of His heavenly kingdom. She was more than ready to be "ravished."

And slowly but surely the days slipped by, swallowed up one by one, until, at last, Mrs. Brush needed to pray no more. On that day, in circumstances no one would ever have imagined, she finally allowed herself to peacefully lean back in the strong arms of her Lord and Savior. There, at last, she found it possible to be enthralled by God and reach out to welcome death with open arms. Had Mrs. Brush or Daisy—or even Old Syd—been omniscient, they would have known the moment of her demise would arrive in the autumn of 1918—on October 12, to be exact.

❧27❧
Oscar Lund

OSCAR LUND SERIOUSLY DISLIKED his father. Some days emotion rose like bile in his throat, making him sick to his stomach. The dislike had been growing for most of his life and filled him. Now, when his father disciplined him, Oscar stood as tall as he could, looking his his father directly—and boldly—in his eyes. Never again would Oscar bow his head and cringe before the man's tirades.

Over the past summer and autumn, Oscar had grown. His head measured past his father's chin and, if he really stretched, he could almost equal his father in height. Oscar stopped flinching as his father berated him for some tiny infraction of his multitude of rules. As angry as his father would become at times, the leather belt remained where it belonged—holding up his father's perfectly creased trousers.

Oscar and his mother tried to maintain a semblance of peace while walking the tightrope that was his father's temper. Having spent so much time on the Island with Henry and his family and with Maggie and her father, Oscar had a new standard for what a parent's behavior toward a child should be. His father failed in all regards. He showed no affection, nor any interest in Oscar's activities at school or church. When his father stood, eyes blazing in disgust at his son's latest transgression, Oscar just stared back, an image of Henry and his father in his mind showing him what his father lacked.

On one occasion the path to the wood shed was supposed to be kept passable and, after the last snow storm, Henry evidently forgot his responsibility, leaving Daisy to scramble through the drifts to get wood for the stove. Hank was upset, yet he sat Henry down across from him at the table and talked to him, one man to another. "This was your responsibility, Henry," Hank spoke sternly to his son. "Your mother and I depend on you to do the tasks assigned to you. We have to work together to get along out here on the Island."

Henry agreed. "I'm sorry, Dad. Sometimes the days go by so fast I forget what my chores are. The next time a blizzard swoops in, I'll be out there in the middle of it with my shovel."

Hank laughed. "We'll let you get by until the snow's done falling, Henry!" The encounter closed with a warm handshake.

As a casual observer, this was a teaching moment for Oscar. Thinking about it later, Oscar was sure he'd willingly shovel his way to the moon for his father—if he ever treated him in such a loving way.

Arthur Lund had become aware of the look in his son's narrowed eyes, a hard look, indicating the boy would no longer tolerate physical punishment. Partially because of this, Mr. Lund spent less time at home. He and his Ford rambled away at all hours of the day or night.

The nocturnal forays down the darkened road, no matter how secretive Mr. Lund tried to be, provided fodder for the gossip mill. His Ford was recognized by laborers heading home from the late shift at the mill. Farmers, coming and going from Carlton to Cloquet, made note of the car as it was parked, supposedly hidden, in the deep shade of the pines. "Now there's a pair that really deserves each another," was the opinion most often spoken as a benediction to the gossip dealing with the clandestine relationship.

And then there was Anna Belle. Oscar loved his mother, and he knew how much she loved him in return. As the months passed, he was pleased to note she was doing much better now as far as liquor was concerned. Actually, Daisy Larson had been a huge factor in her recovery, for Daisy now made it a point to stop by for a visit once or twice a week as she came and went from Mrs. Brush's home.

Anna Belle Lund looked forward to the mornings she and Daisy spent visiting in the sunny parlor. At times, the maid served them a fragrant tea, much to Daisy's delight. Most often on the serving side, Daisy found she rather enjoyed lifting her dainty china teacup after someone else served her tea.

As a wife, Anna Belle Lund had never been the recipient of tender affection and concern from her husband. Even when they were first married, she soon realized she was alone, left to herself. For a time, Arthur came to their bed often, but never with romantic overtures or ardent love. He came, he reached for her, and she was always ready, always hopeful. Freshly bathed and in a soft flannel gown, gently perfumed, hair braided, lying on her side, she waited for him to love her, to caress the curve of her hip. And when he did, for a while, she responded eagerly, thinking that—at last—he wanted to love her and be loved in return.

That was never the case. He pinned her to the bed, entered her forcefully, climaxed, rolled over and turned to the wall. Tears flowed as she lay there, listening to his even breathing, totally oblivious of how she longed for someone to lavish her with love and affection. At first she told herself Arthur must be very busy at the bank making a fine living for the two of them; he must have had thoughts only for the business. That made sense for a year or two. Then, when she found herself pregnant, she felt deep in her heart that a child would unite the two of them and they would finally be a happy family.

But that, too, did not materialize. She was still abandoned, so to speak, but now she had a child to love and care for all by herself. And she loved Oscar with all her heart. Being a devoted mother became her goal in life, and she reveled in the life she was able to live with a baby at her breast, and later, a child toddling at her side holding her hand.

The drinking began when Oscar went off to school and she was left all alone in the big house. Anna Belle felt empty without her child at her side. The hired help was respectful, but distant. And not one of the other socially acceptable young women reached out to be her friend. Arthur Lund had alienated most of the clients of his bank and was, consequentially, not held in high regard by other businessmen. Their wives exercised their social muscles by shutting her out. So, the bottle became Anna Belle's friend.

Now, with Daisy as his mother's ally and friend, Oscar saw a remarkable change in Anna Belle. Together, mother and son were able to survive the storms that often erupted within the walls of their lovely home. Together, as the months passed, they slowly distanced themselves, emotionally and physically, from their constant critic. Together, they told themselves they'd survive and would try to greet the future with hopefulness. And as a true blessing for Anna Belle, Arthur Lund had not darkened the door of her bedroom for quite some time.

She didn't miss him—not one iota. In fact, she was sleeping more soundly now, even without the help of her usual nightcap. And even her dreams became more pleasant as time passed. Thus, she set aside the liquor, carefully placing the bottles inside a decorative cabinet in the parlor, near to the fainting couch by the window. However, she knew exactly where they were stored, and only occasionally, on a extremely trying day, would she seek them out for the sweet escape an occasional drink provided her. After all, she had to be strong for her beloved son. She was all he had.

Anna Belle had no idea of what trauma awaited her and her beloved son. Had she felt any hint of the catastrophe that awaited them because of her fondness for the bottle, she would have immediately poured all the alcohol down the sink and tossed every colored bottle into the trash.

ɞ28ଔ
Friends

HANK LARSON LOOKED FORWARD to spring with a mixture of excitement and anxiety. The spring thaw would send the logs plunging downriver from the logging camps. One year had passed since his unfortunate accident, and every day he sorely missed his life as a lumberjack. Trying to be patient, he sat by his window and watched the other men head north to the lumber camps. He tried to do the various tasks assigned him by the office managers of the mills, thankful he had some income.

He loved being with Daisy and was eternally grateful for her care and concern. Quietly observing her over the past weeks and months, he had come to love her even more than before. As the years of their marriage slipped by, he didn't think he could ever have felt a deeper affection for her, but he was wrong. His love and appreciation for her continued to grow each day. How did he ever deserve such a wonderful woman?

His back and legs had healed to some degree, but the strength that had once been there did not return as he had hoped. His life had forever changed. He realized that the work he loved was not possible anymore, and he struggled to make peace with life as he had to live it.

Even so, he waited eagerly for the shouts announcing the approaching logs and all the excitement that accompanied their arrival. Hank had already made plans with Henry to find them a place in front of the Moose Saloon near the bridge. Together father and son would cheer as the logs tumbled down the river, the river pigs dancing atop them, and watch as they came to rest in the curve of the river south of the Island. Rain or shine, father and son together would welcome the river pigs home again.

For Henry, the spring held the anticipation of the returning horses that had for the past months worked hauling logs forth and back, through ice and snow, to the edge of the river. He had missed his visits to the barns, and especially the time spent with Samson. Henry wondered if Samson would recognize him after the winter away.

Breathing in the odors of the barn, the fragrance of the hay, and the pungent smell of horse dung filled Henry with anticipation. Henry stopped by to help Mr. Kellar get the barn ready whenever he could. Samson would have a stall to be envied by all the other horses—if it were possible for a horse to envy.

Miss Vivian Thoreson had been a delightful and stimulating teacher for Henry, Maggie, and Oscar. Their class had toured the world by way of the magical maps that

Miss Thoreson would draw down for them all to see. They loved seeing the wide oceans, the rivers cascading through the various countries, the mountain ranges that rose up and divided the prairies and the deserts. Ancient cities and historical landmarks stirred their young imaginations along with the knowledge of explorers and pioneers who struggled to claim the land.

Henry took time to share his newfound knowledge with Mrs. Brush whenever he saw her. Sitting on the edge of her bed if she were resting, or sipping a cup of the sugar-laden coffee in her kitchen, Henry more than compensated for the times they had spent together when he was a lonely little boy. After all, she had been the one to plant the desire for knowledge in his impressionable brain all those years ago. Knowing that desire had taken root and listening to his eager recounting of all he had learned made Mrs. Brush happy.

Spring had finally arrived, and the three friends participated in the annual spelling bee, held each year in the high school gymnasium. All three had done well and gone on to represent Cleveland Elementary School at the sixth grade spelling finals. When the day of the contest finally arrived, the students, dressed in their very best, sat in a row on the stage, awaiting their turn to come to the podium. Tension filled the room as student after student hesitated and either spelled—or misspelled—the word given to them.

Henry had to step aside early in the second round when he stumbled on the word "malodorousness." Maggie, one of only three left standing, was stumped by "propinquity," leaving only Oscar and another boy. Oscar maintained an outward calm and spelled "irascibility" correctly while the other boy misspelled "entrepreneur." Oscar was awarded the trophy with much pomp and circumstance.

What he appreciated the most was that he was now declared publically the very best at something. Gazing at the shiny trophy, Oscar could see his smiling face reflected back at him. This made his smile even wider as he looked out over the audience. He sought out his mother's face, and there she was, glowing with pride.

Anna Belle, seated in the large auditorium with her friends, smiled back as tears threatened to slip down her cheeks. All the parents and friends were proud of the young scholars from Churchill Elementary School. Miss Thoreson stood offstage, nodding her head gently in approval.

That evening at home, even Oscar's father took note of his son's achievement with a pat on the back and a mumbled, "Congratulations." Oscar thanked him politely, but never raised his eyes to acknowledge him. When asked to see his award, Oscar held it out, but quietly refused to allow his father to touch the trophy.

"The trophy is mine," Oscar said as he turned away.

An ill-tempered look flashed across his father's face, lasting only a moment. Then he slammed out the back door and made his way to the garage. The black Ford roared to life and Oscar and his mother heard it rumble past the side of the house and down the driveway where it made a sharp turn toward town, leaving behind a cloud of dust. The trophy itself finally found a resting place on the top shelf of the fine oak china cabinet dominating the large dining room. No one ever touched it, except Oscar.

The spring play, a one-act play adapted from Mark Twain's *Tom Sawyer* and focused on the chapter where Tom whitewashed a fence, was the final challenge for the sixth-graders. Henry played Tom and Maggie secured the role of Becky. Together they stole the show. The auditorium was filled with family and friends from town and the Island. The Island fans were a bit more demonstrative with their approval than the more reserved folks from Cloquet. Miss Thoreson, as was her custom, stood quietly backstage and allowed the two "stars" of the show to have their moment in the sun.

The Island hummed with excitement—the occasional fistfight, arm wrestling tournaments, spitting contests, and cards and gambling provided some very testy confrontations. When things got out of hand on several occasions, the city police made their presence known, arresting the brawlers and hauling them off to jail. Each spring, the men returning from the camps needed time to accustom themselves to the pressures of civilization when they stepped back into their routines working for the mills.

Pastor Jenson spent more time on the Island than perhaps necessary. Nothing pleased him more than to put his books aside for a short time and head over the red bridge. Somehow he felt totally at home at the Larsons' table, coffee in his right hand and a fresh donut in his left, or enjoying a crowded supper in Big Jack's boarding house dining room. The conversation never lagged, and Michael came to hold Hank Larson and Big Jack Swanson in high regard as husbands (Big Jack seemed to be approaching this position with Bertha Ness), fathers, men, and Christians. If Michael had ever had the privilege of having a brother, he would certainly have chosen a man just like Hank or Big Jack.

The church had grown very fond of their pastor. Just this past winter, an old lumberjack was found drunk and unconscious on the dark path leading to his tarpaper shack on the north shore of the Island. Almost frozen to death, his good Samaritans rushed him to the hospital. No one knew of any next of kin, so Pastor Jenson was summoned to the side of the dying man. As Michael entered the hospital room, the doctor looked up from his examination and shook his head. "There's little hope that this man will survive," he confided in the pastor. "Whoever he is, he was exposed to the frigid winter weather for far too long." The doctor walked to the door and turned again to the pastor. "There's nothing more I can do for him here. So, Pastor Jenson, you must help him approach the heavenly gates."

Michael stood alone at the foot of the bed. The only sound in the shadowy room was the labored breathing of the dying man. Michael pulled a chair close to the bed, determined to be there until death, on the pale gray horse, came to bear the soul of the unconscious man to his just reward.

Only once did the eyes of the dying man open. Slowly turning his head toward the light from the hall, he looked into the caring face of the unknown man at the side of his bed. Michael reached out and placed his hand in blessing on the head of the dying man before him, smoothed the thin, unruly hair back from the white forehead and found the skin ice cold, rigid beneath his touch. Leaning closer, Michael spoke gently, but firmly, to the man who held onto life with such a fragile grasp. "Don't be afraid. The Lord Jesus is with you." A sudden look of panic filled the rheumy, tear-filled eyes.

Michael leaned to the man's ear and gently spoke what he thought he would like to hear someone speak to him if he were dying. "Just lean back into the strong arms of Jesus and he will care for you. Jesus loves you. He always has and always will. 'Come unto me and I will give you rest.' Those are the words of Jesus, and you can rely on what he says."

Michael gently stroked the furrowed brow of the dying man, watching as his eyes slowly closed and his breathing became more and more shallow. Michael spoke softly, hoping the man could still hear the words. "Jesus loves you, you can be sure of that. For the Bible tells us that He died for your sins and for my sins. Yes, Jesus loves me—and he loves you, as well." Michael spoke those comforting words, over and over, until he felt the breath of life vanish from the man.

The funeral was held at the Lutheran Church the very next day. Only eleven men attended and sat scattered throughout the sanctuary, mostly old lumberjacks with their hair slicked back, each wearing an unfamiliar clean shirt, along with Big Jack and Hank Larson. Michael's sermon dealt with the undeserved gift of grace, centering on the words of Jesus and the thief as they hung on the cross. "Remember me!" the dying thief had begged as death came ever nearer. Jesus responded to his pleading as only He was able.

Michael described the moment when Jesus turned his pain-filled eyes, fixing them on the anguished criminal hanging at his side. "Today you shall be with me in paradise," were the comforting words directed toward the dying thief. Michael repeated the phrase two times, once as it fit in the crucifixion account and once again as he looked out over the ill-kept mix of men who sat before him. Attempting to look each one of them in the eye as he came to the end of his sermon, he firmly concluded by saying, "Since Jesus was able to be so open and inviting to a crook on the cross, think just how sure everyone here can be that Jesus invites each and every one of us to also be with him in paradise."

Big Jack invited all the mourners down to his boarding house for cake and coffee. Bertha Ness volunteered to come early so the coffee would be percolating on the stove when everyone arrived, and the generous pieces of chocolate cake were on trays all ready to be placed on the serving table. The church ladies felt somewhat relieved, thankful they did not have to serve what they perceived to be a very motley crew.

Later, when the ladies came into the sanctuary to straighten up the pews and replace the hymn books in the racks, they suddenly paused at the door. Raising their heads they intently sniffed the air, positive they could detect a definite odor of liquor hovering about the sanctuary. Thank goodness it was a fairly nice day outside so they could throw open the windows and bring fresh, clean air back into the sanctuary. There they stood, each one by a window, waving their ample aprons, summoning the fragrant, almost spring-like air back into God's house.

Michael stayed for supper at Big Jack's, enjoying the acceptance he felt from the mill workers and lumberjacks. Years of living on the farm and doing manual labor gave him a natural rapport with the hard-working men. He had become especially notorious since his knock-down fight in the Moose Saloon. The men of the Island had become very fond of the young pastor who was so open and accepting to all of them.

More Island people found themselves walking over the bridge on a Sunday morning, joining with the townspeople as they worshiped in the Lutheran Church. Michael stood in the pulpit each Sunday and looked out over his flock. He truly loved each and every human being who sat in the pews before him, from the aged down to the newly born, waiting each Sunday for him to open the scripture, the Word of God, to them and help them live more satisfying lives.

Michael often thought that, deep down, he fully understood why Christ had been ready to give his life to ransom the countless people who were to follow throughout the passing centuries. It was really quite simply stated in I Corinthians 13: "Faith, hope, and love. But the greatest of these is love!" And Michael found love in his heart for everyone he met.

ഓ29രു
Summer 1918

Mᴏss Tʜᴏʀᴇsᴏɴ sᴛᴏᴏᴅ, tall and imposing, in the doorway of her sixth-grade room on the final day of the school year. With the work of the morning, a few wisps of hair had come loose from the bun at the back of her neck and floated gently around her cheeks. A pencil protruded from behind her left ear, where she habitually placed it when it was not in use. The students had cleared out their desks, taken down all their artistic works from the bulletin boards, helped stack all their textbooks in the nearby storeroom, and taken one last trip to the library to return their books.

Glancing around the room, she was pleased it appeared to be neat and clean, well organized with the work tables clear and the maps pulled up and once again in their sleeves. Sunlight streamed through the western windows and highlighted the attentive faces of all the students she had come to love over the past nine months. There they sat, looking expectant, their hands folded atop their desk as they had been taught.

Miss Vivian Thoreson felt a lump in her throat each year as she bid farewell to the lively children placed under her authority. There had been success stories, and moments when she felt she had failed to reach the inner potential of a child. And now they were leaving her, to go on to their next educational challenge.

She signaled for them to stand, and she could feel the excitement spilling over in each youngster. After all, twelve weeks of freedom beckoned them. Her directions were given in her most authoritative voice. "Walk single file to the door! Then stand at attention until you're dismissed!" And they did as they were told.

Shaking the hand of each one, Miss Thoreson then sent them out the door with the benediction she always preached. "Always do your very best!" However, once the students passed through her portal and felt freedom beckon them, they picked up speed on their way to the front door of the school, where they burst forth into the summer sunshine.

However, three students remained, quietly standing in the hall near Miss Thoreson. When she turned to go back into her now-empty room, she noticed them—Oscar, Maggie, and Henry. Almost in unison they began to thank her.

"We had such a great year in your class! We learned so much, thanks to you. You always made us feel we could do anything we set out minds to. We'll miss coming to school each morning and spending the day with you as our teacher. We had so much fun!"

Miss Thoreson was not a demonstrative woman, but she could not resist the brief and spontaneous hugs the children bestowed on her. Much against her nature, she found herself hugging them in return.

Then they, too, ran down the hall and out into the brightness of the afternoon. Returning to her desk, she wearily sat and leaned back in her creaky old chair. *Those three are special*, she thought. *I hope the world will be good to them.* Closing her eyes, she lay her head back on the cracked leather upholstery of the chair she'd used for more years than she cared to count. She, too, needed a time of freedom, a time to replenish the energy and excitement she always wished to convey to her students.

Some days she felt all her vim and vigor had just leaked out. Dismissing that negative thought with a shake of her head, she renewed her firm resolution to be positive. Suddenly, straightening herself, she stood, smoothed down her well-worn dress, and picked up her case full of the selection of books she planned to read over the summer. Another school year fast approached, and she meant to be ready when the next group of students tumbled into her room next fall.

As always, there were a few things left to do before she could call it a day. She had to fill out the last of the papers pertaining to final grades, check the storeroom one more time, and wipe down the blackboard where she had earlier written: "READ A BOOK A WEEK IF IT IS KNOWLEDGE YOU SEEK!" She liked the flow of the words.

Summer days arrived with bright blue skies, warm breezes, and temperatures that made everyone wish they could strip down and jump in to the cool depths of the St. Louis River. Many youngsters did just that.

The mills had been working at full capacity ever since the logs came tumbling down the river in late March. Men were summoned to their labor by the shrill whistles signaling the start and the finish of the morning and evening shifts. The huge stacks of cut lumber stretched over vast acres near the river waiting to be shipped all over the country where people had settled and wanted to build homes, businesses, churches, or even saloons.

The eastern point of the Island, stretching out into the river as it flowed toward Duluth, was covered in long rows of finished lumber. The lumber was stacked almost twenty feet high, forming deep canyons as far as the eye could see, with paths between the rows covered with sawdust to protect the wood from being spattered with mud during summer storms. Across the river on the town side, long walls of timber also lined the shore and backed up almost to the main street of the town.

Railroads had ready access to the millions of board feet of lumber ready for shipping; trains constantly came and went, feeding the building boom now erupting in the larger cities to the west and the newly settled communities on the prairies. Townspeople learned to sleep through the constant comings and goings of the trains as they loaded, coupled and uncoupled night and day, and finally chugged their way out of town. The small number of people living permanently on the Island eventually trained themselves to shut out the din of the trains, too, even though the tracks on their side of the river came practically through their living rooms or the pool hall or saloon.

Summer quickly evolved into ball games, fishing trips, picnics, and family gatherings. Children gathered in vacant lots with a bat and ball and a spontaneous "world series" came into being. Girls practiced to perfect the rhythmic timing needed to be an outstanding jump roper. Wagons and scooters traveled over the city streets, up and down the hills, through the park, and across the vacant lots. Henry still considered his wagon to be the epitome of design and function. He and his two sidekicks were a familiar sight on the city streets during the summer, always coming and going with their valuable cargo—Daisy's famous freshly baked goods.

At night the neighborhood children came together after supper and chores to play Hide and Seek or "I'll Draw the Frying Pan." Sometimes, on a clear, dark night, when the sky held all the mysteries of the universe, the children simply lay on their backs in the still, warm grass and gazed into the velvety darkness overhead. The radiant stars appeared so close they felt it almost possible to reach up and capture one of them in an outstretched hand. Occasionally the children would gasp in wonder as they witnessed a rare falling star. "Where did it go?" they wondered. "How fast was it falling? Did it just come loose from where it was before? Why don't any of the stars in the Big Dipper ever fall away?"

Henry, Maggie, and Oscar loved to find a comfortable spot by the edge of the river on a night when the sky was clear and the moon full. They would sit close to the shore and watch the moon rise over the slender remnants of clouds near the horizon. As the orb rose, it cast an almost-magical aura over the land and the river. Reflected in the moving waters of the St. Louis River, the moonlight gave the impression of molten silver spilling down the river on both sides of the Island and past the children as they sat in the grass on the Island's north shore. No one had much to say, for all three youngsters were enthralled by the beauty of the scene.

"I love living on the Island," Henry said. "We'd never get to sit right here and watch this if we lived in town, I bet!" And his two friends agreed with him.

Now that summer had made its grand entrance, Pinehurst Park was filled every weekend with folks pleased to have some free time to enjoy life and meet with friends and neighbors. Picnic dinners on picnic tables or on a quilt on the grass displayed a bounty of delicious homemade food: baked ham, homemade potato salad, deviled eggs, thick slices of fresh bread, freshly sliced tomatoes, cakes, pies, and cookies, all fit for a king. The ordinary picnic became life on the grand scale for the down-to-earth residents of the area. A woman's reputation could be elevated or destroyed by the type of salad, cake, or pie she contributed to a family or church gathering. The bar was set very high, yet the women always seemed to rise to the occasion.

And always on a quiet spot on the river, men and boys practiced the fine art of birling. Everyone was accustomed to seeing a man or boy struggling atop a spinning log, trying to keep balanced—but eventually tumbling into the murky water.

This year the river was often clogged by spectators who came to observe a once-in-a-lifetime event: a girl was among the youngsters preparing for competition. Maggie was being trained to compete against the boys and had signed up for the young people's Lumberjack Days birling competition. Her trainer was none other than Hank Larson, the man considered by local experts to be among the very best of the river pigs.

Earlier that spring, when the snow had melted and warm days finally arrived on the scene, Hank had all but forgotten Maggie's request from the previous summer. But, as soon as the river was clear of ice and school was out, Maggie was at his elbow, reminding him of what he had promised those many months ago. "You said you could teach me to run the logs! You promised!" she lamented. So they began the daily training.

There she was, soaking wet from falls into the water, on top of the spinning log, her long braid flying out behind her. Balance, quickness, confidence, and speed were all factors Maggie was working to develop as she stepped back again and again onto the slippery log. Hank stood on the shore supported by two canes, almost in the water himself, excitedly calling out to her as, together, they fine-tuned her technique.

Hank found Maggie an eager student. Frank Shaw, the champion from last summer's competition, came by as often as he was able to watch the eager young girl practice, work with her directly on the log, and ready himself for the challengers reportedly coming from all the neighboring logging areas. Once the distant loggers heard reports that Hank Larson was out of contention for another year, they immediately had mounting ambitions of tossing Frank from his spinning log, into the churning water, and out of the winner's circle.

The tension mounted as the Lumberjack Days celebration drew nearer. Throughout the saloons wagers were made with most of the loggers' hard-earned money backing Frank. They all hoped for a win. No one paid much attention to Hank and his student.

The number of onlookers grew daily as the date of the competition approached. Many school friends came to watch Maggie practice, cheering her on. At first the boys scoffed at the idea that Maggie could hold her own. Very soon, however, the booing become shouts of encouragement as Maggie seemed glued to the top of the log. Even the girls, skeptical as they had been at first, were now cheering along with everyone else as Maggie remained longer and longer on the spinning log beneath her nimble feet.

On lovely summer afternoons, Beatrice often walked across the bridge from the white house where she and Samuel now lived. By this time everyone in the area could see that she and Samuel were expecting their first child sometime in the fall.

To the casual observer, Beatrice had become even more lovely than usual as the child grew within her. Her eyes were bright and clear and her skin seemed to glow with health and radiance. Walking slowly and carefully, carrying a blue umbrella to shade her porcelain skin from the sun, Beatrice slowly found her way across the bridge to the comfortable chair Big Jack always provided for her in the shade of a large pine tree, close to where all the activity was taking place.

Once she was seated in her comfortable chair, with her umbrella over her shoulder, she could enjoy the commotion and laughter constantly erupting from the ever-growing crowd. Fresh breezes coming downriver, plus the chatter of her friends and neighbors surrounding her, gave her a sense of peace and the comfort of being part of the community.

Beatrice and Samuel were counting the days to the arrival of their first child. By the middle of October, if she had figured correctly, she and Samuel would welcome their already well-loved child into their hearts and home. While seated on her chair in the shade, Beatrice always placed her hand on her rounded belly to feel the baby's movement.

Slightly dusted with flour, Daisy would often bring another chair, plus two cold glasses of lemonade, and sit beside Beatrice while waiting for her dough to rise. They would visit, talking of the approaching birth, the juicy tidbits of gossip floating across from the town, comparing notes on the rumored romance between Big Jack and Bertha Ness, of which they both approved, and slowly sipping their ice cold lemonade.

Daisy always cheered for Hank with great enthusiasm, watching him as he interacted with Maggie, Henry, and all the young people who seemed so interested in this physical feat that came so naturally to a lumberjack, a river pig. In her mind she could always see her beloved Hank as he was before the accident. She remembered how, as the ice disappeared and the waters flowed freely, large crowds gathered near the bank to watch the logs tumbling down the river.

So Daisy cheered loudly for Maggie, and for Hank, always trying to swallow the great lump that would form in her throat as she watched Hank struggle while standing near the shore, attempting to steady himself with his two canes shoring up his uncooperative, still damaged legs. As always, he cheered, admonished, and shook his canes.

Rumors filtered across the river, and soon Miss Thoreson heard reports of "the girl who was entering the birling contest" from several of her horrified friends. Miss Thoreson laughed at their sour outlook toward a girl attempting to try something new and exciting. Curiosity finally got the better of her. On a lovely afternoon in late July she put on her comfortable shoes, picked up her walking stick that always stood by the front door, placed a straw hat at a rakish angle upon her head, and started off to the Island, where all this interesting activity was said to be taking place.

Later that afternoon when Maggie raised her eyes to look at the rowdy crowd now gathered near the river, she noticed Miss Thoreson standing on the shore with the other onlookers. With a small wave of her hand, Miss Thoreson acknowledged Maggie's glance. Maggie smiled, shyly returned the gesture, and readied herself to begin her practice run.

Holding her breath, Miss Thoreson watched as Maggie prepared to mount the log. Maggie was agile, graceful, and strong as she spun the log beneath her nimble feet. Miss Thoreson clenched her hands at her chest while she watched the scene before her. Hank was animated in his method of training, Frank was dramatic as he danced across the logs with such ease and masculine grace, and Maggie simply made everyone smile and cheer for her as—time after time—she crawled out of the river and once more mounted the uncooperative log to try to master its treacherous surface.

That very day Miss Vivian Thoreson was converted as a fan of birling. As she walked home by way of Cloquet Avenue, the people on the street looked at her with mounting curiosity as she ever so slightly hopped, skipped, and jumped, all the while imagining herself atop the twirling log with the river splashing at her feet.

The weeks of summer slipped by, always punctuated by the preparation for and celebration of the Sunday worship service. For Pastor Jenson, most days were filled with a multitude of plans that held no relationship to the church calendar. The pastoral load always lightened slightly during the summer months, with Sunday School classes set aside until after rally Sunday and confirmation classes programmed to begin shortly after school resumed. Having been a shepherd to his flock for just over a year, Michael appeared to relish the freedom of days he could spend calling on the many people who were in need of a helping hand, a shoulder to cry on, or a listening ear.

So far this summer he had been seen riding a tractor, bumping across the rows as he cultivated a field for old Mr. Erickson, incapacitated by a stroke. Another member, out for an evening stroll, had been surprised to look up and see the pastor high atop a ladder painting the trim around the windows of a home where a loved one had recently passed away. Occasionally on a summer evening the pastor put on his overalls, took up his ax, and chopped wood for anyone—member or not—who was unable to do it themselves.

Most of the townspeople thought all this physical labor was admirable for a pastor, though a few thought he should not lower himself to such common labor. To Michael, what others thought did not matter much. He enjoyed the work, appreciated the fellowship, and felt a sense of personal connection when he lingered over a cup of coffee once the chore was completed. Even his hands felt a sense of purpose, especially when he noted the blisters and calluses scattered over his palms.

Several times a week the pastor sat with Mrs. Brush on her shaded front porch. More and more fragile, he would assist her, at times even carrying her gently, to a chaise lounge tucked away in a shaded corner of the porch, where he positioned her pillow just so and tucked in the old, lightweight shawl she preferred around her delicate frame. Mrs. Brush loved to be close to the fragrance of the rose bushes flourishing near the front steps. She would lay her head on the pillow and breath deeply of the rich scent of the roses her very own hands had planted when she was a newly married woman.

When she breathed deeply of the rich bouquet, in her mind she once again became the young, vibrant woman, so eager for the future. When she at last opened her eyes and looked about at the familiar world around her—Old Syd's wrinkled face and Pastor Jenson's kindly smile—she realized that her future had certainly arrived and would soon come to a close. She was at peace. After all, she had lived for almost ninety years. What more could a person expect? So, when Michael took her slender hand into his and they prayed together, "Thy will be done," she knew what she could soon expect, and she returned the gentle pressure of his grip. Surely she felt the passage of each day and did not battle against her mortality. She would go peacefully.

Then, of course, there were always the whispered reports of Pastor Jenson's occasional visits to the Island. Michael offered no excuses for his journeys across the red bridge, his time spent with the Larsons and Big Jack and Maggie. The members of his flock were intrigued by the reports of the men he had helped find their way home when they were under the influence of too much alcohol and the rumors of the fights and arguments where he had brokered peace, when a handshake rather than a fistfight was the ultimate result.

Michael loved his parish, the people he served who were members of his flock, but he also loved the many people of the area who had needs and problems and had no source of support. They were also dear to his heart, and that feeling radiated out to everyone with whom he came into contact during his first year of his ministry. The general opinion of just about everyone who lived in the community could be stated simply: "That Pastor Jenson is a good man!"

August descended on the entire area with extremely high temperatures and little rain. The long, hot days of summer brought constant drought conditions; thus, the season would go into the record books as the driest ever recorded since 1870.

Lush, green lawns turned brown and crisp before their eyes. Garden produce required constant watering or it collapsed, limp and worthless, onto the dry, unproductive earth. The pond in Pinehurst Park seemed to diminish, inches at a time, before the very eyes of the reduced number of city residents who continued to picnic there despite the heat. Sporadic reports of fires igniting in the outlying bog areas filtered into the city and onto the Island. The pungent odor of smoke often seemed to hang in the air, especially if the winds came from the north or west. The locals did not think this to be odd, for a farmer was often seen burning a field or a logger igniting a pile of cut brush.

Old timers nodded their grizzled heads and spoke of days long past when they were young. Then, too, they recalled clearly the warm summer days when the sun burned the crops and the fields dried up. They could remember and were certain those were not "the good old days." But, they would add, with a confident look in their watery eyes, "The rain will come eventually, but only God knows when!" And they would draw thoughtfully on their pipes or hand-rolled cigarettes, nodding profoundly as they slowly blew the smoke dramatically from their nostrils. "Only God knows!"

Lumberjack Days finally took place on a blistering August day. The number of contestants registered for the competitions was down slightly because of the extreme heat, but the organizers were not discouraged. They let their view be made known that only "the cream of the crop" would be taking part in the events set for this year.

And then, of course, the men in charge had to determine the appropriateness of allowing a young woman—of all things—to compete in the birling competition. Most of those in charge firmly put their foot down and said "*No!*" A woman (or girl) had never mounted a log in the contest, and—by God!—no woman (or girl) would enter the competition while they had anything to say about it. That was the end of that!

Even most of the women of the community agreed with the stand taken by the organizers of Lumberjack Days. In their minds, girls had far better things to do to keep themselves busy. Girls needed to concentrate on things such as embroidery, playing the piano, dabbling in the arts, and learning how to cook and clean and keep a home. If girls could develop some of these talents, they would be more than prepared to marry well, to manage a household, and prepare for motherhood. And the women also chimed in and said, "It would be unseemly to have a female flaunting her ability before the eyes of the onlookers!" The competitions would go on without Maggie. She was heartbroken.

As soon as he heard the decision on Friday, Big Jack had a sudden inspiration. He talked it over with Hank and they came to a quick agreement. The two men then brought the proposal to Maggie. She listened carefully, finally raised her head to look the two men in their eyes, and allowed a slow smile to creep over her face. They would have to move fast if they were to get everything ready to execute their plan later on Sunday, after the competitions had all taken place. They had two days.

Three dozen invitations were quickly printed out, by hand. Then Henry and Oscar ran up and down the streets of the town and the Island—even entering the saloons—handing out the announcements to friends and neighbors deemed worthy to receive them. As each of the recipients unfolded the paper and looked at what was printed there, they smiled and read the announcement again, even as the boys were running off for their next delivery.

The flier said, in large letters:

SUNDAY, AFTER LUMBERJACK DAYS CONCLUDES,
COME TO BIG JACK'S BOARDING HOUSE
AT 6:00 P.M. TO WITNESS SOMETHING SPECIAL—
MAGGIE THE MARVEL WILL DAZZLE YOU
WITH HER FANCY FOOTWORK
AS SHE SPINS THE LOG BENEATH HER FEET!
COOKIES WILL BE SERVED FREE OF CHARGE
THANKS TO DAISY LARSON, OUR FAVORITE BAKER

Once the fliers were delivered, Big Jack and his partners had barely one day to put the plan in action. Daisy started baking dozens of cookies immediately and the boys pitched in to help Big Jack set up the logs on the shore of the river. Samuel came across the north bridge and offered his assistance in hauling the benches needed to set up a viewing area once the grass had been cut. A small dingy was anchored nearby and would serve as transportation for Maggie and Frank Shaw, who had agreed to be part of the demonstration, to and from the logs. Frank hoped he would arrive at Big Jack's on Sunday with the Birling Trophy once again in his possession.

Sunday dawned hot and dry. The park filled slowly, for it was very difficult to find a shady area out of the hot August sun. Umbrellas, fans, large-brimmed hats, and hankies moistened with fragrant toilet water assisted female observers as they attempted to stay cool. The men gave in to the oppressive heat, rolling up their sleeves and unbuttoning their collars.

By the close of the competition, several new champions had been crowned. Frank held on to the birling trophy, while Big Jack and Samuel once again took top honors in the two-man sawing contest.

Meanwhile, back at Big Jack's boarding house, Daisy, Maggie, and Bertha had set up the serving table on the porch . Two long tables, one on each side of the front door, were covered with red-and-white-checked tablecloths, trays of cookies, pitchers of lemonade, and pots of coffee. The women estimated perhaps thirty to forty of their friends and Maggie's friends from school would stop by to participate in this unusual event. No matter how many people came, they hoped the event would be a positive moment for Maggie after all her hard work.

By six o'clock ,the bank of the river was lined with friends from church, acquaintances from the saloons, fellow students from Garfield school, and people none of the hosts had ever met before. Over fifty people had rallied to support Maggie and her dream.

The benches were soon taken and the remaining spectators stood and waited patiently for the show to begin. Big Jack was the host and thanked all his friends who had rallied to his invitation. Everyone was aware of how diligently Maggie had worked and were pleased to be a part of this event.

Miss Thoreson had come early and commandeered a seat on the bench, right in the front row. With her cookie and her cup of coffee, she waited eaerly to see what was to take place. She was apprehensive for her student, but also proud and eager to witness just what Maggie was capable of doing on the log.

Hank caught the attention of the crowd. They cheered loudly as he stood before them, leaning heavily on his two canes. With a few well-chosen words he explained the physicality and dynamics of the art of birling. He had the whole crowd laughing as he told of some of the harrowing escapades he and his fellow river pigs had survived over their years taming the wildly churning logs.

Finally he introduced Maggie and Frank who stood and, amid cheering, walked to the shore and climbed into the dingy. Big Jack accompanied them to the waiting log. Frank was the first to mount the log and gave a breathtaking exhibition of his great dexterity. The crowd gave him a long ovation. He stepped back into the dingy and helped Maggie, clothed in her everyday overalls rolled up to her knees, as she mounted the log and quickly set it to spinning—first forward and then backward. Her long braid whipped out behind her and her arms seemed to keep her lifted from the surface of the water-splashed log. Everyone noticed the look on her face—not fear or apprehension, but enjoyment and pleasure at what she was doing. The crowd on shore cheered her on, proud of this young woman who had been so willing to try something new and different.

For a grand finale, Frank and Maggie mounted the log together and set it to spinning. Their timing seemed perfect, but the crowd could tell Frank was being gentle with Maggie. Both grinned and kept the log whirling while they seemed to dance on its surface. And then it happened—Maggie, hesitating a fraction of a second when she tried to restore the rhythm of her agile feet, slipped from the log and splashed backward into the river. Frank had tried to reach for her. Thus, his balance faltered as well and he, too, plunged into the waiting river. The crowd cheered enthusiastically as the two climbed, soaking wet, back into the dingy and headed for shore where their family and friends waited.

The birling demonstration itself lasted only a short time, but Frank and Maggie felt satisfied, though they were both soaked to the skin. And the crowd enjoyed the demonstration and Maggie's premiere. Each wrapped in a towel, the two birlers joined their friends as they emptied the trays of cookies. Only a few crumbs remained by the time the onlookers headed home. The August sun, soon to dip behind the western hills, kept the day extremely warm. Then, suddenly, a light breeze swept down from the hills, bathing the Island in the pungent odor of smoke.

The benches and tables were returned to the dining room by the husky boarders patiently awaiting their supper. Big Jack hastily retreated to the kitchen, where the final touches for supper needed to be made. The men who boarded with Big Jack had been okay with the delay thus far, but now they were hungry and ready to sit down and dig into a generous plate of Big Jack's famous roast beef, mashed potatoes, gravy, and all the trimmings. Big Jack knew better than to push the tolerance of such large, hungry young men.

Maggie, dried off and dressed once again in her working clothes, donned her apron and took her place beside her father as he dished up the plates she would deliver to the tables. Her moment in the sun seemed over. That was fine with her, knowing she had displayed to everyone she was capable of doing what she had set her mind to accomplish. The pride of the moment made her smile, and it was impossible to wipe that smile from her lovely young face. Big Jack, working furiously to get the food out before his diners mutinied, saw Maggie and couldn't suppress a grin as wide as hers.

For a moment their eyes met in acknowledgement of what had been accomplished. Then they heard the unrest in the dining room and quickly returned to slicing the roast and dishing up the vast quantities of mashed potatoes.

The long, dry summer finally drew to an end, and the first day of school loomed large on the horizon. Lincoln High School and all the instructors awaited as the local students prepared to walk through the wide doors of the new school. Recently constructed for grades seven through twelve, Lincoln was a totally modern school, designed and built to last far into the future. The teachers would be able to expand the minds of local children for decades to come. That was the hope, at least.

౩౦ಣ
The Fire

O hushed October morning mild,
Thy leaves have ripened to the fall;
Tomorrow's wind, if it be wild,
Should waste them all.

–"October" by Robert Frost

AUTUMN COLORS ALONG the St. Louis River in 1918 were as bright and vibrant as ever. Local people were pleasantly surprised, pleased the months of heat and drought had not dimmed the final intensity of color before the leaves cascaded to the ground. Daisy took time every morning to stand at the kitchen window, look across the river to the north, and drink in the depth and variety of color covering the hills. She likened the pattern she saw to the colors of a fine quilt, pieced together by a master quilter.

Slender birch trees covered with golden leaves stood out from the deep green of the pines. The birches' burnished leaves slowly fluttered to the ground and from there, blown by the wind, danced into the river, where they floated like golden coins on their way to Lake Superior. The designer of this magnificent quilt incorporated the yellow of ash leaves set next to the vibrant reds and oranges of the maples. Giant cottonwoods maintained their multicolored leaves for as long as possible before setting them free to clatter across the yards and streets of the town. And behind the vibrant colors of the many-colored quilt were the browns and russets and ochers, all set against the brilliant clear azure sky. As always, the rich green of the pine remained after the marvelous quilt of many colors blew away.

A rich fragrance of burning leaves wafted over the city and across the Island. The few flowers remaining were picked, their bulbs secured for planting once the winter snow disappeared. Garden produce was gathered in before the first killing frost, filling root cellars with potatoes, onions, squash, carrots, pumpkins, apples, canned goods, jellies, jams, sauces, preserved meats and gravies to last—hopefully—through the coming winter.

Then, when the final Mason jar had been placed on a shelf and the last bushel of potatoes had rumbled into the bin, the industrious women would take a moment to linger in the darkened cellar, hands on their ample hips. Gazing upon the shelves lined with the jewel-like jars full of delicious foods to be enjoyed in the days to come, all created out of their many hours of labor, they felt a great deal of pride. "Let the winter come," they said as they climbed the steps and returned to the kitchen. "My family will be well fed!"

School was well underway. Daisy prepared breakfast for Henry and made sure he was out the door in time to meet Maggie on the corner. Lunch box in one hand and school books in the other, they headed across the red bridge, picked up Oscar on Cloquet Avenue, and climbed the hill to the beautiful new school. By October, all three had learned to find their classes, were acclimated to their new schedules, kept up with the assignments that seemed more difficult than they were used to, and had made some new friends.

After school the three hurried back to the Island, where they quickly loaded the wagon and once again crossed the red bridge to begin the deliveries of Daisy's famous baked goods. Her fame had spread. Some afternoons they made more than one trip. As was their custom, the three young people finished their day at Oscar's house. Waiting for them, Anna Belle Lund had steaming hot cocoa ready, a warm smile lighting her lovely face.

Before the eyes of all who loved and cared for her, Mrs. Brush seemed to disappear. Her energy and vitality evaporated, little by little, and she became confined to her bed or the couch in the parlor. Daisy, after preparing her bread dough and setting the bowls in the sun where the dough would rise, made it a point to arrive at Mrs. Brush's front door each morning before 10:00 a.m. She marched up the steps to her bedroom, raised the shades and opened the curtains to let in the morning sun.

Lately the autumn air had developed a rancid, pungent odor from the many brush fires burning on the edges of the nearby bogs and open fields. Still, Mrs. Brush loved the autumn breeze that caressed her cheeks as she lay on her goose-down pillow, waiting for Daisy to prepare her for the day.

Getting dressed had changed. A fresh gown and bed jacket were all Mrs. Brush needed. Knowing her hours on earth were numbered, she was only too glad to discuss her upcoming ascension into the heavenly realms. Often, as Daisy braided her hair, Mrs. Brush spoke in great detail about what awaited her once she passed from this life and into the next.

"In my mind I can see myself smack in the middle of a bright light, kneeling right at the feet of the Savior I have loved for so long." Closing her eyes, she would tip back her head, smiling while explaining to Daisy what would happen next. "I'll feel the strong hands of Jesus upon my shoulders as he lifts me to my feet and looks deep into my eyes." She claimed she could even hear his voice asking her one vital question: "Do you love me?"

And she knew already what her emphatic answer would be. "Yes, Lord! You know I love you! There's no doubt about that answer!" And then, she said, "I'll be escorted through those lovely pearly gates." Mrs. Brush had no doubts about the coming event. "I'm so ready," she confessed to Daisy. Having walked through the scene many times in her mind, she was eager to have it take place. Daisy combed the silver hair, blinking back tears as Mrs. Brush foretold of her earthly departure and her heavenly arrival.

By this time Daisy had prepared her for the day, and Mrs. Brush lay back once again on her hand-embroidered pillow. Her fragile hands rested quietly on the blanket covering her. Only on special days—a Sunday, perhaps—would she be carried gently down the stairs by Pastor Jenson. He would stop by after the service and, if she desired, he would gently place her on the couch in the parlor where she'd recline for a short time. Her callers were few—her remaining friends were as frail as she or had already left this world behind.

Her favorite guests were Samuel and Beatrice Berg. Their youth and affection for each other always brought joy and a sense of peace to her. Often Beatrice would sit close to Mrs. Brush as the fragile woman reclined on the couch, take her hand, and place it on her swollen belly. Feeling the movements of the baby always brought tears to Mrs. Brush's eyes.

Pastor Jenson often stopped by for a midmorning cup of coffee and a brief visit with Daisy and Mrs. Brush—his "two favorite women," as he often told them. The church thrived with young families joining the Sunday worship and a number of Island people coming regularly. Of course, some members were vocal in their criticism of the antics of the young pastor and his outreach to the inhabitants of the Island. Michael took it all in stride, greeting each person through the church's door on Sunday with a hearty handshake.

Samson waited each day in the pasture for his sugar lump benefactor to stop by on his way home from school or from the bakery deliveries. Henry was proud of the fact he had almost perfected the skill of producing a loud, sharp whistle, and Samson appeared to recognize his attempts. Day after day Henry would pucker his lips, let loose with the whistle, and smile while Samson came trotting over to the fence, ready for his treat. Maggie often left Henry atop the fence with his hands embedded in Samson's thick, dark mane as she hurried home to assist Big Jack with the supper preparations.

Henry had less time to spend at the stables since school had resumed and his homework increased. Still, whenever possible, he came back to the stable and spent time grooming his favorite horse. He passed the time by brushing, combing, cleaning the stall, filling it with clean hay, and concluding with moments astride the broad back of the gentle horse, his head and hands deep in the thickness of the almost black mane. Mr. Keller smiled and looked the other way. As Henry walked home, school books heavy in his bag, he always felt fulfilled, his heart lighter. And once he entered the door of his warm and fragrant home, where love and affection awaited him, he smiled at his loving parents.

Henry was proud of his father. Hank, with the help and encouragement of Big Jack, had continued in his recovery. Still moving slowly, Hank was able to walk with the use of only one cane or walking stick. Each day, as Daisy headed across the bridge to care for Mrs. Brush, Hank laced up his boots, put on his flannel shirt, picked up his diamond willow walking stick, and visited Big Jack at the boarding house before walking the short distance down Main Street to St. Louis Avenue.

Big Jack, usually peeling, paring, butchering, kneading, slicing, or stirring something that would be served later that evening, would point to the pot of coffee simmering on the back burner of the giant cook stove and Hank would pour himself a mug of the darkest, strongest coffee available. Even adding a shot of cream didn't dilute the biting flavor of the coffee. Hank holding his steaming cup in both hands, he and Big Jack tossed comments back and forth as they laughed together while Big Jack sent peelings flying in all directions.

Once the mug was almost empty with only an abundance of grounds in the bottom, Hank rinsed it out, set it in its place on the cupboard and headed for the door. Most of the time Hank left Big Jack up to his elbows in bread dough or apples for pies needed to satisfy the hungry mill workers.

Selecting a different saloon each day, Hank carefully walked the dusty street until he reached the boardwalk. Then, slowly mounting the steps, he entered the front door of the establishment and ordered a mug of beer. Standing there at the bar with some of his friends from his time working at the camps and in the mill, Hank felt more like his former self. He had always been strong, independent, and ready to tackle any difficulty that came his way. Now, after his accident, he realized just how fragile life could be and just how precious each day of his life had become.

Occasionally, with perfect timing as he left his "saloon of the day," he would look toward the red bridge and see Daisy returning from her visit with Mrs. Brush. He'd watch her as she walked briskly toward him. Most of the time she was deep in thought, unaware that he watched her. He loved when she looked up and saw him there, waiting for her. She would smile warmly, grasp his arm and hold it close as they slowly headed up Main Street to their modest home on the north edge of the Island. Life was good, as long as they faced each day together.

Reports of fires in the outlying areas continued to spread through town and over the Island, but this was not unusual for this time of year. The bogs were occasionally torched by the landowners, loggers piled up scraps of wood that they set afire and often left unattended, campers packed up their tents and left smoldering embers behind as they vacated campsites, and sparks constantly belched from the smokestacks of trains traveling north and south along the tracks running from Duluth, through Cloquet, and on into the northern areas of the state.

The multitude of these tiny sparks gave birth to small fires, now fed by the tinder-dry leaves and brush at the side of the tracks. The wind gradually increased, becoming more and more insistent on igniting what would become a colossal disaster.

BEFORE SUNRISE ON SATURDAY, October 12, Big Jack swung his long legs out from under the quilt, rose to a sitting position, and planted his feet firmly on the braided rug running along the side of his bed. Getting up early, before most normal people opened their eyes, had long been his custom. The more chores he could accomplish before the sun came up, the better the remainder of the day seemed to go. He ran his fingers through his thick, dark hair and reached for the clothes he had set out the evening before. Big Jack had never been conscious of his appearance; he worked hard and was usually covered with a dusting of flour accented by a potato peeling here and there, as well as large fingerprints on his canvas apron made when wiping his dough-covered hands after filling pans with bread dough or sheets with cookies. Neatness had never been one of his sterling characteristics.

Standing over the kitchen sink under the northern window, he took a moment to look out into the semi-darkness. He took note of the flush of crimson in the sky, barely showing over the trees across the river. The past day or two had been unusual—unseasonably hot and humid with a heaviness riding on the wind.

Uneasy feelings about the reports filtering down from the north lingered in his mind. An unusual number of small fires burned across the fields, bogs, and wooded areas. No government people walked the tracks on the lookout for sparks as they did before the Great War. Yet, so far, no one in a leadership position had stated any concerns about the smoke that continued to flow downriver, causing people's eyes to burn and weep. Oh, well! What did he know? He was just the owner of a boarding house and a father to his lovely daughter.

And now, allowing his mind to think about it for just a moment, he realized how deeply he cared for Bertha Ness. He felt she also cared for him. She'd be coming to the Island later that afternoon, having promised to assist him in his last-minute preparation of pies he always prepared for his famous Sunday dinners.

A week ago, she had worked at his side canning meatballs and gravy, as well as fried chicken and gravy, and roast venison and gravy, in large Mason jars. Eighty quart jars were now lined up on the shelves of his root cellar—many thanks to his able "assistant."

In the damp darkness of the root cellar, after many trips carrying the canned goods down into the cool earth, Jack had been bold enough to take Bertha into his arms and kiss her. Bertha leaned into him, her arms about his broad chest while she quietly whispered his name. "Oh, Jack! I've dreamed about kissing you for such a long time." He heard her laugh gently. "I would have kissed you first, but I thought I would have to stand on a chair to reach your lips." She tipped back her head, smiled into his eyes, and he kissed her again—this time longer, with more intensity.

They stood together, both of them lost in the meaning of the moment, then parted reluctantly and climbed the ladder back into the sunlight. Taking his hand in hers, she smiled up at him as they once again entered the fragrant kitchen. At that moment, he truly was aware she loved him in return.

Back in the moment, feeling the stubble on his chin as he scratched his cheek, he knew he had to hurry to prepare breakfast, then the lunches and the roast venison he had planned for supper. Maggie would be up soon, and she was becoming very efficient dealing with the breakfast menu. Pancakes were now her speciality, and she could pour the batter, watch over the bubbling cakes as they baked on the large griddle, turn them efficiently, and pile up mountains of cakes on the platters destined for the tables and the hungry mill workers.

Now that she was almost thirteen, and mature for her age, Big Jack was becoming sensitive to any young worker who paid Maggie the least bit of attention. The men knew better than to cause a problem with the man who housed and fed them.

AS THEY BEGAN THEIR DAY, the weathermen in Duluth reported low barometric pressure. Winds were light thus far, and fair weather was predicted for the remainder of the day. By 10:30 a.m. a small craft warning was issued for the shore of Lake Superior. The wind was gusting occasionally up to thirty miles per hour.

TWO BOWLS OF BREAD DOUGH were covered and struggling to rise on the counter of Daisy's kitchen. However, no warm sunlight coming through the kitchen window could pierce the smoky air outside and warm the dough to make it rise smooth and shiny as a fat lady's belly. After punching it down and covering it once again, Daisy threw a shawl over her shoulders and set out for Mrs. Brush's bedside. Stepping out the door, Daisy could feel the unnatural heat of the day and the ever-increasing wind that buffeted her.

When passing the stables, she waved to Henry, who was brushing Samson's brown coat. He waved in return, causing Samson to lift his head and shake his shaggy mane. Daisy knew Henry would be home in time to load and deliver her baked goods. "What a fine boy!" she would often say to herself.

A short time later, Mrs. Brush lay comfortably tucked into her bed, her favorite quilt drawn up to her chest. Her hair was brushed, her face and hands washed and dried. A light perfume had been applied behind her ears and at her throat. Finally, Daisy helped her put on a linen bed jacket to cover her shoulders and upper arms. The windows had been closed, much to Mrs. Brush's dismay, for she loved the breeze caressing her cheeks. As the morning passed, the wind increased, and the pungent odor of smoke filled the room, even with the windows closed.

When she was ready to leave for home, Daisy heard Mrs. Brush once more call her name. Mrs. Brush said in a halting voice, "I worry about the wind, the smoke, and the heat of the day." She took a moment, as if to gather her strength, and continued. "In all my years upon this earth, I find this weather most unusual." Attempting to catch her breath, she whispered, "Be careful, my dear Daisy. This will not be a pleasant day."

Daisy went to the bed and bent to place a kiss upon the wrinkled cheek she loved so deeply. "Everyone says its just an unusual autumn day—wind and smoke and the last of the heat from the summer," Daisy said, reassuringly, as she smoothed back a rebellious strand of curly white hair and kissed the cool, creased forehead. "I'll come back with some fresh bread and check on you before the sun goes down. Until then, just rest and eat the lunch Old Syd will bring you in just a little while."

With a wave of her hand, she was down the stairs and out the front door. The wind tugged at her shawl, and the smoke-laden air caught in her throat and stung her eyes. By the time she reached the Island, Henry was already home helping Hank repair a clothesline that had snapped under the onslaught of the wind. The freshly laundered sheets, hung earlier that morning, had caught the wind and swelled like sails on a clipper ship. Pulling on the lines, the wind wrestled the sheets and the clothes lines from the poles, flinging them across the backyard. Still damp, the sheets lay crumpled and soiled and full of soot.

AROUND NOON, BILLOWING CLOUDS of smoke moved in from the west and hovered over Cloquet. As yet no one had considered the unusual events to be an emergency. No one felt inclined to flee the city. Some of the old timers claimed that, with all the burning of nearby fields and leftover scrub brush, there was bound to be smoke. Yet deep inside they, too, felt a small sense of dread. Smoke-filled air would be normal, they commented, and was acceptable at this time of year. Even so, this was more than could be expected

Still, when the smoke turned the noon sun blood-red, the old men nervously tried to remember a scene such as this in their past years. Try as they would to recall a memory of any similar occurrence, none rose to the surface. They shook their heads and chewed chaws of tobacco, the juice cascading down their bearded chins.

DAISY WAS APPREHENSIVE as she loaded the wagon with the last of her deliveries for the day. Sending the three youngsters out into these frightful conditions didn't seem like the wisest choice, but she gave in to their assurances they'd hurry back before she could shake a stick at them. With conditions so weird, the delivery seemed a grand adventure, one they could tell tales about in the years to come. "You hurry as fast as you can and get back here before the weather gets any worse!" Daisy ordered, trying to look commanding.

The three friends headed down Main Avenue at a brisk pace. Constantly keeping watch on the clean towels covering their valuable cargo, they battled the wind as they headed across the bridge.

Once in town, they were able to quickly deliver the baked goods from one home to the next. Oscar and Henry did the running from house to house while Maggie guarded the wagon and bread from the wind and falling ashes. Every door that opened revealed the worried face of an adult, one who did not know what conditions the rest of the afternoon had in store for them and their family.

Even Old Syd told them to hurry home as fast as they could when they dropped off a loaf of rye bread for him and Mrs. Brush. Syd took Henry by the shoulder and whispered in his ear, "Tell your mom that Mrs. Brush doesn't look too good this afternoon." He shook his head sadly and retreated into the house, away from the smoke and wind. With the empty wagon bouncing behind them, the children ran down the street as fast as they could, through the smoke and wind, to Oscar's house. Oscar was concerned about his mother and how she was coping with such a terrible day.

WIND VELOCITY INCREASED as the hours passed. Shortly after 3:00 p.m., the force of the wind rose to over forty miles per hour—then up to fifty miles per hour at rare moments. Smoke continued to choke the town and the Island. Residents now knew this wasn't normal in any sense. Finally the people came to the realization they were in danger. But they weren't sure how difficult it would be to leave or the path they should select to escape to safety, should that become their only option.

If the unpredictable weather, smoke, and untimely heat were not enough to deal with, Pastor Jenson had received a frantic phone call earlier that morning as he sat behind his desk in his ever-darkening office, putting the finishing touches on his sermon for the next day. The call was from Samuel Berg. Michael was shocked to hear the stress in Samuel's voice. "Beatrice started having labor pains before the sun came up!" Big, strong Samuel sounded as though he was on the edge of hysteria. "I bundled her up in her favorite quilt and took her by carriage to my mother's house. Now I'm not sure what I'm supposed to do!"

Michael could hear his desperation. Even with Mrs. Berg in charge and Beatrice giving the delivery her heart and soul, Samuel was the one collapsing from the strain.

Samuel could chop down a mighty pine tree, could handle an ax and the giant saws, could wrestle the strongest man into submission, but he was not prepared to deal with seeing his wife in pain and the birth of his first child.

"I need you over here, Pastor. I'm only a man, and my own mother won't let me in the bedroom. Beatrice wants me to wait in the hall!" Samuel tried valiantly to suppress his panic and attempted to be confident his mother could manage the birth with great efficiency, just as she constantly tried to manage everyone else's affairs. Still, Samuel was sure the day would proceed far better if he had his pastor—and his friend—at his side.

Michael said, "I'll be there, Samuel. Take a deep breath and pray. I'm coming!"

Mrs. Berg was only too happy to provide Beatrice with a bed, a shoulder to cry on, a hand to grasp when the pains came, and waiting arms for the blessed child that would be her first grandchild. Having assisted with other births in years past, Mrs. Berg scrubbed her hands and put on a clean apron. A basin of water was placed on the stove to boil and clean towels were set out on the dresser near the bed. Always thinking ahead, the soon-to-be grandmother placed a sharp scissors on the dresser along with a ball of twine.

With Beatrice in Samuel's boyhood bed and Mrs. Berg in control, both women seemed to relax, sure nature would soon take its course. Samuel hovered in the hall, near collapse.

As soon as he received the call, Michael closed his books, slipped his Greek New Testament into his pocket, and grabbed his hat. The intense heat and violent wind hit him as he stepped out the front door of the church, taking him by surprise. Within an instant his best hat had flown away, never to be seen again.

With the wind at his back Michael flew up the block and across the street, where Samuel met him at the door and ushered him upstairs, where the women had finally let him into the room. Beatrice lay there, sweat beading across her forehead. Reaching for Samuel's hand, she clutched it in anguish as pain wracked her body. Trying not to cry out, Beatrice turned her head to the wall. "I can feel the baby coming!" she whispered, tears filling her eyes. Mrs. Berg hustled over to the side of the bed, then ordered the two men from the room once more.

Michael was at a loss, having never seen a human birth. Farm boy that he was, he had more than once reached into the throbbing womb of a cow and pulled the almost lifeless calf, by a hoof or an ear, into the world. However, all he could do now was place his arm about the wide shoulders of his friend and escort him from the bedroom.

As they were about to exit the room and close the door behind them, Beatrice turned her head, looked at them, and reached out to her husband and her pastor. "Pray for me— please—and for my baby," she whispered between the pains. "I do so love this baby!" And once again her lovely face contorted with the pain pulsing through her young body. Mrs. Berg ushered them from the room, firmly closing the door behind them.

Samuel immediately fell to his knees, loudly beseeching God, who, he had to admit, he did not know very well, to watch over his beloved and his child. Michael kneeled at his side and prayed aloud, his voice echoing down the narrow hallway. "Let there be life—for the mother and the child!" Michael prayed. Samuel began to weep. "And bless the loving hands of Mrs. Berg, who labors mightily to bring this beloved child safely into the world."

He turned to Samuel, who had covered his anguished face with his work-worn hands. "Let the Lord know what you desire!" Michael said firmly. "Speak what is in your heart!"

Samuel leaned over so far his head nearly touched the floor. The words he spoke to the Lord he knew were muffled by his tears. Yet Michael knew exactly what he was praying. "I put them both in your hands, God. I give them to you. Please." There was a long pause when all the men could hear was the force of the winds outside and the scraping of the branches against the side of the house. "Please!"

Michael knew that God was totally aware of Samuel's unspoken plea.

The two men remained on their knees for some time, hearing Beatrice's cries from the room behind the closed door. Michael finally rose, but Samuel chose to remain where he was. Occasionally they could hear muffled sounds, some more intense than others. Then there was a pause, a silence that hung in the air. Finally, the cry of the newborn child slipped under the door and into the hearts of the men waiting in the narrow hall.

Immediately Samuel rose, a little unsteady from his long vigil on his knees. He knocked at the door. When it opened, there stood his mother, a bit disheveled but smiling broadly. With a wide smile she motioned for the two men to enter.

Slowly Samuel walked toward the bed where his wife lay, wan but radiant. Beatrice, propped up on her pillow, looked triumphant as she tenderly cradled the small, snugly wrapped bundle in her arms, their daughter. Her name would be Pearl.

After offering words of thanks and bestowing a blessing, Pastor Jenson stepped out the front door and was nearly blown back into the front hallway by the force of the wind coming across the city from the northwest. The smoke and wind roared through the streets and down the alleys, limiting Michael's visibility and hiding the sun somewhere high above the bell tower of the church. "Good grief!" Michael exclaimed to himself. "The situation just gets worse as the day goes on."

He made a mental note to get in touch with the chief of police or the mayor and find out what the danger level of the situation was and what, if any, plans had been made to accommodate the residents of the city. With the wind literally tossing him through the front door of the church, he headed for his desk where, as usual, there was a scattering of books and a pile of sermon notes. He took note of the work that lay before him, but his mind quickly moved to thoughts of Samuel and Beatrice and their precious infant—and Mrs. Berg as well. This was quite the day for tiny Pearl to make her entrance into the world.

THE DANGER APPROACHING was not yet clear to the residents of Cloquet and the Island. Unknown to anyone, approximately seventy-five isolated fires were uniting farther north to form one huge conflagration, one that would be fanned into mammoth proportions by the ever-increasing surge of winds, most of them created by the flames and fires themselves. The residents were conscious of the wind whipping through the streets of the town, but no one realized the searing heat was not the end of a particularly warm and dry summer, but a foretaste of a wall of flame on its way. Flashing across the wall of smoke now covering the sky, the undulating fire was descending on them from the north and west.

Everyone became galvanized into action by the unexpected arrival of a train from Brookston, a small community a few miles north of Cloquet. An engine and several freight cars pierced the wall of smoke and fire from twenty miles north, roared south along the flaming tracks, and came to a screeching halt at the depot in Cloquet.

Brookston, by this time, had already been destroyed by the fire, wiped from the face of the earth. The train consisted of several freight cars filled to overflowing with weeping, dazed, blistered human beings who had fled their homes.

Every scorched traveler shared tales of horror. Wild-eyed, they told of loading the freight cars with the entire population of the town, watching houses and shops burst into flame around them as the engine chugged out of town, away from the holocaust.

Then, after traveling less than half a mile down the track, someone suddenly discovered the final two freight cars had not been properly connected to the train. Thus, some of their friends and families remained behind, trapped in the middle of the burning town, facing certain death, while the train they assumed they were connected to disappeared down the track into the wall of smoke.

As soon as the conductor realized what had happened, he threw the engine into reverse. Backing through the inferno raging through the wooded area surrounding their comfortable little town, no one was sure if their friends and neighbors would still be alive.

With flames raging on both sides of the track, the two abandoned cars still waited. Frantic passengers watched in horror as the cars were quickly engulfed in the blaze. Once the cars were attached the engineer braced himself, put the train in motion, blindly moving through the ever-expanding wall of fire. With God's help he would deliver his passengers to the depot in Cloquet.

The passengers were covered with soot and burns from the blowing ashes and tree branches falling from the flaming trees lining the track. The train crawled at a snail's pace, the engineer directing the train blindly toward safety. Even the paint covering the outside of the freight cars blistered and peeled from the heat on their desperate journey through what many from the crowd of passengers described "as hell itself!"

Realizing the people would not be safe, even in Cloquet, the train carrying the Brookston survivors once again started up and cleared the southern edge of Cloquet on its way to Carlton. Finally the mayor and city leaders of Cloquet began to create their own plan to enable their community to survive what was coming.

The telephone operators began to call all homes equipped with telephones and relayed the message that they should hurry to the depot, where trains would be waiting to carry everyone away from the coming inferno.

For those households without a telephone, Boy Scouts were enlisted to run through the streets of the town, knocking on doors, informing families of the trains.

Meanwhile—and most importantly—Lawrence Fauley, the depot agent, the station master, and the train engineers hurried to put in place all available engines, passenger cars, freight cars, flat cars, boxcars, coal cars and any other car that could be loaded and carry people away from the flames.

By this time, an urgent escape was the priority in everyone's mind as the community set out for the depot. Some people took time to bury their valuables in their backyards or gardens, hoping to find them once again. Others stuffed their pockets, purses, baskets, and wagons with various and sundry items—some valuable, some not—hoping they could smuggle them onto the train. That was not to be possible.

As Lawrence Fauley rushed to put together a string of cars that would take Cloquet's citizens to safety, the winds began gusting at fifty to sixty miles an hour, sweeping the flames down upon the town.

On the western edge of the city, a ravine known as "No. 5 Alley" was where the Northern Lumber Company stored their number five boards. Stacked twenty feet high in long rows, surrounded with deep deposits of sawdust to keep the lumber clean, the boards soon ignited as the fire roared down from the north, causing flames to issue forth in all directions. One by one the fresh, clean boards, each now burning like a struck match, were lifted by the ever-increasing winds and flung far and wide across the city. New fires flared up in all corners of the town.

The fire department soon realized they were helpless in the face of this kind of conflagration. The men left their equipment and fled to their homes to help their own families escape.

All the mills shut down and quickly deployed their workers to help battle the flames wherever needed. The mills' shrill whistles constantly sounded their warning cry, imploring the residents to hurry to the depot. By this time the new school was burning, as were all manner of houses. The business district was demolished, and numerous churches ignited, steeples flaming to the heavens. It appeared that nothing could stem the flow of the flames as the mighty wind, now occasionally bearing down on the area at over seventy miles an hour, drove the flames toward Duluth.

The roar of the wind, and the fires that fed it, was deafening. By now the wall of flame stretched across a front of at least eight miles. There seemed to be nothing humanly possible to do to arrest the fire in its path of destruction.

No one had to be told twice that the expedient thing to do was to flee for their very lives. A torrent of frightened humanity began their frantic race to the depot.

With push carts, wagons, wheelbarrows, and buggies filled with their worldly possessions—family photos, heirloom quilts, hand crocheted doilies, priceless jewelry worn only at weddings or grand balls or funerals, table linens handed down from generation to generation, along with silverware and china that had only been used on very special occasions, books and family records, wedding gowns and fur wraps, antique clocks and valuable stamp collections—the fearful citizens assembled at the depot. Here the station master and the sheriff, both armed, told them there would only be human cargo on the train. All the "precious" belongings had to be left on the station platform. Everything became disposable when life alone was the most valued possession. Women and children crowded into the cars, packed together, even seated on one another, with barely room to breathe.

Slowly the train began to move, and those with access to a window looked back at the inferno trailing after them as the train slowly picked up speed as it left town. Passengers cried and wailed as the cars journeyed through the flames, which reached out to lick the sides of the cars while they proceeded on their way to Carlton or Duluth—and hopefully to safety.

TWO MORE TRAINS were at the ready, with only boxcars and flat bed cars attached to the engine. Again women and children crowded into them. Their faces and clothing were covered with soot, and trails of tears coursed down their blackened cheeks. No one paid much attention to the three youngsters struggling to make their way pulling a loaded wagon through the swirling smoke and ash. Slowly, painstakingly, they made their way to the front of the line where the crowds of frantic people were crawling into the boxcar.

A SHORT TIME EARLIER, in the furor of the afternoon, with sirens shrieking and the Boy Scouts racing through the neighborhoods telling everyone to head to the depot, the three hot and dusty friends made their way through smoke and wind to Oscar's house. Concerned about Anna Belle, they hurried into the front hall and immediately collided with Oscar's father. Shoving them aside, he charged toward the front door, a large satchel in each hand. Eyes wide with fear, his mind set on saving only himself, Mr. Lund stepped over Maggie, who was sprawled on the hall floor, and forced his way past the children.

"Out of my way!" he shouted over the wind. "I don't have time to worry about any of you! I need to get to the bank!"

Oscar took a step toward his father, only to be struck in the chest with one of the large satchels, knocking him into the front door. In a second Mr. Lund was outside, down the porch steps, and lost from sight in the smoke and ash.

A moment later the children heard the roar of the motor of the shiny black Ford and, in a flash, the car careened out of the garage and down the driveway. Mr. Lund, his face shrouded by a scarf and goggles, sat alone in the driver's seat, pausing only a moment as he looked dismissively at the three young people watching him in shocked amazement from the front door of his house. Shifting down, he threw the car into low and sped off down the street, the tires spewing gravel as the car swerved down the avenue.

His father gone, Oscar quickly led his friends to the sitting room, where they were shocked to find his mother laying on the floor, blood from a wound staining the expensive woven rug beneath her. Kneeling beside her, Maggie gently turned Anna Belle onto her back, wiping away the blood from a cut on her lip .

Oscar's mother spoke so quietly the three friends could barely make out her words. "I begged him to take Oscar with him when he left town," Oscar held her hand as she spoke. She continued, "He laughed and said if I wanted to save my son I would have to do it myself." Oscar blinked back his tears. "I told him I'd never want to go anywhere with him—even on such a terrible day. But his son," she stammered, "I thought he might want to save his only son."

She turned away, the tears filling her eyes. "That's when he struck me—and told me Oscar and I weren't worth saving." Her trembling hands reached up to cover her face.

Oscar wiped his runny nose with the back of his hand. Realizing at that moment that he—and his two friends—were now totally responsible for the safety of his mother, Oscar focused on the problem at hand and rose to the occasion. Oscar and his young friends helped Anna Belle to a sitting position, smoothed back her hair, and gently cleaned the blood from her face. A slight aroma of alcohol hung about her, masking the pungent odor of smoke.

Maggie wrapped a woolen shawl about Anna Belle's shoulders. Then, with Oscar on one side and Henry on the other, they assisted her to her feet and headed for the front door. They made their way down the steps of the porch. Maggie grabbed a small, woven tapestry rug in the hallway and, after removing the few baked goods remaining in the wagon from the unclaimed orders, placed it in the bottom of the wagon.

Anna Belle was limp with anguish and despair for her son—and his friends. Oscar encircled his mother with both arms and held her upright, while Henry took her arm and placed it over his shoulders for support. Once they left the front hall and navigated down the front steps, Anna Belle gamely tried to decline their insistence that she sit in the wagon. Under their direction she was finally settled in the wagon where Maggie carefully tucked her dress about her legs, bent at the knees to accommodate the small wagon bed.

Maggie wrapped the weeping woman in the heavy-knit shawl to shield her from the flying debris whirling about them. Oscar dutifully shut and locked the expensive oak front door to the home where he had spent so many stressful years. With one final act of defiance, he tossed the house key into burning shrubbery. *Good riddance*, he thought.

With Henry pulling on the handle of the wagon and Maggie pushing at the rear, the sad little procession made its way through the tongues of flame assaulting them on all sides, through the howling winds blasting in their young, worried faces. Finally, they became part of the throng of people heading to the depot. Oscar walked beside the wagon holding his mother's hand, assuring her that all of them would be fine.

As they neared the depot the crowd swelled to hundreds, and everyone slowed almost to a halt as loading the train cars began. They slowly made their way to a boxcar, where they helped Oscar and his mother board the car. The three determined young people were assisted by other equally desperate people, all trying to find a place to sit in the already overcrowded car.

A strong young man lifted Anna Belle, tapestry and all, positioning her in the front corner of the boxcar where the wall would support her back. Oscar crawled into the corner, sat down next to his weeping mother, and put his arm protectively around her, cradling her battered face close to his chest.

With a quick farewell, Henry and Maggie hurriedly left the boxcar and reclaimed the wagon before making their way again through the crush of the crowd to the Island, where they knew their families anxiously awaited them.

Feeling as though his heart were breaking, Oscar took a moment to glance about the car where women and children were scrambling for a place to sit, a place to stand, any spot to get them to safety. When the boxcar was almost full to capacity, his eyes were drawn to a woman seated on his left, a few people down from where he and his mother cowered in the corner. The woman's eyes widened as they gazed back at Oscar and his mother. And then the woman smiled, creasing her soot-covered face. Oscar suddenly was filled with a glimmer of hope. He knew those eyes, that smile—under all the messed-up hair and the ash-stained clothing sat his favorite teacher, Miss Vivian Thoreson.

In a split second Miss Thoreson heaved herself up from the floor of the boxcar and slowly made her way through the legs and bodies and crying children to Oscar's side.

With a bit of maneuvering she lowered herself to the floor of the car, near the wall close to Anna Belle. As though Anna Belle was just a child, Miss Thoreson gently labored to position the slender woman on her ample lap. Rearranging the scorched tapestry and shawl so they better covered Anna Belle's face and arms, she then encircled the weeping woman with her left arm and pressed her face into her neck and shoulder.

With her other arm, Miss Thoreson gathered Oscar close to her ample breast and caressed ever so gently the weeping boy's heaving back. "Never you mind, Oscar. I'll watch over your mother—and you." She hugged him extra tight before she continued. "We'll take the trip to Duluth together—you and me and your mother!" Oscar, with his slender arms, reached around his beloved teacher, embracing her in return. Miss Thoreson spoke in his ear, in her teacher's voice, "God willing, we will all be safe!"

In the meantime, Henry and Maggie fought their way through the crowd and glanced over toward one of the last cars of the train. Even from a distance they could make out the forms of Pastor Jenson and Samuel as the two men pushed their way through the mass of people and the billowing smoke. Into this scene of mayhem, Pastor Jenson elbowed his way through the crowd on the platform, clearing a path for Samuel Berg, who carried Beatrice in his arms. Not too long ago, a soot-covered Boy Scout had frantically knocked at the front door of Mrs. Berg's house, introducing them to the crisis that awaited the citizens of Cloquet as the fires raged through the city. What a day for their child to be born!

Samuel was consumed with fear for his wife and newborn daughter. Weakened as she was, Beatrice insisted theyfollow the directions of the city leaders and make their way to the depot. They knew their only chance for survival was to find a place on one of the trains and exit the rapidly deteriorating town.

Taking nothing with them but their love for each other and their infant daughter, they began their exodus. Samuel wrapped Beatrice in a heavy quilt his mother had made for him when he was a young boy, lifted her in his strong arms, and headed for the carriage awaiting them at the curb.

Mrs. Berg, with the fervor of a new grandmother, gently wrapped the tiny baby and, pale and trembling as she was, followed close behind Samuel, clutching the tiny being. Only once, much like Lot's wife, did she turn around, just in time to see the roof of her home erupt in flames. In disbelief, she followed her son into the carriage.

On their way they picked up Pastor Jenson, who had just fled the church he had come to love so dearly. His heart was broken, for, as he entered the sanctuary for the final time, the large altar painting of Jesus Christ started to burn. The fire surged out of his office, down the hall, and into the sanctuary. The final image Michael had of his beloved church were the flames devouring the altar, the kneeling benches where untold prayers had been lifted heavenward, and the wooden walls of the sacristy.

Once the flames reached the painting, the heat scorched Michael's face as he paused in disbelief, watching the gentle face of Jesus dissolve into nothingness. With a burst of energy he charged for the heavy wooden doors, also now in flames. Leaping down the front steps of the church, he was relieved to see the Bergs on their way to the depot and jumped aboard their carriage. Samuel whipped the horse, forcing it through the smoke and flames now coming at them from all directions, on the whirling tornado of the winds.

Leaving the carriage on the fringe of the masses of people waiting to board the train, Michael wrapped his arms around Mrs. Berg, careful of baby Pearl, and plowed into the thick of the crowd. For once Michael was not gentle, and, inch by inch, they all made their way to the entrance of the boxcar. Mrs. Berg looked as though she would collapse from fright, but she held the baby next to her soft breast and allowed Michael to direct her steps. Samuel, strong and broad, with Beatrice cradled in his arms, forced his way through whatever or whoever lay before him, followed behind his friend and pastor.

The station master frantically waved the two men away from the line of people filling every boxcar. Pastor Jenson was not to be deterred. Leaving Mrs. Berg with Samuel at the side of the boxcar amd ignoring the station master, even with a pistol in his face, Michael pushed his way to the front of the slow-moving mass entering the boxcar and hoisted himself inside.

"Women and children only!" the station master shouted, with most of his words lost, blown away by the hot wind. Likewise ignoring the pistol, Samuel lifted Beatrice gently into Michael's waiting arms. Her hair had become loose from her braids and fell about her shoulders. Her cheeks were pale and her eyes wide with concern for her tiny child. Weakness filled her body and fear coursed through her heart.

Realizing their desperate situation, a woman in the corner of the car motioned for Michael to bring Beatrice over to her. Several women sitting nearby hastily created a makeshift bed from shawls and jackets on which Beatrice could recline. All the mothers in the boxcar were filled with compassion and helped the two men settle the young woman into the car.

Then Samuel tenderly took the baby from his mother's arms and passed the tiny being up to Michael, who settled Pearl in the waiting arms of her mother. Samuel then hoisted his ample mother into the boxcar and made a space for her next to his beloved Beatrice. Mrs. Berg was pale under the soot and—for once—totally speechless. She reached for Beatrice's hand and held it tight. The baby slept, covered and protected from the soot and sparks that surrounded the train by a soft blanket and her mother's love.

Kneeling before his wife as she lay in the boxcar, with a touch of his lips to her forehead, Samuel said farewell. Michael watched, his eyes filling with tears. The station master finally understood what the two men were doing in the car and put his gun back into its holster.

Around him a constant flow of women and children continued to file into the confines of the car until there was no room left, not even for one person. Michael and Samuel quickly jumped from the car, opening up precious space as it began its perilous journey.

With the cars filled to overflowing, the engine began to pull. The train slowly moved down the track, through the tunnel of flames and the tumult of the wind. In a moment, the train was lost from their sight, hidden in the billowing smoke and flames. Samuel dropped to his knees and covered his face with his blackened hands. Weeping, he called out the names of his beloved, "Beatrice, my beautiful Beatrice!" he cried. "Pearl! My baby! Will I ever see them again?"

The depot platform remained thronged with men, women, and children, desperately waiting to board the next coal car, boxcar, or freight car to take them to safety. No one paid any attention to Samuel, on his knees at the feet of his pastor. Michael reached around the weeping man, sheltering him from the blowing debris and glowing sparks that burned everyone's skin and clothing. Not one of the frantic people boarding the train took note of the soot-covered pastor as he placed his strong hands on the head and quaking shoulders of the young husband and father, nor could they hear the words spoken to the heart that broke before him.

"Lord Jesus!" Michael's words were lost in the roar of the wind. "I call out to you to bring to safety all these people who have need of your care and keeping. I put Samuel into your loving arms as we have put Beatrice, Pearl, and Mrs. Berg into them. We give them to you and your unending love. Be with us all!" The wind continued to howl and the sparks continued to burn, but Samuel slowly took a deep breath, grew quiet, and rose to his feet.

Just as Samuel stood up and wiped away his tears with a soot-covered hand, the station master ran over and shouted in their ears, "After this load the next train will carry men as well as women and children. The exodus has gone better than expected!" He ran off to fill the final car of this train and begin loading the next—and, ultimately, the last—train to head for the safety of Duluth and Superior.

Samuel decided he'd help at the depot before boarding the final train and following his family to Duluth. Michael, on the other hand, decided to go back, against his better judgment, to the church and also check Mrs. Brush's house. He was sure Daisy would have spirited Mrs. Brush away by this time.

After an embrace the two men separated, Samuel helping people board the final train to leave the city, Michael running at top speed back through the wall of people surging toward the empty cars, searching for the Bergs' horse and carriage. Once he found it he leaped into the seat and, with a slap of the reins, guided the frantic horse through the sea of people and headed for the conflagration that had once been Cloquet Avenue.

As though he were heading against a strong river current, Michael steered his skittish horse through the crowds still heading for the depot. Visibility was almost nil and smoke clogged the streets, hindering all foot traffic and carriages. Vast walls of flame were blasted about by the ever-howling wind. The mercantile, the barber shop, the livery stable, the tobacco shop, the department stores, the banks—all were in flames.

Michael took note of Mr. Lund's auto idling in front of the bank, then caught sight of the banker escaping through a wall of flame clutching two large satchels. As Michael forced the horse through the blinding walls of fire, his eyes briefly met the eyes of the furtive banker, who threw the two satchels into the auto and leaped behind the wheel. With the motor roaring, Mr. Lund soon disappeared into the dense smoke, his taillights glowing momentarily through the smoke and blowing debris. Then he was gone.

When Michael approached the corner where his church had once stood so proudly, the horse became more and more uncontrollable as the flames licked at its withers, causing it to buck and rear in terror.

Finally Michael gave up trying to guide the frantic horse through the flames. Pulling to a halt, he leaped down from the driver's seat, unhitched the horse, removed the harness, and with a smack on the horse's rear end, watched as the horse bounded wildly down the street before disappearing into the smoke and flames. Leaving the buggy in the middle of the street, Michael tried to visualize exactly where he was, but there were no familiar signs or landmarks that remained—only the flames surrounding him on all sides.

Then, with a slight change in the direction of the wind, he saw the steeple of his church as it turned into a torch of flame belching into the sky. Suddenly it collapsed into the body of the church, where everything was devoured. Michael frantically reached into his jacket pocket and, sure enough, he still possessed his Greek New Testament. For a moment he felt reassured.

Turning his gaze to the spot where he suspected Mrs. Brush's house had been, he thought he could see a figure in the smoky outline of a doorway. Quickly navigating the hazardous street crossing, dodging the flying debris, he leaped up the soon-to-be demolished porch steps. There he found Daisy weeping, collapsed on the doorframe of Mrs. Brush's once lovely home.

"She won't let me take her to safety!" Daisy was uncontrollable, clutching Michael's shirtfront. "She wants to stay in her bed and die in her home—fire or no fire!" Daisy wept with her head on Michael's chest.

Throwing his arm around Daisy, Michael quickly forced their way into the parlor, which was now on fire from the rear of the house, and then, pulling Daisy with him, he bounded up the stairway that appeared to be intact—for the moment. Daisy, full of fear and trembling, was afraid to let go of Michael. Thus, together they entered what had at one time been a place of grace and serenity, where Mrs. Brush had reigned comfortably in her lovely bed, holding court, so to speak, as her friends came and went over the recent weeks.

Peering into the smoke-filled room, Michael could barely make out the slight form lying on the bed, ever so slightly creasing the quilt. Together Michael and Daisy hovered over the peaceful face gazing back at them from the silken pillow. Loud crashes of flying lumber echoed through the room as burning boards hit the roof and shattered the windows. Flames licked up the walls of the hallway and the bedrooms; it would not be long before the house would collapse upon itself.

Mrs. Brush, adamant in her decision, gazed up at the two beloved faces. Her hair lay spread out over the pillow and her hands were folded serenely across her breast. She was very conscious of the stress and pain in her chest as her heart beat its final strokes beneath her hands. "Bless me once last time, Pastor," she whispered. Michael and Daisy could barely hear the quiet words over the wind and flames that roared about them. "Please," she entreated, "just lay your hands upon me and bless me before I rise to meet my precious Savior." Her breathing became uneven and her eyes closed. For a moment the two friends thought they had lost her. Then her clear blue eyes opened suddenly. "Please!" It was a direct order. She managed a weak smile, beseeching them.

Another crash sounded and Michael was sure it was the roof of the porch. More flaming pieces of lumber smashed into the house and yard. Another flaming board smashed through the bedroom window and lay burning on the rich floral carpet. The house would soon collapse. As he placed his soot-covered hands on the brow of his lovely friend, she smiled gently into his eyes one final time before her lids fluttered and closed. "I place you in the care and keeping of your Lord and Savior, Jesus Christ."

His throat thickened, and he found it difficult to speak. Leaning close to the serene face waiting to hear his words, he almost shouted to be heard above the roar of the fire. "May He take your hand and lead you to the reward in heaven that He has promised to all who believe in him." He made the sign of the cross upon her brow and on her folded hands. Daisy wept silently, kneeling beside the bed of the woman who had befriended her for so many years.

For a split second there was a moment of silence, then the fire raged with new fury around the building now totally ravished by the flames. Daisy tucked the quilt one last time about her friend and ran a hand through the hair she had so often brushed to a silken sheen.

Then, after stroking the aged cheek of his friend one last time, Pastor Jenson reached out, grabbed Daisy by the hand, and plunged down the fire-filled stairway now shuddering beneath them, barely holding up under their weight. As they exited the house, it seemed to ignite like a torch behind them and flame into the smoke-covered heavens.

Mrs. Brush had breathed her last before the roof of her lovely home burst into flame and collapsed. No one but the Lord Himself saw Mrs. Brush as she became aware of the bright light hovering above her. One could imagine her tranquil smile as she felt her right hand clasped in the strong hand enfolding hers, sensing the liberation of her soul as it burst free from her aged body. She was "ravished," "made new" and was eager to answer the Lord's question, "Do you love me?" with the words she had practiced saying for so long. "Yes, Lord, you know that I love you!"

The remains of the house flamed on, whipped by fire-driven winds.

Michael clutched Daisy's hand as together they set out for the Island at a dead run, stumbling over debris, dodging flying lumber and household items that soared by them. A flaming mattress, borne on the wind, almost careened into them and would have flattened them into the wall of the burning building to their right had they not seen it in time.

Smoke and ash filled their eyes and nostrils, making it difficult for them to breathe or see where they were going. Their clothing ignited from the flaming sparks surrounding them on all sides, causing them to extinguish, by hand, any burning area on dress or jacket.

Cloquet Avenue was now full of frantic horses. Released from the barns by the stable hands attempting to free them from the burning buildings, the horses were wild with fright and galloping madly in all directions. Through the flames, dodging the frantic horses, flying debris, the collapsing buildings, Michael and Daisy frantically made their way toward the red bridge.

The streets were nearly empty of people now, the final numbers of the doomed town's population still at the depot boarding the last train. The station master postponed his final departure as long as he dared, straining to see through the dense smoke enveloping the depot. He knew he would not be able to live with himself if there were the slightest possibility that, at the final moment, one last person would materialize out of the smoke only to find the train disappearing into the fury of the surrounding fire and smoke.

In desperation he realized the one remaining train had to begin its flight to safety, the final opportunity to escape from the raging fire. He leaped on the cowcatcher at the front of the engine and, waving his lantern into the smoke-filled air, signaled the engineer to proceed. This train, the last engine and cars available, was his final chance to take his precious cargo to Duluth. Peering through the smoke, searching the surrounding area for anyone needing help, he felt the train lurch forward and begin its journey through the devastated area that lay ahead. The smoke billowed, the fire raged, and he determined there was no one left to save.

By the time the train left Cloquet, the station was totally engulfed in flames, as were all the discarded possessions left cluttering the loading area. Within the time it would take to blink an eye, all the treasures that had been tearfully discarded exploded into flame and were no more.

As Michael and Daisy neared the red bridge they saw mass confusion erupting to their left. They glanced quickly in the direction of the large horse barns located near the road. The roofs of the two large barns were engulfed in flames, quickly fanning out in all directions.

Through the smoke they could see Mr. Keller and his hired men still trying to evacuate the horses and bring them to a place of shelter. Once the barn doors were opened and the horses freed from their stalls, the stable hands clutched the bridle reins, desperately trying to lead the horses outside the flaming building. Daisy and Michael could see the silhouettes of the frantic workers, illuminated by the flames surrounding them.

Prompted by their inherent fear of fire, the horses erupted from the door and bolted, dragging along the men clutching the reins as they attempted to control the animals' exit from the burning barns. Becoming confused and not knowing where to go in the now-unfamiliar surroundings, some horses headed across the bridge to the Island, some galloped down the shore of the river, and some could not be deterred from once again going back inside the flaming shell of the building.

The smell of burning horseflesh wafted across the road and sickened the runners as they made their way to the bridge. Daisy tried to see if Samson was in the group of horses now clustered about the stables and galloping across the pasture. She knew how worried Henry would be about his favorite horse. Severely limited by the ash and soot in the air, she saw no horse that fit the description of the mighty Samson.

After crossing the bridge, miracle of miracles, through the billowing smoke they could discern the saloons rising up before them—all seventeen of them totally intact, not a blaze or fire anywhere. The rampaging fire came from the northwest, then bore down upon the far western point of the Island, totally destroying the railroad roundhouse and the warehouse of the St. Louis Mercantile Company. Flames from the western end of the Island then swirled high into the air, where the wind whipped them into a frenzy and drove the inferno straight across the river to the southwest corner of the town.

The fire, reaching out its tentacles to the stacks of millions of board feet of lumber stored along the shore of the river, erupted into a torrent of wind that picked up the burning lumber and tossed it like toothpicks onto the area of the city bordering the river. Houses, shops, sheds, businesses, warehouses, storage units, equipment barns—everything had become part of the raging inferno.

With the fickleness of fate, the extreme eastern portion of the Island, where stack after stack of dried lumber lay waiting to be shipped, remained untouched. What miracle of nature kept those stacks upright and stationary in the driving wind? Only heaven knew.

Michael and Daisy forced their way into the wind. Passing the open doors of the saloons, their smoke-filled eyes could barely make out the lumberjacks standing warily by the bar, not sure what their plans of action should be. Some lumberjacks had formed a haphazard bucket brigade and were frantically passing buckets of river water up through the lines of men who then threw the water on any and all sparks landing on the wooden boardwalk or the walls or roofs of the saloons.

When they tired, they changed places with others and renewed their strength at the bar. Drinks were on the house. Should they stand by the bar with a drink in their hand, foolishly waiting for the saloons to burst into flame, or should they make a mad dash to the trains and flee the town altogether? A drink in the hand trumped the practical impulse of escape, so there they stood, a bit tipsy but happy nonetheless as they once again took their turn with the buckets, the river water, and the free beer.

The heavy smoke swirled around the Island, causing Michael and Daisy to disappear from view as they made their perilous way up Main Street to the northern shore of the Island where Big Jack's boarding house stood, hidden in the dense smoke, firm against the punishing winds.

Daisy was certain Hank and Henry would be at the boarding house with Big Jack and Maggie. Earlier that afternoon, against Hank's wishes, she had hastened through the smoke and fire intending to rescue Mrs. Brush. Now she was back and relieved to see that, even though it was surrounded by smoke and flying ashes, most of the Island—even their little house—was still untouched by the fury of the flames.

Big Jack met them at the steps, threw his arms around both of them, and all but carried them into the dining area where Hank waited, consumed with worry. "Dear God! Where have you been?" Hank exploded. "I've been worried sick!" At once, with his bare hands, he began to extinguish the sparks and smoldering ashes caught in Daisy's hair and on her skin and burning clothing. Big Jack worked on Michael's singed hair and shirt. Frantically, everyone grabbed a bucket of water and a blanket, then headed for safety in the root cellar at the rear of the boarding house.

Maggie and Bertha, each carrying a lantern, led the small group down the rustic steps and into the fragrant storage area where the produce from the summer would endure until spring. Pastor Jenson and Daisy assisted Hank down the steep wooden steps and seated him comfortably on a wooden bench which usually held bushel baskets overflowing with freshly picked red apples from Pearl's trees. Big Jack, holding the doors against the power of the wind, finally made ready to close the door and bolt it shut.

Suddenly Hank struggled to his feet and looked about him in fear and disbelief. "Henry!" he cried. "Where is Henry?"

Everyone came to a halt, trying to recall the last time they had been aware of Henry being in their midst. All eyes turned to Maggie, who stuttered her hesitant reply, knowing she would be in trouble, whatever she said. She was definitely a silent partner in the matter of the missing young boy. "The horse," she whispered. "He asked me not to tell you that he was going to run to the stables and see if he could find Samson." Her head bowed and tears coursed down her cheeks, making paths in the soot on her face. Finally, she started to weep and buried her face in Bertha's lap. "He should have been back by now. I should have told someone," she sobbed. "But," she took a ragged breath, "I promised Henry I wouldn't tell on him."

Bertha wrapped her arms about the girl and held her close. Overwhelmed by the thought of what might have happened to her only child, Daisy raised her apron to her face and wept. Having just come by the stable area, she was far too aware of the conditions there and the wildly stampeding horses, loose and out of control.

The men huddled together by the cellar stairway, talking frantically, trying to sort out a plan, one that would rescue Henry from the fury of the wind and the flames. Any of these three brave men, once they climbed the stairs and stepped out the door of the cellar, knew they put themselves into a life-threatening situation. The roaring tempest awaited them.

"How long had Henry been gone?" shouted Hank. "How much of a head start does he have?"

Through her tears Maggie choked out, "Only ten minutes or so," she whispered. "Right before Daisy and Pastor Jenson arrived."

Michael suddenly took charge of the situation. "We must have passed him, walked right by him as we came here," he said as ran his hand over his brow. "The smoke was like a wall, so thick we couldn't see!" He began to mount the steps.

"Open the door and let me out!" he shouted to Big Jack.

Big Jack and Hank reached out in protest, but Michael was not to be denied. "You both have loved ones to care for here. I'll go alone—you hold the fort down here."

Big Jack tried to hold him back. Being prepared for this, Michael twisted around, placed his foot on Big Jack's chest, and gave a mighty shove. Shocked, Big Jack fell back, sprawling on the damp floor of the cellar, still reaching for Michael's legs.

"Let me out!" Michael bellowed, pushing against the heavy cellar door until it moved slightly. Caught by a powerful gust of wind, the door finally slammed open, allowing a dense cloud of smoke and ash to enter as Michael dashed up the steps, out the door, into the unknown that lay beyond.

Once again Big Jack forced the door shut, making sure it was securely latched. Only one kerosene lamp remained lit after the burst of foul air descended through the door and down the steps. For a moment the whole group was stunned. They had no idea what Pastor Jenson would encounter as he searched for Henry through the hell that raged over the Island. As a fearful silence choked each of them, they found they could hardly breathe.

Suddenly Hank bent over, his head buried in his hands, and started to cry out in a loud and desperate voice to God Almighty, the only source of strength that remained for the fearful group all but buried beneath the hell that raged above them.

"Please, God," he shouted, "go with Pastor Jenson. Help him, dear God! Please, please, help him!" The remaining lamp sputtered a bit, but held its flame so that darkness did not prevail—at least for the time being. In their heart of hearts, all those left behind in the root cellar reached out for a miracle.

∞31∞
The Crash

B Y THE TIME THE FINAL TRAIN left the doomed city and disappeared into the tumult of churning smoke, violent flames had swept across the entire area, destroying everything as far as the human eye could see. Winds, occasionally reaching sixty or seventy miles an hour, drove the front of the fire to the south toward Carlton and Moose Lake. Later reports from some of the escaping passengers told of flames reaching upwards to 200 feet in the air as the trains tentatively crossed the St. Louis River. Miraculously the trestles, the only path to safety, withstood the heat, fire, and winds until all the trains were safely on the other side.

Before long, the city of Cloquet was no more. At first the shrieking mill whistles, warning of the devastation that would wipe the city off the map, could be heard over the roar of the flames and the howling winds. Finally, even the sirens ceased, the electric company lost power, and the entire area was plunged into darkness. All that was left to illuminate the destruction was the never-ending wall of flame.

All this time, Mr. Arthur Lund was totally confident that, with his brilliant plan firmly in place, he would soon escape the hell now surrounding him. Once he had collected a "bit" of cash from the vault in the bank, shut the vault once again, and stashed his satchels in the Ford, he was prepared for whatever lay ahead. Unfortunately, Pastor Jenson had chosen this exact moment to pass by the bank. Oh, well. Since he was not a member of the church the pastor served, Mr. Lund did not feel he had committed a major transgression of any kind.

Actually, he had no regrets or guilty feelings whatsoever about "borrowing" the money from the bank, or even leaving his family to fend for themselves, for that matter. *Let them take care of each other*, he thought, knowing his wife and child had never become a real part of his life. *After all, I have plans to start a new life once I reach St. Paul*, he mused. *When I finally get there, I have no doubt I'll quickly establish myself as a pillar of that vibrant banking community. I'll let my experience speak for itself.* A smile creased his cheeks, outlined by the black soot covering his face.

He contemplated, only briefly, stopping by to pick up Wilma, but then his common sense took over, telling him she'd only become a burden to him, would never be someone he could display proudly in the higher society he planned to infiltrate. With firm resolve, he told himself he would be far better off by starting his new life with no trappings from his past to encumber his rise to power and wealth.

Wilma, unaware of her lover's change of heart, waited, watching in vain for the auto to appear through the dense smoke and flames surrounding her house. Finally, she packed a valise with piano music, joined the parade of neighbors struggling to make their way to the depot before the final train left, and cursed the spineless man who had been her lover.

Mr. Lund pulled his Ford into the line of cars creeping slowly down the Pike Lake Road leading toward Duluth, to safety and a new life. He patted the satchels sitting regally beside him on the front seat.

Who will ever know what happened to all the cash in the vault? he mused. *The bank will certainly burn to the ground, destroying all the records as well. Thank goodness!* He grinned again. *No sense at all to allow all that money to be destroyed. No sense at all!*

As part of the serpentine caravan moving slowly through the smoke and flames, Mr. Lund saw fire raging about the cars on all sides, the billowing smoke and blowing ashes totally obscuring the drivers' vision. Even with goggles, drivers and passengers could barely make out their own hands in front of their faces. The dim outline of the taillights from the car ahead gave Mr. Lund a small sense of assurance. *Keep calm*, he told himself. *Once I get out of this damned hellhole, I'll be on my way to a new life!* He allowed another small smile slip over his lips as he clutched the wheel with sweating hands, always keeping his eyes focused on the dim taillights flickering ahead of him.

Acres of trees that once towered over the road were engulfed in flames and, thanks to the deadly wind, their branches were being ripped from their trunks, then blown in all directions. Flaming branches crashed into the road and onto the tops of the cars, impeding their progress. Smoke became thicker, making it all but impossible for the drivers to see even the taillights of the car directly in front of them.

The distraught drivers, unaware of exactly where they were on the road, had no memory—or indication—of the deep gully plunging down the right side of the road. On a more pleasant day the gully was usually filled with beautiful trees, colorful wildflowers, and long, thick grasses.

Then, suddenly, the hopes of all the people fleeing the fire in the cars seemed to explode. At the front of the procession, the driver of the lead car and his passengers could see nothing, only swirling smoke, until, suddenly, a flaming tree blew over and crashed in the middle of the narrow road. In desperation, the driver turned his wheel sharply to the right, hoping for a quick passage around the wall of flames blocking the way. Without warning, the driver and his passengers felt the car leave the ground and become airborne, twist in mid-air, and plunge sharply down into the deep gully waiting below. End over end, the auto cartwheeled down the hill, bursting into flame once it crashed into the bottom of the gully where it disappeared, hidden in the smoke and flames below.

One after the other, the drivers who focused on the dim glow of the taillights ahead of them followed the path of the lead car and met the same violent destruction as the first.

Auto after auto crashed into the gully, spilling bodies, luggage, and the contents of their gas tanks, igniting an even greater burst of flame. At the rear of the procession, Mr. Lund gripped the steering wheel, eyes concentrated on the dim, receding outline of the car ahead, and noted when the taillights before him made a slight turn to the right. Slowly, carefully, Mr. Lund peered through the wall of smoke, then turned his steering wheel.

Within a second, an explosion of flames directly in front of him became visible through his windshield. He slammed on the brake just as he felt his shiny black auto leave the road and become airborne through the smoke and flames billowing up from the ditch. And then another car, just behind him, also turned and crashed into the underbelly of Mr. Lund's now-flaming, upside-down Ford. The satchels full of money took only a second before they, too, burst into flame alongside the body of the lifeless bank president.

Before long almost a dozen cars had crashed into the gully. At last, one sensible driver slowed carefully before making the right turn, taking a closer look at the tower of flame engulfing that side of road. What he saw, as he peered into the flames, noting the burning autos and the flaming bodies of their passengers, made him slam on the brakes and bring a desperate end to what remained of the procession of fleeing autos.

Realizing the road was now totally impassable, the drivers halted their frenzied dash for safety and emptied their panic-filled passengers into the road, right in the middle of the fury of the flaming woods. Some were rescued and taken to safety in Duluth; some of the charred bodies discovered later were never identified—Mr. Lund being one of them.

Perhaps Mr. Lund might have been interested in the fact that Oscar and his mother arrived safely in Duluth after being kindly nurtured by Miss Vivian Thoreson, their Good Samaritan.

But then, he probably wouldn't have cared in the least.

‰32‰
Once More into the Flames

As Michael stumbled out of the root cellar, the fire and its ravishing winds continued their deadly onslaught. Once again the smoke burned his eyes and made it difficult to breathe. Peering through the dense smoke, searching for Main Street, he shielded his eyes from the flying ashes as he pressed forward.

The heat from the multitude of fires flaming on the west end of the Island and across the river burned his eyes and skin, and sparks once again ignited his clothing. Quickly realizing it would accomplish nothing if he called out Henry's name, he lowered his head and plowed ahead in the direction of the red bridge. Nothing could be heard over the deafening roar of the wind and flames still reaching to the heavens.

Advancing cautiously through the thick wall of smoke, Michael once again vaguely recognized the row of saloons still standing along St. Louis Avenue where the lumberjacks continued to operate the bucket brigade, their devotion to their sources of liquor admirable.

Michael, working his way through the smoke and blowing debris, approached the figures in front of what he remembered as the Moose Saloon. No one noticed him when he emerged from a dense cloud of smoke and headed for the men manning the buckets. Thinking he recognized a familiar face, even though the features were caked with soot, he set his course for the third man in the line. Hopefully he was correct in thinking the dark figure was Hank's friend Willard Schiebe. Trying not to disrupt the rhythm of the passing of the buckets, he eased his way up the line, thinking that perhaps Willard, or one of his friends, had taken note of Henry if and when he passed this way.

Michael reached out his hand to touch Willard's arm and gain his attention, but even before Michael's hand made contact with Willard's arm, the bucket man looked up into his face and smiled a wide smile, his teeth gleaming white in his soot-stained face.

"God damn, if it ain't Pastor Jenson!"

Grabbing Willard around the neck, Michael thrust his mouth right up against the startled man's ear, hoping Willard could hear him over the wind. As the buckets kept coming, Willard tried his best to keep up the rhythm coming into his hand and leaving a second later, but to no avail. The water spilled over both men as they attempted to communicate over the roar of the wind.

"Have you seen Henry Larson, Hank's son, come by here in the last half hour?" A bucket was passed up the line before Willard shouted his reply.

"I saw a kid run by—I wasn't sure who it was because of the smoke," Willard paused. "It could have been Henry." A puzzled look crossed his face. "What was Hank's kid doing, being out in this mess?" Two more buckets sloshed by, soaking Michael's shoes and trousers.

"Which way was he headed?" Michael shouted. "Just nod your head in the direction and keep passing the buckets!" Willard passed another bucket and nodded in the direction of the red bridge, located somewhere beyond the swirling smoke covering the Island. "Thanks!" shouted Michael as he turned, broke into a run, and disappeared into the wall of smoke.

Desperately searching through the smoke and ashes, he finally found the red bridge, now covered with debris and burning hot to the touch. With a few giant strides, Michael made it to the other side, where he paused to take stock of the situation. Squinting against the swirling smoke, he was able to catch a view of the remains of the stables, now burning and crumbling to the ground. Silhouetted against the flames of the collapsing buildings, he could barely make out several men trying to collect the horses into a herd, one that could be driven over the bridge to the relative safety of the Island or into the river where they might survive the flames and the extreme heat.

In Michael's mind, the moment looked like a scene from Dante's *Inferno*. All at once he felt helpless and was at a total loss of what he should do, where he should look for Henry, how he could conquer the darkness, the power of the wind, the undulating flames, the pain in his lungs, and attempt to rescue Hank and Daisy's precious son.

The extreme heat, the lack of oxygen, the burning ashes stinging his face, and the force of the winds were wearing away at the pastor's strength and endurance. When he neared where the barns had been, he stumbled and almost fell into a watering trough with water still in it. Stripping off his jacket, he plunged it into the little water that remained, and put the jacket back on, sopping wet. The water seeped through his soiled shirt and trickled down his back, cooling him for the moment.

Fighting his way up to what was left of the stables, he was conscious of the panic filling the horses still remaining in the area. Eyes wide with fear, the huge horses charged blindly in all directions, unable to return to the comfort of their stalls. The stables were gone, totally unrecognizable with only flaming piles of collapsed roof and walls remaining where the horses had been housed so comfortably such a short time ago.

Trying to sheild his eyes from the soot and ash, Michael stumbled and crashed through an unseen remnant of a glass window hidden under a pile of debris near a stable door. Buried beneath the fallen timbers and layers of ash from the stables, the pane of glass shattered as his leg plunged through it, sending shards of glass cutting through the fabric of his trousers and slashing into his leg. His body twisted in pain.

Stunned for a moment, he realized his leg was injured. Reaching down, he could feel the blood flowing through his trousers and the shards of glass now imbedded in the flesh of his calf. Slowly, painfully, he struggled to free his leg, then knelt in the soot and smoke and flames, all that remained of the once lush, green pasture.

Now very conscious of the nasty wound to his leg, he tried to remove some of the larger pieces of glass protruding through his trousers. The pain made him weak, and he wasn't sure how to stem the bleeding. Attempting to catch his breath, he bent almost double, covering his nose and mouth, trying to draw some good air into his lungs. His lungs burned, his breath came in short gasps, and his leg throbbed with pain. Finally able to stand upright, he struggled to take a step and fell again.

Never before had he felt so vulnerable, his life so fragile. Then, all at once, the face of Jesus from the painting above the church altar came into his mind. In the final moment spent in his burning church, Michael had looked up and into the eyes of his Lord as the flames devoured the altarpiece, and yet the Lord lived on—and Michael believed he would as well. Now, however, he needed to focus on finding Henry, whatever the cost to himself.

"I'm ready, Lord!" he shouted into the wind. "Help me find my friend!"

Almost smiling through the pain, he visualized himself literally black as soot, burned and bleeding from the glass shards, the flying ash and debris, and now sprawled in what he was sure was a pile of horse manure. Evidently he was closer to the barns than he had first thought. The horse handlers had finally given up their battle with the horses and fled the scene. Most of the horses had also disappeared, galloping wildly through the smoke in every direction.

Slowly and painfully Michael struggled to stand once again on his feet. Wiping his face with the front of his shirt, hoping to clear away some of the soot—and manure—that seemed to cover everything and impair his vision, Michael peered through the flying soot and ash trying to determine where Henry could have gone, or where he might have tried to hide from the flames.

Then Michael noticed a large, dark shape off to his left where the stable door had once been located. The smoke billowed in waves, back and forth, obstructing his vision. Moving forward carefully, favoring his injured leg, he thought he could see the faint outline of what he thought—and prayed—was a horse, standing strangely quiet near a small portion of fence that still remained. The horse was still as a statue, standing with its head down, reins seeming to touch the ground, as though the animal had become too weary to raise its eyes and look at the world as it flamed around him.

Michael moved slowly, painfully, ever closer, straining his eyes until he finally noticed an object on the ground between the four legs of the horse. At first Michael thought it could be a wounded dog, or a horse blanket blown there by the wind, or maybe just a piece of lumber that remained from what once were the stables.

Trying not to spook the horse, Michael reached out to stroke its neck, then gently took the reins in his left hand, only to find that the reins were secured to whatever lay between the still legs of the horse. Bending down and brushing away the ash and cinders covering the object on the ground, Michael was shocked to discover a human body. And miracle of miracles, the still form lying there at his feet was Henry Larson!

Grimacing in pain, Michael knelt, then carefully turned Henry onto his back, trying to make an assessment of the young boy's condition. The horse—evidently Samson—whinnied softly and shook his shaggy head. "Easy, boy," Michael reached up to stroke Samson's quivering neck. "You'll have to help us out of this hellhole, so keep calm!"

Once again Michael directed his attention to the still body before him. Henry was breathing evenly, his arms and legs appeared to be intact, his heart beat regularly in his young chest. The only cause for concern that Michael discovered was a large gash in Henry's right temple.

Michael surmised that one of the finely milled pieces of flying lumber had blown through the air and crashed into Henry as he sat astride his beloved horse. Falling unconscious to the ground beneath the horse's hooves, the reins remained twisted around Henry's wrist. And Samson, the blessed horse, evidently stepped over the unconscious boy, carefully placing himself to shelter Henry from the sharp hooves of the frantic horses milling about the area. There the two had remained until Pastor Jenson found his way through the smoke and flames to save them both.

Gently untangling the reins from Henry's wrist, Micharl lashed them around his own strong arm. After wiping Henry's bloodstained face with his handkerchief, dampened with some water still remaining in the trough, Michael gently lifted the young boy from the ground, trying not to spook the horse. Samson, except for a shake of his head, seemed to understand the urgency of the moment and stood very still, even as the burning ashes burned into his mane and coat.

Remembering his days on the farm when he worked with his father's livestock, Michael spoke softly to the horse. "Hey, there, Samson," he soothed the quivering horse, "you and I have to work together to get Henry out of danger." Cradling the boy in his arms, Michael lifted him carefully, then placed him on Samson's broad back. Henry's head hung forward and lay limply in the matted mane he had so often brushed.

"Good boy! Henry would be proud of you," Michael stroked the horse's neck and positioned the limp boy securely before making a move. Henry had sat there so many times in the past, with his face and hands buried in the thick mane covering the horse's neck, that Samson accepted his silent passenger and stood quietly through the whole operation.

Once the boy was secure, protected from the flying ashes and soot by the pastor's damp coat, Michael gently pulled on the reins and the threesome—an unconscious boy, a wounded man, and a defeated horse—slowly and carefully started down the hill, limping through the blinding smoke toward the bridge. The path was deserted. The last train had left the depot a short time ago. The mill sirens were silent, leaving only the roar of the wind. The town was black, with only the flames to light the darkness.

THE BEER STILL FLOWED FREELY and the bucket brigade was hard at work by the time Willard finally took another break. Needing time to catch his breath, he grabbed a beer and sat down to rest on the water-soaked boardwalk before returning to his place in line. So far, Willard and his friends assumed full credit for not allowing even one saloon to fall prey to the fire. He leaned back and took a long, loud swallow of the over-heated beer, then wiped his mouth with the back of his hand.

Suddenly, blinking his smoke-filled eyes between gulps, he stood upright and stared in disbelief at what he saw coming slowly toward him through the smoke. Tossing his glass of beer into the air while shouting to the working brigade members as he ran by them, he pointed south toward the bridge.

Faintly visible through the dense wall of smoke, Willard could barely make out the silhouette of a man leading a horse toward the saloons, the horse laden with something that, from this distance, could be a boy.

"By God! It's the pastor!" His throat swelled as he proclaimed the good news. "He's found the boy!"

‍‍ℬ33ℛ
A New Beginning

By 3:00 a.m. Sunday morning, the panorama of the city was most spectacular, flames raging like demons battering against the churning, smoke-filled sky. Nero would have enjoyed the view as the flames swept through Cloquet, then sped on their deadly path to communities farther to the south. The city was plunged into total darkness—the land burned black and barren, buildings demolished, charred skeletons of trees left standing, silhouetted against the black sky. The war-torn lands of Europe could barely hold a candle to the desolate remains of the once-thriving city on the St. Louis River. Still the fire continued its frenzied and turbulent journey, borne on powerful winds that ushered it steadily to the south. In years to come this fire would come to be known as "the greatest fire since the San Francisco fire."

Then, with the fickleness of fate, the winds suddenly turned upon themselves and began to blow from the east off of Lake Superior. Lo and behold, the fire was forced back upon the barren landscape it had just devoured and found nothing left to feed its insatiable appetite. Slowly, ever so slowly, the monster fire burned itself out and was last seen as a flickering flame dancing from twig to twig, bush to bush, hay bale to hay bale. The wind took a deep breath, paused, and became a breeze instead of a tempest.

Incredibly, only four lives were lost in the city. A report on the fire later stated that "one aged woman died of fright in her own bed," (the writers had evidently never met Mrs. Brush) "and three men who decided to stay and see it out were suffocated." The report also somberly stated that several bodies, burned beyond recognition, were found in the wreckage from the mulitple-car crash on Pike Lake Road.

A few adventurous spirits refused to leave Cloquet and waited out the inferno in the pond at Pinehurst Park, so recently the site of so much excitement and joy at Lumberjack Days. Even if they greatly exaggerated the accounts of their escape, no one was more surprised than they that they came through alive.

The $100,000 "fireproof" high school was left as a pile of dust. The churches in the area looked like their cousins in war-torn Belgium and France. Residents were left to wonder at the strange remants of their town, such as telephone poles which apparently burned straight down, leaving only piles of ashes in the holes in which they had so recently stood proudly.

The Island was largely untouched. Two blocks of saloons—eighteen buildings in all—escaped the fire unscathed, leading at least one journalist to comment, "The Devil certainly takes care of his own!" The Northern Lumber Company yard, just next door, was destroyed. Train tracks were twisted masses of serpentine-like steel.

The article should have mentioned that north of the Island stood a neat white house that also escaped the flames. A small group of apple trees also survived, even though the fire raged on all sides.

The residents of Cloquet were eager to discover the fate of what had once been their comfortable homes. Anxiously returning to the city, they found no buildings, no telephones, no water, and no electricity. Family after family cautiously stumbled across the stark landscape, looking about them in disbelief at the desolation. Some families had taken time to bury the family silver and other precious possessions in their backyards or gardens before leaving. Now they could not even discern where their lots had been located. All at once the entire population of the city was on equal footing—every one of them was homeless.

Troops of the Fourth Regiment of the Minnesota National Guard arrived on Sunday. The city was now under martial law, with the National Guard watching over safes and vaults that survived the fire as well as keeping looting to a minimum—but then, there was hardly anything left worth looting.

Within forty-eight hours, the executives of the mills voted for large sums of company money to be set aside and made available to families determined to rebuild in the area. The lumber barons also looked at the limited amount of lumber that survived the fire and decided to make it available to anyone wanting to build housing of any kind before the winds of winter howled down from the north. Thus, a shanty town of sorts sprang up, each hastily constructed shack housing up to two or three families.

Basements, some miraculously surviving the fire, were cleared of debris and ashes. Metal objects in the houses above which survived the flames tumbled into basements as houses were consumed by flames. Bed springs, tools, pots and pans, unrecognizable objects melted in the heat, all were hauled up and away before the basement area could be roofed over and made ready to house a family once more.

Smokestacks from the simple stoves used to heat the rustic dwellings rose up and pointed like narrow, blackened fingers to the sky. Smoke belched from each stack as the residents living beneath the newly constructed roofs struggled to keep the cold at bay. A new nickname came into being for the city of Cloquet—people now affectionately christened their hometown " Smokestack City."

As the citizens of Cloquet labored diligently to reclaim their lives, the Red Cross set up tents where they provided coffee and donuts for the soot-covered residents. Nothing would ever taste better than that hot cup of coffee and the crisp donut handed out as the people labored to bring back the life they once knew and loved.

By October 14, the authorities reported that the fires were well in hand. However, areas of smoldering embers found in many locations continued to be a menace and were constantly under observation by firefighters. The copious rains that fell on October 19 were an answer to many prayers and finally put an end to the threat. Mills—those still standing—could now resume a semblance of normal operation and once again begin to employ the men of the area.

Overnight, the Island was turned into a haven of refuge for the homeless. People were incredulous when it became common knowledge that none of the saloons or boarding houses had been touched by the fire. The most often heard response to that news was an incredulous, "God must have quite a sense of humor!" The Northeastern Hotel was quickly refurbished as a hospital staffed by the Red Cross, caring for those injured while escaping the fire. Not only were the sick and injured cared for there, but medical help could also be found at a number of the saloons. Families with no place to find shelter also migrated to the Island, where they were grateful to find a roof over their heads, a wood stove to warm them, and a blanket to wrap about themselves as they lay down to sleep. Lumberjacks and families all shared the rooms in the overcrowded boarding houses.

The Garfield School, which had somehow survived the flames, was turned into the headquarters for government assistance programs as well as the Red Cross operation.

The insurance inspectors, drawn like bees to nectar, flooded the area. They soon determined that the origin of the fire was north of Brookston, and was ignited by the sparks from a train at milepost sixty-two. According to the inspectors' report, embers from the smokestack of a Great Northern Railroad train lit a pile of debris from leftover forest products located near the tracks.

The United States government was held responsible, for they had taken over the management of the railroads after the start of the Great War. 278 residents from the Cloquet area eventually filed claims against the U.S government for damages resulting from the fire. Many years would pass before the first payments were issued.

At last, the sun came out from behind the smoky haze and wispy autumn clouds drifted across the deep blue October sky. The sounds of hammers and saws filled the air from dawn until dusk, when the sun slipped silently behind the now-treeless hills to the west.

Blowing in from the northwest two weeks after the fire, a gentle snowstorm quickly changed the appearance of the entire area in one short evening. Soft, white snow fell like feathers from the clouds, and, little by little, the blackened earth was transformed into a carpet of pure white. When the adults and children awoke and gazed out their small windows, they were awed by the unblemished purity of the snow that glistened before them. All at once the whole world looked clean.

༄34ༀ
Life Goes On

NEWS OF A CHURCH SERVICE, scheduled by Pastor Jenson and to be held in the Moose Saloon on November 3, the first Sunday of November, quickly circulated through the town and across the Island. Other denominations had also held services in unusual places. Space large enough for a service of any kind was difficult to come by, especially with Garfield School filled to capacity with government officials and Red Cross workers. Now the search was on to locate enough chairs, stools, benches, boxes, crates, or anything on which the people coming to worship could sit.

Expectation was high, for people of the community assumed that since Pastor Jenson had scheduled the service, he would be the preacher. Everyone had heard the story of his heroic search through the smoke and flames for Henry Larson. Rumors circulated that he had been seriously injured and might be recalled from his pastorate, but, thank God, that was only a rumor.

And just about everyone felt the need to gather in a church service and give thanks to God for the gift of survival, the simple gift of being alive. No one would ever be able to estimate the number of prayers for safety—and salvation—that continued to batter the doors of heaven on the day of the fire—and the days since.

November 3, dawned clear and bright. A slight breeze gently made its way across the river from the north and stirred—just a bit—the light layer of snow covering the blackened earth. By noon people from town walked toward the red bridge, now scarred and warped by the fire. Crossing over to the Island, they joined the lines of young and old stepping up on the boardwalk and entering the doors of the Moose Saloon, where candles and kerosene lamps cast their warm glow.

Once inside the doors, the air became comfortably warm, thanks to Big Jack's attention to the fire blazing away in the potbellied stove in the far corner. Hats were removed and mittens stuffed in jacket pockets. Cheeks grew rosier as the people warmed up and found a place to sit while waiting for the service to begin. The moose heads on the walls loomed over them.

The rickety upright piano in the corner was being beaten into submission by a saloon regular who often played for his own pleasure when he came to the saloon, if not for the pleasure of those listening. At the moment he was hammering out a hymn somewhat resembling the melody of "Oh God Our Help in Ages Past." His repertoire expanded as time passed and the gathering congregation was serenaded by the player's renditions of "Oh happy home, where thou art loved the dearest," "There is a green hill far away," and finally "On our way rejoicing," all played with great enthusiasm. Occasionally the pianist would lean to his left and let go with a great spit of tobacco juice, which hit the nearby spittoon dead on every time. The virtuoso was most pleased that Pastor Jenson had invited him to play for the service, and he intended to perform at his very best.

At last, when everyone was seated and warmed clear to the bone by the music and the stove, Pastor Jenson entered the saloon from the rear. He wore a plaid flannel shirt and a pair of heavy canvas trousers borrowed from Hank Larson. His alb and stole were gone forever, but no one even noticed. Everyone seated there saw only their pastor, a friend they admired. No outward signs were necessary to show he was their shepherd.

He walked with a definite limp, due to his injury sustained when searching for Henry, and slipped in behind the long, polished surface of the bar. He placed his Greek New Testament—now his only biblical reference book—and a small folded sheet of paper with some notes, barely visible to people in the congregation, on the polished wood. He raised his eyes to look out over the people crammed into the space before him, by now all warmed and content, and then—of course—he smiled his winsome smile.

Some thought he looked pale; his color wasn't as ruddy as they remembered and his eyes appeared larger than usual because his face seemed thinner. There were wounded areas about his head and face where flying embers and debris had ignited his hair and burned his skin. When he raised his arms toward heaven to begin the service, all eyes went to the cuts and bruises and scabbed-over burns scattered over his hands and arms.

Spontaneously, everyone began to applaud. Some even stood as they clapped with enthusiasm, recognizing the courage and affection this young man had for everyone he had met during his brief sojourn here as a pastor. Finally, Michael signaled the congregation to settle down. The group quieted, sat down, and Michael began to speak.

"In the name of the Father, and of the Son, and of the Holy Ghost," he began, and the service started with the singing of "A Mighty Fortress Is Our God," a hymn most people knew by heart. Three men from the community, whose Bibles had miraculously survived the fire, took turns reading three Psalms: 23, 100, and 121. The opening words of the twenty-third Psalm now had special meaning to everyone: "The Lord is my shepherd. I shall not want." For a moment, everyone felt content with whatever they now called their own—no matter how scant their possessions were. They still had their Shepherd.

Michael spoke freely, using no notes, just the words he felt rise up from his pastor's heart. He told stories related to him by people who fled the fire and felt the Lord's presence as they boarded the trains that traveled through the very flames of Hell. He related how people reached out in love, willing to sacrifice themselves for the good of others. He named the heroes of the evacuation process and gave credit to all the railroad employees who delivered their precious living cargo to a place of safety. He cited many small acts of kindness he had witnessed or were told to him by the recipients of the gift of grace. Over and over he stressed how, even in the throes of danger and terror, the grace of God flooded the hearts of those who beseeched Him with fear and trembling, leaving behind a "peace that passes all understanding."

The people who listened to his words thought of their own experiences, the kindness they received, the strength they felt when someone held them close, the relief they felt when realizing their loved ones were safe. A universal wave of thanksgiving swept over the motley congregation that clustered in the Moose Saloon. Yes, indeed! God is good! What a gift it was to be alive! Tears of joy and relief flowed freely over the cheeks of the men and the women present.

In closing the service, Pastor Jenson announced that what would happen next would probably never happen again in any service—or in any church. Taking a moment to explain what would follow, he exclaimed, "We are still a community! Thus, we need to share in the celebrations that occur in our lives. And that is exactly what we are going to do today."

Michael walked out from behind the bar and came to stand in front of the congregation. Spreading his arms wide, as though to include everyone, he began, "Today is our day to rejoice in the combination of events we all experience in our life journey." He went on to explain, "We are going to celebrate the gift of new life by witnessing a baptism." He indicated a white bowl near a pitcher of water. "Next we will celebrate the gift of human love by taking part in a wedding ceremony." He held up a simple gold band for all to see. "And finally, as the grand finale, we will commend one of our beloved community members to the arms of Jesus Christ, our Lord and Savior. That should be a fitting conclusion to our service here today."

People in the congregation moved about, sitting up straighter to gain a better vantage point for what was to come. And there they were—Samuel, beaming with pride, Beatrice, more beautiful than ever with the aura of motherhood about her, and baby Pearl, sound asleep in the arms of her father. With smiling faces, they walked up to the counter of the bar where Oscar Lund had just poured a pitcher of slightly warmed water into a bowl, usually filled with mashed potatoes at Big Jack's boarding house. A clean white cotton napkin, also from Big Jack's, lay beside the bowl. Daisy and Hank rose from their chairs in the second row and slowly made their way to the bar, where they would become Pearl's godparents.

The Larsons stood at the front of the congregation, overcome by what they felt in their hearts. Looking at Pastor Jenson as he stood there smiling at them, ready to minister to any and all, they knew how much they loved him. What a debt of gratitude they felt for this kind and loving friend.

They would never forget the night when he went forth in the tumult of the flames to find their beloved son. Nor would they ever be able to put into words what they felt as they finally heard the commotion outside the root cellar when the pastor—and five lumberjacks who temporarily put aside their bucket brigade duties—returned with their son on the back of his beloved horse. Samson now lived, temporarily, in Big Jack's shed with one cow and some chickens. He was Henry's horse—now and forever—but it didn't take long before Daisy had also fallen in love with the sturdy, old work horse. Samson now received more sugar lumps each day than he had ever thought possible.

Gently taking the three-week-old infant into her arms, Daisy felt her eyes fill with tears. Three times Pastor Jenson dipped his large hand into the bowl, scooping up the water to baptize the child. "In the name of the Father—and the Son—and the Holy Spirit." He thought of saying, "You truly are a pearl of great price," but common sense controlled his tongue as he dried the drops of baptismal water from Pearl's dark hair.

Michael took the baby into his arms and walked about the room, through the maze of boxes, chairs, stools, feet, and children, letting the congregation get a closer look at the newest member of the Lord's family, a baby born on that desperate day in October. Pearl finally opened her eyes, looking about in quiet amazement at the faces peering into hers. Then, enough was enough, and she peacefully dozed off once again as she was carefully placed in the waiting arms of "Grandma" Berg.

Samuel and Beatrice remained at the front of the room while the pianist, with a perfectly aimed shot at the spittoon, toned down his music and quietly played a popular number called, "I Love You Truly." While the romantic music flowed over the curious people in the room, who had been expecting another rousing hymn, Big Jack and Bertha rose from their chairs and walked hand in hand to the bar, where Pastor Jenson waited.

Looking into the caring eyes of his pastor, Big Jack's mind flashed back to the night of the fire, when he and the rest of the group in the cellar waited anxiously for the pastor to return from his rescue mission. Big Jack recalled finally hearing someone beating on his cellar door, calling his name. Leaping up the stairs, Big Jack forced open the door against the power of the wind—and there they were! Willard Schiebe held fast to Samson's reins, and four soot-stained lumberjacks carried Pastor Jenson's unconscious body. The valiant pastor had finally collapsed after crossing the red bridge.

The reality that everyone was still alive on this special day, and that he was about to marry the woman he loved proved to him that God truly worked miracles. Big Jack worked hard to blink back tears.

Once the quartet of people had rearranged themselves—Big Jack and Samuel on one side of the pastor, Bertha and Beatrice on the other—Michael addressed the curious people assembled before him.

"After living through an experience such as we have, all of a sudden life and love become the most important qualities—and gifts—of our lives." He reached out for Big Jack's large hand. Then he reached for Bertha's slender hand, placing it in Big Jack's hand as he folded Big Jack's hard-working hand over it so they were symbolically bound together.

"First we promise to love and serve our Lord and Savior—thus Baptism. Then God gives the gift of love and service, to be shared with another person whom we love and forever desire to share our life, to become as one in His name." The pastor smiled into the eyes of the couple standing before him, and recited the wedding vows from memory—since his occasional service book had helped fueled the flames in his office. The words were familiar and came easily. "Do you take this woman ?" "Do you take this man?" "I now pronounce you man and wife."

And when all was said and done and the golden band placed on Bertha's left hand, Big Jack gathered Bertha close to his chest for a giant embrace, then swooped her up in his strong arms and carried her back to their seats. The congregation erupted in applause as Bertha wrapped her arms about his neck and kissed him firmly on the lips. As they parted Big Jack blushed furiously, then reached out for Maggie, and the three of them embraced amid the cheers of all their friends.

After singing a verse of "My God, How Wonderful Thou Art," Michael once again stood behind the counter of the bar. "If you will bear with me for one more event in this service, I would be forever grateful." He reached for the folded page he had earlier placed upon the shiny surface of the bar, cleared his throat, and swallowed as though he had something caught in his throat.

"I have in my hands the plans Mrs. Brush and I made last fall for her funeral service. As you know, she was swept up into the arms of her Savior just as her home erupted into flames." He carefully unfolded the page of white stationery. "I lost just about everything in the fire, all my books, my notes, my references, my sermons. Everything, that is, except my Greek New Testament, which was tucked into my jacket pocket throughout the entire ordeal." He held up the battered book for all to see.

"And inside the cover of my Greek New Testament were Mrs. Brush's wishes for her final worldly celebration." Once again he paused before he could continue. Everyone in the room was perfectly still, hanging on his every word, as he smoothed out the creased paper as it lay upon the bar.

"Mrs. Brush gave me three specific directives. She wanted a memorable service, and her instructions are as follows, in her very words and as written by her very hand:

'Pastor, I insist that you keep my service very simple and uncomplicated. I tried to live that way, and I hope you will send me on my heavenly journey in such a manner. These are the three things I would like to have at my service:

'1. Implore Old Syd to sing my favorite hymn "Rock of Ages, Cleft for Me." He has a beautiful voice. For years I could always hear him humming about the place, but he would never sing me a song, no matter how many times I asked. Pastor, you must make him sing for me this one time.

'2. Please ask Henry Larson to read my chosen scripture verses and one sonnet of my choosing. As a young child he often read aloud for me when we sat together; one more time would be such a gift.

'3. If anyone should choose to come to my service, I would like to have each of them rewarded with a selection of Daisy Larson's delicious cookies. Should I make it through the gates of heaven, I will be surprised if anything—even in heaven— tastes as delicious as one of Daisy's cookies. Oh, yes—one more request; no sermon. Let the sermon be my friends enjoying each other's company and celebrating the gift of friendship. Thus, you are freed from having to take the time to write a sermon to send me on my heavenly journey.

'Thank you, Pastor Jenson, for your friendship and your spiritual guidance.

Sincerely, Mrs. Brush. (My given name is Helen, in case you didn't know.)'

Pastor Jenson looked out over the silent group before him. "How many of you remember occasionally receiving a helping hand from Mrs. Brush?" Almost every hand went up. "Well, now we are privileged to fulfill her wishes, and remember what she meant to all of us."

Pastor Jenson walked to the stool where Old Syd sat with his head down, gazing at the floor. Michael gently took him by the arm, raised him to his feet, then led him to the front of the room where he positioned the frail, old man on a stool in front of the bar. Old Syd raised his head and gazed out over the crowd of curious people. A smile slowly crinkled his wrinkled cheeks as he looked into their eyes.

"I would do anything for Mrs. Brush. We had been friends ever since we were children, and—she was right—I never did sing a song for her, but I truly enjoy singing for myself." He pulled on the front of his ill-fitting jacket, straightened up as much as his rigid, old spine would allow. "I always figured nobody would ever want to hear a crazy old man like me singing," he said, and he cleared his throat. "Well, my dear friend, this is my parting gift to you. Just me, singing for you."

No one expected anything spectacular to issue forth from that aged throat and mouth. When Old Syd started to sing with no accompaniment, very quietly at first, there was something winsome about the sound as it carried through the room. His voice was surprisingly deep, coming from that lean, old body. It was a baritone voice, clear and clean. Even the expression on his face changed from crestfallen to triumphant as the music rose from his soul and filled the saloon. The words of the song were perfect for Mrs. Brush's memorial, and there was not a dry eye to be found in the room.

When Old Syd came to the final stanza, he reached into his jacket pocket and retrieved a large white handkerchief which, pausing for a moment, he used to blow his nose and quickly wipe his eyes. The words he sang next, in his rich voice, were a perfect tribute to his friend of so many years.

"While I draw this fleeting breath
When mine eyelids close in death,
When I soar to worlds unknown,
See thee on thy judgment throne,
Rock of Ages, cleft for me,
Let me hid myself in thee. Amen."

The room was still, with the exception of a few people sniffling or blowing their noses, while old Syd let his head fall to his chest as he made his way once again to his stool, holding the arm of the pastor.

Then, generous applause filled the room, causing Old Syd to look out over all his friends who never realized he could sing a note, much less touch their hearts. He smiled his almost toothless smile and signaled for them to stop clapping, which they did as soon as he sat down.

Henry Larson strode to the front of the room next. People looked at him and commented to their neighbors on the scars he still bore on his face from his battle with the fire. Quietly they whispered to one another how much he resembled his father, how much he had grown over the past year, how blessed he was to come under the wing of his beloved mentor, Mrs. Brush. What a miracle it was that he survived his battle with the fire. He held in his hand a handwritten translation of the scripture, made from Pastor Jenson's Greek New Testament.

Henry announced his readings. First he would read I Corinthians 13, the great love chapter that exclaims in its final verse, "Faith, hope, and love. And the greatest of these is love!" He then read the scripture verses that told of the thief on the cross, crucified next to Jesus. Mark 23:42-43—"'Jesus, remember me when thou comest into thy kingdom.' And Jesus said unto him, 'Verily I say unto thee. Today thou shalt be with me in paradise.'"

Henry could not resist adding, "Mrs. Brush always had empathy for the thief. She always said that if he made it to paradise, she felt she would be welcome, too."

And finally, Henry folded his papers and put them in his pocket. He looked around the room at Oscar and his mother sitting by Miss Thoreson, the new Swanson family, and of course his mother and father who were bursting with pride. "Mrs. Brush's favorite sonnet was a love sonnet by Elizabeth Barrett Browning. I came to know it by heart when I was only eight years old because we read it together so many times."

With one glance at the ceiling and a slight clearing of the throat, he began. "How do I love thee? Let me count the ways." His clear, young voice carried well in the crowded saloon. With rapt attention the listeners held onto his every word, especially when he arrived at the final three phrases:

—I love thee with the breath,
Smiles, tears, of all my life!—and, if God choose,
I shall but love thee better after death."

The room was hushed. Henry finished, "Dear Mrs. Brush, thank you for loving us—all of us. You will always be memorable to us."

He quickly walked to the back of the saloon, accompanied by Oscar, Maggie, Daisy, Bertha, and Anna Belle Lund, then entered the kitchen, the swinging doors closing behind them. Pastor Jenson stepped to the front of the assembly once more and spread his arms wide. The words of the benediction flowed over the bowed heads of the people.

"The Lord bless thee and keep thee. The Lord make his face shine upon thee, and be gracious unto thee. The Lord lift up his countenance upon thee, and give thee peace: In the Name of the Father, and of the Son, and of the Holy Ghost!"

Adults and children, seated close together across the floor of the saloon, began to stand up and turn to one another, smiling, visiting, and shaking hands. The younger children crept away from their parents to investigate the mysteries that lay behind the brass rail and the large wooden bar—a perfect place to play hide and seek.

Then Big Jack called for everyone's attention. "Our grand finale for Mrs. Brush is about to take place. As you recall, she specifically ordered all of us to partake in one—or perhaps even two—of Daisy Larson's excellent cookies." Just at that moment the doors to the kitchen swung open and Oscar, Henry, and Maggie entered the room, each carrying a huge tray filled with cookies in a multitude of flavors.

Chocolate, vanilla, molasses, oatmeal, sugar, coconut, ginger snaps, date, almond, ice box, peanut, frosted, not frosted, cookies to dunk, cookies not to dunk—Daisy hadn't missed a one. Once the trays were placed upon the bar, cups appeared from under the bar and two huge pots of fragrant, hot coffee were carried to the bar by Samuel Berg and Willard Scheibe. Cream and sugar lumps appeared next, along with spoons to stir, like magic.

Big Jack and Bertha poured while Daisy and Miss Thoreson managed the cookie trays, trying to see that everyone was served and satisfied before the cookies disappeared into the eager hands of the youngsters who returned again and again, until the last crumb was gone.

Pastor Jenson stood quietly near the bar, watching the interactions between the men, women, and children milling about with their hands filled with cookies and cups of coffee. Suddenly feeling weary, he sought a place to sit before the chairs, benches, and stools disappeared from the Moose Saloon and returned to their places of origin. Actually, he needed two chairs—one to sit on and one on which he could prop up his damaged leg. The wound throbbed, healing slowly but surely, once the doctor had attended to the nasty lacerations and gashes resulting from his fall near the stables. The stitches had been removed and the inflamation had almost gone. Soon he'd be good as new, the doctor said.

As the congregation once again prepared to enter the cold and head for home in the late afternoon sunshine, Michael could hear people calling back and forth, making plans to assist one another with all the work and construction needed to bring the demolished town back into being.

They were planing a community sauna, a fully stocked mercantile, a new hospital—not that they didn't appreciate the generous space provided at the Northeastern Hotel—and a new school, hopefully completed by the autumn of 1919. Poor Garfield School would be bursting at the seams until then, educating children from grades one through twelve. A movie theater, library, barber shops, millinery shop, bakery, tobacco shop, auto shop, livery stable, and bank would be in the next wave of buildings. The list went on and on—and then someone had a revelation. "We need to rebuild the churches—and soon!" Every one cheered, especially Pastor Jenson.

Within a few minutes everyone was gone, each to their place of shelter. The late afternoon sun dipped down behind the naked hills on the western horizon, and the chill winds of evening began to blow. Pulling up the collar of the fleece-lined jacket and slipping on a borrowed knit hat, Pastor Jenson was the last to leave the saloon before the nighttime regulars arrived.

As he stepped out of the door of the Moose Saloon and onto the boardwalk, he was greeted warmly by the lumberjacks arriving for their evening libation. With slaps on the back and handshakes all around, he slowly worked his way through the crowd while making his way down St. Louis Avenue. He headed north to Big Jack's boarding house, where he would stay until other living arrangements could be made.

As he walked he allowed himself to dream. A new church! A new parsonage! A vision flooded his imagination, so real he could behold in his mind an entirely new city, rising from the ashes of the fire. He felt the excitement of what could be possible as the whole area was made new. Aware of the confidence and determination shown by the families returning to the area desiring to rebuild—to create a new city with new opportunities, new sources of employment, new schools for a fine education, a new main street with shops and stores to fulfill everyone's desires—Michael's confidence in the future ignited within him.

At last he thought about the Island and smiled, wondering what God might have in store for this small piece of real estate, now that it had survived the flames in such a miraculous manner. Taking his time walking up the steps to the boarding house, Pastor Jenson said aloud and with feeling, "I like it here! Yep! I like it here!"

And once the words escaped his lips, Michael began to laugh, remembering the first time he had uttered those very same words. He had just stepped down from the train almost eighteen months ago, and was standing at the depot—alone—sweating in the summer heat, flies buzzing about his head.

"I like it here!" was his initial response, and it had never changed. He meant those words then, and he surely meant them now. The pain in his leg seemed to diminish and his spirits lifted as he opened the door to the boarding house. With a wide smile, he returned the greetings of the lumberjacks making their way to the dining room. Pausing in the hallway, he took in a deep breath, the aroma of Big Jack's famous roast beef and gravy flooding his senses.

After hanging up his jacket and joining the men already seated at the tables, Michael and the lumberjacks were prepared to polish off every morsel of beef, drop of gravy, and slice of bread—not to mention every slab of chocolate cake.

With only a few moments left before Big Jack would come bursting through the kitchen door, Willard Schiebe claimed the chair next to Michael and struck him firmly across his back. "Good to have you with us, Pastor." Willard smiled, then asked boldly, "Do you suppose you could offer a prayer for all us scoundrels seated in this room?"

Another slap on Michael's back followed before Willard, looking a bit more serious, added, "I think all of us could all use a prayer or two after everything that's happened." He turned to the other men. "What do ya think? Could we all use a prayer or two?"

Heads turned toward the pair, nodding. Pastor Jenson smiled, slowly rose from his chair and looked into the faces of all the men around him, men who had become his friends.

"I would consider it an honor to pray with all of you. Thank you for asking."

An unusual stillness settled over the room. "Please join me in prayer," he said as he folded his hands. The large, gruff men around him bowed their heads.

"Dear Lord Jesus, thank you for life, thank you for this place, thank you for each of these hard-working men, thank you for the Island, and, most of all, thank you for loving us just as we are—sinners each and every one of us."

He paused for a moment. It was silent. No one stirred.

"Help us to move on into the future, to rebuild, to celebrate a new beginning." With a flourish, Michael then closed with, "And last but not least, thank you for Big Jack's wonderful food! Amen."

The men echoed with another robust "Amen!" while executing a quick reach for the nearby bread and butter.

And with that, the kitchen doors swung open. Big Jack, Maggie, and Henry entered the dining room laden with roast beef, gravy, mashed potatoes, and all the trimmings. Bertha could be seen in the kitchen slicing the chocolate cake for dessert. A contented stillness spread over the room as the men filled their plates to overflowing.

Michael sat down once again, grinned at the men seated around him, rubbed his hands together in anticipation, and said, again, for all to hear, "I like it here! I really like it here!" quickly followed by, "Please pass the potatoes and gravy!"

Epilogue

THE GREAT WAR CAME to an end on November 11,1918, barely a month after the fire. Soldiers from the Cloquet area returned home to find an even greater desolation in their own backyard than they had seen overseas.

Prohibition began when the Eighteenth Amendment was passed on January 16, 1920, forcing the Island out of the liquor business. Some saloons resorted to selling ice cream instead. Somehow it never caught on with the lumberjacks, and the mystique of the Island quickly faded away.

BY THE END OF 1919, the church was rebuilt as a sturdy brick structure, and Bishop Hanson came for the dedication. Michael Jenson felt honored to serve as the pastor for fifteen more years. The fall after the fire, when the schools were finally up and running, several new teachers were employed and moved into the community. One in particular, Mary, joined the Lutheran Church, where she caught the eye of the pastor. They were married the following summer and were blessed with three children—the firstborn girl being named Helen. After his fifteenth year as a pastor in Cloquet, Michael was called to teach Greek at Luther Seminary in St. Paul. He always carried his battered Greek New Testament in his jacket pocket.

Old Syd died in 1921 at age ninety-one. He chose to live alone, supported by the small inheritance willed to him by Mrs. Brush. He barely spent a cent and left the bulk of the money to the Lutheran church. He never again sang in public; however, people who heard him sing at the service in the Moose Saloon never forget his one and only solo performance.

The Larsons decided to remain in their small Island home. After using part of their inheritance from Mrs. Brush's estate to add indoor plumbing, a larger kitchen, and a genuine bedroom for Henry, they felt comfortable. Hank ran for mayor and was elected to the office in 1924, the year Henry left for the University of Minnesota, where he would fulfill his dream of becoming a writer. Daisy continued to bake and deliver her goods until the delivery crew grew too mature to be seen pulling a wagon about town.

Miss Thoreson insisted Oscar and Anna Belle Lund move into her comfortable—but empty—home. She felt it a miracle that her house should be the only dwelling to survive the fire that had demolished her entire neighborhood. Being only one block from her precious Garfield School, which also survived, she felt twice blessed. The Lunds became the family she never had. Oscar would graduate at the top of his class (Miss Thoreson would settle for no less!) and pursued his dream of becoming a lawyer at Harvard Law School. Anna Belle never shed a tear for the loss of her husband. Scant remains of Mr. Lund had been found in the gully with all the other incinerated bodies and twisted wreckage—only his silver money clip could be identified as belonging to the bank president when the gully was cleared of bodies. Anna Belle never remarried, but kept a warm and welcoming home for Miss Thoreson.

Moving the Berg family to the white house north of the Island was a shrewd move for all. They loved living in Pearl's house across the bridge. As the years flew by, baby Pearl grew into a feisty little girl. Samuel and Beatrice added two sons to their lovely family, and Mrs. Berg became the ultimate grandma. Strangely enough, since she instigated the attack on the brothel those many years ago, she now took devious pleasure in inviting her friends to visit her parlor/bedroom on the second floor. She adapted quite well to occupying one of the infamous brothel rooms, especially when her friends—while sipping tea—would gasp in disbelief when she filled in the details of what, at one time, occurred in this *very* room. She found the old four-poster bed to be extremely comfortable and the morning sun that shone into the room to awaken her quite pleasing.

Big Jack and Bertha had a grand time working together in the boarding house. Bertha's copy of *The Woodsman's Handbook* no longer had any emotional value and was left on the bottom shelf of the book case. Six years passed quickly, and before they were quite ready, Maggie graduated from high school and headed off to college in Duluth. She then returned to Cloquet to teach English and girls' physical education at the high school. One of the spring and summer activities open to girls who desired to learn was the art of birling. Maggie and Henry saw each other every summer during school breaks, and eventually married. After a number of years, Big Jack and Bertha sold the boarding house, moved into town, and opened a popular café well positioned on Cloquet Avenue. It was affectionately named The Tall Timber Café—famous for its roast beef dinners, chocolate cake, pies, and Daisy Larson's delectable breads and pastries.

The End

Acknowledgements

I would like to take a moment to sincerely thank the following:

· Our friends in the parish of Bigfork and Effie, Minnesota, who first introduced us to the rhythms of a logging community;

· My precious elderly acquaintances in Cloquet, Minnesota, who shared the stories of their youth and their traumatic flight from the 1918 fire, as we spent peaceful afternoons in the '70s sipping coffee and playing Scrabble together;

· My six children, their mates, and their families, who have always been so positive and supportive as my novel evolved,

· Most of all, I would like to thank my beloved husband, Pastor Gilbert (Gib) Lee, for allowing me to accompany him and share his life for fifty-five years.